ISBN: 1517395828
ISBN-13: 978-1517395827

HUNT FOR THE SAIPH

Book 3

Of

The Saiph Series

Books by PP Corcoran

The Saiph Series:
Discovery of the Saiph, book 1
Search for the Saiph, book 2
Hunt for the Saiph, book 3
Book 4 Coming 2016

Ghost Soldiers (shorts):
The Province

Most books also available in ebook and audiobook.

Visit www.ppcorcoran.com

CONTENTS

CHAPTER ONE
The Dyson Sphere

2287 LIGHT YEARS FROM EARTH

The small ship reenters normal space and its sensors sweep the surrounding area. Penetrating the blackness of space, its systems register the nearby gas giant, invisible to the naked eye. More lifeless planetoids are detected at the very edges of the system by the astrogation computer, which compares the sensor readings to the data stored in its core. It confirms the ship has indeed reached the desired destination its makers programmed into it nearly ten centuries earlier. The ship adjusts its position and ignites its powerful intersystem engines, which come to life, pushing it toward the heart of the dark and lifeless system. Appearances, however, can be deceiving. No light reaches out from a central star to kiss the outer planets. No radiation is detected to hint at the presence of a hidden star at the center of the planetary system. The planets seem to have formed against all known theories of system formation. Where is the system's star?

The engines power down and the ship coasts along its course, moving toward the center of the impossible planetary system. In the darkness the sensors pick something up, a very weak signal but definitely there, a latticework like a giant spider's web which forms a complete globe at least two AUs in diameter and situated exactly where the system's star should be.

As the spacecraft closes in, it becomes apparent there are small bulges at some of the junctions where the fine latticework meets.

Closer still and the true size of the bulges are revealed as the structures dwarf the ship. The seemingly smooth, seamless skin of one of these structures splits, and a brightly lit docking area is revealed. The ship enters and the structure's skin closes behind it like the mouth of a shark.

The ship moves silently through the cavernous hangar passing the sleeping behemoths of kilometer-long warships. All were painted the same inky-black as the night sky. Flattened hulls with weapons' pylons protruding above and below the main body like fins of some enormous deep sea predator. Gliding through another armored port, the ship passes yet more machines of war until it finally settles into a snug docking cradle. Powering down its engines, the onboard computers link with the overarching Artificial Intelligence. The AI receives the information the small ship brings, detailing the fate of the Chosen People at the hands of the Commonwealth forces. For what would be an eternity for any flesh-and-blood brain, but is in fact mere thousandths of a second, the AI ponders its next move until it finds the most compatible file. Instructions flash out to long-dormant equipment.

"Awaken!"

CHAPTER TWO
Survivors

PLANET II - STAR SYSTEM 52980
107.3 LIGHT YEARS FROM EARTH

Planet II of System 52980 steadily orbited its G-type main sequence star. The planet consisted of six large continents, making up about one-third of its surface. The remainder was covered in liquid water, forming deep oceans.

Planet II was ideally located in its star system to be a viable life-bearing planet, but the 'Others' ensured whatever civilization may have sprung from its fertile ground would never have the chance to reach its peak.

According to the drone's readings, the planet was subjected to an orbital bombardment sometime in the past four years. The bombardment had scoured the surface clear of life and plunged the planet's ecology into a new Ice Age, brought about by the nuclear winter clouds that still blanketed the planet's sky. Maybe in a few thousand years, when the ice began to recede and the radiation levels dropped, life would return to this dead world.

For what it was worth, the perpetrators of this destruction suffered the same fate. Second Fleet, under the command of Admiral Robert Lewis, descended on the Others' final sector base like avenging angels. The sector base was built into a large asteroid circling a gas giant so massive it put Sol's own Jupiter to shame in a star system fifteen light years from its intended target.

If nothing else, the Others were consistent. They seemed only to build two types of base. The first was the sort the forces of Fifth Fleet encountered on 70 Ophiuchi: An orbiting facility designed to facilitate naval vessels, supported by a large ground installation. The second was of the type that faced Admiral Radford and Third Fleet out of Garunda: built into a large asteroid and surrounded by fire support bases mounted on smaller asteroids.

Whichever style of base, they were always located in an adjacent system to the intended target. Therefore, if one knew the location of the base, it was a relatively simple matter of scouting nearby systems to find a planet that piqued the Others' interest and so must be slated for destruction.

Now, though, the fourteenth and last enemy base was neutralized. When the Others' home on Narath was destroyed by its Artificial Intelligence, many thought it a simple matter of wiping up the remaining sector bases the enemy left behind. This cleanup operation took three years of hard fighting and cost the Commonwealth forces dearly in both ships and crew.

Following the battle around Earth and the destruction of Narath, only Second Fleet retained its full strength, so to Admiral Lewis fell the mission of taking down the surviving enemy bases until First and Third Fleets had licked their wounds and regained their former strength.

The first target of Second Fleet was the Others' outpost in System 24901: A nondescript red giant star that had consumed the majority of the planets which once orbited it until what had probably been an icy moon of a now-vanished planet was its sole remaining satellite.

This dwarf planet had developed a thin but breathable atmosphere around which the Others built an orbital facility to support the two Buzzards and one Vulture that patrolled the system and the surrounding space. On the dwarf's surface was a fortified complex exactly like the one on 70 Ophiuchi, which had cost the lives of so many marines in their futile attempt to capture it.

Many of the Commonwealth's scientists and politicians refused to believe the detonation of nuclear weapons on 70 Ophiuchi and Narath was anything other than intentional. Lewis, however, was not one of them. He had read the paper written by now-Lieutenant (Junior Grade) Terrance Wilson, his wife's nephew, and it left Lewis in no doubt that the Others, although not directly controlled by an artificial intelligence, certainly took direction from one. Lewis was determined that the waste of life, both friendly and enemy, would never be repeated.

His initial assault plan was almost identical to the one employed by the ill-fated Fifth Fleet. Second Fleet emerged from fold space and launched a merciless missile attack on the orbital base and its warships. In fewer than five minutes, the orbital works and enemy warships were nothing more than floating wreckage. With the space-borne threat neutralized, Second Fleet moved into low orbit, and as the rotation of the moon brought the surface base over the horizon, Lewis began his Kinetic Energy Missile bombardment. The missile strikes threw tonnes of debris into the air but ground-penetrating radar continued to identify targets for the fleet's missiles. Anything and everything looking remotely like a weapon or command-and-control facility was targeted.

When the tactical officer was satisfied there were no viable targets left, Lewis ordered the deployment of the High Altitude Electro Magnetic Pulse (HEMP) weapons. Blinding flashes lit the night sky high above the Others' base as the weapons detonated in the stratosphere and their gamma rays were converted into a prodigious electromagnetic pulse. Every piece of unprotected electronic equipment within 100 kilometers ceased to function.

Buried deep below the base, the artificial intelligence of the Coltus noted that all feeds from the surface had been lost. The "Self-Destruct" protocol was activated and the electronic signal triggering the ULF transmission and nuclear demolition charges was sent. It never reached its intended destination. Although the Coltus was housed in a hardened bunker, the cables and equipment it was trying to activate was not. The HEMP rendered the unprotected systems nothing more than expensive junk. When confirmation of the completion of its instructions was not received, the Coltus moved to the next step in the protocol and initiated the thermobaric explosives embedded in the walls of its own bunker. The AI ceased to exist, leaving the soldiers on the surface to fight on without its guidance.

The marines of Second Fleet dropped right on top of the base and no enemy fire rose to meet them. As they disembarked from the assault shuttles, they were met by enemy defenders, whose high-tech weapons were disabled by the HEMP pulse. But still they attacked. They were reduced to swinging their useless weapons like clubs. Picking up rubble and broken masonry to use as additional weapons, they flung themselves upon the marines.

As reports from the ground flooded into the flag bridge,

Lewis came to a decision. He ordered his marines to switch to non-lethal weapons unless they were faced with no choice. Lewis understood this increased the risk of casualties among his marines but he refused to slaughter his enemy out of hand. On the surface, the marines slung their plasma rifles over their shoulders, pulled out their PEP pistols, and faced their charging enemy.

In the end, the marines managed to secure over 2500 prisoners. It was the largest number ever captured alive and Lewis was forced to request additional resources to help secure, house, and care for them. Units of the Garundan Army were shipped in and construction began of a vast prisoner-of-war camp. Their former enemy was now their responsibility.

Over three years of conflict, this method of neutralizing enemy surface bases had been successfully deployed on five occasions and netted the Commonwealth nearly 15,000 prisoners, spread over five different star systems. However, they had not devised a similar method of minimizing casualties on the two enemy bases housed within asteroids.

The Combined Joint Chiefs of Staff, given no choice, ordered the assault fleet to stand off at a safe distance and pulverize the asteroid until there was nothing left except dust if the enemy commander failed to signal his surrender. Enemy fatalities were inevitably total.

Images of the lifeless planets the Stealthy Reconnaissance Drone (SRD) returned to the fleet from the target planets of these enemy bases soon negated whatever pity was felt over the slaughter caused by the Others refusal to surrender.

With grim resolve, the sailors and marines went about their task of removing the threat the Others represented to innocent life in the galaxy.

Robert Lewis pushed himself back from the desk in his quarters on board the Bismarck class battleship TDF *Tsushima,* musing over the report he'd been reading on the terminal while absently rubbing a hand over his tired face. The analysts had pored over the SRD's data and noticed an anomaly. It was certain that whatever life existed on Planet II was long gone, but as the SRD had egressed the system, it passed close to Planet II's single moon. The compact electronic sniffer package on the probe, originally designed to detect stealthy enemy warships, had sniffed what the analysts were calling a "non-natural occurring power source." So either the Others had left something on the small moon or there was some other party out there who was yet to reveal themselves. Well, there was only one way to find out. Some lucky soul was going to have to go and take a look.

#

The Tanto class shuttle lurched slightly as it moved clear of the marine assault ship *Sheridan*. The heads-up display on Philippa's Wraith suit was configured to show the small ship's approach profile. The *Sheridan* had come out of fold space on the dark side of the small moon, exactly 180 degrees opposite the location of the power reading the reconnaissance drones had sniffed when they passed the moon during their final sweep of the dead planet it silently orbited. The Tanto carrying Philippa and her platoon mates was to spiral down to a height of fifty meters from the surface of the moon and then approach the area flying 'nap of the earth'. A quaint military phrase for flying as close to the ground as possible without running into the ground. The idea of which was to fly low enough to avoid enemy fire. It may have been uncomfortable for the passengers but Philippa was willing to sit through a bumpy ride if it increased the shuttles chances of making it to its target in one piece.

Unfortunately, the brief glimpse the SRD had gotten

only allowed the analysts to narrow the search area down to a few square kilometers so the Tanto's crew was forced to fly a search pattern and use their more powerful equipment to localize the source.

Philippa and her fellow marines were there to baby-sit the scientists who would actually look at whatever was generating the power source. *If they ever find it and it wasn't just a glitch in the SRD's data,* Philippa thought. The blinking incoming message icon appeared in her HUD.

"Go for Papadomas." Said Philippa accepting the call.

The slightly nasal voice of Lieutenant Travis came through her ear bug. "Corporal, five mikes till we reach the search area. Give your big brain types a gentle reminder the initial pass will be on passives only. Let’s not go active on anything which may be mistaken for a fire control radar until we know more about what we're dealing with here, OK?"

"Understood, sir." A small sigh escaped Philippa as she cut the link. She’d been lumbered with the unenviable task of herding the small scientific tech team while the platoon commander coordinated with the crew of the Tanto and the marines under the first sergeant, who would deal with the security of the site when and if they needed to put boots on the ground.

Philippa turned her head slightly so she could see the displays of the tech team’s equipment and verify the systems were in passive mode. The senior scientists saw her and gave her a weak smile. Philippa's face, blank under her helmet, stared at him until he turned away in discomfort. Before leaving the *Sheridan,* she had a quiet word with the senior scientist and made it plain to him that if he questioned her instructions in any shape or form, she would personally ensure he spent the next few weeks in the *Sheridan's* sick bay.

Now, the scientist wasn't a small man by any means. He was proud of his near-daily workouts in the *Sheridan's* small gym. But one glance into the diminutive marine corporal's steely eyes convinced him that perhaps following her instructions was a good idea.

The Tanto slowed as it entered the search area and the scientists' focused their full concentration on the search for the elusive power source. The Tanto crisscrossed the search grid for nearly half an hour before the lead scientist cried, "We've got it. 1300 meters at 168 degrees. Definitely not a naturally occurring source. If I were to hazard a guess, I'd say it's a condensing nuclear reactor. Pretty old tech but if properly maintained it could run efficiently for decades."

Philippa only had one question. "Is it the Others?"

The scientist shook his head. "We've never come across them using this type of tech, so my money is on 'no'."

Good enough for Philippa. Changing channels, she called Travis. "Lieutenant. The eggheads have a hit. 1300 meters at 168 degrees. They're calling it a condensing nuclear reactor. Most likely not the Others."

"Understood, Corporal. Let's firm up an exact location. Permission granted to go active on all sensors. Travis clear."

It took another ten minutes while the Tanto flew in a wide, sweeping circle, but eventually the senior scientist was satisfied his team had narrowed the location down to fifteen meters below the dwarf planet's surface in an area maybe 100 meters squared. It was as good as he was going to get. Philippa relayed the message to Travis, who came to a quick decision.

"Corporal, tell the scientists to seal up. I think it's time we stretched our legs. Between our suits' sensors and their portable gear, we should be able to get an exact fix on this thing. If it's buried, we need to know where to dig."

Travis had the Tanto set down a couple hundred meters from the source. As the dust settled, Travis' marines disembarked and shook out into a skirmish line, while Philippa and her scientist charges, along with two more marines as escorts, followed close behind.

The marines advanced toward the lip of a large meteorite crater, its bottom shrouded in darkness thanks to the high sides of the crater's walls blocking out the light from the distant red giant. Travis bounded to the lip and used his suit's passives to give the crater floor the once-over. Nothing. However, Travis had learned to trust his instincts and the tickling sensation at the back of his neck was telling him something wasn't quite right about this. Well, his mission was to locate and identify whatever was generating the power source and the only way to do so, apparently, was to go inside the crater. He chose to ignore his instincts just this once and activated his link to the platoon's first sergeant.

"First Sergeant. Take half the platoon around the lip of the crater and set up a fire support position at ninety degrees to our current location. Sergeant Morales will go firm here with the remaining marines while I go forward with Papadomas and the eggheads and check out the crater floor."

As the marines sprang into action, Travis continued to scan the crater's floor with his passives. Nothing seemed out of place, but buried in the center of the crater, not a hundred meters from him, was a functioning nuclear reactor. The question was: Who did it belong to? A telltale signal in his HUD changed from amber to green. The first sergeant was in position and happy with his marines positions. Travis continued to ignore the tickling sensation at the back of his neck as his well-honed instincts told him something was not quite right here; he took a deep breath before activating his link to Philippa and her charges, "Let's move out. Eyes sharp, marines."

With the two scientists between them, Travis and Philippa stepped over the lip of the crater and descended into the darkness below. As the inky blackness swallowed her up, Philippa switched her suit's optics to image intensifier mode and the floor and walls of the crater jumped out at her in mixtures of green and gray. Cautiously, they advanced, reaching the center of the crater's floor without incident, but the nagging sensation at the back of Travis' neck was still there and judging by her overly cautious movements, he guessed the normally ice-cool Philippa could sense it too.

"Are you getting the same bad feeling I am, Corporal?" Travis asked over their link.

"You betcha, sir. I can't quite put my finger on it, but I get the distinct feeling we're not alone down here. I'm going to go to thermals to see if it makes any difference. Suit," she ordered. "Thermal image mode."

The world around Philippa shifted to a mixture of blues, reds, and yellows as the suit showed her the crater according to temperature variations. The crater's floor and walls were in shadow and should have been a uniform cool blue, but as Philippa scanned one small patch of wall, it appeared slightly warmer than the rest.

"Lieutenant, I have a heat variance on the crater wall at ten o'clock."

Travis switched to thermal imagery himself and quickly spotted the anomaly. "OK Corporal, go check it out. I'll cover you from here."

"Aye-aye, sir. Moving now."

Travis dropped to one knee, brought up his rifle, and placed the targeting dot on the heat source. A command to his suit pushed the aiming point over his link to the first sergeant and the fire support team. This action allowed everyone to see where Travis had his rifle aimed at. Now Philippa had the amassed firepower of the majority of the platoon to back her up if it all went wrong.

Philippa noted the lieutenant's aiming point in her suit and was slightly reassured as she slowly approached the heat source. She noticed the heat source grew bigger as she moved closer and her optics got a better look at it. The source expanded in her HUD until a perfect horizontal line formed, about a meter and a half across. Faint red lines dropped vertically away from each end of the horizontal line, fading into a cool blue as they went, "Are you seeing this, Lieutenant? It looks to me like heat escaping from a badly sealed hatch."

Travis called the image up to the corner of his own HUD. *Damn if she wasn't right!* Nature abhors straight lines and those heat lines were perfectly straight and joined at right angles. "Sit tight, Corporal, I'm coming to you." Travis opened his link to the two scientists. "Can your gear get me a good reading on whatever the hell that thing is?"

"Get me close enough Lieutenant and our equipment should be able to penetrate anything but battleship shielding," replied the lead scientist.

"OK, you pair stay behind me and shout when we get close enough for you to get a good reading. Move out." Travis moved off with the scientist trailing a few steps behind him.

Just as they came level with Philippa, the scientist spoke over the link. "That's close enough. I'm pushing the image to you now. It's some sort of airlock door to a narrow corridor cut into the rock, it slopes down at a shallow angle away from our position before skirting around and disappearing out of range about fifteen meters below the surface..." The pause in the scientist's report got Travis' full attention.

"And?" Travis asked, trying to keep the impatience out of his voice. For the briefest of seconds the scientist said nothing, then Travis saw in his HUD that both scientists were backing away.

"And there's something in the airlock now and it's cycling."

Crap! "Corporal! Heads up, we're about to have a visitor!" Travis' warning call came not a moment too soon.

In Philippa's HUD, the thermal image bloomed as the airlock opened. Outlined in its center was a figure in cooler blue. Philippa's rifle came up, her aiming mark centered on the chest of the unidentified figure only scant meters from her. The alien seemed as shocked to find the marines outside the airlock, as they were to see the alien.

Philippa saw the alien take a step back into the airlock. If whoever or whatever it was raised the alarm, the marines could be in for a world of hurt. Before she realized she was doing it, Philippa sprang forward, her rifle falling slack on its sling and freeing her arms as she tackled the figure. She took it to the ground in a tangle of arms and legs.

Philippa's Wraith suit's servos should have given her an unfair advantage, but as she tried to pin the alien to the ground it managed to hold her off. Either it was incredibly strong or it was being aided by its own mechanical suit. The fight came to swift end as Travis entered the airlock behind Philippa and leveled his PEP pistol at the alien's obscured faceplate. The space-suited figure got the message and assumed the prone position on the airlock's floor.

Philippa pushed herself back to her feet, taking out her own PEP and quickly scanning the small airlock for threats. Lying by the door was a large metal case with the lid propped open. She took a tentative look inside to see a neat stack of a multitude of tools. *Is this guy on the floor a maintenance tech?*

"Looks like some kind of tools to me, Lieutenant," she said as she completed her scan of the airlock. Satisfied they were alone, Philippa relaxed slightly but kept her PEP at the ready. Maybe the alien still lying on the floor had friends on the other side of the airlock.

Philippa moved to the airlock's open outer door. A cursory examination identified the control cables for the door's mechanism, "Lieutenant, if I cut this control cable, it should stop the door closing from the other side of the inner airlock. If their systems are anything like ours, it should be impossible to open the inner door while the outer one is still open. Might buy us some time to figure out our next move."

"Good thinking, Corporal. Make it happen."

Holstering her PEP, Philippa reached into her leg pouch and pulled out the small plasma cutter she always kept there. On activation, plasma as hot as the surface of the sun lanced out, its thin arc cut through the control cables in seconds and disabled the outer door. Philippa moved back toward Travis, her PEP back out and leveled at the alien.

"I've got this, Lieutenant."

Travis took a step back toward the outer door, pausing to inspect Philippa's handiwork. The outer door was out of commission and her swift action gave him a few minutes to collect his thoughts. "Good work there, Corporal. Quick thinking with the tackle and the door." A slight movement of Philippa's Wraith suit's helmet in silent acknowledgment was all Travis got in return for his plaudits.

Travis recalled that he had been incredulous when the First Sergeant recommended Papadomas for the job of shepherding the scientists. Travis would have much preferred that one of the sergeants had the job. Papadomas was the junior corporal in the platoon, less than two years out of training; nevertheless, the First Sergeant was quite insistent. If there was anything they taught you in officer training, it was to listen to your senior noncommissioned officers, so Travis bowed to the First Sergeant's greater knowledge of the platoon.

Watching Papadomas in action, he was glad he had. She reacted more quickly than he to the rapidly developing situation. First putting the alien out of action, then disabling the outer airlock door and securing their position for the moment. B*ack to the situation in hand,* thought Travis.

They had one prisoner but God knew how many more were on the other side of the inner door. Of course, there was no definite proof that whoever was on the other side of the door was aggressive. If they wanted to get into a fight with his marines, they would have sent more than one lone individual who, from what Travis could see, was not even armed.

Travis gambled that whoever else was on the other side of the inner door did not know the marines had been on the surface. Activating his link to the Tanto, he called the pilot. "Whistle up the *Sheridan,* it looks like we may have a first contact situation here. I'll pass you a copy of my visual data packet so they can make their own appraisal. Tell the *Sheridan* I'm requesting a full diplomatic team to take the lead here and I need additional marine units to secure the surrounding area out to at least a kilometer. If we've found one airlock here, there might be more scattered around and I don't want to be blindsided. Break. First Sergeant, let's get the men spread out into all-round defense, we may be here for a while." In his HUD, a sparkling of points appeared as the First Sergeant repositioned the marines. Maneuvers completed, Travis turned his attention to the still-prone figure on the floor.

Two arms, two legs, and a head. Any facial features were obscured by the tinted visor of the helmet. The pressure suit the figure wore looked a bit battered and had received some obvious repairs. On closer observation, Travis saw the suit seemed more bulky at the joints than it should. The way he'd been able to hold off Papadomas might be explained by a battery-powered exoskeleton built into the suit. Well, they weren't going to learn much more until the First Contact Team arrived, at which point this particular problem wouldn't be his anymore, it would belong to someone on a much higher pay grade.

A small beep signaled to Travis that his suit was trying to get his attention. The suit had detected a radio signal being generated from beyond the inner door and being received by the figure on the floor. Travis' suit could easily block the signal but he decided not to. Any information they gathered on these aliens was advantageous to the work of the First Contact Team. "Suit. Record all transmissions received and transmitted from the prisoner. Relay through the Tanto and mark it as priority information for the First Contact Team." The suit emitted a single beep as it acknowledged his orders.

#

Time seemed to creep by slowly as Travis, Philippa, and the two scientists, along with their prisoner, waited in the airlock. In reality, it was only ten minutes since Travis passed his first contact report to the crew of the Tanto. The two scientists laid their equipment on the floor in one corner and used it to scan beyond the inner airlock into the corridor beyond. Travis didn't like what the scans were telling him. Ghostly figures were moving around at the edges of the equipment's detection range and they appeared to be sealing the corridor from floor to ceiling. If Travis was to hazard a guess, he would say they were building a makeshift airlock, allowing them to decompress the corridor beyond the inner airlock, which would then allow them to open the inner door without endangering the corridor beyond. At the rate they were building, Travis reckoned they had another fifteen minutes, maybe less, until they were finished and he and his small party would get some more visitors. The transmissions between the suit of his prisoner and whoever was beyond the airlock were almost continuous and Travis could only hope the computers of the First Contact Team had been able to make head or tail of the aliens' language, or this was all going to go south real quick. Just as Travis was thinking it was time to retreat to the crater edge or even the Tanto, the double tone of an incoming message sounded in his helmet: "Go for Travis."

"Travis, Captain Zubek, Echo Company. I'm two minutes out with Charlie Company five minutes behind me. The admiral has chopped two cruisers for fire support and they should be in position before I land. The First Contact Team is assembling now and they'll follow on as soon as they're ready. What's your current status?"

Travis' relief was palpable. With two companies of marines on the ground with him and two cruisers overhead, he was confident he could fend off any assault on his position if he withdrew to the crater's lip, allowing his increased firepower to come into play while the forces assembling in the corridor would have to come at him through the narrow airlock door, "Sir. I have an unknown number of aliens constructing what I believe to be an airlock in the corridor beyond my position. I estimate completion in fifteen mikes. It is my intention to withdraw to the lip of the crater with my prisoner and go firm there awaiting the arrival of the First Contact Team."

Zubek's voice was all business. "Understood, Travis. Echo will come in hot and deploy to reinforce your perimeter. Charlie to make a deliberate deployment and secure a landing site for the First Contact Team." Zubek's tone softened slightly. "Good job, son. Keep your head and I'll be with you as soon as I can. Zubek clear."

Travis appreciated the confidence the captain showed in him but right now, he needed to get moving. "Corporal, round up the eggheads, we're leaving. I'll take care of our friend here."

Philippa got to work hustling the two scientists who were packing their equipment as fast as they could, glad to be getting away from whatever would shortly be coming through the inner door. Travis took a step toward the prisoner and used the barrel of his PEP to indicate he was to stand up. The alien slowly got to its feet and Travis motioned for it to make its way through the outer airlock. Hesitantly, it did as it was directed but once outside it stopped dead in its tracks, confronted by the sight of four Tanto combat shuttles dropping a company of marines onto the moon's barren surface. Travis was forced to give the alien a gentle nudge to get it moving again as they climbed up the shallow incline of the crater wall to be met by Captain Zubek.

Zubek took a moment to give the alien suit a head to toe appraisal before activating his link to Travis. "Let's get your prisoner over to Charlie Company's Landing Zone to await the First Contact Team. Admiral Lewis must have lit a fire under them as they're already on a shuttle and on their way down. I'm sure they're chomping at the bit to have a chat with him..." Zubek chuckled softly, "Or her, come to think of it."

"Aye-aye sir. Papadomas, you're prisoner escort with me." He turned to the scientists. "You two head over to our Tanto and hole up until I need you. And thanks for a job well done." The two scientists did not need to be told twice and headed off at a dead run for the relative safety of the Tanto.

The small group of Travis, Philippa, and their prisoner moved off across the powder-like surface, skirting craters as they went. After a few minutes, they reached the lip of a large crater and saw that the four Tantos of Charlie Company were spread out on its floor. Marines poured out of the troop doors and took up positions along the lip of the crater, securing it for the arrival of the First Contact Team. The alien paused as he looked down at the deploying marines, his head slowly moving from left to right as he took in the scene. Travis gave him a gentle nudge to coax him on, but what had been intended as nothing more than a "hurry up" took a turn for the worse as the alien stumbled and the loose surface underneath him gave way. He tumbled down the crater's steep side. Travis and Philippa leapt after him, only to have a large boulder intervene in their headlong chase. Philippa reached the crumpled alien first and went to her knees, turning him over and immediately noticing a large tear in the pressure suit, which was venting atmosphere. Philippa automatically reached for her emergency suit repair kit.

"Lieutenant, his suit's ripped pretty well all the way through!"

Philippa worked quickly, knowing every second counted. The life-giving atmosphere escaping from the suit in a jet crystallized as it hit the coldness of space. Philippa's movements were drilled into her. Spray the glue. Fix the patch in place. Press down hard. Hold for one... two... three.

Check for leaks. Philippa's eyes fell on a few lone crystals still escaping from the top edge of the patch. Her heart pounding in her ears, Philippa fumbled for her repair kit but she had dropped it onto the powdery surface in her haste to attach the first patch. Travis saw her frantic search and realized what she was looking for. Popping his own kit, he forced a second patch into her hand. With the second patch applied and no sign of a leak, Philippa sat back on her heels as Travis moved the alien into a sitting position, propping him up against the boulder that had nearly been the death of him.

Philippa became aware of an armored hand resting on her shoulder as she slowly regained control of her breathing.

“Quick reactions there, Corporal, I think you just saved our friend’s life," said Travis. His head turned skyward as his eyes caught sight of a lone shuttle dropping into the crater to settle in the middle of the marine cordon. "That’ll be the First Contact Team. What say we go hand over our prisoner and let them take it from here?"

Philippa nodded and pushed herself to her feet. She stretched out an arm to the alien, who was still leaning against the boulder. The alien hesitated, then took the proffered hand and used it to pull himself upright. For a moment, the two suited figures looked at each other through feature-hiding helmets before the alien slowly crossed its arms over his chest, gloved hands touching his shoulders and gave a small nod of his head.

"I think that was a ‘thank you,’ Corporal," chuckled Travis.

Philippa mimicked the alien’s movements, in an attempt to acknowledge the thanks, before the three of them set off for the waiting shuttle.

The outer airlock of the shuttle was already open as they

reached it and there was a suave suited civilian and a gaggle of suited Navy techs waiting for them.

"Lieutenant Travis, I'm Clare Honeywell, part of Ambassador Jelav's First Contact Team. We'll take the prisoner in first, sir. If he's from Planet II, his atmosphere is richer in nitrogen than Earth's norm so we have a pressure chamber set up with his requirements. Once he's through we'll bring you in and you can brief the ambassador personally."

Travis and Philippa waited at the foot of the ramp as Honeywell gestured for the alien to follow her into the airlock. With a glance back at Philippa, he slowly walked up the ramp and Philippa lost sight of him as the airlock closed.

Travis opened his link to Philippa. "So we get to brief the ambassador personally. Huh, when was the last time you heard of a civilian listening to what a couple of lowly marines had to say? Five gets you ten we get a pat on the back and a mumbled thanks for your help before we find ourselves back out in the cold."

"You never know, sir. Jelav is a Garundan so he might do things a little differently."

"I'll believe it when I see it, Corporal."

The airlock door cycled open and both marines entered. The airlock cycled quickly and moments later Travis and Philippa were able to remove their helmets. Both gave their crew-cut hair a good rubdown as they did so. It was probably the most irritating thing about wearing the Wraith suit for long periods, no matter how much you tried not to think about it, you just wanted to rub your head sometimes. The day someone invented a way to scratch your head without removing your helmet would be a very happy day for many a marine. The inner door slid open and Travis and Philippa stepped into the shuttle proper. The well-lit personnel bay, which normally held twenty Wraith-suited marines and their gear, was instead full of bustling civilians, all seemingly talking at the same time. Not knowing what to do next, the two marines just stood by the airlock and waited patiently. The sea of civilians parted as the form of an elderly, but remarkably sprightly, Garundan made his way over to the marines.

"Ah, Lieutenant Travis and Corporal Papadomas. Welcome, welcome. I believe it is you we have to thank for our guest."

Travis answered, "We didn't really have much choice but to bring him with us, Mr. Ambassador..."

Jelav waved a dismissive hand at the lieutenant's attempt at an explanation. "However it came about, Lieutenant, you have allowed us to meet a new race, something which doesn't happen every day." The ambassador glanced toward the rear of the cabin, as if in a hurry to return. He hesitated and then asked, "Would you like to meet our guest in the flesh, so to speak?"

An excited, "Oh yes!" slipped out of Philippa's mouth before she could stop it.

The diminutive Garundan gave the small open-mouthed laugh of his people. "This way, then." The animated civilians parted as the ambassador strode to the rear of the cabin and stopped in front of the protective plasteel window. Hard as steel but clear like glass, plasteel was the perfect alloy for jobs like pressure windows and habitat domes in unfriendly atmospheres.

Seated in the small chamber was the still-partially suited alien. Philippa had no idea what he looked like beneath his pressure suit and was eager to find out. Looking through the plasteel, Philippa was confronted by what she could best describe as the head of a bird of prey atop a hominid body.

Two large, round, brown eyes stared back at her unblinkingly from a head covered in bright white feathers, which changed to darker brown as they disappeared under the pressure suit's neck joint. Where a human mouth should be there was a protrusion of yellowed bone curving eloquently to a sharp point.

The alien stood and approached the plasteel until it stood directly in front of Philippa. The hands came up and formed the same cross-body move as before, but this time the suit gloves were off. Philippa's eyes widened in surprise as six thin, bony fingers touched shoulders before giving a short nod of the head. Philippa returned the gesture and the alien retook its seat.

Another soft chuckle came from Jelav as he noticed Philippa's reaction. "That's right, Corporal Papadomas. Our guest has six fingers. It looks like this is our first encounter with a race who escaped Saiph DNA manipulation."

Ever since the discovery of Saiph DNA manipulation on nine different worlds which had been intended to bring forth a species to climb to the top of their respective intelligence chains and become the foremost species of their planet, scientists had prophesied we would, undoubtedly, run into a race who's development had been free of Saiph interference and who had reached a level of development which would be comparable, if not superior, to our own. And here, behind the plasteel looking back at Philippa, stood a member of that race.

"How are we doing with the translation software?" Jelav called to no one in particular.

A harassed-looking tech off to one side of the chamber answered without raising his head from his terminal, "We've run all the radio transmissions through the computers, Ambassador, and I think I've got the algorithm close enough for you to understand each other. The computer will automatically refine itself as you go."

Jelav gave Philippa the open-mouthed grin of his race, "Shall we, Corporal? It was you, after all, who brought us our guest."

Philippa cleared her throat before stepping hesitantly forward until her face was inches from the plasteel. "Hello. My name is Philippa. Philippa Papadomas of the Commonwealth Union of Planets and we mean you no harm. What is your name?"

Inside the chamber, the bird-like head cocked to one side as the speaker repeated Philippa's words in his own language.

The alien regarded Philippa with unblinking eyes for a few seconds before saying, "I am Weloo. First Grade Technician. I see your computing machines are very advanced." Again the cocking of the head to one side. "Have you come to kill the last of us?"

Philippa hesitated in her response, taken aback by the matter-of-fact question. Jelav took her hesitation as his chance to speak, "Weloo. I am Ambassador Jelav. As Philippa stated, we have no intention of harming anyone. We seek only peaceful contact with your species."

Weloo looked from Jelav to Philippa and back again, "You are not of the same kind?"

Philippa regained her composure and answered calmly, "No, we are not the same species. The Commonwealth we belong to is made up of different races from different planets. Who are these people you talk of? Are they the ones who destroyed the planet around which this moon orbits?"

Weloo's fingers balled into fists and he became very still. His mind's eye seemed to conjure the image of his irradiated home. "Six cycles ago they came. Eighteen huge ships. We tried to speak to them. Our best scientists used radio, laser, and even went so far as sending up a small spacecraft to make personal contact with them, but instead they just kept coming on in total silence. When they reached high orbit they opened fire. Bombs fell on every city. Every town and then every village until there was nothing left. In less than two rotations, Edasich was no more."

"Edasich? Is that the name of your people?"

Weloo looked up as the vision of his destroyed world cleared. "We who remain came from many countries on Edasich and before the destruction, we each claimed to be a citizen of that country alone. We had already established a small subterranean base here on this moon for scientific research. A joint venture between the different nations. However, neither they nor their people remain, so we survivors are all just Edasich now. Nothing more and nothing less."

"But how did you survive the attack?"

"Our base commander, Felan, saw the first bombs fall and ordered every non-essential system shut down in the hope we would evade detection. We kept the radio receivers on and heard the calls for mercy on every frequency. Their pleas were never answered. When the last bomb fell, the silent ships turned around and simply left. Felan ordered the power levels kept at minimum in case they somehow discovered us. For forty rotations, we stayed the same way. The recycled air was always stale and the cold... many succumbed to the cold while some took their own lives in despair. We had nearly reached breaking point, so Felan allowed the reactors to be brought back up to full power. The hydroponics labs, which had only been experimental, were now our only hope for food so they were expanded and we mined for water trapped in the ice below ground. It has been a struggle but we have survived."

A double tone in Travis' ear bug alerted him to an incoming signal. "Go for Travis."

"Travis. Captain Zubek. It looks like your prisoner's friends are massing just inside the airlock."

"Hold on, sir, I'm going to put you on speaker." With a touch of his suit controls Travis activated his external speaker. "Go on, sir."

"I'm expecting some sort of breakout imminently. If they come out shooting, it won't end well for them. I have a company plus on the crater lip. Tell Ambassador Jelav if he's going to do something then now's the time."

"Understood, sir." Travis cut the link.

Inside the chamber, Weloo looked distraught. "Let me speak to them. They probably think, as I did, that you are the same people who attacked us before and are back to finish what you started."

Jelav looked at Travis, who shrugged. "It's your call, Ambassador. All the way here, Weloo was allowed to use his suit radio to speak to his base so they know our rough numbers. They probably don't know our dispositions but if they come out the airlock firing Captain Zubek, will cut them to shreds."

Seeing he really didn't have a choice, Jelav turned back to Weloo. "Weloo, please tell your people to wait. Tell them we will defend ourselves if they fire upon us but we will make no attempt to enter the crater. I'd very much like to speak to this Felan. If he's willing, I'll meet with him at a time and place of his choosing."

Weloo was already speaking animatedly into his suit's pick-up. His head took on the now familiar cocking movement as he listened to the reply.

Through the corner of his eye, Jelav saw the comms tech give him a thumbs-up, so he was prepared for Weloo's next statement.

"Felan has ordered all personnel to hold their positions. He asks you meet him by the airlock and orders me to remain here as your... guest until your safe return."

Jelav waved a hand dismissively. "I don't believe that's required, Weloo. I'd prefer for you to accompany me to this meeting." Turning to Philippa and Travis he said, "Would you be so kind as to make yourselves available as escorts, Lieutenant? We leave as soon as I suit up." Jelav headed for the suit room.

#

The walk back to the crater holding the airlock door for the sub-surface base took the small group of Travis, Philippa, Ambassador Jelav, his assistant Clare Honeywell, and Weloo less time than it had taken to reach the First Contact team's shuttle. Understandably, Weloo was anxious to get back to his own people and Philippa was forced to place a restraining arm on his shoulder a number of times so that the diminutive Garundan ambassador could keep up. When they finally arrived at the crater's lip, it appeared to be covered in a solid wall of marines. Each one had their weapons trained on the still-open airlock door that Philippa had disabled with her plasma torch.

The sight of the amassed marines caused Weloo to stop in his tracks. His head scanned left and right as he took in the firepower on display. The voice of Jelav broke into his study of the marine lines. "Would you like to tell Felan we are approaching the airlock now?"

Weloo dragged his attention back to the ambassador. "Of course. One moment please, while I change channels."

Behind his mirrored faceplate, the ambassador let his eyes cross over to where Honeywell was standing directly behind Weloo. Her position was no accident. Part of her job was to monitor the Edasich communications. It wasn't that the ambassador didn't trust Weloo, but in his experience it always paid to have a little insider knowledge in any negotiations. Honeywell's thumbs-up signal coincided with Weloo coming back onto the inter-suit channel.

"Felan is making his way to the airlock now and requests we join him there."

"Please lead on, Weloo."

The Edasich stepped over the crater's lip and headed down its steep walls, closely followed by the Commonwealth delegation.

The double beep of an incoming signal sounded in Philippa's ear and a quick check of her HUD showed it was Travis. "Go for Papadomas."

"If this all goes to hell, Corporal, you grab Honeywell and I'll take the ambassador. Try to get clear of the line of fire and let the covering force do their jobs. Understood?"

"Oo-rah, sir."

The party approached the open airlock and came to a halt. Unnoticed by either of the diplomats, Travis and

Philippa had taken up flanking positions within easy arm's reach of each of their chosen charges.

A figure stepped from the airlock, dressed in a similarly beaten and bedraggled spacesuit as Weloo. Crossing the small distance between them, Weloo stopped in front of what, presumably, was the figure of Felan. With more flourish than he had shown to Philippa, Weloo crossed his arms, gloved hands to shoulder blades, and bowed deeply, holding the position until Felan stepped forward and touched his right hand to Weloo's left shoulder. Weloo straightened and Felan leaned his helmeted head forward until it was touching Weloo's helmet.

Sneaky, thought Philippa. With their helmets touching, both Edasich could hold a conversation without having to use their suits' radios, as their voices could be heard through the touching helmets. They'd need to shout but it effectively prevented anyone from listening in. Philippa had to give him her grudging admiration.

By the way, the Edasich's helmets bobbed up and down, they were having a very animated conversation, which went on for a number of minutes until they finally separated and Weloo stepped to one side. For the first time, Felan addressed the Commonwealth group directly.

"If I am to believe First Technician Weloo, you have the top of the crater lined with soldiers. Correct?"

"Base Commander Felan," began Jelav, "My name is Ambassador Jelav, representing the Commonwealth Union of Planets. What Weloo has told you is correct. There is a large number of soldiers and warships are in orbit above us, but they are there as a precaution only."

"A precaution, Ambassador? A precaution against what? Was it not your soldiers who attempted to enter our home?

Was it not your soldiers who kidnapped one of our own? Have we made any aggressive moves toward you? I demand you withdraw your soldiers and send your warships away at once! This is our home and you are not welcome here."

Jelav paused before answering in his most conciliatory tone. "If you so desire, Base Commander, we will withdraw from this place and leave you in peace. We have no wish to force ourselves upon you. But... if I may?"

Even though he was dressed in a spacesuit, it was easy to see the reluctance in Felan's jerky arm movement, which Jelav took as permission to continue.

"First Technician Weloo has indicated to us you are the last survivors of the Edasich and life is hard for you here. As a sign of our peaceful intent, may I offer some food stuffs from our stores to bolster your hydroponics?"

Everyone could hear the skepticism in Felan's voice even through the computer-aided interpretation. "And you would do such a thing why? You know nothing about us and I have already told you to leave."

Jelav raised his arm and pointed at the dead planet low above the horizon. "Because, Base Commander, not too long ago these humans who stand beside me gave my people succor when we were in need. They did not do so because they had to, they did it because it was the right thing to do. It is a lesson that my people have taken to heart. You are in need and I can help, so I choose to."

For a long moment, the six individuals from three different races fixed their eyes on a dead planet hovering millions of kilometers away in complete silence.

"What of the soldiers and your warships?" Felan asked in a less argumentative tone.

"Lieutenant."

"Yes, Ambassador."

"Please tell Captain Zubek to contact the cruisers and order them to withdraw to the edge of the system. Once he has done so, he is to embark all his marines and return to the fleet. Only my shuttle is to remain on the surface. And when I say all his marines are to return to the fleet, I mean you and the corporal too."

Travis could not believe what he was hearing but like a good marine, he followed his orders. No sooner had Zubek acknowledged the order than the small group made out the shadowy figures of marines leaving their firing positions and heading for their shuttles on the double. Less than five minutes later, all but one of the marine shuttles were loaded and their straining engines lifted them clear of the moon's surface. They angled away on course for the waiting fleet.

Beep. Beep. "Go for Travis."

"Heads up, Lieutenant. I'm holding the last shuttle for you so hustle up, it's a long walk home," said Zubek over the link.

"Understood, sir, we're on our way. Travis clear." With a quick tap, he changed channels and opened a link to Philippa. "Our ride's waiting, Corporal, let's bounce."

"Aye-aye sir," Philippa turned, prepared to double time it to the waiting shuttle, but something stopped her. Turning to face Felan, she replicated Weloo's earlier respectful bow. Holding it for a few seconds before standing back upright she spun in place and set off after Travis who was already bounding up the crater walls on his power-assisted legs. A call on the open radio channel stopped both of them in their headlong dash.

"Wait!" Called the unmistakable sound of Felan.

Both Travis and Philippa came to an instant halt.

"Perhaps I was too hasty in my earlier statements, Ambassador Jelav. You've withdrawn all your soldiers and warships, as you said you would. Even these last two, leaving yourself unprotected and defenseless in front of me. How do you know I won't now take you hostage and demand your people supply the things I need, rather than wait on your charity?"

Over the open mike, the slight Garundan's distinctive chuckle was heard. "Trust is a thing to be earned, Base Commander, and I choose to use myself and my colleague as collateral."

The radio channel hissed quietly and all caught Felan's glance at his dead world before he again looked at the Garundan. "Would you like a tour of the base, Ambassador, you and your escort? And may I formally request whatever assistance you and your people are able to supply?"

Travis activated his link to the waiting marine shuttle. "Looks like we're staying a little longer, sir. See you back at the fleet."

CHAPTER THREE
Keep It in the Family

SLIVINO VALLEY - NORTHERN ITALY - EARTH - SOL SYSTEM

The stable hand bent back to his work as Seaton Anderson, astride his favorite chestnut stallion, left the stable complex situated behind the main house in the center of the sprawling 170-square kilometer estate that dominated the Slivino valley of northern Italy. Since being placed under house arrest on his estate Seaton had taken to going riding nearly every morning, spending hours weaving his way through the thick pine forests covering the estate.

Many of the staff commented on how their billionaire master seemed un-phased by his indictment for charges ranging from bribery to murder.

Seaton had been removed from his position as chair of one the Commonwealth's biggest conglomerates, Zurich Lines, and forced to remain on his palatial estate while his army of lawyers fought the government every inch of the way. The media were reporting it could take years, if ever, to bring Seaton to trial. And all the time he lived the life anyone could ever dream of. Waited on hand and foot. His every want tended to. The stable hand shook his head in weary resignation as the horse and rider disappeared from view. Picking up the pitchfork, he shoveled fresh hay into the stall, ready for the stallion on its return.

Seaton Anderson's nonplussed exterior could not have been further from his real state of mind. Seaton was a worried man. For thirty years, he had spent every ounce of his considerable energy building the shipping line left to him by his father into one of the biggest in known space. Go to any port in the Commonwealth and you were guaranteed to find a Zurich Lines flagged ship there. Buy any item manufactured or produced off-planet and there was a very good chance it had been carried aboard a Zurich Lines ship at some point.

Now though, the company he gave two marriages and his entire adult life to build was crumbling around him. It was not the court indictments that bothered him so much. His lawyers assured him he would never see the inside of a courtroom in his lifetime. It was not even the fact some of his bankers had called in the loans he had used to finance his expanding fleet, a requirement to establish and service the new colonies springing up like fresh seeds after a spring rain. The company had enough revenue and reserves to cover the costs. No. It was President Coston's plan to grant independence to Janus that worried him. An integral part of the president's plan was the restructuring of all of Janus' debts. Debts which were made up in a significant part by the shipping costs incurred during the establishment of the colony world and the infrastructure required to maintain and expand it as it grew to a point where it was self-sustaining. Zurich Lines was owed billions by the colony and if Coston's plan was successful, these debts would be restructured over a much longer timeline, cutting the company's expected revenue by nearly forty-five percent. Combine the revenue loss with the withdrawal of investment and the company was left in a precarious financial position. Seaton made himself a solemn vow: No matter what it took, he would not allow his company to be destroyed!

The difficulty was, Seaton was no longer directly involved in his own company and the question of who he could trust to continue in his stead was undecided. His most trusted confidant, Daya Thomas, had spent the last three years locked up in solitary confinement in a federal maximum security prison on Titan after the former intelligence chief had been caught trying to smuggle Seaton's personal files containing embarrassing information on various highly placed legal, political, and military figures off the planet during the Others' attack. Seaton's lawyers' most arduous efforts were not enough to release her, leaving Seaton with only one choice. In his deliberations, Seaton had remembered a favorite phrase of his father's: "Keep things in the family."

It presented Seaton with a bit of a quandary. He had no children of his own but had always been close to his sister's son, Bryer. With his sister and her husband's unfortunate passing Seaton had kept a watchful eye on the boy's naval career. Making sure he remained out of harm's way. Not an easy task in a time of war but with the right word here and there it was not an impossible task either. That was until Bryer fell afoul of the same Admiral Elizabeth Wilson who was leading the investigation into Zurich Lines and its involvement in the Empire of Alona's scheme to gain access to the gravity drive, a technology which was deemed a state secret.

At the tap of a key, Bryer had been packed off to some back-of-beyond job in the asteroid belt. His carefully orchestrated naval career in tatters. Well, maybe it was time for Bryer to come home.

When the Federal Investigation Bureau swooped on Zurich Lines' offices and Seaton's own home armed with court warrants, they seized every computer and data storage device they found, but like many raised in the electronic age, their prejudice against anything appearing outdated was a fatal flaw. They never even thought to look for something like paper records. Not that there were any to find in the company's offices or Seaton's home.

The Seaton estate was only centered on the main house. Scattered throughout the sprawling estate grounds were various other smaller hunting lodges and derelict farmhouses which had once been the homes of families who had worked the rich farmland for generations before the land had been procured by the Anderson family. The majority of those farmhouses had not had a visitor in decades, becoming overgrown and derelict. Why would the FIB bother to search them?

Seaton spent two hours winding his way through the fragrant pine trees and long meadow grass until, apparently by chance, he came upon one of those long abandoned farmhouses, which to any casual observer, looked no different from the others spread around the estate.

Patting the stallion's neck affectionately, Seaton dismounted and tied him to one of the towering pines. The dried pine needles on the forest floor deadened the sound of his footsteps as he approached the front door, which stood at an angle in its warped frame. Reaching into his pocket, Seaton retrieved his cigar cutter. An item anyone, friend or foe, would attest to as a plaything – he had an annoying habit of fiddling with it during virtually every meeting.

With a practiced motion, Seaton depressed and released the cutter. A muted beep came from above the doorframe as the explosive charges set in the floor and walls disarmed and reinforced steel locking bars slid silently into their recesses. Pushing the rickety-looking door open, Seaton stepped inside. Low intensity automatic lighting came on, illuminating the stark interior. Walking to the center of the small living room, Seaton dropped to one knee and pressed a hand onto a burnished metal plate. The biometric lock accepted him and a section of the floor dropped a few centimeters before silently sliding to one side. More low-level lights came on, revealing a set of steep steps. Making his way down carefully, Seaton was forced to duck his head as he took the last few steps to avoid hitting the Permacrete-reinforced roof.

As he reached the bottom step, the false floor above him slid back into place with a nearly inaudible click. With the room now sealed, the ceiling lighting sprang to life to reveal a row of ancient five-drawer filing cabinets lining one wall of the cramped room. A low wooden desk was placed against the opposite wall, upon which sat an archaic adjustable desk lamp and a single chair pushed neatly under the desk. That was the whole of the room's furniture. There was no computer or electronic communications device to be found anywhere. Nothing for any snooper, be they government or competitor, to piggyback in on.

Seaton's father had first brought him here years before. His father had been a secretive man, some said paranoid, and he had spent a small fortune having the farmhouse above the room painstakingly taken down one brick at a time by hand, only to have it rebuilt exactly as it had been a few weeks later. The laborers carrying out the work were told the farmhouse held sentimental value to the aging Anderson. He had wanted to replace it with an ultramodern hunting lodge but on seeing its demise, reconsidered and decided to retain the original building.

They did not know about the complete underground unit built off-site by a defense contractor who thought he was building a prototype fallout shelter. The unit was collected from the contractor's factory for trials, which he was subsequently informed were unsuccessful, and the project was shelved. Like so many new ideas, this one was consigned to the scrap heap. In reality, a separate set of contractors installed the entire unit in just three days. They were told it was for a rich family who feared another nuclear war and wanted somewhere to live through it. Each of these contractors had been flown in to the site in the dead of night and remained there until the job was finished.

On completion, every person signed a nondisclosure agreement before being airlifted out of the site with a substantial bag of cash.

When it came to rebuilding the farmhouse, the men carrying out the work had no idea there was now a secret bunker below.

Seaton moved to the desk and switched on the lamp, throwing a bright light onto the well-thumbed ledger book sitting in the center of the wooden desk. Seaton bent over and blew the fine film of dust from the ledger's cover before opening it and running his index finger down the alphabetical list of names until it came to rest on one in particular. He let out a satisfied "Hmmm." The same finger traced horizontally across the page until it came to the correct cabinet, drawer, and index number. Closing the ledger again, he used his index fingers to ensure it was returned to its exact place. A small idiosyncrasy he had picked up watching his father in this very room.

Turning his back to the desk, he went to the second filing cabinet and pulled open the bottom drawer. The drawer opened with a creak. Seaton made a mental note to bring a small bottle of lubricant with him on his next visit.

Reaching in, he lifted out the correct file, then took a seat at the desk and flipped it open. The file contained about a dozen neatly handwritten sheets of paper. Attached to the top sheet was a color photograph of a young, self-assured navy ensign. Flicking to the second page, Seaton skipped to the last line of the bio. And there in his neat handwriting were the words: "Assistant to the Chief of Naval Personnel."

Seaton allowed himself a wry smile. Perfect! He leaned back and began to memorize the file's contents, reminding himself of what indiscretion the young ensign had committed all those years ago which had led to his name joining the list in the ledger and, more importantly, what leverage it now gave Seaton to secure Bryer's release from naval service.

Returning to the ledger, Seaton searched out two other names, removed their files, and set them down on the desk. It wasn't enough to secure the release of Bryer, he had to ensure his position as head of Zurich Lines was as strong as possible, and the only way to do so was to have friends in high places. Exactly what Seaton had in mind, even if he had to bring down a government to do it.

CHAPTER FOUR
Survey Command

CHARON BASE - ORBIT OF PLUTO - SOL SYSTEM

Christos Papadomas leaned back in his comfortable office chair, closed his weary eyes, and rubbed the bridge of his nose in what he knew was a futile effort to avert the dull pain behind his eyes from worsening. As he straightened back up, his eyes fell upon the small, silver-framed portrait standing in pride of place on his desk. The picture showed his three girls, Philippa, Maia, and Odysseia, playing in his mother's garden on Crete with his wife, Kayla, hovering like a mother hen in the background. The picture had been taken fifteen years before when the children were so much younger and his life was so much happier and much less complicated. A veil of sadness descended on him as his eyes fixed on the beauty of Kayla.

Kayla had been a doctor working in the Lunar Colony's Central Hospital when the attack came. Dedicated to her profession, she ensured the safety of her children in the deep mines before she returned to her post. A direct hit from an enemy missile on her workplace cut her life short and stole her from him and their children.

When Christos heard of her death, his heart was ripped from him and he became like a zombie. He withdrew to the seclusion of his quarters on his flagship, TDF *Cutlass,* rather than mix with his crew and the inevitable words of consolation and the sympathetic looks. When *Cutlass* arrived at the Lunar Colony and he left his quarters to head to the shuttle bay, crewmembers pressed themselves against bulkheads to move out of his way as the shell of what was once their smiling, happy commander walked past, his eyes vacant and unseeing.

Christos had vague memories of the shuttle ride down to the lunar surface with a worried Nicholas Schamu in the seat beside him. When the shuttle touched down and the sound of the engines died, Christos walked past the saluting crew chief without recognition and before he knew it, he was holding Maia and Odysseia in his arms. The tears finally came and he bared his soul to the world in a shuttle hangar surrounded by the hulking Persai form of Force Leader Verus and the six other equally intimidating Persai who challenged anyone to intrude on their commander's grief.

The protective circle of Persai had opened to admit Nicholas Schamu and the short, elderly, apparently frail form of Mrs. Victoria Brown. Mrs. Brown had been the Schamu children's nanny and had shown them the love and affection their parents seemed incapable of. Over the coming days, Mrs. Brown was there to see to the needs of not only the Papadomas children, but also Christos.

Philippa had been on Earth during the attack and Nicholas moved heaven and earth to get Christos' eldest daughter passage on a shuttle to return her to the Lunar Colony. Mrs. Brown happened to mention to William Schamu, governor of the Lunar Colony and brother to

Nicholas, that perhaps the family would like some privacy on the shuttle's landing. When Christos and his youngest children arrived at the shuttleport to meet Philippa, they found the arrivals area secured by lunar police and the normally busy concourse completely empty. As the shuttle bay doors opened to admit Philippa, her father was glad of the privacy as once more, the tears came and his grief overwhelmed him.

Now, three years later, he had come to terms with the loss of Kayla. It wasn't that he'd forgotten her, not a day passed when he didn't think of her and her smiling face, but he no longer sat up alone late at night until he fell asleep in his armchair, only to find at some point Mrs. Brown had quietly entered the living room and placed a blanket over him. She always ensured she made just enough noise to accidentally wake him as she moved around the kitchen the following morning, preparing the children's breakfasts, so he had time to shower and change, making himself presentable before the children got out of bed.

Mrs. Brown's foresight had saved him from embarrassment and probably saved his career a few months after the loss of his wife, when he received an unexpected visitor.

The chiming of the front doorbell was the signal for the customary mad rush by ten-year-old Odysseia in her mission to beat anyone else in the Papadomas household to the door. Christos shared a knowing look with Maia and Philippa as he pushed away from the breakfast table and headed for the door, passed by an unhappy Odysseia stamping back toward her cereal bowl.

"It's for you, Poppa."

Christos tousled her hair as she passed. "One day it will

be a vid star come to whisk you away." *Over my dead body,* thought Christos, pressing the door release as the beginnings of a smile tugged at his lips. All thoughts of vid stars fled his mind as the door slid aside to reveal the figure of Admiral Jing, newly appointed Chief of the Combined Joint Chiefs of Staff, standing in the corridor in a neat pinstriped suit he wore as if it was the uniform Christos was so used to seeing him in. The sight of the admiral in civilian attire caused Christos' brain to react slower than it should, but he recovered quickly and brought himself to attention like a first-year recruit at the academy.

With a wave of his hand Jing said, "Please relax, Christos. I am calling at your home so let's dispense with the formalities, shall we?"

"Of course, sir... please come in. You'll have to excuse me, the children are just finishing their breakfast before going to school." Christos stepped back to allow the admiral entry and was surprised by the sight of Odysseia and Maia, school bags in hand, ready to leave. From the kitchen came the sounds of dishes being placed in the dishwasher and the table being wiped. Mrs. Brown appeared and with a "Good morning, Admiral Jing," shepherded the children out the door and away.

"Well, it appears the children are finished with breakfast and off to school." Christos let the door slide closed before leading the way into the living room, where he ushered Jing to a seat before turning to fetch them both coffee. Philippa, who was carrying a tray with two steaming coffee cups, cream, and sugar, stopped him in his tracks.

"Mrs. Brown told me you prefer decaf, Admiral," said Philippa as she placed the tray on the low table between Jing and Christos' seats. She retreated to her room as a wide-eyed Christos stared.

A small chuckle escaped Jing as he reached for his cup. "It would appear you've been the subject of a very well-executed ambush, Christos."

Taking his seat, Christos could only nod. "Mrs. Brown is very... formidable."

"Indeed," agreed Jing as he took an appreciative sip of his coffee. With a satisfied, "Ahh," he placed the cup down on the tray again. "She even managed to get my favorite brand. I didn't think they had this on the colony. I have to get mine shipped from Earth."

"Friends in low places, sir." Christos was going to have a few choice words with Nicholas Schamu the minute the admiral left. "So to what do I owe the pleasure, sir?"

Jing sat back in the padded armchair and his hands fell into his distinctive steepled pose. *Uh-oh,* thought Christos.

"I've a problem and I think you can assist."

"Any way I can, sir." Christos answered, waiting patiently for the other shoe to drop.

"The war is drawing down and there's going to be a radical shift in government policy and, of course, the navy. Indeed, the whole of the armed services will have to adapt to meet the new policies."

Christos was confused. "What policy changes, sir?"

"Colonization, Christos. Colonization. Not one planet at a time, as with Janus, but mass colonization. A diaspora like we've never seen," he paused. "Look, the people and big businesses were never slow to see the potential of the gravity drive – it's opened the universe to us. Only the fear of the Others kept them reined in. When that threat goes, there are multiple planets in multiple systems, hundreds, possibly thousands of light years apart, that groups are eyeing as ripe for exploitation. For mining, colonization or both."

"The president and other Commonwealth leaders are already in discussions to form a single colonization program with a single department to run it, the Bureau of Colonization I believe it's called. Well, whatever they come up with, we need to radically rethink our own business."

Christos sat back in his chair and considered the impact of mass colonization. "The navy will be spread real thin trying to protect a whole array of new worlds, sir. We don't have enough ships for that. Even if we used every capital ship in every fleet, we wouldn't be strong in any single system and would be exposed elsewhere."

Jing pointed a bony finger at him. "Exactly, Christos! If we spread ourselves too thin, we end up not covering the major planets in the Commonwealth and we place them all at risk. That solution is simply unacceptable."

Christos mulled on Jing's predicament while sipping his coffee. *If we break up the fleets and spread our main fighting power throughout the Commonwealth, it would take time, even with faster-than-light gravity drive communications drones, to reassemble the fleet ready to face down any threat. If you don't disperse the fleet, the only solution is to build new ships to cover the colonies. With the war all but over, Jing will be hard-pressed to get a budget for new ships approved, never mind finding the personnel to crew them.*

Christos had never served under Admiral Jing personally, but his reputation preceded him. Jing was a planner. If he was here speaking to him, then he already had a solution in mind and was just waiting for the right moment to reveal it. *Mrs. Brown and the admiral must have been cut from the same cloth,* thought Christos.

"I take it you have a cunning plan, sir."

A lopsided grin broke Jing's serious expression. "Well, of course I have, Christos. We're going to speed up the construction of Fortress Command. Dedicated capital ship units will supplement the forts, with their fixed defenses. Smaller than the current fleets, we have protecting the major planets at the moment, but their lack of numbers will be offset by the added firepower of the forts. As and when the Colossus carriers come on line, they will become the core of a new type of fleet unit, one which hasn't been seen since the last major wet navy engagements of the late 21st century. The Carrier Strike Group," he paused. "Each CSG will be completely self-sufficient. The Colossus carriers will carry a complement of seventy-two Mosquito space fighters, have their own dedicated escorts, and two complete BatFors to give them some added heavy firepower. In case there is a need for a surface action, the CSGs will have an integral marine element of one assault ship carrying a complete Marine Expeditionary Unit. As the CSG may have to operate at some distance from a fleet base, there will also be a fleet train of fast colliers carrying everything from food and water to missiles and reaction mass for the ion drives."

"That's a hard-hitting package," said Christos, impressed by the admiral's plans. "The reduction in the size of the standing fleets will free up the personnel and ships required to equip the CSGs. The Only problem I foresee, is if we start colonizing on a large scale, surely the CSGs can't be everywhere?"

Jing nodded sagely. "That's where, unfortunately, we must live within our means, Christos. There's no way we can build and crew enough CSGs for every world we're going to colonize. So, I've come up with a stopgap solution. It's not perfect by any means, but we'll just have to make do. As you know, running a single Bismarck battleship is an expensive business. Just the routine maintenance, never mind upgrades, costs a small fortune. My bean counters tell me for every battleship I put into mothballs or cancel construction of outright I could build and run four light cruisers. So that's exactly what I intend to do."

Christos snapped his fingers as he realized what Jing intended. "You're taking a leaf from the old colonial navies of Earth's books. You cannot have battleships everywhere but you can send independent cruiser squadrons on long cruises where they do multiple port visits of the colonies. Basically, you're going to fly the flag and if the cruisers come up against anything too big to handle, they call up a Carrier Strike Group who bring in the big guns."

Jing sat back with that grin on his face, watching Christos work through the plan in his head and after a few moments' thought, Christos was ready to ask his next question.

"So if you're going to have these cruiser squadrons running around the colonies, presumably they have to have a central base to work out of, say, within a single sustainable fold, giving them a maximum area of operations around 5000 light years in diameter, dependent of course on how many colonized worlds are within that area. The more colonized worlds, the smaller the area of operations. And that central base in turn would be where the CSG is stationed."

"Correct, Christos. As each quadrant is colonized, there will naturally be a single planet that becomes the center of that quadrant. The fleet will establish a base there, which will expand in line with the size and importance of the colony. Once the colony reaches sufficient size and economic capability, like Janus, the planet's defense will be handed over to Fortress Command and the CSG will move on to the next quadrant, ready to repeat the process."

"I'm impressed, sir. You really have thought this one through."

Jing let out a soft laugh. "Believe me, Christos it wasn't all my doing. There are quite a few staff officers who have been working day and night to make my ideas into reality."

As Jing's laugh subsided a frown wrinkled Christos' brow. "I'm sorry, sir, I still don't see where I fit into all this." The frown disappeared as Christos sat upright in his seat and his face took on a worried expression. "With all these new units, you're going to need experienced commanders, sir. If you intend to appoint me to a position that takes me away from my children, then I must politely refuse. If you insist on it, I'll put my refusal in writing and my request to resign my commission. My children come first now, sir, my family and I have given enough."

For a moment, an awkward silence filled the room before Jing leaned forward and looked Christos square in the eye. "Christos, you are a good officer and a better father. I have no intention of taking you from your family."

A tidal wave of relief washed over Christos.

"However, that said, with the damage suffered by Charon Base and the unfortunate death of Admiral Catney, it leaves Survey Command without a home and a figurehead. I want you to be that figurehead. Rebuild Survey Command for me and make it the kind of command we need it to be. Survey Command will be at the very tip of the spear as we move out into the universe. It will be their ships, your ships, which will be first into new star systems. Your ships will decide whether we send miners and colonists. I need a man in whom I have the utmost confidence to get the job done and I want you to be that man, Christos."

"I'm flattered, sir, but as I said, I have responsibilities

here. I cannot just leave the children with Mrs. Brown and disappear out to the edge of the solar system. No, I'm sorry, sir, I'm not willing to do it."

Jing regarded Christos over the brim of his coffee cup and took another sip before speaking again. "Christos, I'm not asking you to leave the children behind. Survey Command is going to see a massive expansion in ships and personnel over the next few years. Charon Base will need to be rebuilt to accommodate all the new personnel who will run it, which is why the decision was made to allow those personnel to bring their families if they choose. There will be housing, schools, and offices. We expect the final numbers to add up to around 10000 men, women, and children on the base." Jing chuckled softly. "Not only will you be the commander of Survey Command, but you will be the mayor of a small town. What could be better than a family man for that job? So what do you say, Christos?"

Without thinking, Christos' eyes wandered the room. Everywhere he looked, he could see the influence of Kayla. She had brought her own individual touch to transform a standard accommodation module into a family home. Everywhere he looked, he was reminded of her, as he was sure, were the children. Maybe a change of scenery would help them in the process of healing.

"OK sir, I'll do it."

Jing clapped his hands as he stood, then reached over to shake Christos' hand. "Thank you, Christos. I appreciate what you're doing. I know it'll be hard for you and the children, but maybe this will go some small way to making up for it." Jing reached into his jacket pocket and pulled out a small black leather box, which he handed to Christos.

Christos accepted the box and opened it. Sitting inside

were two sets of three golden stars.

"Congratulations, Vice Admiral Papadomas, and may I say a well-deserved promotion. Now I'll be on my way. I've taken up enough of your time."

Christos walked Jing to the door, dazed by his sudden and unexpected promotion. As the door slid closed behind Jing, Christos made his way back into the living room where a nervous-looking Philippa was now sitting on the edge of the chair recently vacated by Jing.

"I take it you heard?" Christos' voice came out a little more gruffly than he intended. Philippa nodded without saying anything, so Christos sat down and forced himself to relax. Philippa was an adult now and deserved to be treated like one.

"I'll speak to Mrs. Brown and ask her if she's willing to stay on and help with the children until we get settled on Charon. It sounds like the family houses won't be ready for a while yet, so there's plenty of time for you to keep searching for a suitable college."

Philippa averted her eyes. Christos realized whatever was troubling his eldest daughter, it wasn't his decision to take the job. Leaning forward, he cupped her hands in his and his voice was a low whisper. "What's wrong, Philippa?"

"I don't know if I want to go to college, Poppa. I thought I did. I thought I wanted to be a famous ambassador like Nicholas and fly between the stars preaching the power of diplomacy and peace. But that was before they took Momma away."

Christos' voice caught in his throat as he heard the depth of loss for his Kayla in his daughter's voice. "You still can be, honey. My new job is an administrative post. I won't be on a ship. There's no reason you can't go and pursue your dreams."

Philippa raised her head and Christos could see the glistening tears she was trying to force back, but there was something else. A determination he hadn’t seen before. A look he had seen so often in her mother’s eyes as she worked so hard to become a doctor while raising young children with a husband aboard a ship somewhere out in the solar system.

"They took Momma from us and I don't want that to happen to anyone else. Somebody needs to stand up to them just as you did. Maia and Odysseia need you here now so you can't be that person anymore... but I can... I want to enlist, Poppa."

The tears came to his eyes as he wrapped his arms around his daughter and held her close. "If that’s what you want, honey. I know your mother would be as proud of you as I am."

The soft double tone of his desk comms panel snapped Christos back to the present and he pressed the acceptance key.

"Your daughter’s shuttle is on final approach, Admiral."

"Thank you, Yeoman. Could you call my quarters and let Mrs. Brown know?"

"She's already been in touch, sir and told me to tell you she and the children will meet you at the landing pad."

"Of course she did." Christos replied with a smile. *One day I'll get something past that woman... well at least I can try,* he thought as he headed for the door.

#

The maglev car slowed as it came to its destination and the bare rocky walls of the tunnel gave way to the brightly lit terminal bustling with people. The car halted and its doors opened with a small hiss of hydraulics. The original Charon Base was small enough that one could walk from point to point but now that it was home to thousands of service members, support personnel, and their families, it far outstripped its original boundaries. Fortunately, the planners had the foresight to design a maglev network to connect the various hubs of a base, which now covered over forty square kilometers.

As Christos stepped from the car, he was greeted by the sight of Mrs. Brown, holding the hand of the twelve-year-old Odysseia, trying desperately to hide her impatience, and a very mature-looking Maia hoping no one would see through her air of nonchalance and spot that she too was impatient to see her sister again. At eighteen years old, Maia was a carbon copy of Kayla at the same age, tall, raven-haired with high cheekbones, and eyes which were as piercing as lasers. Christos hardly failed to notice the admiring looks she got from the many single young men on the base. He shook his head, realizing it was only going to get worse when she flew the nest and began college back on Earth.

"Something wrong, Poppa?" asked Maia with a blinding smile.

Christos mumbled something under his breath as his parental radar fixed on a couple of marines looking in Maia's dirction as they headed for another landing pad. Quick to notice they were the target of Christos' hawk-like stare, they picked up their pace and began an animated conversation, averting their eyes from the admiral and his party.

"Now Christos, that's no way to treat potential suitors for your daughter's hand, is it?" Mrs. Brown said in a stage whisper loud enough for Maia's cheeks to take on a red tinge.

Christos gave the elderly woman a withering look before mumbling a few more choice words under his breath.

Odysseia tugged at his hand. "Can we go now, Poppa? The board says Philippa's shuttle has landed and we don't want to miss her."

Looking down into the screwed-up face of his youngest, Christos could only smile. "I don't think we have to worry about that. Just remember who the boss is around here."

The girl's face turned serious before she said, "I thought Mrs. Brown was the boss." She skipped out of reach as Christos' hand moved to playfully swat her behind.

The small group headed into the arrivals area and on seeing the three stars glinting on the admiral's collar, military and civilians alike stood back at a respectful distance. With a soft hum, the bulkhead leading to the shuttle bay slid open and a mix of military and civilians began to enter the arrivals area. Odysseia was virtually bouncing from foot to foot as she tried to spot her elder sister and Maia was forced to keep a restraining hand on her shoulder.

"There she is! There she is!" Squealed an excited Odysseia. Maia looked to her father for approval. He gave her a small nod and all at once, the whirlwind that was Odysseia Papadomas flew across the arrivals area, ducked under the barrier separating the arrivals gate from the waiting families, and pounced on an unsuspecting marine corporal still in the process of showing her travel orders to the military police officer staffing the gate. The police officer was about to say something when he spotted the approaching admiral. Taking a second look at the marine's identity on his PAD, he made the connection. Corporal Papadomas, daughter of Vice Admiral Papadomas. Like all good soldiers when the brass were descending, he made himself scarce. With a brusque wave of his hand, he passed Philippa and her limpet-like sister through and into the main arrivals area.

Maia gave her elder sister a hug before lifting Odysseia from her arms. "You can't hang off a marine like that, you little monkey."

Philippa turned to face her father. She brought herself to attention and gave him a parade ground salute. Christos assumed the position of attention himself and snapped off a salute of his own. From behind him came Mrs. Brown's exasperated voice. "If you've finished with the military stuff, Christos, may I remind you, you haven't seen each other for two years? Perhaps you'd like to welcome your daughter home properly?"

Christos' face broke into a large smile, mirroring Philippa's. Stepping forward, his powerful arms pulled his daughter to him. "Welcome home, Philippa."

Philippa closed her eyes and breathed deeply, enjoying the feel of his protective arms around her. "Thanks, Poppa. I've missed you all."

Christos sensed her weariness, a weariness he recognized from the many times he had returned from an arduous mission and fell into Kayla's warm embrace. Releasing her, he held her at arm's length. For the first time he noticed how old her eyes looked. His little girl was grown up and her expression told him she'd seen a few things that would stay with her the rest of her life. Being a marine in combat did that to you. Philippa caught her father's look of concern and she gave him a small smile to deflect his concerns.

"I'd kill for a decent cold beer."

Christos let out a loud laugh, turning heads among those

still milling about. "I'm sure I have one or two in the fridge but I warn you, Nicholas is coming for dinner tonight and he'll be horrified you're drinking beer and not his fancy wine."

Now it was Philippa's turn to laugh. "What does he expect from a marine?"

Arm in arm, the corporal and the vice admiral headed for the maglev terminal while the three sisters shared two years' worth of gossip.

#

The evening had been filled with random, nonsensical chatter as Philippa tried in vain to satisfy her younger sisters' seemingly insatiable appetite to know every second of her life for the past two years. Philippa had spun her tales of marine boot camp and life on board ship like a master storyteller, but Christos and Nicholas had both noticed the way she avoided the subject of combat and glossed over the details of the worlds she had seen laid to waste by the Others.

As the two younger Papadomas girls were ushered into the kitchen to help Mrs. Brown clean up after dinner, Christos decided to broach the subject he had been brooding over for the last few days and one he now mentioned ever so casually. "I received an interesting request the other day, Philippa."

The bottle of beer paused halfway to her lips for a fraction of a second before continuing on its journey. Philippa took a slug of the cold beer before answering in an equally casual tone, "Oh? I thought you admirals had minions to filter out the crap before it got as far as your inbox."

"A veritable army of them, my dear Philippa," commented Nicholas as he studiously contemplated his wine glass.

Christos spared him a glance, a none-too-subtle order to stay out of this particular father-daughter chat.

"It would appear one of my minions, as you so politely call Yeoman Givens, thought a request from my eldest daughter's platoon commander was worthy of my personal attention. A lieutenant who felt so strongly about something, he was willing to sidestep the chain of command and contact a vice admiral directly. An act, which could in all honesty have some devastating repercussions for said lieutenant's career if his own superiors found out what he had done. Care to guess what your lieutenant had to say?"

Philippa carefully placed her bottle on the table, suddenly finding the picture of her father's first command on the wall extremely interesting. She refused to meet her father's eyes, unconsciously chewing her lower lip as she played for time, her stomach churning, trying to control her burgeoning anxiety. Her mind replayed the conversations she had had with Lieutenant Travis and Captain Zubek. *Damn them! I told them both no. I'm not ready*. Steeling herself for the inevitable browbeating from her father, she was surprised when the conciliatory voice of Nicholas intruded on the lengthening silence.

"If I may interject? Before voices are raised and things are said which may not so easily be forgotten perhaps a small cautionary tale is in order."

Christos' expression soured while Philippa's eyes pleaded with Nicholas to intervene. The continuing silence gave Nicholas the green light to proceed.

"I seem to remember a similar situation to the one we face here occurring some years ago. A young sailor showed quite extraordinary potential, a fact those above him were quick to recognize, and he rose swiftly through the ranks. But no matter how hard his superiors tried to convince him to take the next step and become a commissioned officer and fulfill his potential, he repeatedly sidestepped their attempts to push him down that road. Eventually, his constant refusals frustrated his commanding officer so much, the officer decided to try a different tactic. The next time the ship was in port the CO ensured said sailor was held up on board for a couple of hours while the CO threw the rulebook out the window and called on the sailor's wife at home. The CO had no way of anticipating how his turning up unexpectedly at the home would be taken.

"The sailor's heavily pregnant wife met him at the door while cradling another child in her arms. The CO begged her pardon for his intrusion but explained he needed to speak to her about her husband. She invited him in and he spent the next hour explaining to the sailor's wife that her husband was the most promising candidate for officer school he had ever come across. His peers and superiors held him in such high regard that on more than one occasion he was given responsibilities well above his rank and performed them to such a high standard he put others to shame. However, for whatever reason, he refused to take the next step. The CO feared his constant refusal would eventually lead to a point where the offer of a commission would simply be withdrawn and, in his opinion, this would be a complete tragedy. The wife sat and listened patiently to what the CO had to say and had apparently mulled the problem over for a few minutes while the CO waited. She stood and showed the CO to the door, promising that her husband would be outside his office the following morning to fill in the required paperwork."

Philippa, so deeply engrossed by Nicholas' story, jumped when her father let out a loud "Harrumph!" The mischievous look in his eyes did not match his stern expression.

"That was Kayla's version of events. I seem to remember it differently," said Christos as a grin cracked his lips.

"Say what you like, Christos, but I never doubted her," replied Nicholas.

Philippa's words caught in her throat as she realized both men were referring to her mother. And if the story was about her mother, then the sailor had to be her father. Philippa's open jaw closed with a snap, which earned a hearty chuckle from Nicholas.

"Ah, I see Philippa has put two and two together, Christos." Pulling himself out of the chair, Nicholas headed for the kitchen door. "Time to refresh my wine, I think," he said, leaving Christos and Philippa alone as the kitchen door slid closed behind him.

"I... I... I didn't know it was Momma who pushed you to take a commission Poppa. I always thought it was something you decided."

Christos smiled as he leaned forward and took his daughter's hands in his. "Oh Philippa, I would still be taking orders and saluting ensigns fresh out of the academy if your mother hadn't given me a swift kick in the ass that day. I knew I was good enough to be an officer, but sometimes you just need someone to grab you by the scruff of the neck and shove you down a direction you know is the right one, even if you don't have the confidence to go there yourself."

Philippa could only look at the man who had always been her rock, who had always known the right thing to do, who had never seemed to need to consult another living soul when a hard decision had to be made. Now she understood how deep her parents' relationship had actually been. Momma was *his* rock and when she was wrenched from him, it left a void, which would never be filled again. He wasn't angry she refused to take a commission, he just didn't know how to give her the gentle nudge in the right direction Momma had given him.

Lifting her chin and straightening her spine Philippa looked into her father's dark eyes. "I'll do it Poppa. And I promise to make you and Momma proud."

The kitchen door slid aside and revealed Nicholas standing there with a topped-up wine glass and a frosted beer bottle, which he handed to Philippa. "A toast. To the latest recruit to marine officer training. God help them."

CHAPTER FIVE
Earth First

HOUSE OF THE SENATE - GENEVA - EARTH - SOL SYSTEM

The Speaker of the Senate House banged his outdated but traditional wooden gavel on his equally traditional wooden lectern. Modern electronics, concealed within the very fabric of the lectern, transmitted the bang of the gavel to speakers placed throughout the Senate Chamber.

Slowly, almost begrudgingly, the assembled senators grew still and awaited the first business of the day: a statement by the Chair of the Colonization Oversight Committee, Senator Mathias Grant III. It didn't escape the speaker's notice that, for what was billed as "a mundane report on the issue of colonization license application procedures and the funding of mining operations," there appeared to be a surprising number of senators present in the chamber. The speaker smelled something off and quietly sent a messenger to alert the president's office.

Senator Grant was the latest in a long line of Grants to take his place in the Senate. His family was from what was euphemistically called “old money” and generations of Grants had walked the political tightrope, always working behind the scenes creating and exerting their influence on matters which, if you listened to the skeptics, enriched their own power and influence, rather than that of the people they had been elected to represent.

Recently, however, Mathias Grant III had emerged from the shadows. More and more he was held up as the leader of the group known as the Earth First Movement. The movement appeared shortly after the Others’ assault on Earth, riding the wave of fear and hatred the attack had spawned. The Earth First Movement preached an anti-Commonwealth policy, insisting that Earth abandon its allies and go it alone.

If the TDF had not gone to the aid of Garunda, the Others would’ve remained unaware of human existence and would have been no threat to humanity in the first place, Earth First said.

If First Fleet hadn’t rushed to defend the Empire of Alona, an empire which committed interstellar theft by stealing the gravity drive technology and placing a stranglehold on Commonwealth commerce within the Empire, then the fleet would have been in a position to easily defeat the Others, Earth First said.

Their version of the facts, however skewed, was appearing more and more in the news vids. This Senator Grant intended to become the king and not the kingmaker as his ancestors had been.

The speaker banged his gavel once more before announcing, "The Chair recognizes Senator Grant."

The hush that followed the loud bang of the speaker’s gavel seemed somehow to intensify as all heads in the ornate chamber turned to regard Grant. For the senator’s part, he allowed the silence to continue unbroken for a few minutes as he absently arranged the items on his PAD display, giving the impression he was unsure of how to begin.

The speaker was not deceived for a second and he surreptitiously sent another message to the president's office urgently requesting she contact her supporters in the House and get them to the chamber. Something was in the offing here and the speaker knew if it came from Grant then it was not good for the government.

Looking up from his PAD, Grant cleared his throat. "Mr. Speaker. My fellow Senators. Today I was due to give you a report on the progress I and my committee have made over the issues involving our colonization program, but instead I beg the chamber's indulgence and request I be allowed to speak on a separate matter."

Damn, thought the speaker. He knew Grant was up to something, but what? He needed to delay whatever it was long enough for the government's supporters to reach the chamber.

"Perhaps the esteemed senator could deliver his report first and then a vote could be taken by the members present to gauge whether they are inclined to hear your follow-up statement?"

From his seat, Grant gave the speaker his best conciliatory look. "I fear, Mr. Speaker, that what I have to say is of more importance than a simple update on committee progress..." A brief wolf-like smile passed over Grant's face. "I move a vote should be taken immediately to allow the chamber to hear my statement."

Before the speaker could utter a word of protest, a voice from the upper reaches of the chamber called, "I second the motion."

The speaker had no need to check the board in front of him to see who had seconded. The smooth, feminine voice of Senator Dikul was unmistakable. The government had been ambushed. With the motion proposed and seconded, chamber procedure left the speaker no choice. A vote must be called. "Very well. The motion is Senator Grant should be allowed to make a statement to the chamber. Please vote now." The vote was a forgone conclusion. With the government's senators thin on the ground, Grant's motion was easily passed.

"The motion has passed. Senator Grant, you have the floor. Please continue." The speaker settled into his seat and could hardly fail to notice the vid cameras swinging toward Grant as he stood.

"Mr. Speaker. Fellow Senators. Citizens of Earth. I speak to you this morning with a troubled heart. I have wrestled with my feelings throughout the last few days and my conscience will no longer allow me to remain silent. I speak of yet another decision made by the faceless, nameless servants of the so-called Commonwealth, which places the brave members of our armed forces in the front line once more and costs tens of millions of your tax credits without even having the common decency to ask you, the voting public, what you think." Grant clenched his fists and bowed his head as he leaned on the railing in front of his seat. The speaker, a long in the tooth politician, knew enough to know this was all an act for the camera and the public watching at home; however, he knew it had the desired effect of projecting Grant as a man wracked by internal conflict.

"I refer of course by the decision of the Garundan-born Ambassador Jelav to provide the survivors of Edasich with millions of credits worth of aid on his own authority and then the decision by the leaders of the Commonwealth to expand the aid to include engineering and technical equipment, along with the necessary advisers to instruct them on the use of the equipment. Indeed, enough to support them until they become completely self-sufficient. The Commonwealth has arbitrarily committed itself, and therefore Earth, to an aid program forecast to last at least five years and costing billions of credits. A cost that will be borne in no small part by the citizens of Earth." Grant paused, allowing his last statement to sink in with the viewing audience. "Now, I am known as a compassionate man. The terror and destruction the Others have caused to the various races we have encountered cannot be underestimated. The planet Edasich was subjected to the Others' standard orbital nuclear bombardment and its surface has been reduced to a radioactive wasteland. A wasteland we, of all the members of the Commonwealth, know will take decades of hard work and vast sums of money to repair. We know because we have been there! But, and this is something I cannot imagine the leaders of the Commonwealth have failed to consider, the position which Earth found itself in following the war which caused such devastation to our own home is not one which the Edasich find themselves in." Grant looked around the chamber and could see he had the complete undivided attention of his audience. "No. The Edasich have a choice we never had." Grant paused melodramatically. "So flabbergasted was I by this latest decision by the Commonwealth, I ordered my staff to research an alternative to the Commonwealth's decision to support the Edasich and their moon base while beginning the massive task of making their home planet habitable again." Grant lifted his PAD and raised it above his head like some kind of holy grail. "On this PAD is an extract from the navy's Survey Command's own database. A database to which my office has access, due to my position as Chairman of the Colonization Oversight Committee. The navy's own database lists at least nine planets which could easily be colonized by the Edasich at a fraction of the cost which the Commonwealth has projected to complete their current plan."

The murmur of hasty conversations reached the speaker's chair. Where the hell were the government senators? Only a senator from the floor could request the speaker bring this tirade of anti-Commonwealth rhetoric to an end, but looking around, the speaker could only see either Earth First supporters or the undecided. And it was those undecided who held the true balance of power today. The viewing figures were being repeated on their terminals as they were on the speaker's, and they had been rising steadily as the major networks cut into their normal programming to bring Grant's speech into people's homes. The speaker was in no doubt Grant and his Earth First movement had used their influence behind the scenes to orchestrate this with the networks. The speaker was brought back into the House as Grant continued his oratory.

"If the Edasich were simply relocated, then not only would the cost be lower, but the expense involved would, with the correct repayment plan, be recouped by the Commonwealth within a fixed term; similar to that of our own colonization program. I point to Janus as a shining example of what can be achieved with hard work. So why has the Commonwealth decided not to pursue this course of action? Sadly, my committee and indeed this chamber, has no authority to question the decisions of the Commonwealth. Perhaps we should call on President Coston to explain to this chamber, and the citizens of Earth, how this decision came to be made?"

Calls of agreement from Grant's supporters filled the chamber. *And there it is*, thought the speaker. Grant had moved from questioning the motivation of the Commonwealth to questioning decisions made by the president herself. But Grant wasn't finished yet.

"At a time of military overstretch, with many of our patriotic volunteers who flocked to join the Terran Defense

Forces returning home in triumph following the successful conclusion of the war against the Others, the question has to be asked: Is the added burden of providing protection for yet another world the straw which will break the camel's back?"

Another chorus of agreement rang around the chamber.

"The fleet is already being forced to mothball many of its larger vessels due to lack of personnel, so why take on more commitments?"

The speaker noted Grant failed to mention the decision to mothball some of the fleet's heavier units had nothing to do with lack of trained personnel. Rather, it was a conscious decision by the Combined Joint Chiefs based on the fact the navy would be better able to support the program of colonization by introducing groups of lighter, more flexible cruiser units while retaining the core heavy units, expanding Fortress Command and the new Carrier Strike Groups.

Why let facts cloud a good political speech?

"Since the inception of the Commonwealth, it has been Earth followed by Janus, which has not only been the industrial but the military bulwark of the Commonwealth. Was it not the TDF that saved Garunda from destruction? Was it not the TDF who suffered such horrific losses at 70 Ophiuchi? Was it not the TDF who rushed to the aid of the Alonan Empire and left Earth near defenseless in the face of the Others' sneak attack? If not for the bravery of Admiral Chavez and her valiant sailors I, all of you in this very chamber, and many watching this vid cast from home, might well not be here now. Time and time again, it seems our brave military personnel are thrown into battle to defend others. And for what? Yes, we defeated the Others. But what thanks have we received from the Empire of Alona?"

"None!" Came a voice from the chamber floor.

"At a time when we are reducing our forces, we are also supplying gravity drive technology to a race, the Benii, which has already successfully colonized two star systems without it. Not to mention the fact the Benii have a significant standing navy and have been training for years how to use it to best effect. Am I the only one who sees the folly of our current leadership?"

"No!" Was the cry from the floor.

"We need change and we need it now! We need to put Earth's interests and the interests of our citizens first! I have spoken to my family, my friends, and my esteemed colleagues of this Senate and I have come to a decision... I intend to put my name forward as my party's nomination in the upcoming presidential elections and I will stand on an Earth First policy!"

The speaker could only watch as the chamber erupted into applause.

#

Clement Bradshaw, Chief of Staff to President Coston, silenced the holo cube in the corner with an undisguised snort of disgust. "Well, at least we know who the enemy is now."

Rebecca Coston placed her steaming cup of tea down on the low table before replying. "True Clement, that little speech of his was well-planned and the speed with which the networks picked it up goes to show he has friends in the media."

"Hmm... it would appear the senator got all his ducks in a row before declaring his intention to run against whoever we eventually decide on."

Rebecca couldn't hide a little wince at the comment. "Any luck finding out from the party leaders who they favor as our candidate next spring?"

Clement shrugged. "Your guess is as good as mine, Madam President. I think they, like us, thought Arnie Harriman would jump at the chance, but when he announced his intention to retire at the next election it left them without a clear nominee. Perhaps I could still persuade you to run?"

Rebecca let out a short laugh. "If you think you could get the Senate to change the constitution and allow me to run for a third term, then you go ahead. By the time you do that, I'll be hiding out in Aaron Beckett's cabin incommunicado until the results of the election have been declared."

With a small sigh, Clement sat back in the comfortable seat. "Well, it was a nice thought at least... But seriously. Grant has got a head start and unless we find a suitable nominee very soon, Grant may have the election all sewn up before we get in the running."

"Do you have anyone in mind?"

Clement closed his eyes for a moment as his brain ran through a list of likely candidates. It was a very short list. He, like everyone else in the party, thought Vice President Harriman was a shoo-in, so nobody bothered to seriously look for a challenger but now that was all changed.

Harriman's announcement that he was retiring from public life so he could spend more time with his family had come as a body blow to the party's election planning, leaving the party leadership running around like headless chickens.

The president publicly voiced her support for his decision but Clement knew she was furious and there had been more than a few cross words between them. Clement suspected there was more to it than met the eye and had already placed a few feelers out there to try to find the underlying cause of Harriman's radical U-turn. Opening his eyes, he fixed his gaze on Rebecca.

"I know that look," Rebecca said. "It's the look you give me when you're going to say something you know I'm not going to agree with but you're going to say it anyway. Go on, get it over with!"

Clement inched forward until he teetered on the edge of his seat. "Senator Kris Madkin."

In the two decades Clement had been her friend, confidant, and political adviser, Rebecca had learned that whenever he made a suggestion, she should give it serious consideration before making a decision and this was definitely one of those times.

Senator Madkin was a second-term senator. He had come late to the political scene. Having completed a five-year hitch with the marines straight out of high school, Madkin had used the government sponsored ex-military bursary to put himself through law school. On passing the bar, he had become a prosecutor working closely with the Federal Investigation Bureau and leading more than a few high-profile cases. From there he moved into politics, where he ruffled a few feathers with the party hierarchy when he refused to follow their voting orders on the odd occasion. Instead, he voted as he believed the people of his constituency wanted him to. His voting policy did not make him many friends at the top; however, it proved him a man of conscience and that was something both the president and the voting public admired.

"He won't have much in the way of a campaign machine and the party may not like such an inexperienced senator facing off against Grant," Rebecca said.

"But on the plus side, there's never been even a whiff of

any scandal surrounding him, either politically or personally," Clement said. "His previous service in the marines should allow him to connect with all the returning service men and women. His voting record proves he is his own man and does what he thinks is best for people, whether he crosses party lines or not. In these times of uncertainty when nobody knows what's waiting for us around the next corner, he may be just what the people need." Clement could tell Rebecca was still not convinced. "With the right guidance, I really feel he could be our man."

Rebecca understood Clement's passion. If Madkin raised such strong emotions in him, it would do no harm to at least explore Madkin's candidacy. Her main concern was his inexperience in top-level politics. He would need someone around him who knew his or her way around the system and could watch his back, just as Clement had done for her over the years... A wicked smile spread across her face. Clement knew whatever was coming next would give him a headache for days.

"OK Clement, let's approach Madkin and sound him out. If he's up to it then I'll give him my blessing, which should get the party leadership on board."

Clement was pleasantly surprised by her reaction but he knew she was not yet finished.

"I'll back him on one condition."

Here it comes.

"If you really think he has a chance of winning against Grant, then he'll need a damned good Chief of Staff. This race is going to get real dirty real quick and Madkin hasn't been around long enough to know where all the bodies are buried and who the real power brokers are..." Rebecca pointed a finger at Clement. "But you do."

A loud groan escaped Clement and he realized he had just talked himself into a corner. His plans for his upcoming retirement from politics had just been put on hold indefinitely. "Deal," he mumbled.

Rebecca clapped her hands like an excited pupil. "Excellent. Now, moving on. Where are we with the Janus vote?"

"For once, I don't think we have anything to worry about. The results of the plebiscite were pretty plain. With over eighty-two percent of the voters opting for independence and strong support from all parties in the Senate, the vote is really just a formality. By this time next year, Janus will be an independent nation. The other heads of the Commonwealth have already expressed their willingness to grant an independent Janus full membership."

At the mention of the Commonwealth, Rebecca’s enthusiasm waned. "If we’re still part of it next year."

Clement noticed the change of mood. "Madam President, I think we seriously have to look into the ramifications of Earth pulling out of the Commonwealth. We, and any candidate we decide on, needs to make it damn clear to the public we are better off in the Commonwealth than out and to do so we need solid, indisputable facts and figures."

Rebecca knew, yet again, that Clement was right. "Agreed. The whole idea behind the Commonwealth is it makes us all stronger both economically and militarily." The president sat quietly for a minute as she considered her next course of action. Finally, she made up her mind. "Set up a meeting with Doctor Bath for me. I want her to head up a small team to look into the pros and cons of Commonwealth membership and what the results would be if we were to follow Grant and his Earth First model."

Clement nodded and tapped a few notes into his PAD.

Rebecca waited until he had finished before going on. "So, anything else?"

The conversation turned to the more mundane minutia of running a planet-wide government.

CHAPTER SIX

Out of the Wilderness

CARSON CITY - EARTH - SOL SYSTEM

Lieutenant Terrance Wilson sat with his feet up on his desk, staring at the slowly rotating black circle with the emblazoned red X floating in the holo cube. Terrance had, whenever his other duties allowed over the last three years, tried to fathom some connection between the Others' use of the symbol and the fact that the Saiph database assigned the exact same symbol to the designation "military prisoner." Stuck to the wall behind the holo cube were scraps of paper that bore the few precious fruits of his labor. A computer-generated timeline starting with the destruction of Balach, the original home of the Others, on or around 1000 AD, followed by the Others' attack on the Saiph home-world in 1187 AD. Moving along, he reached the attack on the Rubicon world around 1482 AD. Then there was a huge empty space of nearly 600 years until the destruction of the original Pars in 2038. Things had moved swiftly from there. Humanity's first contact with the Others in 2186 was swiftly followed by the First Battle of Garunda in 2188. It was this fateful battle which introduced Earth to their Persai allies who, along with the Garundans and subsequently the Benii, had stood faithfully beside them in the war which raged on for a long seven years, back and forth across tens of thousands of light years and cost nearly a million lives on the allies' side alone. Nobody knew how many Others were killed in the fighting, but it all paled into insignificance with the exploding nuclear weapons on the surface of Durav and the deaths of hundreds of millions of souls.

His earlier assumption, which many now accepted as fact, of the Others being controlled by highly developed artificial intelligence, led him to be given a near free hand in his research. Research in which he waded through so much data that, at times, he thought he would drown in it.

Slowly but surely, he had managed to piece together what he believed to be a realistic picture of how the Others had waged their campaign of Ehita, or holy war, through the stars. As humanity and its allies moved through the fourteen known sectors of Others-controlled space, they had found civilization after civilization laid waste. Terrance believed the hole in the timeline between 1482 and 2038 was explained by the time it had taken the Others to travel to, identify, and build up sufficient forces to destroy a new target. The grim discoveries only substantiated Terrance's theory. Not only were the Others targeting planets where the Saiph had manipulated the DNA of indigenous species, they were intent on wiping out all life which was not of their own. No matter how abhorrent this practice was, it raised an interesting question. If the Others had been the subject of Saiph manipulation on Balach, which allowed them to develop into the dominant species roughly equating the level most Earth humans had attained by the Middle Ages then who devised the Saiph-specific bio weapon which killed the majority of the population but left some immune? Furthermore, why would a race who obviously had star-drive technology themselves then bother to relocate the survivors to Durav, where over the course of the next 150 years they educated these same survivors to a level where they could now travel among the stars and carry out some pseudo-religious murder spree? Why not just do it themselves? And were they still out there? What he needed was a time machine to transport him back to 1000 AD so he could just follow this so-called Creator to wherever the hell he came from. Fat chance!

An incoming message on his comm link broke into his chain of thought. Activating the terminal on his desk, he accepted the call. His worries fell from his shoulders at the sight of Maggie's smiling face filling the screen. "May I remind the lieutenant his pregnant wife and unborn child are patiently waiting at the clinic for his arrival?"

Terrance's eyes flew to the clock on the wall. *Oh, crap!* "On my way now, dear, I'll be there in ten minutes... maybe twenty."

"You, Mr., need a better clock. Now get a move on, or else! Love you." Maggie laughed as she cut the connection. Terrance fled the office in the direction of the nearest elevator, thoughts of distant stars forgotten.

#

MAINTENANCE AND SUPPORT STATION 13
ASTEROID BELT – SOL SYSTEM

Commander Bryer Anderson attempted to keep a look of unbridled joy off his face as he stood waiting for the personnel airlock's door light to turn green. Three years he had been banished to this pimple on the rump of Sol system and before that, a year as a supply officer on a research station beyond the orbit of Neptune. Now though, now he was coming home and all he had to do was hold it together for another few minutes until he boarded the Zurich Lines yacht sent by the company, *his* new company, to transport him back to Earth. For a fleeting moment, he felt the old anger stir in him as the vision of Admiral Elizabeth Wilson came to him, that smug smile of hers plastered on her face as she threw him out of his plush office at Naval Intelligence Service headquarters in Carson City. His mind replayed the moment as it had nearly every day since she had so succinctly signaled the death knell to his naval career. *Bitch! Well we shall see who has the last laugh.*

Bryer had laughed aloud when he received the private and confidential message from his uncle, Seaton Anderson, some six weeks prior. The message informed him Seaton's army of lawyers had set to work on releasing Bryer from military service in order for Bryer to continue the Anderson bloodline as Chairman of Zurich Lines, the largest freight line in the Commonwealth. Bryer's release from military service would be no easy thing to achieve. Technically, the Commonwealth and the Terran Defense Forces in which Bryer served were still in an active state of war, so pursuant to the Emergency Powers Act, all members of the armed forces were ineligible for release from their duties without a review of their circumstances by the head of the Bureau of Naval Personnel herself. The very same admiral who signed the orders that sent him to this hellhole in the first place. Seaton's lawyers argued, successfully, that officers should be afforded the same rights as enlisted personnel, large numbers of whom were being released back into civilian lives with the drawdown of military forces. The war was won so why should a technicality chain officers to the service while other ranks were free to leave.

It was also the case that Bryer was the only person who could legally take up the reins of the vast Zurich Lines while a federal court order prevented his uncle from exercising control of the company. The lawyers made mention of a large and expensive lawsuit aimed at the admiral in charge of the personnel bureau, which would potentially prevent said admiral taking any promotion. Knowing the admiral was on the short list for the position of Chief of Naval Operations, her aide pointed out it would be far easier to simply sign Commander Anderson's release papers than spend the next few years fighting it in court while the opportunity of a lifetime, the position of CNO, passed her by. Reluctantly, the release orders were signed, and as of 12.00 hours today, Commander Bryer Anderson became Mr. Bryer Anderson.

Lieutenant Cathy Allenby trembled with anticipation at the thought of her stuffy, sexist commanding officer finally leaving the station. "Station" was an overly generous title. Maintenance and Support Station 13 was nothing more than a converted decommissioned freighter the navy had picked up at a rock-bottom price from some scrap yard somewhere. A couple of weeks in the naval dock yards added living quarters for fifty-four officers and other ranks There was also a shuttle bay big enough to hold three shuttles and, more importantly, the workshops and stores which were the true purpose of the station.

Maintenance and Support Station 13 was one of over 200 stations spread throughout the asteroid belt that maintained the thousands of emitter buoys that made it impossible to operate any form of gravity drive within the inner Sol system, and the Sherlock surveillance platforms that kept a watchful eye on anything approaching the system. The station's shuttles were employed on regular runs out to the buoys and platforms within its designated area of responsibility to carry out routine maintenance and, where necessary, repairs or replacement. It was a mundane but necessary task and one that, perversely, the station crew took pride in doing. Probably because the usual length of a tour of duty on this type of station was only twelve months and the station commanding officer was normally a senior engineering lieutenant, so life on the stations was more relaxed than on a ship. Not so on Station 13, though. When Allenby had first received her orders, she had been quite excited. Command of a station, even out in the middle of nowhere, would be a challenge for the young officer. It was only when she reached the end of her movement orders and read that she would actually be second-in-command of the station did she realize her dreams of a command were on hold. The station CO was a Commander Anderson. What the hell was a full-fledged commander doing on a maintenance station? When Allenby had made a few discreet inquiries, she was horrified by what she heard about the commander. He reputedly treated his crew like serfs, especially the women. He insisted on inspecting the station twice a week and if he found anything he considered below standard, *his* standard, not naval regulation standard, he wrote up the crewmember and their section chief. Worst of all, he had been in command of the station ever since it came on line, nearly three years ago.

Somebody high up in the chain of command clearly had it in for Commander Anderson, and he in turn vented his anger on the people below him. Allenby had contacted the Bureau of Naval Personnel directly, asking for a change of orders, but her request had been refused. The only light at the end of the tunnel was a small note at the bottom of the message which stated that all entries in her personal file made by Commander Anderson would be subject to review by the Bureau of Personnel and if found unsubstantiated they would be removed without prejudice. Further, on completion of her tour of duty, the Bureau would make all efforts to ensure she received her preferred choice of next tour. Obviously, someone in personnel was aware of the commander's reputation and had taken steps to ensure that whatever his beef was with the higher echelons of the navy, it would not have an adverse effect on those who served under him.

Her four months on the station proved that everything she heard about Anderson prior to her arrival was true. The man was a pompous ass who strutted around the small station like a feudal lord, reprimanding crew for the tiniest infringement of regulations. Allenby soon learned to make copious notes during his frequent inspection tours and made sure that when a crewmember fell afoul of the CO and was written up, she added her own comments to those of Anderson before forwarding any entry which would appear in the crewmember's personal file. Hopefully any future CO of the unlucky sailor would be wise enough to read between the lines and see Anderson's rebuke for what it was, complete BS!

The soft tone and a steady green light indicated the pressure equalizing in the airlock and the station's chief petty officer tapped the locks controls, allowing the inner door to slide effortlessly aside. With a casual glance at her wrist comm, Allenby checked the time. 12.01 hours.

Bryer Anderson was a stickler for protocol even when it meant he was forced to acknowledge those he considered beneath him. This was one of those times. Turning to face Allenby, he waited for her expected salute, which was his due as the senior officer. It never came. Instead, she remained in the at-ease position and simply called past him to the CPO.

"Please ensure Mr. Anderson clears the station safely, Chief. I'll be in ops." And with no acknowledgment of Anderson, she turned on her heel and jauntily strolled off down the corridor. Bryer Anderson could not believe what he was seeing. Anger boiled over and his face flushed red. How dare she ignore him! He opened his mouth to scream his derision at the back of the retreating Allenby, but a large, beefy hand on his shoulder spun him around and he looked directly into the face of a smiling CPO.

"I would advise against saying anything, Mr. Anderson. I may be forced to defend the honor of a real officer and as you are still on navy property, I would take great pleasure in kicking your ass. So why don't you pick up your bag and ship out?"

Bryer was dumbstruck. Did this Neanderthal just threaten to physically harm him? He took one more look at the grinning CPO and the look in his eyes. Yes, he really would do it. With all the pride he could muster, Bryer picked up his bag and walked down the length of the personnel tube connecting the waiting yacht to the naval station. All the time he swore he could hear the derisive laughter of the Neanderthal. When he reached the far end, the yacht's airlock opened and the smiling face of a Zurich Lines flight officer greeted him.

"Welcome aboard, Mr. Anderson. Allow me to escort you to the passenger lounge. Is there anything we can do for you to make your flight more comfortable?"

Bryer looked down at his naval uniform. "I would like to change into something more comfortable."

"Certainly, sir. I'll have one of the cabin crew show you to your quarters where you can change. They'll ensure your uniform is cleaned, pressed, and re-packed for you."

"Re-packed? No need! Eject that piece of crap into space. I won't need it ever again, thank God!"

The plastic smile slipped momentarily before returning to hide the disgust the flight officer felt as he closed the airlock doors. He himself had proudly worn that same uniform for ten years before moving into the private sector. Bryer moved past him to follow the cabin crewmember, who miraculously appeared as if from nowhere, taking him toward his cabin and his new life.

#

CAMBRIDGE - ENGLAND - EARTH

Clement Bradshaw closed the door of the car and turned up his coat's collar against the chill of the early morning. The birds were still sounding their dawn chorus as his feet crunched up the gravel driveway and reached the cobbled doorstep of the compact, single-story, brown brick house surrounded by thick hedges, screening it from the neighboring homes. It could not have been further from an artist's impression of the home of an ex-vice president of the Terran Federation.

A close enough glance showed regular raised mounds in the grass just inside the tree line, which hid the motion sensors linked to the security office hidden away above the detached garage. Arnie Harriman always made it perfectly clear he had no interest in the multi-layered security that surrounded President Coston wherever she went. Arnie had been in politics a long time and was the perfect running mate for Rebecca when she made her bid for president. However, his price was the reduced security. It drove the Presidential Security Office insane.

On election night when the votes were counted and Rebecca was announced the winner, a dozen agents appeared as if by magic outside Arnie's hotel room. The sight of the dark-suited, imposing, unsmiling PSO officers terrified Arnie's three grandchildren and it took all of their mother's ministrations to calm them.

Arnie wasted no time in calling Rebecca and bluntly telling her that if the officers were not withdrawn immediately, she would be looking for a new VP before the night was over. A call from the president-elect to the head of PSO reduced the number of officers to three, and for the next six years, there were never more than three officers in

Harriman's protection detail.

Until the day Arnie Harriman tendered his resignation, he was an irascible but effective VP and a shoe in for the party's nomination for president.

Something stinks and it was time to find out what, thought Clement as he reached for the antique brass doorknocker. His fingers halted in midair as the oak door opened to reveal the tight face of Arnie Harriman.

"I should have known you would end up on my doorstep eventually," said Arnie through clenched teeth, "You'd better come in, you're letting the heat out."

Clement followed the man who had been his friend and political ally for four decades into a cozy kitchen heated by an open fire in the corner. A battered metal kettle was reaching the boiling point on the stove. He shuffled along like an old man with the weight of the world on his shoulders. Where was the energetic, sprightly man of only a few months before?

"I see Julie still hasn't persuaded you to install any modern appliances," Clement joked in an attempt to lighten the mood. It failed.

"Look Clement, I know Rebecca's pretty pissed at me, but I've given six years of my life to her administration. Thirty more before that in the senate and local government. I missed Julie's first steps, her first day at school, and damn near missed her graduation. Now the grandkids are getting older, and I want to spend what time I have left with them. I'm sorry if my family inconveniences the party's plans, but my decision is final and nothing you or Rebecca can say will change it!"

Clement stood open-mouthed at his friend's outburst

and as he searched for something to say in reply, he covered his silence by pulling out a chair from the kitchen table and sitting down heavily while Arnie conducted a noisy hunt for teaspoons in a drawer. Not finding what he was looking for, he slammed the offending drawer closed, the loud bang reverberating around the quiet kitchen. Clement sat very still, watching Arnie's back as the man rested both hands on the countertop and his shoulders rhythmically moved up and down in time to his labored breathing.

"Arnie? Arnie, what is it?" Clement pleaded in a low voice. "We've been friends longer than I've been married. For God's sake, Arnie, our kids grew up in each other's pockets. Julie is as much my daughter as she is yours. If you can't tell me, then who can you tell?"

Arnie turned around. His face was wan and his eyes glistened with unshed tears. In silence, he reached into his pocket and passed a small PAD over to Clement with shaking hands. Taking the proffered PAD, Clement activated it and a picture of a smiling, well-groomed thirtyish man appeared on the screen. Clement recognized him immediately. As he should. Will Barr and his wife Julie, Arnie's only daughter, were frequent dinner guests at Clement's home. The picture changed to show what looked like a hotel reception desk and again, Will was in the picture, but this time he was accompanied by a woman who was most definitely not Julie. The picture changed again, this time showing Will and the unknown woman sharing an intimate candle-lit dinner. When the picture changed again, it was obvious it had been taken by a hidden camera in a hotel bedroom. The camera may have been concealed but the image was a good enough quality for Clement to make out a naked Will and an equally naked woman. Tearing his eyes from the PAD, Clement looked up to see tears running freely down Arnie's face.

"Keep watching, there's more."

Clement forced his eyes back to the PAD. Another hotel. Another woman. Clement's anger built, anger at Will for not only betraying Julie, but for betraying the kids. The pictures of Will's infidelity at last ended but the next set stole the breath from Clement. A series of pictures of Arnie's grandkids being dropped off at school. The last picture was frozen with a rifle's crosshair superimposed on each of the smiling children's faces and below the images was a simple message: "You cannot protect them. Resign now."

Horrified disbelief was evident on Clement's face as he slumped in the chair. Any words of consolation escaped him.

When Arnie recovered enough to speak, he did so sotto voce. "I found this PAD in this very kitchen. Somebody got past the perimeter security, entered the house without leaving a trace, and left the PAD. My PSO detail reviewed the security cameras' recordings on the pretext a fox had been at the trash. They showed only members of the detail entering or leaving the house. Either the security recordings have been tampered with or the person who left the PAD is in my own detail. Targeting me is one thing, Clement. I'm a politician and I can take my licks, but this... this is too much. They're only kids, for Christ's sake..."

Clement stood and embraced his sobbing friend, his own voice coming out in a hoarse whisper. "You did the right thing, Arnie. Anybody would have done the same. However, I promise you this. I will find out who is behind this and there is no rock they can hide under. And when I do find them, prison will be the least of their worries."

CHAPTER SEVEN
Compassion for My Enemy

COMMONWEALTH UNION OF PLANETS
SECRETARIAT BUILDING
GENEVA - EARTH - SOL SYSTEM

Rebecca Coston entered the plush conference suite on the 102nd floor of the sparkling glass edifice that was now home to all things Commonwealth. The view through the floor-to-ceiling windows was breathtaking. The sun glistened off the still, blue waters of Lake Geneva and Rebecca's eyes followed the shoreline as it flowed from its natural beauty into the technological brutish gray and white of Geneva city on the far side of the lake. Rebecca was not alone in admiring the view. Leaning heavily on a thick, highly polished wooden stick was the still impressive figure of Chairman Tarrov. The Persai was now nearing his 168th birthday and the last five years had not been kind. His once-powerful frame was bowed and his lush fur showed more silver than black. Rebecca's advisers told her, from their analysis of research into Persai aging, that once a Persai began to deteriorate physically, the aging process accelerated rapidly and the end came within a matter of months. A small tear welled in Rebecca's eye as she thought of a future without Tarrov's calming influence and his sage advice, which had served her so well over the turbulent last few years.

Surreptitiously wiping her eyes, she fixed her most pleasant politician’s smile on her lips, straightened her back and walked to the chair.

"Chairman Tarrov, I see I am not the first to arrive."

Tarrov slowly turned his whole body to face Rebecca and she was sure she could detect a faint grimace of pain as he did so. "No indeed, Madam President. Although I must admit I do not know why our friend Bezled has asked for this extraordinary meeting. Surely with the Others’ end in sight there are no matters too pressing that they could not have waited until the next quarterly meeting? The selection process for a new Chairman of the Council of Twelve is due to begin shortly and my presence will be required on Pars."

Rebecca gave a most apolitical shrug. "I'm in the dark as much as you."

"I note you are not accompanied by Governor Crothers today."

A frown wrinkled Rebecca's forehead at Tarrov's observation. "My advisers thought it best, what with the impending vote in the Senate concerning my bill to allow Janus to become an independent world, that Governor Crothers’ time would be best spent shoring up the votes we need to ensure defeat of this so-called Earth First movement."

The Chairman released a sharp, barking laugh. "Perhaps, Madam President, you should join me in my retirement."

Rebecca let out a small laugh of her own. "Believe me Mr. Chairman, the elections next March cannot come speedily enough." Again, a frown creased her forehead. "These Earth First people worry me, though. They're advocating the dissolution of the Commonwealth now that the threat from the Others has been dealt with. They want Earth to go it alone and implement a complete isolationist policy. Don't they see? Just because we've dealt with the Others, there's no reason to believe we're not going to encounter another hostile race out there as we expand." Rebecca bowed her head and shook it slowly in frustration. "It still amazes me how some people can be so shortsighted."

The elderly Persai placed a large, comforting hand on her slim shoulder. "Do not fret, Rebecca. In my experience, extremists of all views have a very limited lifespan. The people will see through them soon enough."

The moment passed as the meeting room door opened and the tall, waif-like figure of Representative Hoolas of the Benii entered, accompanied by Prime Minister Bezled. On seeing Rebecca and Tarrov already present, Bezled made directly for his seat. "As we are all here, shall we get straight down to business, ladies and gentleman?"

Taking their assigned seats, the others waited as Bezled settled himself. "Friends. The people of Garunda have a proposal, which I have been instructed to present to you in person, hence our unscheduled meeting here today. Before I proceed... I think it important for me to explain the Garundan context in which this proposal has come about."

It was obvious by the normally animated Bezled's hesitancy that he was unsure how the Garundan proposal was going to be received.

"If I may interrupt for a moment, Prime Minister," came the deep baritone voice of Tarrov. "It has always been our unwritten understanding that all member planets of the

Commonwealth will get a fair hearing before any decisions are made, so please do not fear what you have to say will not be considered with the appropriate level of importance."

The Garundan gave Tarrov a grateful nod before continuing. "In Garundan culture, we have an honor code which our warriors have followed for as long as we have had the written word. We call it Yolva. I believe in English it translates to "succor." Following the defeat of an enemy, it is the duty of the victor to provide for his vanquished enemy's needs. The widowed spouse and children of a deceased enemy soldier would become the responsibility of whoever killed that soldier. Over the centuries as my people progressed from simple tribes to city-states to true nations, Yolva has been rigidly followed. Not to follow it is a stain on the very honor of my people..."

The penny dropped for Rebecca and her mouth opened slightly as she realized what Bezled was about to say and what the political ramifications would be.

"Garunda intends to provide Yolva for the remaining Others!" Bezled stated resolutely.

And there it was. Rebecca could not believe what she was hearing. Forget the Earth First movement, what would her own people have to say about the Garundan proposal? Never mind the Alonans. "Prime Minister, perhaps in the case of the Others, Yolva may not apply. After all, they were intent on wiping out your entire race, all our races for that matter. We have all seen the images of the dead worlds that the Others destroyed. Do you think they would have shown you mercy?" Rebecca looked desperately to Tarrov for support but the old Persai remained implacable. Hoolas, on the other hand, looked as shocked as Rebecca.

Before Rebecca could frame a stronger argument,

Bezled continued. "Ever since your intervention, which prevented the Others' assault on our world Madam President, my people have struggled to come to terms with our new place in the universe. The sudden influx of advanced technology which you humans and the Persai have so freely shared with us have allowed our young from every nation to realize their dreams of going to the stars. Our standard of living has reached heights we would never have believed possible. However, there are many among us who see these gifts as changing who we fundamentally are as a people. Because of this, alongside the new sciences and the knowledge they bring, we have been determined to fully educate our young in our history, lest they forget where we came from and the very essence of who we are." A small smile crept onto the prime minister's face. "Indeed, it was a group of our young ones who took it upon themselves to petition the government to invoke Yolva. It seemed we of the older generation had become so engrossed in the conflict and our eventual victory, we forgot our duty to the vanquished."

As Bezled stopped speaking, an uneasy silence settled in the room. Rebecca was still marshaling her thoughts when Tarrov cleared his throat. His deep rumble filled the room.

"Bezled, my friend. The Persai watched as the Others wiped our home-world and all our people from the stars. We vowed that one day we would have our revenge on those who carried out that most heinous of crimes. Seeing the humans come to your aid gave us hope, so we revealed ourselves and found our faith in them was not wasted. We became allies and when the humans' hour of need arose, the Persai, Garunda, and our new friends, the Benii," Hoolas gave a small bow of her head, "stood shoulder to shoulder with them. We defeated the Others and I never thought I would feel a prouder moment... until today. You, Prime Minister, put the rest of us to shame. We defeated the enemy, is now not the time to do the honorable thing and ensure we treat survivors as we would wish to be treated?"

Rebecca was flabbergasted. The old Persai was agreeing with Bezled. *What the hell*? Did he not see the political wasp's nest this move would stir up?

Tarrov pointed a fur-edged finger at Rebecca, "In your history Madam President, following the end of your second world war, did the victors not rush to the aid of the starving, defeated enemy? Aided them in rebuilding their homes and factories. Treated them as equals and welcome them back into the fold of the world community?"

Memories of long past history lectures flooded back to Rebecca. Of course. The Marshall Plan. An American economic aid plan, which pumped billions of dollars into the war-weary economies of not only Western Europe but Asia. Within seven years, the countries receiving aid not only reached prewar economic production, but exceeded it. The plan was seen as a great success, not only did it reinvigorate the world's economy, it had the added effect of bringing former enemies together in a common goal. That cunning old dog's knowledge of human history never ceased to amaze her.

Tarrov forced himself to his feet and ever so slowly walked around the table until he stood beside the Garundan. "The Persai will follow where Garunda leads in this matter."

Rebecca looked across at Representative Hoolas, who was yet to comment. "Representative?"

Hoolas looked from Rebecca to Tarrov and Bezled before she spoke, "I cannot claim to have as deep an understanding of human history as Chairman Tarrov, nor have my people suffered the loss of so many of our people as other member planets of the Commonwealth during its struggle against the Others. Furthermore, we have no culture of Yolva like our Garundan allies. However, I do understand the Garundan position in this matter and I find myself inclined to agree with Chairman Tarrov. What gives us the right to stand idly by and watch the remaining members of a race, even one as inherently evil as the Others, simply die?"

Rebecca had been a politician long enough to see when she was on the losing side. She said, "It seems I find myself outnumbered, Prime Minister. May I inquire how you propose to fulfill your duties under Yolva?" Rebecca sat back with her best game face on. If you cannot win by sound argument, then tie them up in technical details.

Unfortunately, Bezled was prepared. He reached into his jacket and produced three more PADs, which he passed to each delegate. "Phase One is the expansion of our current prisoner-of-war facilities on a suitable planet. By 'suitable,' I mean a planet that is capable of supporting sufficient food production now and in the future, and has adequate natural resources for a minimal level of industrialization. We believe we have identified such a planet: Planet IV in star system 84137. Phase Two. The transportation of all POWs from their current location to Planet IV..."

Rebecca saw her chance and jumped at it. "There are a lot of POWs to move, Prime Minister and I'm not sure when the shipping vehicles would become available to transport them."

The Prime Minister went on, completely unperturbed. "If adequate transport is not immediately available, then Garunda is willing to suspend its colonization program in its entirety to make the hulls available to complete the movement of the POWs."

This comment took the whole room by surprise. The

drive to colonize as many planets as possible as quickly as possible had become not only a political but economical imperative for the entire Commonwealth, and here were the Garundans willing to put it all on hold in their need to satisfy Yolva. Rebecca's next statement was made with newfound respect. "Excuse my interruption, Prime Minister, please continue."

"Phase Three. Security. We understand that not all the peoples of the Commonwealth may be happy with our need to honor Yolva and as long as the Others exist then they could be deemed to be a threat, so as part of the project we intend to build a series of secure compounds. These compounds will house adequate medical facilities to see to the wellbeing of the POWs and they will also contain sufficient military forces to subdue any localized uprisings by the POWs. In orbit will be a single space station based on the planned orbital fortress design and a network of surveillance satellites. This station will be equipped with a number of assault and cargo shuttles. The station will also house an army brigade, which will be on call to support the compounds as required. A flotilla of destroyers will patrol the system at all times."

"That's a significant military presence, Prime Minister," commented Hoolas.

"Garunda is willing to provide all the necessary naval ships and army personnel," stated Bezled matter-of-factly.

The Garundans have certainly thought this through, Rebecca thought.

"Phase Four. De-programming. I think I speak for all of us gathered here that we are all of the opinion the Others were simply puppets being controlled by some unseen puppet master."

There was a mumbled agreement from all present. “A

puppet master whom we have yet to meet, and I fear such a meeting will be an unpleasant affair," said Tarrov.

After a moment's reflection, Rebecca realized a consensus was reached. "It will be a hard sell for me to get it passed in the Senate Prime Minister, but I think I can do it."

"The Persai Council will not allow your honor to be besmirched, Prime Minister," growled Tarrov.

Hoolas stood and stretched her long arm across the table to touch Bezled's arm in a very human gesture. "The Benii agree to your proposal."

Bezled sat back, relieved the proposal had won their support. Now all they had to do was make the proposal a reality.

#

Rebecca Coston entered the underground rail car with her small entourage and security detail for the short journey back to her offices on the far side of Lake Geneva, her thoughts a mix of the Garundan proposal, the Earth First movement, and repeated images of the aging Tarrov. The Garundan decision to invoke Yolva on behalf of the Others was going to cause her a big political headache and it could only provide more ammunition, if any was needed, to the Earth First movement. She could already imagine the news vids full of strutting, self-centered senators, airing their opinions. A faint sickly feeling entered her stomach at the thought of them, preaching their isolationist views to all and sundry. Had these people never bothered to read human history? Isolationism didn't work! The Earth First advocates asserted Earth's interests were best served by keeping the affairs of other planets at a distance. One possible motivation for limiting inter-planetary involvement was to avoid being drawn into dangerous and otherwise undesirable conflicts.

There was also a perceived benefit from avoiding inter-planetary trade agreements or other mutual assistance pacts. Rebecca suspected the real reason behind the growing Earth First movement was the pressure being put on certain political representatives by big business, who thought being outside the Commonwealth economic and trade treaties would give them more bargaining power, as well as allowing them a free hand when it came to exploiting mining and colonization rights. *It always comes down to money,* thought Rebecca, shaking her head.

"Jacob," she addressed her aide, "could you reach out to Secretary Helsett and Secretary Manning and ask them to make themselves available for a meeting with me this afternoon?"

"Certainly, Madam President." The young aide began tapping away furiously on his PAD as he sent requests off to the staffs of Secretary of Defense and the Secretary of Finance, warning them the president required their presence at a time to be confirmed. Then he began shuffling through Rebecca's appointments for the day, in an effort to find the most convenient time in her schedule for the meeting. No mean feat.

Rebecca allowed herself a small moment of amusement as she reflected on how much mayhem she had now caused two cabinet secretaries and a presidential aide. The moment evaporated when the carriage slowed as it passed through the blast doors before coming to a smooth stop adjacent to the platform deep below the skyscraper housing the offices of the president. The doors slid silently apart and Rebecca stood as her security detail formed its protective bubble around her. *Oh well, back to work.*

CHAPTER EIGHT
Awakenings

SLIVINO VALLEY - NORTHERN ITALY - EARTH - SOL SYSTEM

Seaton Anderson urged his horse up the steep path as the loose rocks slipped from under its hooves, cascading down the bluff and into the valley below. The rider behind him let out a half-concealed curse as his own horse sensed the doubt of the lead horse, but a quick prod with his spurs and the horse moved up. Reaching the top of the bluff, Seaton reined in his mount and got down from the saddle to watch his companion cover the last few meters of the path.

A sweating and out of breath Bryer Anderson dismounted and joined his uncle, who was staring out over the valley. Bryer went to say something but for some reason he hesitated and instead cast his eyes over the breathtaking beauty of summer in Northern Italy. Here and there, you could just make out the roofs of the ultramodern hunting lodges used by Seaton's guests poking up through the trees, but even those stylish lodges were put to shame by the massive edifice, which sat at the far end of the valley. Rising like a rock outcropping from the green forest sea that was the valley floor stood the imposing five-story mock-medieval castle that was Seaton Anderson's home and, since his indictment, prison. A magnificent prison, but a prison all the same.

Since his arrival on the estate two days before, Bryer had attempted to speak to his uncle of his plans for the future, but each time Seaton avoided the question and instead engaged in mundane conversation. However, over breakfast this morning, he had invited Bryer to go riding with him.

Bryer hated riding and had only learned at the insistence of his father, who firmly believed that every gentleman should know how to handle a horse. However, Bryer caught the unspoken order in his uncle's request. He changed into the riding clothes the servants laid out for him and joined his uncle on what turned out to be a more arduous ride than he ever imagined. After three hours, they reached the top of the bluff. It seemed Seaton was at last ready to take a break.

"Isn't the view spectacular, Bryer?"

"Yes it is, Uncle," Bryer answered, struggling to keep the exasperation from his voice.

Seaton turned to face his nephew and saw that the tone of Bryer's voice was reflected in the obvious frustration on his face. "Bryer. As you know, because of this infuriating court business, I am restricted to living on this estate and even more annoyingly I'm no longer in direct control of the company I spent my life building. All that ends today."

Bryer's frustration left him only to be replaced by a strong sense of occasion, *a forthcoming announcement of momentous proportions*, he thought.

"This evening, we are having dinner with my chief legal adviser, who will bring with him papers for me to sign. Those papers will transfer my stock in Zurich Lines to you. With it, you will have complete control of the company and once more an Anderson will be at the helm."

Bryer's breath caught in his throat and he actually took a step backwards at his uncle's news. He knew Seaton must have something up his sleeve when the old goat somehow managed to release him from his naval service. Bryer had had his suspicions. He had dared to dream. Now, Seaton had confirmed that he was indeed handing him control of the single biggest shipping line in Commonwealth space. A company worth billions.

Seaton gave his nephew a few moments to take in the news before he went on. "Bryer, our family has a great many enemies both in business and in government who would like nothing more than to see my life's work destroyed before my eyes. With this court ruling, they've effectively sidelined me and think they have a free hand, but with you in charge, we can stop them. I, of course, cannot take any active part in company affairs..." A sly smile creased the older man's face. "But I'm sure you'll be open to taking a little friendly advice from your uncle now and then?"

Bryer snorted with laughter. "Your advice is always welcome, Uncle."

"I believe our first order of business must be to insulate the company from the financial madness of the Coston government. It's too late to stop her from signing the independence of Janus into law, but it's not too late to ensure that our investments in future colonies are protected."

Seaton paused, waiting to see if Bryer could envisage the plan the older Anderson had formulated on the long, lonely nights spent in his gilded cage. A spark of understanding came to Bryer's eyes.

"Coston may be retiring after the next election, but we need to prevent her successor from granting the same loan moratoriums to more colonies potentially wanting independence. We would have to radically change government policy..."

Seaton waited patiently, letting Bryer work through the problem.

"And the best way to change government policy is from within... We would need a president who thinks the same way we do."

"Exactly, Bryer. A president who believes any colony Earth establishes should remain the property of Earth, no matter what those damn Commonwealth idealists have to say. A president who is willing to stand up to the Commonwealth and whom puts Earth and Earth's businesses first and if the Commonwealth doesn't like the idea, then the president must be willing to tell them to go to hell. Pull out of the Commonwealth and go it alone. Let's see how well they would do without the industrial might of Earth propping them up, eh?"

Bryer warmed to the subject. For his uncle, this may all be about securing the future of Zurich Lines, but with the power that control of the company would bring him, combined with a friendly president, there would be nothing to stop Bryer from settling some very personal scores. First things first, though. Business, then pleasure.

"I take it, Uncle, you have a man in mind for the job?"

Seaton turned away from the view of the lush valley and remounted his horse. "I do, Bryer. But first I have something to show you which may give us the leverage we need to ensure our man gets elected."

Bryer, reinvigorated, swung himself up onto his own steed. "Would it have anything to do with how you managed to release me from my naval duties so easily?"

Seaton tapped the side of his nose with a finger as he led the laughing Bryer off down the trail and into a heavily wooded area.

#

2287 LIGHT YEARS FROM EARTH

The faint, regular rhythm of his beating heart came to him as his brain fought to disperse the fog of his long sleep and he struggled to full consciousness. The tingling sensation all over his body, like static electricity, slowly dissipated. His breath passes over chilled lips. Voices, faint to begin with, but now becoming clearer, come to his ears.

"Supreme Leader. Supreme Leader, can you hear me?"

With effort, he forces his eyes open and squints in the harsh artificial light. He tries to speak but only a crackling croak escapes him.

"Water for the Supreme Leader. And be quick about it!" He hears the insistent voice clearly now.

Focusing his vision, he turns his head on its stiff neck in the direction of the speaker, who slowly swims into vision.

"Stop fussing like an old woman, Lorai. I just need a moment."

"Of course, Supreme Leader, excuse my unprofessional outburst. It is just that we have waited so long for your return and now the time is at hand I find myself overawed by the moment."

Lorai's comment brought a burning question to the

Supreme Leader's lips. "How long have I been in cryogenic sleep, Lorai?"

"According to the master AIs clock, you have been sleeping for 1132 years."

The Supreme Leader let the enormity of the number sink in. He and his followers had known that by selecting the lesser half-breed race they had stumbled upon while fleeing from the Elders, it would ensure they bought the requisite time to allow Lorai and her fellow geneticists to produce the tools to achieve his goal of his people becoming the true inheritors of the stars. Not those filthy, inferior half-breeds to whom the Elders were willing to sacrifice their own people's place in the stars.

Time had been the key. Time for the automated shipyards to build the required number of warships but, more importantly, time to build an army of faithful followers to operate those ships.

But 1132 years. How the universe must have changed while he and his followers slept, watched over by the master AI. Bracing himself against the sides of the cryogenic cylinder, he sat up. His head was dizzy and his limbs weak.

"Assist me, Lorai."

Lorai and one of her team immediately moved to the Supreme Leader's side, lifting him clear of the cylinder and into the waiting chair. Once his brain cleared again, he was ready to ask his next question.

"And what of the others, Lorai? Have they all survived?"

The slightest hesitation in her voice suggested the answer might not be to his liking. "As per programming, the master AI awoke myself and the medical team first. I am happy to report that ninety-three percent of all those placed into cryogenic sleep survived."

"Who did we lose, Lorai?"

When she failed to reply, he went to ask the question again but he held his tongue instead, looking deep into her eyes. "Harama?"

Lorai did not trust her voice to reply. She cast her eyes downward and nodded slowly.

The Supreme Leader and his wife Harama, along with all the others, knew the risk of such a long cryogenic sleep. Nevertheless, it had seemed the only way to ensure enough time passed for the leader's plans to come to fruition. His mind brought to him the final view of Harama's warm, loving eyes looking back at him as the cylinders sealed closed. His eyes screwed tightly shut as he repelled his grief and locked it away until he could find the time to mourn properly. Another martyr to the cause whose life would be celebrated after the ultimate victory was achieved.

"Anyone else?"

"A few officers and other ranks but all the senior officers and scientific staff have survived remarkably well."

"And what of the breeding program?"

"If I may, Supreme Leader?" At his nod of consent, Lorai approached the seat and with the tap of a small control, the chair raised itself a few inches off the metal floor on its repulsors, allowing Lorai to move it easily with one hand until she stopped it in front of an innocuous-looking metal wall. The touch of another key and the seemingly solid wall seemed to shimmer in front of his eyes until it became clear as the highest quality glass. The Supreme Leader's breath caught in his chest. Laid out before him were curving green fields. Farm buildings surrounded by crops interlaced with streams and rivers. In the distance, he saw larger settlements, their buildings low and spread out on the edge of where the rivers flowed into a shimmering rich blue sea, upon which he could barely make out the sails of tall ships. Light, fluffy clouds moved slowly in the sky. And there, hovering so close you thought you might reach out and touch it, was a pale red star.

Lorai could not keep the proud look from her face. "Supreme Leader. I am happy to report as of this morning, we have 1.3 billion of pure blood at your command."

The Supreme Leader grasped the sides of the chair and forced himself to stand on legs still not adjusted from their long sleep. He pushed himself away from the chair and leaned heavily on the window, marveling at the achievements of his chief scientist and the engineers. Lorai had convinced him that, given sufficient time and resources, this amazing construction project would indeed be possible. The scale of what she envisaged was unbelievable, but what choice did they have? Once his move against the Elders failed, he had been tried like a common criminal and forced to wear the brand of one. When he was imprisoned, he managed to get word to his followers to put in place his alternate plan.

It took nearly six whole years before they were ready to act and when that day came, his followers assaulted the prison holding him, with Harama at their head. When she opened his cell door, he moved to leave, but hesitated and retrieved the prison jacket with the despised emblem of his conviction on it.

Harama ensured his plan was followed to the last letter. Before the Elders could gather their forces, he was aboard one of the disused starships that the Elders, in their blind faith, decreed were never to be used again. And so, with his followers crowded aboard six starships packed to the gunnels with everything needed to begin again, they fled out among the stars in search of a new home. One where they could rebuild the race. A place where he and his followers' ideals would shape the future, free from the restrictions placed on them by the simple-minded Elders.

They traveled from star to star in their search until they had stumbled upon one of the half-breed worlds the Elders chose to be the legacy of the race. His first reaction was to order the half-breeds erased, as one would any other infestation, but Lorai approached him with an interesting idea. One that had a certain appeal to it.

Why not use these half-breeds against the very ones who conceived them? Lorai had always provided him with good counsel and this time was no different. His six starships held only 5000 of his followers. Barely enough to establish a strong bloodline, so he could ill-afford to waste any in a futile war against the Elders. Lorai's idea held promise but first he had to find a secure base from which to operate. A place where the Elders would never find them. Eventually they emerged in a system the engineers guaranteed held all the necessary ingredients to begin.

It took decades of construction. The self-replicating construction robots, although initially few in number, went to the system's asteroid belt and began the process of extracting the necessary raw materials to not only build his and the engineers' vision, but to build more of themselves. For every construction robot he built, another duplicated itself, and so their numbers rose exponentially.

Within a decade, there was no longer an asteroid belt left, so the robots moved on to the inner planets. Reducing them to raw materials and adding them to the growing construction. Slowly it came together. A shell completely surrounding the system's star, hiding it from prying eyes. And on the inner surface of the shell would be the new home of the race.

With the shell nearing completion, he decided it was time to put Lorai's plan for the Half-breeds into operation. They returned to the world of the Half-breeds where Lorai selected a group she considered the most pliable and began the process of exterminating the remainder. When the numbers were whittled down to something more manageable, he transported them to his starship where he presented himself to them as their god.

As an example of his power, he allowed them to watch as the last pieces were put in place by the construction robots hiding the glowing red star from the universe. The Half-breeds fell to their knees in awe of his power and so began the process of psychological manipulation, which would see the fall of the Elders and all they had conceived.

Lorai, however, did not rest on her laurels. With the construction of their new home complete, she immediately set to work in securing the most vital part of his plan. If the race was going to flourish, it would need something which could not be manufactured overnight. It would need children.

Lorai and her staff constructed the artificial embryo banks and harvested the females among the followers for their eggs.

Cloning was an option, but he was against it. The chances of genetic failure in the future was something he was not willing to risk. He wanted strong, pure members of the race. His decision against clones meant it would take hundreds of years to produce the numbers required, so volunteers were sought to stay awake with the soon-to-be young so they could be educated in the true beliefs of the race and taught the skills they would need in the inevitable war to come.

The construction robots were put to work on a new task. The building of the warships and ancillary equipment that would be needed, as well as the maintenance of the habitat shell. With everything in place, he and his remaining followers took to the cryogenic cylinders for their long sleep, hoping to awake in a universe cleansed of the half-breeds.

Turning his back on the green fields, he addressed his chief scientist. "Convene my officers, Lorai. I want a complete update on our current strengths and weaknesses and the progress of your half-breeds."

"At once, Supreme Leader."

As Lorai rushed off to carry out his orders, a sudden chill like a cold breeze brushed against the light brown hair covering his entire body. He dismissed it as a hangover from the long sleep. His body was yet to regain its full strength. Walking unsteadily back to his cryogenic cylinder, he retrieved his jacket. The same jacket he wore the day of his rescue from the prison. Slipping it on, he glanced down at the symbol the Elders had forced him to wear. One he now wore proudly. A black circle with a simple red X on it.

#

The Leader sat at the head of the long, burnished metal conference table. Pointedly, at his right hand side was Harama's empty seat. The Supreme Leader making his point by highlighting her sacrifice to the cause.

The news his officers brought remained incomplete but they, like him, had only been awake for less than a day and all those implications were yet to be thoroughly analyzed. What was obvious though, was that the half-breeds they fostered to do his bidding had achieved much but ultimately had been defeated. The victorious forces concerned him.

From information gleaned from the ship that brought news of their demise, it appeared the victorious forces were an alliance of the remaining half-breeds that the Elders had somehow successfully hidden from him. *Damn them all to hell!* The sound of his fist crashing down on the table brought all conversation in the room to a halt. Stifling his anger, he addressed his fleet commander.

"What of the fleet, Star Commander Foral?"

"I have only completed a rough inventory, Supreme Leader, but it would appear the construction program put in place before we entered sleep has been exceeded by a factor of four. It was necessary to construct additional yards to cope with the extra hulls. However, there was a flaw in the original programming, which has led to the construction of far more lighter units than heavier ones. It has left the fleet unbalanced. But I believe it will not adversely effect the fleet's effectiveness in the longer term."

Foral and the Supreme Leader had been friends and allies throughout their careers, so if Foral was satisfied with the forces at his disposal, then the Supreme Leader was willing to accept that.

"What of the crew, old friend? Are they prepared for what is to come?"

"From what I have seen so far, I am very impressed. We have sufficient crewmembers for every ship in the fleet and all have been drilled from youth for their position. Those who volunteered to remain awake while we slept aided by the AIs have made improvements and innovations I have as yet to fully comprehend and I would not be willing to give my full backing to these changes until I have witnessed them in combat."

"A wise precaution, Foral. The information I have reviewed on the fleet, which managed to destroy the half-breeds shows aspects of Saiph technology being employed, although I believe our ships and weaponry are still superior to theirs. We must seek out a suitable target of opportunity to try out our new fleet. We need better intelligence on what we face out there and any cracks in this unholy alliance of half-breeds we can endeavor to exploit for our own benefit. Use the intelligence downloaded from the half-breeds' AI before they met their end and deploy scout ships to the systems controlled by this... what was it they called themselves... this Commonwealth. Compile a list of targets in order of ascending force levels. Let us tread carefully until we know the true strengths of our enemy."

Dismissing Foral, he turned to the only face at the table he did not recognize. Geoll was the product of Lorai's breeding program and he had inherited the position of Caretaker of the Race from his father, who had inherited it from his father, and so on. It was the Caretaker's role to ensure the race would be ready when the Supreme Leader and the others wakened from their long slumber and if the initial information reaching the Supreme Leader was to be believed, he and his ancestors had done a job worthy of praise.

"Caretaker..." Geoll raised his chin proudly as the Supreme Leader addressed him by his title, surely a mark of respect. "We have much to thank you for. Your diligence and that of those who came before you show the true strength of the pure race."

"I live to serve, Supreme Leader. I am but one of many who have striven for this day."

"Your modesty serves us all well, Geoll, and is an example of the dedication required to fulfill our dreams of ridding the universe of the half-breeds created by the Elders and ensuring the Saiph and the Saiph alone take their place as the dominant species among the stars."

CHAPTER NINE
A New Command

EDGE OF THE ASTEROID BELT - SOL SYSTEM

The courier carrying John Radford re-entered normal space and the crew slowed the small ship to a dead stop. The captain double-checked the Identify Friend or Foe (IFF) beacon was transmitting the correct codes for the day. It wasn't that the courier's command crew were incapable of ensuring the IFF was activated, but the sight of so many grazers and missile tubes on the patrolling warships tended to encourage any ship's captain to do a double-check.

In the cramped passenger lounge, John viewed the space around the ship via the courier's passive sensors. He gave a low whistle of appreciation. This was the first time he had been back in the Sol system since the defeat of the Others three years before. As commanding Admiral of Third Fleet, he had of course been instrumental in the battle against the Others and the final assault on Durav; however, for the last thirty-six months, he and his fleet had been kept busy alternating with Second Fleet, under Admiral Lewis, as they planned and executed what the politicians had come to call

Operation Clean Up, literally a cleansing of the remaining Others bases. John pursed his lips as he thought of the hundreds of sailors and marines under his command who had perished during Op Clean Up.

Mentally berating himself, he returned his attention to the display. Gateway Station was certainly an impressive piece of engineering. One of the key recommendations of the Combined Joint Chiefs of Staff following the near catastrophic Others attack on Earth was to take a lesson from the Alonan Empire. No ship was allowed direct transit into the Alonan home system without first being required to halt and have its identity verified at the system's outer marker. Earth thus instituted a similar system but with a few modifications. When the Others launched their attack on the Sol system, they had prevented help from reaching the beleaguered defenders under Admiral Chavez by placing buoys in the area, which generated an artificial dampening field negating the Commonwealth navy's gravity drive. Any ship that attempted to use its gravity drive while in contact with the dampening field suffered catastrophic engineering damage and was left floating uselessly in space. If it weren't for the handful of experimental cruisers equipped with a modified gravity drive by Jeff Moore's research teams on Zarminda and used by Admiral Glandinning to successfully destroy the enemy buoys, then the battle would have undoubtedly been lost and humanity's home destroyed.

Following the battle, a number of these buoys were recovered and transferred to Zarminda, where those same scientists adapted the technology to generate a rotating dampening field covering all the frequencies a gravity drive could work on. Fortress Command then seeded the entire inner Sol system with the dampening buoys, which resulted in any form of gravity drive being useless anywhere within the asteroid belt.

Another lesson learned from the enemy attack was the need for a dedicated fleet of heavy units, their sole purpose being the defense of the Sol system.

When the Others launched their feinting attack on Alona, First Fleet, home ported at Earth under the command of Admiral Jing, rushed to their aid. Jing had already summoned units of Second Fleet from Janus to reinforce Chavez's battle-weakened Fifth Fleet, which remained in orbit around Earth following its punishing victory at 70 Ophiuchi. However, before any of these units could arrive, the Others sprung their trap and activated the dampening buoys, leaving Fifth Fleet to stand unaided against the invaders.

Now Fortress Command retained sole control of these heavy units, outside of the normal chain of command, ensuring there were always sufficient mobile naval units in the system to deal with any potential threat.

All this naval firepower was something John had seen before. While in command of Third Fleet, he had had just as much firepower readily available. But what he did not have then was filling the center of his sensor display now. Gateway Station.

As a fleet commander, John was privy to the schematics of the proposed station, but seeing it in real life was something else. At a little over two million metric tonnes and with more firepower than five Bismarck-class battleships, the station looked for all the world like someone had stuck two mushroom caps together, joining them with a thick, short stalk. And just like some varieties of mushroom, this one could be extremely hazardous to your health.

Nestling in the center of layer upon layer of grazer and missile platforms reaching the station would be a mighty task for any attacking enemy. Gateway held another nasty surprise for anyone stupid enough to try to take it on. Six squadrons of Mosquito space fighters called the station home. The TDF's version of the Benii Freiba, the Mosquito class fighter consisted of a two-member crew and was just as swift and agile as its Benii forerunner. The Mosquito, however, thanks to those researchers at Zarminda, was powered by a miniaturized fusion generator derived from Saiph technology, which meant its twin needle grazers were fully capable of punching through even a battleship's armor at close range, and when the promised High Velocity Anti-Matter Missile (HVAMM) became reality, then these particular Mosquitos would become even more deadly. It was these little ships and how Admiral Jing intended to employ them that was bringing John back home to Earth.

The double tone of his wrist comm sounded and John absently tapped the accept key.

"We have permission from Gateway Station to complete the transit to Earth's orbit, Admiral. We're just awaiting confirmation of the buoy deactivation along our route and we should be on our way shortly."

"Thank you, Commander. Please let me know when we reach Earth."

"Aye-aye sir."

As good as his word, not five minutes later the courier vanished from normal space and the sight of the imposing Gateway Station. An instant later, it re-entered normal space, within touching distance of Fortress Command itself. John was forced to reduce the scale on his display several times before he was able to get a complete picture of Earth's primary orbital defense station. If he thought Gateway Station was impressive, it paled into insignificance against Fortress Command.

The gigantic station was the same basic design as Gateway but easily three times the size. Six million tonnes of battle armor, grazer, laser, missiles, and plasma guns were stowed in Fortress Command and the cloud of space forts and overlapping weapons platforms surrounding the Earth it controlled was the last line of defense against any attacker. Admiral Jing, serving as Chairman of the Combined Joint Chiefs, and his planners had spared no expense in ensuring Earth's safety. The other member planets of the Commonwealth were so impressed by what Jing and his designers achieved that they were all in the process of building their own variations of the fortress concept and if current projections held true, then every major planet in the Commonwealth would be secure behind its own web of forts and weapons platforms within four or five years. John was still taking it all in when a call from the flight deck came through.

"You have a priority call from the president's office, Admiral."

John automatically straightened his uniform before replying. "Put it through."

In John's display, the presidential seal appeared briefly, before the face of Patricia Bath replaced it. Her green eyes seemed to flash mischievously at him as he heard her smoky voice.

"Well hello, sailor."

John's heart beat ten to a dozen times faster as he struggled to control the twitching in his cheeks, they so wanted to break into a huge smile at the sight of her. With all the control he could muster, he kept his face deadpan.

"Ah, Doctor Bath. How good to see you again. I see being an adviser to the president allows you the use of the priority communications channels."

The smile in her eyes moved to her lips. "The job has its perks, I suppose, and a small abuse of my position to ensure I at least get a word with my future husband before those horrible navy types sequester him away in some hole in the ground for God knows how long isn't too much to ask, is it?"

The little-girl-lost look she gave him was enough to elicit a snort of laughter from John. "Admiral Jing promised me that after a short debrief at Mont Salève, I'm free to spend what's left of my bachelor life cavorting in various bars until I finally put on the shackles of marriage."

Patricia screwed up her face and stuck her tongue out at him. "You tell the dear admiral I'll hold him to that and remind him my boss is his boss and all I have to do is walk along the corridor, knock on her door, and he'll find himself looking for a new job."

"I shall be sure to use that as my opening line."

"OK, I'll see you later. Oh and by the way, my parents are in town and we are having dinner with them tonight. Bye."

Before John could reply, she cut the link. Dinner with the in-laws... welcome home, John.

#

CENTRAL COMMAND - MONT SALÈVE
EARTH – SOL SYSTEM

As the briefing room door slid aside, John Radford stepped through and snapped to attention, saluting the Chairman of the Combined Joint Chiefs of Staff, Admiral Ai Jing. From his seat at the head of the spotless gray carbonite table, Jing stood and strode toward John, his hand outstretched. As Jing went to greet John, the other gathered uniformed officers who had already been seated also stood. John spared them a fleeting glance before Jing descended on him. The mix of Human, Persai, Garundan, and Benii uniforms in the room was hard on the eyes, as their various colors clashed, but one thing stood out as common to all: A single black patch with silver wording high on the right shoulder stated that all were part of CSG *Itus.* Below the wording was a pair of crossed swords in the same silver embroidery.

"Welcome, John. Please be seated, I'm sure you're eager to hear of your new command's progress before you take the well-deserved leave you've been promised for so long."

Releasing Jing's hand, John took the indicated seat opposite Jing and waited patiently while the chairman retook his. Without pausing, Jing got straight to the point. "Ladies and gentlemen. After years of design and building we have reached the point where we are ready to take the next step in the Carrier Strike Group concept."

Around the table, all eyes were on Jing. This was something some of them had worked on day and night since Jing first conceived the idea of the CSGs over two years before and they were eager to see the fruit of their labors.

"With the arrival of Admiral Radford, I feel we are at last ready to move on to the final stages of fleet trials. I know Admiral Radford has missed the initial trials due to the unavoidable delay in his being relieved as CO of Third Fleet, but now that he's here, I want to press on at full speed. The longer it takes to get CSG *Itus* operational, the longer our colonists will be reliant on the heavy units of our main fleets to protect them and, as you all know, these same fleets are in the process of draw down so their heavy units are becoming scarcer every day."

Jing saw the various species around the table nod in understanding. "With that in mind, I expect CSG *Itus* to be fully operational in no more than six months from today's date."

There was a sharp intake of breath around the table and John said, "Aye-aye sir. Six months from today and not a day longer."

Jing stood abruptly, bringing everyone else in the room to their feet. He nodded to John and made his way from the room. As the door closed behind him John, let a lazy smile spread across his face. "OK people, it looks like the clock is ticking and I just made the admiral a promise that it'll be up to you to keep."

The assembled officers chuckled. Sitting back down John let out a small sigh. *Looks like I'm going to be late for dinner*. "So, where do we start...?"

CHAPTER TEN
Meet the Neighbors

SS CHARLOTTE DUNDAS - SELENE SYSTEM
272 LIGHT YEARS FROM EARTH

"Captain, call the bridge! Captain, call the bridge!"

"What now?" Captain Lucio Vela grumbled as he dragged himself out of the comfortable seat in the officers' lounge of the SS *Charlotte Dundas.* He had been sipping his steaming coffee and looking through the plasteel porthole, observing the gathering clouds on the planet below. Now he headed for the comms panel by the entrance hatch. Vela hated the wrist comms he was supposed to wear at all times so he tended to "forget" to wear it unless a member of the Zurich Lines hierarchy happened to be aboard. These days that was most unlikely, given the difficulties the company was going through. *Charlotte Dundas* and the other eight Elephant class 250,000 tonnes cargo ships were in high demand these days. Only ships like the Elephant class had the load capacity to carry and sustain complete mining or colonization operations like the one currently taking place on Selene, so they were very rarely in port long enough for the bigwigs to decide to visit.

Keying the comms panel by the entrance hatch, Vela established a link to the Duty Bridge Officer and made no attempt to keep the irritation out of his voice. “Captain speaking. This ought to be good, Givens, or you’re going to be doing night watches for the rest of this cruise."

"Captain, sensors are showing a group of ships closing in on our position from behind the orbit of the planet’s second moon."

Vela’s jaw dropped in surprise. *Charlotte Dundas* had been in orbit around Selene for over two months now as the embryonic colony on the planet’s surface fought to establish itself. If all went according to plan, then Vela and his ship would remain a further three months and then head home for a quick shore leave and maintenance cycle before heading out with another load of colonists.

"Have you sent them a hail? They could be another colonization operation who haven’t gotten the word yet that we've secured the rights to Selene." Even as he said it, Vela knew he was grasping at straws. It took months to organize a project the size of colonizing another world and before anyone could even start getting the finances together, they had to secure a license from the Bureau of Colonization. They certainly were not going to make the mistake of issuing two licenses for the same planet.

"Yes, sir. So far there’s no response to our hails."

Vela heard the touch of concern in Givens voice. It was no secret that the cargo of a colonization ship like the *Charlotte Dundas* was worth a small fortune and many a ship’s captain, like Vela, wondered why some enterprising individuals had not yet thought to hijack a ship just like his and sell off the cargo on the black market or ransom the crew.

In the days before the invention of the gravity drive and the war with the Others, the Sol system had had its problems with privateers. A problem the then-small navy of the TDF had struggled to contain. With the invention of the gravity drive, the expansion of the navy, and the surveillance platforms which were seeded throughout the Sol system, the age of the pirate appeared over. Nevertheless, out here, hundreds of light years from home, there was a resurgence of this particularly nasty art.

Yes, if you got a comms drone away in time it could fold and reach Colonial Support Command (CSC) almost instantly. Unfortunately, there was no guarantee there would be a naval vessel in a position to respond immediately. The navy called it overstretch. Vela called it bad planning.

"What's their ETA?"

"If they maintain their current course and speed they should rendezvous with us in... fifty-eight minutes."

"OK Givens, let's get a drone away to CSC on Ganymede. Download our logs and sensor data and request immediate assistance. Put an all-hands call out, quietly though, no need to worry the remaining colonists on board just yet. Let's secure all the outer hatches and tell the master-at-arms to pass out the side arms. Better safe than sorry. I'm on my way to the bridge now. Vela clear."

Vela headed for the bridge, knowing the handful of side arms in the ships armory had little chance of stopping any serious boarding action but it was all he had. For the first time since they arrived at Selene, he wished he were with the colonists who had already set up a base on the windswept planet below.

#

GANYMEDE - SOL SYSTEM

The dull early morning routine in the operations room of what was euphemistically called Colonial Support Command, housed deep in the bedrock of Ganymede, Jupiter's largest moon, was something the duty officer, Lieutenant Pizarro, could have done without. He had been up late the night before celebrating the promotion of his roommate and was feeling a little under the weather this morning, particularly at the prospect of another long tour in the dim room lit only by subdued lighting and the glow of terminals manned by equally bored sailors.

CSC had been established in response to the wave of colonization that was sweeping the Commonwealth. CSC was tasked with acting as the intermediary between Survey Command, the Bureau of Colonization, and the various shipping firms that were providing the actual colony ships. Hence, some unknown sailor had christened the operations room the “Hub” and the nickname stuck. It had even become part of semi-official parlance. CSC did not actually own any navy ships. If there were a requirement from a colony or shipping line for naval support, the Hub would consider the request, prioritize it, and pass it on to the Office of Joint Naval Operations who again would consider the request, prioritize it, and let CSC know their answer, usually within ten days. Nothing moved fast in the administrative world.

"Drone arrival! It’s transmitting a priority message code, Lieutenant."

The call from the Communications Section brought Pizarro to full wakefulness as adrenalin flooded his system. "Accept the message and pass it to my terminal." Pizarro tapped his desktop repeatedly with his stylus as he waited for the drone’s message to be downloaded and passed to him. As the message header appeared on his screen, his brow furrowed. The SS *Charlotte Dundas* was not a name he immediately recognized and Pizarro keyed a query into the computer for the stats of the ship and its destination as he continued to read the message. His breath caught in his chest as he reached the part about three unidentified ships on an intercept course for the defenseless colony ship.

"Comms. Flash Signal. Copy the message and logs from the *Charlotte Dundas* and download it to our drone. Make your destination First Fleet. Add our recommendation for immediate naval support and launch when ready."

A Flash Signal was the highest priority message in the navy. It automatically overrode all other traffic and set alarm bells ringing when it arrived at First Fleet. A big call for a mere lieutenant to make but Pizarro was confident he had taken the correct course of action. Pizarro sat back in his seat, having done all he could. He just hoped help reached the *Charlotte Dundas* in time.

#

SS CHARLOTTE DUNDAS
SELENE SYSTEM - 272 LIGHT YEARS FROM EARTH

All eyes on the cramped bridge of the *Charlotte Dundas* were fixed on the main holo cube. Although not as well equipped as a modern naval vessel, Lucio Vela was still immensely proud of his ship and ensured it was kept in tip-top condition. Though it was times like this when he wished she was equipped with military grade sensors.

Vela forced himself to keep a calm exterior as the three unidentified ships closed on his position. Despite repeated hails, the ships continued their approach in total silence. Either they did not understand his hails or they were intentionally ignoring them.

As the ships closed the distance between themselves and

the *Charlotte Dundas,* the merchant ship's sensors at last got a good read on them. What they revealed made Vela's blood run cold. These were no pirate ships.

Each of the approaching ships was identical and they flew in tight formation. A typical pirate ship was a hotchpotch of converted merchant ships and scrounged or stolen military hardware.

Vela looked at the sleek lines of the ships he was facing. A bulbous bow swept rearward before breaking into five pylons sharply angled away from the main body of the ship. Vela overheard one of the bridge crew liken them to starfish. He could see the resemblance, although these "starfish" were a deep red and likely weighed in at around 70,000 tonnes. Vela's ship could easily outweigh all three of the starfish ships combined, but the grazer points at the end of each of the pylons and the missile tube covers spaced in two rows evenly spread along the main body of each ship meant the *Charlotte Dundas'* meager point defense system was vastly outmatched.

"They're slowing, Captain."

Vela checked his repeater display to confirm his navigator's call. Yes, there was no doubt about it, they had slowed their approach. What the hell were they up to? They were already easily within any conventional weapons range.

The next few minutes seemed to stretch into hours as the three warships slowed and eventually came to a halt less than 100,000 kilometers from the hovering *Charlotte Dundas*.

"Incoming signal! Audio only."

Vela anxiously leaned forward in his seat. "Let's hear it."

A strident, un-intonated voice in Standard English filled

the bridge. "You have infringed on the territory of the Turak. You will remove yourselves within one rotation of the planet or suffer the consequences."

The bridge was silent for a heartbeat after the message ended, then burst into a cacophony of noise as the whole crew attempted to talk at once.

"Silence!" With Vela’s single command, peace returned.

"Communications. Open a link." Vela swallowed to wet his dry throat as the link was established.

"This is Captain Lucio Vela of the Commonwealth Union of Planets’ starship *Charlotte Dundas*. We were unaware you have laid claim to this planet. We operate under a license to colonize the planet, issued by the Commonwealth Bureau of Colonization. May we meet to discuss this misunderstanding?"

Silence, interrupted by bursts of static was the only reply. A nod from the comms section senior bosun confirmed the link was still open. The silence stretched on until Vela gave the bosun a throat-slicing motion and the link was terminated.

Think Lucio. Think. One rotation of Selene was around twenty-six hours. Without moving in his seat Vela called out, "Options, Diane?"

Diane Williams, second-in-command of the *Charlotte Dundas*, uncurled herself from where she was sitting to one side of the bridge watching the unfolding situation and slowly began pacing back and forth across the small bridge, "Before I answer your question, Captain, perhaps it would be wise to consider what we know so far."

"Go on."

"We are facing three warships which our sensors tell us easily outgun us."

"Agreed," Vela replied grimly.

Diane got into her stride, "For whatever reason, they decided to mask their approach by concealing themselves in the shadow of the second moon."

"OK. If I wanted to ambush a ship, I would want to get in as close as possible without being detected. It's just good tactics."

"True, though that in itself also shows prudence on their part. A reluctance to expose themselves too early."

"Again, Diane, good tactics. They couldn't have had any idea of our capabilities until they got close enough to get a good sensor read on us and discover we're only a freighter."

"My point exactly, Captain. They weren't sure what we were until they got closer... so how did they know to hail us in Standard English?"

The silence Vela enforced on the bridge evaporated, he allowed the animated discussion to continue while he grappled with Diane's statement. If you followed her line of thinking, it could only mean the Turak had been observing the Commonwealth for some time but had not made a move until the *Charlotte Dundas* encroached on their territory. A flick of his wrist signaled Diane to continue.

"Option One. Do nothing. Wait for the navy to arrive and see what happens next."

Vela smiled despite himself. "Somehow I get the feeling the Turak mean business. Next?"

"Option Two. Evacuate the colonists from the planet.

Get as many back on board as possible within the time constraints and hightail it out of here."

Vela shook his head slowly, "Diane you know as well as I we have nearly 4500 colonists spread over the entire planet. We simply don't have the lift capability to get all of them and their equipment back on board in time. Is there an option three?"

Diane stopped her pacing directly in front of Vela. As his second-in-command and alter ego, it was her job to lay out all the options. No matter how unpalatable they were. Steeling herself, she forced herself to speak, her voice coming out tautly. "Option Three. Abandon the colonists and head for home."

The shocked expression on the face of the captain caused any who heard Diane's final option to turn away in distaste.

Vela leaned in close to Diane, fighting to control his anger. "I will not abandon these people to their fate, Diane. I don't care how you do it, you get every last one of them off that rock and back on board. Do you understand me?"

Diane nodded in understanding. Nothing further was needed, the captain had given his orders.

Vela took a deep breath as he regained control of himself. "Communications. Open a link to those ships." Comms quickly obliged. "This is Captain Vela. I'm about to launch shuttles to recover the colonists. This is not a sign of aggression. I repeat. It is not a sign of aggression, I'm simply doing as you requested. I'll also launch a communications drone to inform my superiors of your request, there are no weapons onboard and it is of no threat to you. Please acknowledge."

Only stony silence broken by moments of static came from the bridge speakers. Nothing more than Vela expected. He cut the link and addressed his bridge crew, "OK people, we are about to get really busy, really fast. Many angry colonists will be arriving here soon so let's be as pleasant as we can but remember! We are on the clock. Let's get it done!"

#

The next six hours passed at an accelerated rate as the shuttles raced back and forth between the massive freighter and the surface of Selene in a vain attempt to corral the widespread colonists.

Vela had to admit, Diane performed minor miracles as she planned pick-up points and timetables for the colonists to converge on them on the hoof. All the time under the open mouth of the Turak warships' guns. It took only one hard look at the numbers in his display to tell Vela everything he needed to know.

Despite Diane's and the shuttle pilots' heroic efforts, they simply were not getting the colonists onboard at the breakneck speed they needed to. Current projections overran the Turak deadline by at least nine hours.

"Status on the Turak ships?"

"No change, Captain. All three remain stationary at 100,000 kilometers off our starboard quarter. No reply to our hails and our sensors have detected no transmissions between them."

Vela ground his teeth in frustration. He was trying to raise the Turak to explain his need for an extension on their deadline but the ships remained stoically silent. Well, the Turak could go to hell. The *Charlotte Dundas* was staying exactly where she was until the colonists were safely back on board and that was the end of it!

In the blink of an eye, the tactical read-out in the holo cube changed.

"Status change! Fifteen new contacts... correction twenty... computer is calling them warships, Captain."

Vela's shoulders slumped. His ship had little chance of defying three Turak warships, but twenty-three?

"Receiving a general broadcast, sir."

"Put it through the bridge speakers," said Vela as he resigned himself and the colonists to their fate.

"Turak warships, this is Admiral Analisa Chavez, Commanding Officer of First Fleet, Commonwealth Union of Planets. The *SS Charlotte Dundas* and the colonists on the planet below are under my protection. Any attempt to fire on either the *Charlotte Dundas*, the planet's surface, or my vessels will result in my immediate and deadly retaliation. I order you to withdraw your vessels beyond the orbit of the second moon where you may remain and observe the evacuation of the planet. Failure to comply with my orders will result in the use of deadly force. You have five minutes to comply. Chavez clear."

The loud cheer echoing round the cramped bridge was nothing compared to the relief washing over Vela. For the first time today, he allowed himself a smile. "Communications. Update First Fleet on the status of our recovery operations and our projected timetable." Addressing the bridge in general, he said, "Back to work people, we still have a lot of colonists to move."

#

TDF RESOLUTION - SELENE SYSTEM
272 LIGHT YEARS FROM EARTH

"Admiral. The *Cutlass* is signaling its arrival.

Ambassador Schamu reports he is ready to proceed."

Analisa Chavez lifted her eyes from her tactical repeater where she was reviewing the latest from her intelligence section's best guess as to the Turak ships' weapons and capabilities. The section chief came to some surprising conclusions. In his estimation, the Turak were also equipped with a form of gravity drive not too dissimilar to those employed by the CUOP. The data collected by Captain Vela regarding the Turak weapon capabilities were not too far off the mark either. Each ship had two rows of missile tubes, and the covering for each launch tube was smaller than those on an equivalent CUOP heavy cruiser, which meant the missile itself had to be smaller. However, there were more missile tubes on the Turak ships so having smaller missiles may be offset by having a greater number in each salvo.

The section chief then highlighted the number of heavy grazer points. With five grazers, a Turak cruiser would outgun one of her cruisers five to three, meaning at energy weapon ranges, the Turak would have the advantage but at longer ranges, her cruisers could throw a heavier missile weight.

At this particular moment in time, it was a moot point. When the flash signal from the Hub was received at First Fleet, it had been akin to kicking over an ant nest. First Fleet forwarded the flash signal to the Combined Joint Chiefs where Admiral Jing was heard to repeatedly curse CSG *Itus*, the unit specifically designed to deal with exactly this kind of incident, and which was still three months from being operational.

Never a man to hesitate when time was of the essence, Jing ordered Analisa, his replacement as CO First Fleet, to assume command of the ready BatFor and prepare for immediate departure. Analisa and the navy's speedy response had all been for naught as the Commonwealth Council refused permission for the fleet's deployment.

Clearly, they were wary of repeating their mistake in sending First Fleet rushing to the defense of Alona during the war against the Others. That move had left Earth open to the surprise attack which ended in the destruction of Fifth Fleet and the near extinction of the human race. The Council was refusing to authorize the deployment of a single BatFor until each of the member states of the Commonwealth agreed.

Even with the speedy comms drones feeding information to politicians, the Council decision delayed any action until each government considered the pros and cons of deployment. Minutes became hours while Analisa and her relief force could only cool their heels and await their political masters' decision. When it came, a long five hours later, Analisa did not wait for Jing to terminate the communications link before she folded for Selene.

Much to her relief, she arrived to find the stalemate between the hulking freighter and the Turak still in place. With the firepower of an entire BatFor to back up her demands for the Turak to withdraw, whoever was in charge over there decided withdrawal was the better part of valor. The three warships withdrew to just beyond the second moon where they had remained, silently, for the last thirteen hours.

Analisa's sensors detected numerous launches from the center vessel of the three-ship formation. The analysts called it the flagship. The frequent launches, they figured, and Analisa agreed, were most likely communications drones, as almost immediately after launch they accelerated sharply and disappeared into fold space. Analisa wondered if they were calling for backup. She could be in for a shooting war yet. This possibility was the main reason she greeted the news of the *Cutlass'* arrival with a sense of relief.

"Inform the ambassador he may continue." Unconsciously, Analisa's fingers sought out the delicate gold necklace she always wore. A gift from the widow of her late mentor and friend Stephano Ricco killed in the bloodbath of 70 Ophiuchi four years ago. The blue icon representing the *Cutlass* moved away from the massed ships of her BatFor on course for the three unmoving Turak cruisers. *Good luck, Ambassador. For all our sakes.*

#

Nicholas Schamu outwardly appeared not to have a care in the world as he sat on one of the few spare seats on the bridge of SurvFlot One's flagship, TDF *Cutlass*. Only two hours ago Nicholas had been enjoying... perhaps "enjoying" was too strong a word... dinner with his sister Madeleine and her insufferable husband, Senator Mathias Grant III. A priority call summoning him to the austere offices of the Head of the Diplomatic Corps himself had come at a most opportune moment as he had about had enough of the self-inflated ego of Mathias Grant III and he was just one more bland sound bite away from telling him where he could politely shove his ideas of the Earth First movement.

The military flyer which landed on the back lawn of his sister's house made an unsightly mess of the blustering senator's immaculate rose bed and elicited a chortle from the normally mirthless ambassador as he watched the politician mouthing a curse and shaking a fist at the flyer as it took off. The last remaining heads of the roses were separated from their stalks and blown across the neat, now scorched, lawn.

Whatever small amount of joy Nicholas may have taken from his brother-in-law's futile efforts to save his beloved roses was thoroughly suffocated as he opened the secure briefing package on the PAD the crew chief handed to him on boarding. Nicholas, over the years, developed a talent for speed-reading any document and picking out the salient points. In his opinion, the situation at Selene was a hair’s breath away from going from a standoff to armed conflict. As the flyer broke the sound barrier in its headlong dash for distant Geneva, Nicholas tapped a key on his armrest activating his link to the flyer’s pilot.

"Change of destination. Get me to the Geneva spaceport and don’t spare the horses."

"But Ambassador, I have direct orders from Secretary Beckett to take you to the Diplomatic Corps headquarters."

Ah, these military types, always following orders. "And I'm changing those orders. Don’t worry, I’ll sort it out with the secretary, just get me to the spaceport *tout de suite*."

Terminating the link, Nicholas could tell the pilot was not happy but he felt the little flyer bank and knew he was on course for his new destination. A few more taps of his armrest controls and he established a link to Secretary Beckett's private number. The lined, balding head of Aaron Beckett appeared in the display mounted in the headrest in front of Nicholas. Before he could say anything the Secretary wrong footed him.

"I see you’re headed for the spaceport, Nicholas. Luckily I requisitioned a courier ship and it’s warming up on the landing pad."

Instead of replying immediately, Nicholas gave one of his rare chuckles. "I see you understand the importance of haste in the current situation, Mr. Secretary."

Now it was Aaron's turn to laugh. "I only ordered the flyer to bring you here to see if you were still willing to follow your gut instead of blindly following your superiors’ instructions. I'm glad to see, even after knowing you for thirty-odd years, you are still willing to question, if not downright ignore, those instructions."

Nicholas tipped an imaginary hat at the pick up. "I learned from the best, Mr. Secretary."

"Sycophant," laughed Aaron before his demeanor turned all business again. "Back to the matter in hand, Nicholas. The courier ship will take you to Charon Base, where Admiral Papadomas has put the *Cutlass* at your disposal..."

Aaron must have seen the quizzical look on Nicholas' face.

"The admiral was quite insistent. If you're going into a potential war zone, then you will be aboard one of his cruisers, not an unarmed courier ship. He made some reference to a Benii carrier and a shuttle craft, as I recall"

Nicholas smiled ruefully. "Yes. Christos will never let me live that one down, I fear. In this case, he may be right. Tensions appear quite high and perhaps being on board an armored warship is better than being on a defenseless shuttle craft."

"Let's hope you don't have to find out, Nicholas. However, enough of this melancholy talk. *Cutlass* will be at your disposal and I've already sent word to Admiral Chavez, you will be joining her as expeditiously as you can. All the latest information we have is already loaded onto your PAD, including your mission specifics."

Nicholas cocked an eyebrow at the image of the secretary in his display. "Which are?"

"In a nutshell, to make sure we don't find ourselves in another shooting war. Find out as much about these people as you can and try to establish some form of peaceful relations with them."

"From what I've seen, the Turak come across as pretty belligerent, Mr. Secretary."

Aaron frowned and the mood turned somber. "That's what I'm afraid of, Nicholas. Do your best."

Nicholas looked into the tired eyes of his friend for a second before replying. "Yes, of course, you shall have it, Mr. Secretary."

With a nod, Aaron terminated the link. Nicholas picked up the PAD again and began going through the data line by line, hoping to glean even the smallest detail that could help him with the Turak as the flyer sped onwards.

#

"All stop."

"All stop, aye, Captain."

Captain Denise Parks spun her chair until she faced the dapper diplomat in his seat along the rear bulkhead of the *Cutlass*. To her surprise, he was sipping tea from a bone china cup and looked as if he was completely unperturbed by the sight of the three Turak warships hovering 500,000 kilometers dead ahead. Admiral Papadomas had given her strict instructions before departing Charon regarding the ambassador's well-being.

Ambassador Schamu was in charge of the mission and she was to follow his orders to the letter. If the ambassador's orders compromised the safety of the *Cutlass* and her crew Parks was to use her best judgment, the admiral would nonetheless take a very dim view if she were to allow said ambassador to come to any harm by reckless behavior by, say, taking an unarmed shuttle and heading out to meet three warships. If Schamu's reputation for grandiose gestures were anything to go by, those instructions may prove a hard task to complete.

"We are at the limit of what we think is the Turak effective weapons envelope, Ambassador."

Schamu put his cup down carefully on a small table by his chair and put on his best game face. "Thank you, Captain. Perhaps you would open a video and audio link to the Turak ships."

Parks gave her comms officer a nod and the link was established.

"Turak vessels. I am Ambassador Nicholas Schamu of the Commonwealth Union of Planets and I have come here at the request of the Commonwealth to hopefully establish peaceful relations between our peoples and avert any accidental misunderstandings."

There was no reply from the Turak, just stony silence.

"Comms, are we sure the link is still open?" Parks asked.

"Yes, ma'am. My board shows the link is good. The Turak are receiving both our audio and video feed."

"Let's give it a minute, Captain, if you please," said Nicholas.

The seconds crept by and as the bridge clock ticked four minutes later, the harsh, Standard English of the Turak erupted from the bridge speakers.

"You have infringed on the territory of the Turak. You will remove yourselves from the planet or suffer the consequences."

"As you can see, we are doing as you ask and we

apologize for any offense we may have caused. We did not know the Turak claimed this system. If I may make a suggestion? So we may avoid any further misunderstandings in the future, perhaps an exchange of information, a list of systems under Turak control in this quadrant of space to prevent any unintentional ingress. We would of course reciprocate and supply you with a list of systems occupied by the Commonwealth." With a small nod from Nicholas, the comms officer transmitted the pre-prepared data.

Again, the seconds seemed to stretch as Nicholas awaited the Turak's reply.

"Captain, we're receiving a data packet from the Turak... looks like navigational data."

Nicholas let out a small sigh. Progress at last. "Thank you. May I request we establish video communications as well as audio?"

The answer this time was immediate. "No. We have supplied the data you need. Ensure there are no more intrusions into Turak territory. Next time, no opportunity to retreat will be given and if you believe we have taken no action because of the presence of your warships, behold the strength of the Turak!"

The wailing of alarms filled the bridge of the *Cutlass* and the tactical holo cube filled with the blood-red icons of Turak ships. Ten. Twenty. Thirty. Forty. Fifty capital ships, each the size of a Bismarck class battleship filled the holo cube.

Mocking laughter reached Nicholas through the sound of the alarms. "Go now and do not return unless you want war!"

CHAPTER ELEVEN

Misunderstandings

BALAT - SYSTEM 23890 - 22 LIGHT YEARS FROM ALONA

The Alonan colony world of Balat circled the GV type star, the system's primary, at the outer edges of the life-giving Goldilocks zone. Balat was the youngest of the three colonies the Empire rushed to establish in the face of the feared Commonwealth expansion.

From his vantage point high on the ridgeline, Major General Siloz drank in the lush green valley, the home of the courageous all-volunteer colonist force.

The valley floor looked like a maze of construction. Ranging from accommodation buildings to the bio-domes where they cultivated the colony's seedlings before implanting them in the newly rotovated fields surrounding the colony proper.

Siloz came up to this vantage point alone on an almost weekly basis. He told his subordinates it was to check the outstation's progress, but really, he needed time away from the never-ending hubbub that governorship of an ever-expanding colony generated.

Siloz was no fool. He knew the Empire was poorly prepared to establish colony worlds outside of the home system. It had taken a long and arduous thirty years to develop Geta, the second habitable planet of the Alonan home system, into a self-supporting entity. But times were changing.

When the merciless Others attacked the Empire, the Commonwealth fleet's intervention alone saved Alona. At the time, the sparseness of gravity drive cruisers limited the Empire's own naval capability, a grave circumstance that led to a dishonorable act. The Emperor was forced to go cap in hand to the Commonwealth for assistance. When the Commonwealth chose to conceal the existence of the Others from the Empire, they also concealed the real danger they posed to every living thing.

Things were different now. The Empire would never again be treated like a poor relation to the all-powerful Commonwealth. The Emperor aimed to make the Empire a multi-star system affair, complete with the teeth to defend what was theirs. They used technology procured by various government agencies in a race to match the Commonwealth's technological edge. Volunteers filled the colonist ranks as they established habitats in suitable worlds, posts filled almost as quickly as worlds could be found.

Siloz well remembered the list of volunteers wishing to be Balat colonists – the list had been oversubscribed tenfold! Kathan and Opero were equally popular with the volunteers. These three colony worlds secured the immediate future of the Alonan Empire, though deep suspicion remained over the Commonwealth's true intentions toward the empire.

In Alonan tradition, the people had put their shoulders to

the wheel. Construction of naval vessels was at an all-time high and there was no shortage of willing recruits. Siloz's heart swelled with pride as he pictured his own beaming children in their shiny new uniforms of the Imperial Navy.

A gust of cool wind brushed over him and with it, a drizzle of rain settled on his soft brown fur. Siloz looked westward beyond the towers of the atmospheric purification plants, which would one day render the small re-breather over his mouth outdated. He saw burgeoning black clouds rolling toward the valley. The fading light indicated an almighty thunderstorm was imminent. The first clap and then roll of thunder reached him through the heavy air. He sighed as he headed back to his all-terrain ground car. The rich, fertile soil would soon turn to a thick, sticky quagmire under his feet and the dirt track back to the colony would bc difficult even for his ground car.

The chirp of the communicator at his waist reached him through the drip, drip of the steadily increasing rain. Lifting it from his belt he pushed accept. It was his adjutant, Major Froli.

"General! *Kuna* reports four warships have exited fold space. They are shaping an intercept course for him! *Kuna's* sensors indicate the unknowns are in the heavy cruiser range and are powering up weapons. *Kuna* is preparing to engage!"

Siloz stood stock-still in the rain as it ran in rivulets down his face. *Kuna* was one of the Empire's first fold-capable frigates, it was simply visiting Balat as part of its shakedown cruise and the cruisers would have it massively outgunned. Siloz would not waste the crew's lives in some futile gesture. "Order the *Kuna* to break orbit and return to Alona now! Appraise Fleet Headquarters of our situation and return with reinforcements. I'm on my way to Colony Control now and will be with you shortly."

Siloz cut the link and headed for the ground car, pausing he allowed his eyes to feast on the darkened landscape one last time, knowing in his heart he would never look upon the view again.

#

INS KUNA - ORBITING BALAT

Captain Warat and the crew of the *Kuna* raced to prepare the frigate for departure. The trip to Balat had identified a slight variance in the primary fusion generator, prompting Warat to grant the Chief Engineer time to investigate the problem before continuing to Opero. Despite the fact that the yards in Alona could find and fix the issue in half the time his crew could, Warat decided the crew needed the experience. Now that four unknown warships were closing in, he regretted his decision.

On the tactical display, Warat saw the fast-closing icons and realized the *Kuna* was out of time. Even if the chief got the reactor online right away, it wasn't enough time to avoid entering the advancing warships' firing range.

"Communications! Get the drones away now!"

The comms officer's eyes met and briefly held her captain's she understood the unsaid implications. She turned back to her board and set about downloading the destination coordinates into each of the drones' computer brains.

"Download complete, Captain!"

Captain Warat stole a glance at the tactical display, his heart sank as he saw the wave of smaller icons separate from the larger masses representing the warships. Missiles were heading for his poor *Kuna*, he must tell those at home what was happening here.

"Launch the drones! Tactical. Weapons free. Give them everything we've got!"

Five communications drones burst from the belly of the *Kuna*. In their wake, the spread of anti-missile fire from the *Kuna* seemed pitiful in the face of the avalanche of missiles falling on her. Two drones succumbed to enemy energy fire but three made the transition to fold space. Two headed for Alona, the third did not.

In her haste, the comms officer missed the fact that Drone 5 was still locked into the war game the Tactical Section had been playing before real life interrupted. The drone followed its pre-programmed instructions. It headed for Waypoint 4, the nearest Commonwealth base. The final navigation checkpoint before entering Alonan space which, after the breakdown in relations between the Empire and Commonwealth, became the home to a complete Commonwealth Battle Force and the base of its Empire surveillance operation.

#

WAYPOINT 4 - 5000 LIGHT YEARS FROM ALONA INTERSTELLAR SPACE

The Operations Center was a picture of quiet efficiency. Commander Talan, Duty Officer at Waypoint 4, sat relaxed in his chair on its raised dais. The Garundan flicked his eyes around the various workstations filling the small room. All seemed tranquil and sedate as the assorted watch officers tried to fight off the onset of boredom.

The tactical plot remained virtually unchanged since the departure of BatFor 4.1 earlier in the morning. As tended to happen when you coordinated military units over such vast distances, the replacement BatFor, BatFor 2.3, encountered an unexpected delay in its departure from Janus. A delay of twenty-four to thirty-six hours and was late to relieve the

Persai covering force of BatFor 4.1.

The commanding officer of BatFor 4.1, Force Leader Palas, was well aware of the Combined Joint Chiefs of Staff (CJCS) decision that BatFor 2.3 would be the last Commonwealth capital ship unit deployed to Waypoint 4. The colonization program was gaining momentum, as was the operation to secure the last of the Others' bases. The waning plan of CJCS commenced with the re-prioritizing of the use of capital ship heavy units such as the BatFors.

They planned for a future where the BatFors remained primarily in the home systems and the CJCS relied on smaller, more flexible destroyer and cruiser squadrons to police the colonies. The first of this new breed of destroyers was already at Waypoint 4. TDF *Sorcerer*, fresh from yard hands, was refurbished and upgraded with the latest offensive and defensive systems. *Sorcerer* was the lead ship of four in the new Destroyer Division 5.1.1.

Force Leader Palas was happy with this plan, in fact so much so, he saw no measure of danger in folding for home as scheduled without waiting for the now-delayed relief force. After all, the only other ships he'd observed in the area in three months were cargo ships, hauling goods between the Empire and the Commonwealth. Palas was certain the new, secretly deployed Dupin surveillance platforms dotted around the Empire's three colony -worlds should give Waypoint 4 adequate advance warning of any suspicious activity by the Alonans. The Dupin platforms were specifically designed to be as stealthy as possible, while remaining capable of keeping an eye on the Empire.

Commonwealth and Alonan affairs had taken a nose-dive after the attack on Alona by the Others. Even though First Fleet responded to the Empire's call for help, it was obvious the Empire blamed the Commonwealth for the attack in the first place. In the aftermath of the attack, the Empire placed even more stringent conditions of entry than before into what it saw as Alonan space. The regions around the three colony-worlds became a no-go area for Commonwealth shipping. Commonwealth ships were now only allowed as far as the outer marker of the Alonan system, where they transferred their cargoes to Alonan transports at the partially completed Emperor Yalo IV spaceport. The expanding Imperial Navy performed constant sweeps of the inner system for any intruders, so it was deemed too risky to place any Dupin platforms in the Alonan system itself, but by employing the stealth capabilities of a long-range Talos shuttle, the Commonwealth managed to place the Dupins in position around the colony systems.

Talan's lower jaw dropped slightly as he quietly chuckled. *How the universe changes, one day they hail us as heroes for saving them from the Others, the next? We're banned from their systems like lepers!* He unintentionally snorted, a little too loudly, and surreptitiously looked around to see if any of the other staff had noticed. The beep from his terminal alerted 'status change.' Talan hauled himself upright and tapped a key to expand the message. The detection grid was picking up a small object that had just folded back into normal space.

The seaman at the Tactical Station called out, "Commander! Computers are calling Bogey One an Alonan communications drone, it's holding at 500,000 kilometers."

Talan scratched his lower jaw with one pointed claw, "Communications! Lock onto the Alonan drone and send an interrogation query. Let's see what it's doing here."

The Garundan petty officer operating the comms desk carried out his orders and the reply took just seconds to arrive. "Commander! I'm receiving a reply in plain language…Computers are translating now."

"Throw it across to my screen, PO." Talan toggled his screen from tactical display to comms read-out. The translation of the Alonan message popped up. "Holy shit!" The profanity favored by one of his human navy instructors inadvertently escaped him. Talan read the message again. He flipped up the clear plastic cover over the large red button on his desk and without hesitation, he mashed his finger down on it.

The battle station's alarm whooped throughout Waypoint 4.

#

TDF SORCERER - 2000 KILOMETERS OFF WAYPOINT 4

Sorcerer's corridors gleamed almost as brightly as the fresh commander's leaf on Kenichi Sutou's collar. He walked briskly through the Havoc class destroyer, heading for the bridge. Crewmembers dodged around him as they rushed for the battle stations the klaxon called them to.

Kenichi's pace slowed as he approached the bridge entrance, the armed marine on duty by the door keyed in the lock sequence and granted him entry.

It was unusual for a ship of *Sorcerer's* size to have her own marine complement on board, but her original task in the Sol system was to board and inspect merchantmen, and to do so they required a full platoon of marines. With her new policing role in Waypoint 4 space, the admiralty had deemed it prudent to keep them aboard.

Kenichi marveled that the *Sorcerer* was still in commission at all. After the damage the destroyer had sustained as part of Admiral Chavez's desperate defense of Earth, Kenichi fully expected to see his ship scrapped. The authorities, it transpired, had other plans for Kenichi and *Sorcerer*. Once emergency repairs were completed, the *Sorcerer* folded out to Janus. The colony's undamaged shipyards repaired the damage to the little destroyer.

Kenichi's eyes were drawn to the seamless, gleaming roof of the bridge where the Others X-ray laser had once penetrated it. The single hit nearly destroyed *Sorcerer*. The bridge was opened to vacuum, the comms officer and three crewmembers were lost before they had the chance to seal their helmets, but that wasn't the worst of it. The powerful laser carried on through the deck plates until it reached the forward missile hold. Only the quick thinking of a bosun's mate prevented the *Sorcerer* from becoming nothing more than stellar dust as two of the multi-megaton missile warheads went critical. The bosun locked down the hold and activated the emergency decoupler. A large section of *Sorcerer's* outer hull armor explosively detached to allow the entire forward missile hold to be ejected from the ship, accelerating clear on chemical rockets. Kenichi rolled the ship away deploying his still-intact side armor over the rapidly moving hold and only just in time. The missiles detonated at a distance of less than eighty kilometers, rocking the *Sorcerer* to her core. Bosun's Mate Ashley Dison and two missile specialists were still in the hold when it detached. Their sacrifice saved the rest of the crew, a cold comfort to the bereaved families, but one Kenichi stressed in his letters to them.

Kenichi took his seat. "Tactical. Report."

"Sir! Three minutes ago, sensors detected the arrival of an Alonan communications drone. Less than a minute later, Waypoint 4 went to battle stations. Our threat board is clear, but as per SOPs, *Sorcerer* has also gone to battle stations." Kenichi's brow furrowed as comms announced:

"Incoming priority signal from Waypoint 4, sir! It's Commodore Chand."

"Put it through." Kenichi spun his chair ninety degrees and activated his small holo cube, it flickered briefly before the image cleared into the pointed features of the commanding officer of Waypoint 4.

"Commander Sutou, I'll get straight to the point. The Alonan communications drone carries a plain language message indicating Balat is under attack from four cruisers of unknown origin. The drone belongs to the *Kuna*." Chand paused, then pursed her lips. "The drone confirms the *Kuna* was destroyed."

Kenichi recalled the specs for the *Kuna* class frigate. For a small ship, it could pack a heavy punch, but against four cruisers, it would only end in crushing defeat.

"I've dispatched a drone to reach Force Leader Palas before he arrives at Pars, I've requested his immediate return. I've launched drones to BatFor 2.3 and Central Command, they carry details of my intentions."

Kenichi raised a quizzical eyebrow. "Your intentions, Commodore?"

"Your orders are to take the *Sorcerer* to the Balat system. Rendezvous with our Dupin surveillance platform and download its take. If there are no further indications of hostiles in the system, you are to proceed into Balat close orbit and ascertain the condition of the colony."

Kenichi listened in disbelief. "Commodore. You must realize if the *Kuna* managed to get a drone away to Alona, then their own navy will respond in force. The *Sorcerer* emerging in the outer system to download Dupin data is excusable but if the Imperial Navy finds me sneaking around

Balat then it's conceivable they will mistake us for the destroyers of the *Kuna*."

In the holo cube, Chand's cheeks flushed as she fixed Kenichi with a steely stare. "Unless I am much mistaken, I am in command. These are my orders. You will carry them out expeditiously and to the letter or you will suffer the consequences, Commander!"

Kenichi swallowed. "Aye-aye, Commodore."

Chand cut the link, leaving Kenichi staring into blank space trying to figure a way out of the danger Chand was directing the *Sorcerer* toward.

#

BALAT - SYSTEM 23890 - 22 LIGHT YEARS FROM ALONA

The first phase of *Sorcerer's* mission went off without a hitch. Emerging at the edge of the system, the Dupin platform was exactly where it was supposed to be. Minutes later, *Sorcerer's* whisker laser lock was secured and the Dupin's data was transferred into her memory banks.

Kenichi waited with barely concealed impatience as the tactical section carried out an initial analysis of the surveillance platform's data before finding what they were looking for. Kenichi and the entire bridge crew sat glued to their seats as the events of barely three hours ago replayed on the main bridge holo cube.

The footage started peacefully, the *Kuna* in sedate orbit around Balat, high above the gathering storm clouds, which obscured the colony from visual sensors but not from the array of electromagnetic and thermal ones. Without warning, four ships appeared and shaped a course for the *Kuna*. In the display's sidebar, Kenichi saw the energy readings from the *Kuna* rise sharply, but not as sharply as those of the four intruders. The missiles, too small to be seen by any human eye, were automatically highlighted in the holo cube as they left their parent ships.

The *Kuna* returned fire, a paltry effort, as the first enemy missile struck the *Kuna,* the intruders pressed forward and soon energy armament flashed between the intruders and the minnow-sized target.

Kenichi found himself willing the *Kuna* to break orbit and flee into fold space, but the brave little frigate held its ground as it faced the waves of missiles and whipping energy fire. The battle was concluded in minutes. The *Kuna* took hit after hit until finally she simply exploded in a ball of blinding light and expanding gases. Then the inevitable happened. The intruders, without pause, formed up directly over the colony. The holo cube displayed the missiles as icons flushing from tubes but this time targeting the planet's surface. The storm clouds dissipated as the heat of thermonuclear explosions ripped through the atmosphere.

Kenichi counted fifteen detonations starting at the heart of the colony and spreading out in an even circular pattern, destroying the colony with surgical precision.

As the rain of missiles on the planet stopped, the Dupin's sensors swept the area of the colony and the surrounding areas and caught the four intruders breaking orbit, powering away from the decimated colony before disappearing into fold space. Their mission apparently complete and peace seemingly returned. The clouds rolled in and re-covered the planet's surface.

Breaking the silence Kenichi, despite his dry throat, said, "Holo cube off. Tactical. Bomb Damage Assessment?"

"BDA is 100 percent. In my estimation, the colony has been… totally destroyed."

"And the ships' weapons capabilities?"

"Initial analysis shows the ships are the size of large cruisers, but their missile capability is comparable to a Bismarck class battleship. They appear to use lasing and grazing techniques similar to ours but the throughput is well above what we can achieve. I need more time to get a closer look. Honestly, sir I can't give you the answers you want just now."

"Honesty appreciated, Lieutenant. Engineering, what do you have?" Kenichi asked, well aware of Kendricks' second-to-none knowledge of engine design.

"They're definitely using Saiph gravity drives, sir, and from the power readings, they're running at almost maximum efficiency. At least ten percent more so than our most modern ships." Kendricks paused. "Even the Persai's best is not this good. There's no doubt, sir, these people have formidable engineering."

"So… these cruisers have more firepower than a Bismarck battleship and engines more efficient than any from the Commonwealth. Kendricks, have you seen anything like this before? Anything that might give us a clue as to who these people are?"

"Sorry, sir, can't say that I have."

A wave of unfamiliar indecision washed over Kenichi. Despite his feeling that taking the *Sorcerer* any closer to Balat would achieve little, Commodore Chand's orders were explicit.

"OK, people, let's go take a closer look at Balat. Navigation, plot us a fold." The screaming of the collision alarm drowned out his words.

Young's fingers flew across her board. "Sir. I have four… correction, six ships bearing down on us…It's the Alonans, sir! Two cruisers and four destroyers. Weapons are powering up." Her eyes were glued to her display. "Vampire! Vampire! Vampire! Missile separation. Impact in twenty seconds."

Kenichi spat his orders like machine-gun rounds. "Tactical! Weapons free on all defensive systems. Navigation! Cancel my last. Plot us a course home and fold when ready. Communications! Get the ready-drone downloaded and away."

"Ten seconds. Anti-missile missiles away. Laser Defense Clusters firing."

"Hold on, people, this is going to be rough!" Kenichi grabbed the chair restraints, knowing he couldn't secure them in time.

On *Sorcerer's* outer hull the small high-intensity lasers that made up *Sorcerer's* area denial weaponry fired from their pods positioned the length of the destroyer. A swathe of coherent light cut into the approaching missiles. High-speed anti-missile missiles joined the fray, destroying more of the incoming barrage. Inevitably, *Sorcerer's* defenses were breached.

The kiloton yield Alonan missile exploded a scant 200 meters from *Sorcerer's* armored bow, ripping through the first layer of ablative armor like tissue paper. The second layer slowed the progress of the shock wave, but it still wrecked the forward sensors, Grazer One, and Number Two plasma turret. *Sorcerer* staggered under the impact but Commander Kendricks' engines didn't let them down as *Sorcerer* powered on through the expanding plasma cloud.

On the bridge, Kenichi clung to his seat's armrests, as

others were tossed from their seats and landed heavily against equipment and the deck. The navigator, though tossed from side to side, was securely clamped to his seat. With a single keystroke, the *Sorcerer* vanished and reappeared moments later in the peaceful space surrounding Waypoint 4.

CHAPTER TWELVE
Tilting at Windmills

TDF POLARIS - OUTER MARKER
MESSIER 54 - 50000 LIGHT YEARS FROM EARTH

The unarmed courier ship entered normal space a bare 100,000 kilometers from Emperor Yalo IV spaceport and within scant seconds her computers screamed their warning. The defenseless ship was being locked up by multiple fire control systems. Sitting calmly in a jump seat in the cramped flight deck, Admiral Ai Jing could feel the tension in the air. His coming to the Alonan home system was a gamble he knew could go horribly wrong if there was an itchy trigger finger aboard any of the Alonan warships the tactical display showed maneuvering to surround his ship.

The nervousness in the young Communications Officer was apparent as he spoke. "Incoming signal from the spaceport, sir. Message reads: Commonwealth vessel, you have illegally entered Alonan space. Power down your systems and prepare to be boarded. Failure to comply will be taken as a hostile act and you will be fired upon. There will be no further warnings."

"Communications. Transmit in the clear, please. To Commanding Officer Emperor Yalo IV. From. Admiral Jing, Chairman of the Commonwealth Combined Joint Chiefs of Staff. Admiral Jing requests an urgent personal audience with Emperor Paxt."

The reply came back swiftly. "You are ordered to return to Commonwealth space and inform your admiral his request will be forwarded for consideration."

Jing knew it was time to play his ace in the hole. "Communications. Open a video link to the station."

With a wary glance back at the admiral, the comms officer complied and a few seconds later the forward holo cube flickered to life, revealing the impassive face of an Alonan colonel. "Commonwealth ship. I shall not repeat my order..." The colonel's voice faltered as he realized that instead of a lowly courier ship's communications officer, he was looking directly into the face of Admiral Jing, the human who had led the Commonwealth fleet, which was responsible for saving the Empire from certain destruction at the hands of the Others. His head reflexively bowed in supplication and his voice became deeply respectful. "Admiral Jing, forgive my tone. I was unaware you were aboard. My standing orders are to allow no Commonwealth vessel access to the home system. Even if the vessel carries the savior of the Empire. Please accept my apologies."

"Your diligence to your duty does you honor, Colonel. Nevertheless, I must speak to the emperor as a matter of urgency on a subject that I fear, if not resolved, may lead to war between our two great nations."

"A moment please, Admiral."

The colonel's face disappeared from the holo cube to be replaced by the emblem of the Imperial Navy, the stylized winged beast, its talons grasping the sword carried by the very first emperor. As the seconds became minutes, Jing forced himself to relax, but as the wait reached eighteen minutes, even Jing could feel his concern building. Was his last-ditched attempt at averting war a waste of time? Were the Alonans going to deny him an audience with the emperor? The urgent movements of the comms officer caught his eye and then the holo cube came to life and the face of the Alonan colonel filled the cube.

"Admiral, my orders are no Commonwealth vessel be allowed entry into Alonan space..."

Jing felt his hopes for a peaceful resolution to the burgeoning conflict drain away.

"However, there are no such orders referring to individual members of the Commonwealth. As such, I am transmitting your ship docking instructions. Once docked, I have arranged for your immediate transfer to the INS *Topa,* which will carry you onward to Alona where you may make your request for an audience in person."

The normally inscrutable Jing could not quite keep the tone of relief from his voice. "Thank you, Colonel. I am in your debt."

The colonel's face reddened slightly but he said nothing, simply bowing his head before the link was terminated.

Well, we are still in one piece, now all I need to do is get to speak to the emperor, Jing thought as the small craft began its approach to the spaceport.

#

THE IMPERIAL PALACE - ALONA

Admiral Jing absently looked out of the floor-to-ceiling

windows upon the vast expanse of the ornate gardens surrounding the emperor's palace, which was situated like an island of some past world in the sea of advanced industrialization that was Bozra, capital city of the Alonan Empire. In an attempt to hide the apprehension he could feel gnawing away at his stomach, he forced himself to appear relaxed and give the outwardly impression of a man admiring the view. The thick glass deadened the noise of the sprawling city in the valley below into an almost-imperceptible dull drone. The soft whoosh of the large doors opening into the throne room caused Jing to turn away from the colorful garden vista and face the impeccably presented captain of the Imperial Guard.

"Admiral Jing, the emperor is ready to receive you now."

Jing took a small breath and straightened his uniform. With a grateful nod to the officer, Jing walked through the doors and into the imperial throne room. It was just as Aaron Beckett had described. The rows of large windows on either side of the room allowed the light to flood in and the deep pile carpet quieted the sound of his boots as he approached the raised dais at the far end of the room. Emperor Paxt sat rock-still on his seat, flanked by Grand Admiral Raga, commander of the Imperial Navy and the Empire's foreign minister, Minister Hozal.

Halting at the bottom step of the dais, Jing brought himself to attention and gave the emperor a deep bow from the waist, Alonan style. Straightening, he gave a respectful nod to Admiral Raga and Minister Hozal in turn. Minister Hozal opened the conversation.

"Admiral Jing, it is an honor to meet you in person at last. Your actions and those of the men and women of the ships you commanded, will not soon be forgotten by the

Empire, no matter what unpleasantness has led to the current state of affairs between the Empire and the Commonwealth."

Jing moved his head slightly and addressed the emperor directly. "With the emperor's permission, it is this very state of affairs I wish to address today, Minister."

With a barely noticeable flick of his wrist, the emperor gave permission for Jing to continue.

"Your Majesty, I stand before you today at the express order of the leaders of the Commonwealth. The Commonwealth believes these words should be heard from a soldier who stood shoulder-to-shoulder with soldiers of the Empire in its defense. A soldier like myself and not a civilian diplomat who has not once used his own body to protect others."

"Indeed, a wise and considered move by the Commonwealth to send you before us, Admiral but... It could also be mistaken for a shrewd political gambit designed to use our cultural respect for our own military and for you to veil the Commonwealth's true intentions," Minister Hozal said.

"That could be true, Minister, however I promise on my honor as an officer that my intentions here are to prevent what seems to be the inevitable slide into conflict the incident surrounding Balat has put us in."

"That incident, Admiral, cost the lives of 25000 colonists! One 185 fine sailors! Are you denying it was the Commonwealth who carried out the attack?" said Admiral Raga.

The emperor held up a hand and Admiral Raga lowered his head in silent apology for his outburst.

"Whoever was responsible for the attack on Balat, I

promise you it was not the Commonwealth, Admiral Raga. We have all lost people, Admiral. Civilian and combatants alike, and it is my job and yours to ensure we give our leaders the best intelligence and advice we can to help them make the best decisions and right now I don't think you have the best intelligence on which to base your advice." Jing was ready for another outburst from Raga but a raised hand from the emperor forestalled anything the admiral may have wanted to say. Jing took the emperor’s intervention as permission to continue.

"Your Majesty. However regrettable the loss of life at Balat was, it once again reiterates a lesson that history has taught us again and again and we so often forget. When two nations do not trust each other, this lack of trust can very quickly turn into open hostility. Hostility very rapidly becomes a move toward armed conflict..."

This time, the emperor's raised hand was not enough to stop Raga as his nostrils flared and the veins on the side of his neck popped out. "Trust! You dare talk of trust! My ships searched the Balat system after your cowardly attack and guess what we found? A surveillance platform! One of your surveillance platforms, Admiral. I ordered searches of the Kathan and Opero systems and we found yet more surveillance platforms. Your precious Commonwealth is spying on the Empire, Admiral and we can prove it! I dare you to deny it."

For a few seconds, Jing said nothing. If the Empire had truly discovered the surveillance platforms that were run out of Waypoint 4, then denying any involvement in their construction and use would only prove an obstacle in any future talks.

"I admit that the Commonwealth did deploy surveillance platforms in those systems..."

"A-ha! I told you, Your Majesty, the Commonwealth cannot be trusted." Raga said elatedly.

"I would ask however, Admiral Raga..." continued Jing in a convivial tone, "if a bordering nation, one who had completely closed its systems to you, refused any kind of contact beyond a single diplomatic mission which operated under blanket restrictions on its movement, a nation which in the past had already shown its willingness to use covert techniques to secure the purchase of restricted military secrets, what would you have done?"

The veins were visible on Raga's neck again as he spluttered an angry retort. "What we did was for the protection of the Empire, nothing more! It was you who left the Empire open to an attack by the Others. If you had told us of them we would have been better prepared..."

Jing cut him off in midsentence. "You have no idea how much I personally regret not informing you of the Others' threat. However, was it not Commonwealth men and women who put their lives at risk to come to your assistance? We had nothing to gain by helping you. If the Commonwealth wanted you destroyed, then we could simply have left you to your fate. Instead, good sailors died defending Alona." Jing could feel the anger stirring in him but he could not stop it. It had been simmering within him a long time and now it burst forth like lava from an erupting volcano. "And where was your gratitude? I was only doing my duty, but what of the families of those sailors who never came home? How was I expected to tell them their husbands and wives, fathers and mothers, brothers and sisters died defending people who never once said thank you for their sacrifice? Three years, Admiral. Three years and not a word. Well, Admiral Raga, I'm here now. What do you have to say to those families whom you have led to believe that their loved ones died for nothing?"

The throne room had not witnessed a tirade of this kind in living memory. Doors were flung open as members of the Imperial Guard burst in, weapons drawn, ready to defend the emperor but the sight which greeted them caused them to falter in their headlong charge. Emperor Paxt slowly rose from his throne and stepped down from the dais until he stood directly before Admiral Jing. To the entire room's astonishment, the emperor bent his knee and bowed deeply to the human admiral. Following the emperor's lead, every Alonan in the room bowed and averted their eyes. The emperor spoke without raising his head.

"Admiral Jing. Please accept the Empire's deepest apologies for the failing on our part to honor the families of the fallen. It is a shame on our honor that it takes an outsider to remind us of our duty. They are all heroes of the Empire and as such their names will join those of the fallen who fought and died so the Empire may survive. Each and every family will receive a personal letter of thanks from myself. Again, I ask your forgiveness for our failing."

Jing was flabbergasted at the turn of events. His anger subsided as the more clinical part of his brain regained control. "Your apology is accepted, Your Majesty, and please accept mine in return for my outburst."

Regaining his throne, the emperor smiled briefly as the guards retired from the room. "Perhaps it is good at times to allow our true feelings to show, Admiral."

"You may be correct there, Your Majesty." Jing said with a smile of his own.

Minister Hozal took this as his cue to join the conversation. "I assume you have a proposal which may avert any future... er... misunderstandings, Admiral?"

Jing was glad to get back to the original subject.

"Indeed, Minister. The Commonwealth proposes we introduce a system whereby the Empire and the Commonwealth each station observers in the other's systems to monitor fleet movements and war games above a certain size. These military observers would be allowed unfettered access to any system and, within reason, any military base or ship within said system. The idea being that both the Empire and the Commonwealth can keep tabs on each other's military. If neither one side nor the other can make secret preparations for hostilities without the other noticing, the threat of conflict is vastly reduced. We saw something similar on Earth in the late twentieth and early twenty-first centuries and it helped keep the peace for over eighty years."

Hozal cast a glance at Raga, who gave a barely perceptible nod of approval. The emperor similarly gave his silent approval. "Your proposal has merit, Admiral and is certainly worthy of more discussion. Perhaps a short recess would be in order to allow the emperor to consider it. Would it be convenient for you to return tomorrow?"

"The Commonwealth Ambassador has graciously provided rooms for me in the embassy. I shall wait there until I hear from you."

"Until tomorrow, Admiral."

And with that, Jing was dismissed with the satisfied feeling he accomplished a good day's work. As the doors closed behind him, the emperor turned to Raga. "Well?"

The admiral took his time before answering as he considered what he had heard. "The human's reaction, although more heated than we had anticipated, was as assumed. His denial of any involvement in the attack on Balat was only to be expected. However, I believe him. The analysis of the data recovered from the *Kuna's* communications drones and the subsequent reports from the ships we dispatched to Balat to recover the *Kuna's* wreckage and make complete sensor sweeps of the system show that the weapons employed to destroy the ship and the colony were not of any known Commonwealth design. Therefore, we can only presume the colony was destroyed by an enemy who is, as of now, unidentified."

"And what of his proposal we exchange military observers?"

A frown creased the Grand Admiral's brow. "As you know only too well your Majesty our own surveillance technology is still years behind that of the Commonwealth and despite the best efforts of our intelligence services we have been unable to keep track of all the Commonwealths fleet movements never mind getting access to their latest military hardware. After our procurement of the Gravity Drive they tightened up on their security. The idea that I could put a trained intelligence officer on board any ship or base of theirs I please is a gift we would be foolish to turn down."

"And what of the idea of Commonwealth officers on our ships?" Queried Hozal.

"Bah! Let them come." Snorted Raga dismissively. "We are the ones who have more to gain from this so called exchange. The new shipyards we are building in the Foram system are restricted to only those with need to know and the Foram system itself is so far off the beaten track that keeping the prying eyes of the Commonwealth away from the yards should be easy enough."

With a slap of his thrones armrest, the Emperor stood to leave. "It is decided then. Minister Hozal please contact the Commonwealth embassy and set up a meeting with the

Ambassador, Admiral Jing and your people to flesh out the proposal. Grand Admiral Raga get together with your friends in intelligence and draw up a list of officers suitable for the exchange program."

Both men bowed as the Emperor went to leave but he stopped short of the door leading to his private chamber. "One more thing Minister..."

"Yes your Majesty?"

"Ask the Ambassador to forward a list of all members of the Commonwealth forces who gave their lives in the battle for Alona to my private secretary."

"Of course your Majesty."

#

2287 LIGHT YEARS FROM EARTH

"So Foral, you are pleased with the results of the test?" The Supreme Leader asked without turning from the window which gave him a magnificent view of the surrounding fields bathed in the warm red light of the star hovering constantly overhead.

"A resounding success Supreme Leader. The frigate proved no match for our cruisers. If this is an example of what we are likely to encounter then I believe we have little to fear from these lesser beings. There weaponry was inferior to ours, as I predicted, and what missiles of theirs managed to evade the cruisers' defenses wasted themselves harmlessly against the energy shields. A technology which our attack has proved the enemy do not possess."

Tearing himself away from the captivating view, the Supreme Leader turned to face Foral, and his face reflected his cautious tone. "Let us not judge our enemy's capabilities yet, my friend. We chose this world because we knew the technology of this Alonan Empire was less capable than any already available to the Commonwealth. Our monitoring of the Commonwealths unshielded vid broadcasts also indicates they have encountered another potential threat to us, these Turak. It is imperative we keep these differing groups from aligning against us. I suggest our next target needs to be of more significance. A target against whom your fleet can truly test its mettle."

The pair sat in silence for a few moments as each considered their next move. Foral fiddled with the controls inlaid into the table at which he sat and a hologram image came to life at the end of the room. Foral raised himself from his seat and circled the glowing image. It showed dozens of construction vessels floating adjacent to an incomplete spherical structure. In a protective globe around these were several warships varying in size from smaller frigates to hulking battleships. The Supreme Leader left his place by the window and moved to join Foral.

"This should suit our needs, Supreme Leader. Our scouts have been monitoring the progress of the construction of this armed space station at the edge of one of the Commonwealth-held systems. Our analysts estimate it is some eighty percent complete. A fleet of fifty warships protects it and we have detected what we believe to be minefields or energy weapons platforms being seeded in such a way as to restrict ship movement around the station. It should provide an ideal proving ground for our heavier units. I am not sure we have had sufficient time to practice our larger fleet maneuvers as of yet, but within a few months we will be proficient."

The Supreme Leader clasped Foral's shoulder. "Hmm. If we target one of the Commonwealth's core systems, imagine not only the military but also the political repercussions. A system attacked by an unknown enemy. There will be cries for warships to be stationed at every vulnerable point, especially the major planets. Your plan is a good one, but I think we need to go a little further."

Foral raised an eyebrow in query, awaiting the Supreme Leader's explanation.

"The scout ships have intercepted news vids which speak of a planet where the Commonwealth first encountered the Turak. The Turak made it quite plain any incursion into their space would be countered by force. What if we were to launch a raid on this planet as we did on the Alonan colony? The Turak have no reason to suspect we exist, so the only logical conclusion would be that the raid was carried out by the half-breeds, and if they hold true to their word..."

"They would retaliate."

"Yes they would, Foral. Yes they would." The Supreme Leader walked slowly around the shimmering hologram as his mind explored the possibilities. Weighing up the options and his enemy's likely reactions.

"You will first attack the Turak planet. Annihilate their warships and turn the planet into radioactive slag. You will then move to attack the half-breed space station. Suspicion will be rife. Is this the Turak responding to the attack on their planet? Is this Alona seeking revenge on the Commonwealth for the attack on their colony world? If we then select a second Alonan target to attack, will they in turn not think it is the Commonwealth who are responsible? Let these half-breeds fight each other while we continue to conserve our strength for what is to come."

"Once more, Supreme Leader, your skill at seeing the greater plan among the sea of smaller parts only reinforces my faith that with you at our head, the Saiph will be victorious."

The Supreme Leader let out a short laugh as he clapped his friend on the back. "And with you leading our fleets, Foral, I have no need to fear the half-breeds will overcome us."

Walking once more around the holographic projection, the Supreme Leader was sure his plan would come to fruition.

"So tell me, Foral. What is the name of the Commonwealth planet in this system?"

"They call it Garunda."

CHAPTER THIRTEEN
Diaspora

PARS - 6400 LIGHT YEARS FROM EARTH

"As I stated before, Madam President, at this moment in time, our current assessment of the attack on Balat is that it was carried out by a technologically superior force." The naval commander giving this intelligence briefing to the assembled heads of the Commonwealth was having trouble keeping the frustration from his voice as he repeated the same information for the fourth or fifth time. Couldn't these politicians get it into their heads they simply did not know who was responsible for the massacre of the Alonan colony? When the assembled heads of state failed to ask him another question, he looked longingly toward Admiral Jing seated at the far end of the conference room. The admiral, to his relief, indicated silently for him to withdraw from the room. The door had only just sealed closed when Chairman Volak, the man chosen by the Council of Twelve to replace the aging Tarrov, spoke. His deep voice seemed to make the very fabric of the building shake.

"My fellow leaders. It would seem we are no further on

than we were when Balat was destroyed four months ago. There have been no further attacks on either Alonan or Commonwealth colonies and no reported sightings of any unidentified warships."

"I bid you to remember that we've become aware of the existence of the Turak since then, Mr. Chairman," interjected Prime Minister Bezled.

"Our Garundan friends have a point, Chairman Volak," commented Representative Hoolas softly. The tall, overly thin Benii had been a guest of the Persai prior to the conference, as the Benii had been negotiating a deal for Persai computer cores, still the best to be found anywhere in the Commonwealth, so she was the one most familiar with the new Chairman. Thus, Rebecca Coston took her lead from Hoolas.

"Unfortunately, we also have no proof it was in fact the Turak. The military are telling us the warships our spy platform observed carrying out the attack on Balat were not the same design as those we confronted in the Selene system." Rebecca spun in her seat to face Admiral Jing, who up until now had remained steadfastly silent as the politicians interrogated the hapless commander.

"That would be the intelligence community's view, would it not Admiral Jing?"

Jing suspected the Earth's president was making a rhetorical statement, but he decided to reply anyway. "You would be correct, Madam President. Our intelligence at this stage does not prove conclusive either way, so although we cannot definitely rule out Turak involvement, it would be my gut feeling that there is another player in this game who is yet to fully reveal their hand."

Jing could see Chairman Volak was working himself up

to have a dig at him but fortunately Thomas Crothers anticipated Volak and decided to get there first.

"And what steps have been taken to prevent any further confrontation with the Turak, Admiral?" Thomas asked.

"The boundaries of Turak space passed on to Ambassador Schamu have been distributed to every major civilian shipping and Colony Company throughout the Commonwealth. Survey Command as a matter of course do not now conduct operations within ten light years of Turak space. The Alonan Empire, via the Observer Exchange Program, has been given copies of the boundaries as a matter of courtesy, although it should be pointed out the information supplied to Ambassador Schamu does not extend out as far as the Empire."

"And what about naval protection for the colonies and our home planets?" Volak demanded.

Jing forced himself to take a deep, calming breath before answering the Persai. "Mr. Chairman, it is simply not possible for our navies to be everywhere at once. This point has been raised on more occasions than I choose to remember. We are in the process of developing the Carrier Strike Groups, but it takes time. Each Commonwealth world is building its own version of the layered defense approach taken by Earth. Our own Gateway Station has only been on line a few months and that was after two years of construction. Janus, Pars, and Garunda are all in the advanced stages of completing their own, and Benii is only now laying down the inner frame. The Joint Chiefs have siphoned off as many cruisers from the existing BatFors to patrol the new colonies as we consider prudent. The lack of cruisers and the necessary support vessels is something the Joint Chiefs have highlighted repeatedly. The answer to the lack of naval support for the colonies is simple: Stop establishing new colonies until the naval building program has caught up with colony ship construction." Jing's matter-of-fact statement came as a bit of a shock to the gathered leaders. Rebecca was the first to recover.

"I think you are well aware, Admiral Jing that the public clamor to immigrate to new worlds is like nothing my or any other government in history has had to deal with before. The best analogy I have is the opening of the western parts of the North American continent in the 1800s. Normal, everyday people see a chance to improve their lives, to have an adventure; and big business is investing heavily in colonization and mining operations. I am sure the situation on Earth is comparable to that on the other Commonwealth worlds."

Around the table, the various dignitaries nodded. Rebecca pressed on.

"The move to colonize is one which is politically unstoppable. Even Janus, a planet which started off as a colony itself, is already establishing settlements on two more worlds."

"We find ourselves in a similar position, Madam President," said Hoolas. "Since the Benii Federation has been given access to your gravity drive, not only has the home world, through the auspices of Survey Command, identified planets suitable for colonization, but our two established colonies of Baut and Gossol have requested permission to seek out worlds for themselves to colonize. The Survey Command units attached to Benii estimate that at the current rate, it will have identified and surveyed eleven suitable worlds by the end of the year. How are we to tell our people that these new worlds are off-limits because we are failing in our duty to protect them?"

As the room lapsed into silence, Jing was aware all eyes were upon him. Slowly and deliberately, he steepled his fingers in front of him and forced himself to relax in his seat. "Ladies and gentlemen. My latest numbers from Admiral Papadomas at Survey Command are that his probes have identified 3845 potential planets within the various Commonwealth planets' proposed spheres of influence, of which 961 have been identified as being able to support our particular type of life. The number of potential colonies is staggering. We are faced with a diaspora of not only human life, but of all civilized peoples, and we as a Commonwealth are simply not prepared to cope with it. We have not even taken into account what other civilizations we may find out there. We have already encountered the Edasich, the Turak, and possibly a third, as yet unidentified, race. Who knows what else is awaiting discovery out there? I urge you to exhibit caution, ladies and gentlemen, because if we keep expanding at our current rate, it is only a matter of time before we come across someone who, unlike the Turak, will shoot first and ask questions later. I'm not saying we should slow down the work of Survey Command, but we should seriously consider slowing or halting completely the number of licenses granted for mining and colonization until the new cruisers and CSGs come on line. For all our sakes."

Once more, silence descended on the room as each world's leader considered the sobering words of caution uttered by their military chief.

#

SLIVINO VALLEY - NORTHERN ITALY - EARTH - SOL SYSTEM

Liveried servants moved around the French polished mahogany dining table, quietly removing the remains of the lavish dinner's final course. The four diners retired to an equally ornate library, sinking into overstuffed armchairs as more servants poured brandy into 100 year-old crystal glasses before retiring from the room. As the thick wooden doors silently closed, Seaton Anderson activated the electronic shield, which would stop anyone trying to eavesdrop on the conversation of the library's occupants.

"I must congratulate you, Seaton, the meal was delicious," purred Katria Dikul as she admired the quality of her brandy.

Seaton waved a hand dismissively as he reached for the humidor holding his favorite cigars. "A guest of your standing should expect no less than the best, Senator." A small hiss escaped the humidor as Seaton extracted a cigar whose cost equaled the monthly salary of one of the liveried servants who poured his brandy. Catching Dikul wrinkling her nose, he graced her with a smile as he depressed a control built into his chair and the soft whirring of an extractor fan directly above his seat reached his ear. Removing his cigar cutter from an inner pocket of his jacket, he deftly snipped the end of the cigar and with a flourish, struck a match which seemed to have appeared from nowhere, puffing deeply as he brought the cigar to life.

"Ah, Seaton, you think of everything," chuckled Mathias Grant III from his chair, before taking a sip of his brandy.

"Uncle Seaton likes to be prepared for any eventuality, my dear Mathias. Preparation is the key to success and the reason for tonight's dinner invitation," Bryer Anderson, the final member of the foursome, commented.

Seaton allowed himself a deep intake of the cigar's smoke, holding it in so he could truly appreciate its fine aroma, before he exhaled the thick smoke, which was quickly gathered up by the extractor.

"To business then, my friends. I see our friends in the

media have been giving Coston a hard time in the press for her decision to support the Garundans setting up camps to care for the Others, never mind these rumors of new restrictions being placed on colonization and mining."

Mathias' fists clenched his reddening face as he let out a strange strangled sound. "The Garundans are idiots. There isn't a chance in hell those genocidal maniacs will ever be rehabilitated. Coston is just pouring good money after bad and the people know it. If I had my way, I would leave them all to rot and good riddance!"

Katria Dikul reached across and patted Mathias' hand like a mother would with a wayward child. "Now, now, Mathias. Let the Garundans waste their resources on these few remaining creatures. The more Coston becomes involved with them, the greater will be her failure, and if that young upstart Kris Madkin pins his flag to her as well, he may find it quickly turning into a stone around his neck. For the time being, I think our short-term aim should be to muster support within the mining corporations in case Coston does impose restrictions on their off-world operations. Perhaps you may be of assistance there, Seaton?"

"Bryer has more day-to-day dealings with them now than I do since he took my place as chairman of the board. Bryer?"

"It's no secret that the larger players in the market have heavily invested in equipment and licenses. Our bulk transports are in higher demand than ever, and the shipyards cannot keep up with the production demand for colony ships. With great foresight, Uncle Seaton bought up what shipping was available before others realized there would be such a high demand, so Zurich Lines has a virtual monopoly on both types, which we project to last until certainly after the election next March. I think a few calls to the right people should be enough to light a fire under the mining and colonization fraternity."

Seaton absentmindedly tapped some ash into the crystal ashtray on his chair arm. "And what about Madkin? My people report he is neck and neck with you in the polls. There are only five months left until the election, Mathias."

"Madkin is an amateur, Seaton. He has neither the experience nor the stamina. It goes to show how desperate Coston and her people really are that they would choose a two-term senator to go up against me. Madkin’s campaign will run out of steam before Christmas, I guarantee it."

Seaton continued to look at the blustering politician a moment longer before addressing Dikul. "And what are your thoughts, Katria?" Out of the corner of his eye, he caught Mathias sitting back heavily in his seat and crossing his arms like the petulant child Seaton knew him to be but, as he reminded himself constantly, beggars couldn't be choosers and with Mathias as president, Seaton would have carte blanche to do virtually anything he wanted. Katria Dikul, on the other hand, was a completely different kettle of fish. Dikul was the mistress of back-room politics and it would be she who would be the true power behind any throne Mathias found himself sitting on. The very reason Seaton always made sure he was paying attention when she spoke.

"Madkin may not have the depth of experience that Mathias does, but Coston is not stupid. She has set Madkin up with her own Chief of Staff and Clement Bradshaw is nobody's fool. Bradshaw has run and won more campaigns than anyone else in Zurich. He's the real danger." Dikul settled her eyes on Seaton. "It's a pity he could not be persuaded to retire like Harriman."

"Best thing that could have happened," blustered

Mathias. "He was nothing but a Coston sycophant anyway."

It took Bryer a few seconds to realize his uncle and Dikul were still looking at each other. Seaton broke off and regarded the still-huffing Mathias before moving his eyes to Bryer, who understood the implicit command. Standing up, he walked over to Mathias and placed a friendly hand on his shoulder.

"Uncle tells me you are quite the horticulturist, Mathias. I would be grateful if you could spare me a few minutes to examine our pitiful attempts in the greenhouse. Uncle tells me I am wasting my time with our roses, but maybe all I need is your experienced eye."

Mathias jumped at the chance to show off. "Of course Bryer, it would be my pleasure. Roses can be fickle things, you know."

Seaton ensured the electronic shield reengaged as the door closed behind the still-chatting men before he returned his attention to Dikul.

"I take it you have heard something of interest, Katria?"

Dikul took a sip of her brandy and eyed him over the fine crystal.

"My sources are telling me that Bradshaw has ever-so-quietly been meeting with high-ranking officers of the PSO and subsequently over the last few weeks, all of Harriman's protection detail have been rotated out to other duties."

Seaton kept his voice free of inflection for fear of giving something away in the presence of this political shark. "Surely it would not be unusual for the Presidential Security Office to replace their more experienced officers with others, now that Harriman is no longer vice president?"

"You would think that would be true, but you then have to ask yourself why the PSO has now requested a special dispensation in their agreed-upon budget because of an unexpected overrun that they have put down to extra protection required by a raised threat level at a senior retired official's home."

"Although an interesting piece of gossip, Katria, I cannot for the world see what it has to do with me."

A playful smile crossed her lips. "Come now, Seaton. Do you forget that I am chair of the Armed Forces Oversight committee? The military and the FIB may have tried to keep it quiet, but I know all about Daya Thomas being detained while in possession of files which listed some very powerful people in and out of government. The contents of those files are still a closely guarded secret, but from what I have heard, those files, if in the wrong hands, have the potential to end a lot of careers. Maybe even result in jail time for a few unlucky individuals." Dikul paused as she took another sip of her brandy. Seaton suspected this was more to add to the suspense than because she was thirsty. She was enjoying this moment of intrigue.

"You run a very tight ship, Seaton. There's no way Daya would have been in possession of those files if you didn't know about them, and a man as well-organized as yourself would always make sure he had copies." When she paused this time, she ensured that she kept her eyes on Seaton. "All I'm saying is perhaps those files contain something which could take Bradshaw out of the picture, so to speak. With him gone, Madkin would be a lame duck and Mathias could walk away with the election."

Seaton was forced to admit that he had underestimated Dikul. Not only was she willing to do everything in her political power to win, she was hinting she was willing to go beyond simple legalities to ensure victory. Her expectant face told him enough. Time to take the game to a new level.

"Unfortunately Bradshaw's name is not among those you will find in the files. However..." Dikul's obvious disappointment became expectation. "Perhaps a more direct course of action could be taken in this particular case. I am aware of an individual who has been useful in the past in this type of situation..."

As Dikul listened to Seaton's proposal, she began to understand the true depth of this man's willingness to succeed. No matter what he was forced to do. And she admired him for it.

CHAPTER FOURTEEN
Piggy in the Middle

PLANET IV - 23 LIBRAE SYSTEM
83.7 LIGHT YEARS FROM EARTH

It was past two o'clock in the morning ship's time and the ensign on duty at the Tactical Station aboard the research ship TDF *Henry Moseley* was struggling, mostly in vain, to keep his eyes open when an incessant beeping eventually penetrated his groggy consciousness. Rubbing his eyes, he canceled the alarm and checked his panel. The sensors were picking up a ship on approach and by the course it was shaping, it was headed for a low-orbit insertion. The *Henry Moseley* was in high orbit of Planet IV, known as Uolas by the Deres and Wapal by the Nilmerg. Neither side could agree on a single name for the planet and were not likely to any time soon, was the ensign's understanding. The *Henry Moseley* was here in support of the scientific expedition on the surface of the planet, which the Commonwealth simply referred to as Planet IV. The fact that the mission was the combined effort of the Commonwealth, Deres, and Nilmerg was a minor miracle in itself. The arrival of SurvFlot Two and Rear Admiral Torrance three years ago had brought about a ceasefire, albeit a precarious one, in the hundred-year war that had raged between the Deres and the Nilmerg. Both sides had suffered horribly in the conflict and their hatred of each other was so deeply etched into their psyche, even getting them to sit down at the same table had taken the Commonwealth Ambassador, Amber Isa, over two months. The ceasefire she negotiated was only made possible with the promise that the Commonwealth navy would be its guarantor and that the navy would constantly maintain sufficient resources in 23 Librae system to enforce the ceasefire agreement. At present, that force consisted of the four Lynx-class cruisers comprising Cruiser Squadron 1.2.2 under the command of Commodore Mkhize, currently engaged in war games on the edge of the system.

With a few keystrokes, the ensign commanded the tactical computers to run an ID on the approaching ship, which they dutifully accomplished a few seconds later, throwing the results up on the tactical holo cube. The ensign half turned in his seat to face the duty bridge officer, an engineering lieutenant who was so completely engrossed in her PAD displaying details of the latest declassified specs on the new Colossus carriers, she did not even notice the tactical display's update. "Ma'am, we have a Deres freighter on approach to low-orbit insertion."

Without raising her eyes from the PAD, the lieutenant replied, "Probably just the monthly resupply with more of that stringy stuff the Deres call food. Log it, then inform Base Control to expect visitors."

"Aye-aye, ma'am." Message sent, the ensign shuffled in his seat to find the most comfortable position and returned to his battle with boredom.

#

EXPEDITION BASE - SURFACE OF PLANET IV
23 LIBRAE SYSTEM

Sarah Boone took one last look up at the stars through the clear plasteel dome enclosing the base and holding back the thin, barely breathable atmosphere as she closed the door to her cramped quarters on the surface of Planet IV with an audible sigh of relief, her ears still ringing from the constant whining of Gils Sarar and Ull Fors. Both the Deres and Nilmerg expedition leaders respectively had been a pain in her proverbial ass since the base had been established six months ago. It appeared neither could agree with the other on anything. If one said something was black, the other would immediately state that it was white. The latest disagreement was over who would be first to enter the cave five kilometers below them. A cave which, if the power readings detected by the *Rapier* during its first visit to the planet, and the subsequent surveys the Deres and the Nilmerg had carried out were to be believed, held blockhouses identical to those found over a decade before on the Rubicon planet in Proxima Centauri. Blockhouses that Sarah knew undoubtedly contained another complete Saiph database. Even through her fatigue and frustration, a small shiver of excitement passed up Sarah's spine. During the original Rubicon expedition, she had been the Chief Structural Engineer and remembered as if it was only yesterday the day they discovered the five blockhouses constructed by the Saiph so long ago. When she was approached to head up the Commonwealth expedition to Planet IV, she had jumped at the chance. Little did she know what she had been letting herself in for. Kicking her boots off and discarding her coveralls, as she walked to the bathroom, Sarah headed for the welcoming embrace of a hot shower and then bed. Sarah only made it as far as the bathroom door before the double tone of her wrist comm interrupted her plans. *Give me a break!*

"Go for Boone."

"Director. Willis in Base Control. Signal from the *Henry Moseley*. They report a Deres freighter entering orbit."

And? Sarah bit her tongue. Willis was only doing his job. "Thank you, Willis. I'm sure they know we're in the middle of the night here so unless it's urgent, tell them we will be prepared to receive supplies when the morning shift comes on."

"Yes, Director. Sorry to disturb you. Good night. Control out."

And good night to you too. Now for a shower, thought Sarah.

#

If the bridge crew of the *Henry Moseley* had bothered to make visual contact with the inbound freighter's crew, they might have been curious as to why, instead of the usual white uniforms of a Deres merchant vessel's crew, they would have seen the space-black uniforms of the Deres Space Force, but after months of coming and going, the Deres had satisfied themselves the Commonwealth ship's crew were becoming lax. And it was about to cost them dear. The freighter's navigator turned to the ship's captain and did his best to ignore the presence of the squat, older Deres who sat beside the captain, with the ever-present hulking bodyguard directly behind him. "Orbit achieved. We are now geostationary directly over the Commonwealth base and the research vessel is holding station 28000 Jils above us, sir."

"Very well." The captain turned his head sideways to address the true commander of the vessel. "With your permission, Marshall?"

Marshall Poll, Commander in Chief, Deres Space Force,

paused a heartbeat before answering. Relishing the moment as months of secret planning were about to come to fruition. Poll cursed the politicians who denied him permission to take the secrets of the Saiph database buried deep below the surface of Uolas and use them to finally bring the long war against the Nilmerg to an end. An end which would see the Deres victorious and the Nilmerg annihilated. No. The politicians would rather listen to the words of the cowards who had forgotten how the Nilmerg had killed so many with their treacherous, unprovoked attack so long ago. The same cowards who insisted there could be peace between Deres and Nilmerg. Fools! Did they not realize if the Deres did not seize the alien library then it was only a matter of time before the Nilmerg did and then it would be they, not the Deres, who would be victorious? Poll had been a soldier all his life. He had shed his blood in defense of his world and had watched too many of his friends pay the ultimate sacrifice to let some spineless mouthpiece in the House of the People belittle their sacrifice by seeking peace when the tools of victory were so close to hand. No. Never!

His voice came out in a whisper, but it was loud enough for the captain to hear. "Execute."

"Execute! Execute!" Repeated the captain, and seconds later the bridge crew experienced the craft shudder as explosive bolts fired. Along the entire length of the freighter, false hull plates fell away to reveal evil-looking assault shuttles full of Deres soldiers sitting in their drop cradles. This particular freighter was something humans would have called a Q Ship. An armed merchant ship which only revealed its teeth when its prey was close enough. As the plates reached a safe distance, the shuttles were released and their pilots tipped their noses downward and began a screaming, maximum power descent into the atmosphere. Just as the juddering of the released shuttles halted, a fresh set of tremors rolled throughout the ship. Along the upper spine of the freighter, a second set of explosive bolts blew, the hull plating cleared the ship and exposed the ugly snouts of a hidden battery of energy weapons, which swung on their mounts and oriented themselves onto the *Henry Moseley*.

"Target locked, Captain."

With only the briefest of glances at the marshall by his side, the captain called, "Fire!"

#

The bridge crew of the *Henry Moseley* returned to their quiet routine as the freighter slipped into orbit. The quiet was shattered by the ear-piercing wail of the missile warning alarm. The sleepy ensign's eyes flew open and he nearly fell from his seat as he leaned forward to read his display. To his horror, the computer was telling him that what he and the rest of the bridge crew had presumed was an unarmed freighter had just fired a dozen missiles toward the surface... wait... hold on... the bogeys were too slow for missiles. The computer was now calling them small craft. Before he could tell the lieutenant, a fresh alarm sounded. His eyes flashed to another corner of his display. *Oh God!* A targeting radar had acquired them. "Lieutenant..."

He never finished. The near light-speed energy weapons mounted on the freighter's spine fired, and at such close range the minimal battle armor of the *Henry Moseley* may as well have been tissue paper. The outer hull simply evaporated under the intense bombardment. The inner hull was sliced open as the terawatts of energy sought to turn itself into heat. On and on the beams went, evaporating flesh and steel without pity until at last they punched through the outer hull again. As the beam weapon mounts slowly tracked along the length of the research ship, it was only a matter of time before they connected with a critical area. In less than five seconds they found it. The area took the form of the forward-fusion bottle. In an instant, containment was lost, and in a blinding flash the *Henry Moseley* and her crew were no more.

#

"Target destroyed. Energy banks recharging. Radar shows no further targets within range, sir."

Poll clapped his hands together and let out a loud, "Ha! I told those fools we could defeat these meddling Commonwealth pale skins. Captain?"

"Yes, Marshall."

"Transmit the go code to the fleet, we need them here as quickly as possible. There are still Commonwealth warships lurking in the system somewhere and we cannot be sure the research vessel did not have time to get off a call for aid."

"At once, Marshall." The captain gave the comms officer a curt nod and with that, phase two of the marshall's plan was put into operation. The captain wholeheartedly agreed with the marshall that they needed the fleet here if they were to stand a chance against Commonwealth warships and not simply a poorly armed research ship. He just hoped the fleet got here first.

#

The high-pitched whining of turbofans rudely wakened Sarah Boone. Very close turbofans if she could hear them through the dome walls. Her hand scrabbled about the top of her bedside cabinet as it searched for her wrist comm in the darkness. Retrieving it, she pulled it toward her and activated the link, her tired brain making no effort to keep the irritation from her voice. "Control! Willis! What the hell is going on? I thought I told you to tell the Deres not to unload till the morning and what the hell are they doing setting down so close to the dome anyway? If they puncture it we'll all be wearing breathers until it's repaired and I don't know anybody who will be happy with that."

"Eh... Director, you had better get in here. Those aren't supply shuttles. The airlock cameras are showing armed Deres soldiers entering the dome."

Sarah sat bolt upright in bed, her eyes searching the pitch-black room as if she could see the soldiers coming. The base was a civilian affair, there wasn't a single weapon or soldier on it. That had been a specific clause in the agreement in setting up the combined three-way expedition. *Crap!*

"Contact the *Henry Moseley* and make them aware of our situation."

"I've been trying to raise the ship and all I'm getting is static." The sound of desperation was apparent in Willis' voice.

If they couldn't raise the research ship it can only mean two things, thought Sarah. *Either it's folded away or the Deres have already dealt with it. Whatever, there's no chance of help arriving in the next few minutes.* "Well, get a general signal off on all frequencies then. Hopefully Commodore Mkhize will hear it and come running." Sarah didn't wait for Willis to acknowledge. She cut the link to the Control Room and then entered her director's code into the wrist comm. A single tone informed her she was now linked to every wrist comm and speaker on the base. "Attention! Attention! This is Director Boone. An unknown number of armed Deres have entered the base. All personnel are ordered to offer no resistance. I repeat, no resistance. You are to comply with all instructions given to you. Good luck. Boone out." Having done what she could to warn her people, she flung back the covers and started getting dressed. She was just putting on her boots when the door was flung open and in the doorway she could make out the shadow of a Deres soldier pointing his weapon at her.

#

DSN VOLAR - GEOSTATIONARY ORBIT - DERES

Twelve minutes after the comms officer on board the freighter transmitted the go signal, it was received aboard DSN *Volar*, flagship of the Deres Space Navy in orbit around its home planet of Deres. The *Volar* and the majority of the fleet, some forty destroyer-sized ships weighing in at around 16000 tonnes each and armed with two main heavy energy weapons and forty-eight missile tubes apiece were a formidable force, and one which Fleet Admiral Toro was justly proud to command, but at this precise moment his mind was elsewhere. For what seemed the thousandth time in the past hour, his eyes were drawn to the bridge clock located directly above the main view screen. If all was going to schedule, the marshall should be launching his attack about now.

When his mentor first approached Toro and outlined his plan to seize the alien database, Toro had been shocked. Marshall Poll had guided his career from Toro's earliest days in the navy and Poll had always expounded the merits of loyalty and discipline, so to hear him so blatantly discussing treason was a tremendous jolt. But the more he listened to the marshall's argument that it was not he who was the traitor, it was in fact the members of the House of the People and Commissioner Malas himself who, by allowing the Nilmerg access to the alien secrets, were the true traitors, the more he saw the logic of it. Poll had not pushed Toro to join him, but over the coming days, Toro thought long and hard about what his mentor had said to him and slowly but surely he found himself agreeing with him. By the end of the week, Toro became the second member of the marshall's coup d'état. Over the coming months, Toro and the marshall sought out officers in key positions whom they knew to be like-minded, until the day came when the marshall declared them ready to begin the operation which would see the end of the Nilmerg threat forever.

The communications officer left his station and approached the admiral. Stopping in front of him, he spoke in a voice just loud enough for only the admiral to hear. "Admiral. We have received the go code from Marshall Poll."

"Thank you, Rana. Please take up your post." The officer nodded once and then, apparently without any real purpose, strolled over to the *Volar's* commander, Captain Wol, and struck up an idle conversation. Once the captain was suitably distracted, Toro punched a code into his armrest's comms panel. The call was answered immediately.

"Aft Weapons. Lieutenant Possa."

Toro took a second before uttering the single word that committed him to his path. "Auro." The Deres word for vengeance. With that, Toro closed the channel and punched a complex code into the panel. This code was known to him and him alone. It was a code which, when entered, bypassed the normal communications channels and connected him directly with the captains of fifteen of the fleet's destroyers. Captains who had aligned themselves with the marshall. A small light on the comms panel went from red to green as one after another, each captain acknowledged the signal.

The raised voice of the tactical officer broke the normally hushed conversations on the bridge. "Captain! My panel is showing Tube 15 loading a mark four ground-attack missile. Outer doors are opening and a launch sequence has been entered!"

Wol lunged out of his seat and raced to the side of the tactical officer, bending over his shoulder. "Cancel the launch command!"

The tactical officer's hands moved urgently over his panel, but he wasn't quick enough. The *Volar* shuddered slightly as the missile left its tube. "Initiate the self-destruct," ordered the captain. The required commands were entered but still the missile sped onwards.

"I'm sorry, sir, I've been locked out."

The captain spun around, intending to head back to his chair. The comms panel on his chair allowed him to override any lockout and he would destroy the missile before it could do any damage. The last thing he expected was to find his communications officer, Lieutenant Rana, blocking his path. Wol was about to push past him when he noticed Rana's arm was raised and in his hand was a small pistol. The sharp crack of the pistol echoed around the bridge as Rana pulled the trigger and shot the captain right between the eyes. The small caliber round exited the rear of the captain's skull and sprayed brain matter and blood over the horrified face of the tactical officer. The bridge crew froze in place as the captain's body crumpled to the deck. Rana swept his arm back and forth, ready to deal with any crewmembers who tried anything.

From his seat, Toro initiated a ship-wide call. Throughout the *Volar*, crewmembers stopped whatever they were doing to listen to address. "Crew of the *Volar*. Fellow Deres. This is Fleet Admiral Toro. I speak to you now on a matter of national security. Some months ago, Marshall Poll and I became aware of a number of traitorous activities being committed against our government and our people. The traitors have infected the highest echelons of our government and of our beloved navy. Even here, on our navy's flagship, the traitors hide in plain sight. Captain Wol was one of these traitors. Today, under the direct orders of Marshall Poll, loyal officers have taken control of key parts of our military and have begun arresting the traitors. Those who resist arrest will be executed on the spot. We must show no mercy to these traitorous elements. Not since the first attack by the Nilmerg has there been such a threat to the very existence of our people. The traitors will try to subvert you with their promises of peace and reconciliation with the Nilmerg, but in your hearts you know the truth. The Nilmerg cannot be trusted. So I call upon all loyal officers and men to follow me and Marshall Poll as we secure the future of all Deres."

Toro scanned the bridge to gauge the reaction of the bridge crew as he spoke. They were getting over the shock of the sudden and violent end of Captain Wol. Toro could see the doubt in their eyes. Could it be true? The captain was a traitor? They all knew Commissioner Malas had announced his intentions to hold more peace talks with the Nilmerg. On the other hand, why would the fleet admiral lie to them? He and Marshall Poll had led them into battle against the Nilmerg. Risked their own lives side by side with them. A growing number of the bridge crew began to nod. He had them.

"I ask nothing more of you than that you do your duty. In a few moments, we will be breaking orbit along with other loyal ships of the fleet and will be charting a course for Uolas, where we will join Marshall Poll, who has secured the alien database for the Deres people. With its secrets, we will forever rid ourselves of the Nilmerg threat and the traitors in our midst. Long live Deres!"

Toro sat back in his chair as throughout the ship, crewmembers began to chant, "Long live Deres!"

#

Deputy Aral Lex was running late and his constant haranguing of his driver was not going to help matters, so he forced himself to sit back in his comfortable ground car and relax. Opening his secure briefcase, he decided his time would be better spent reading the commissioner's proposals for the next step in turning the ceasefire with the Nilmerg into a permanent peace deal. Aral frowned. There were a few in the military who were deeply opposed to any talk of peace, and the commissioner believed Marshall Poll was inactive in quelling voices of discontent. The commissioner believed, as did Aral, that it was not the military's place to decide government policy and he was willing to take measures, however unpopular with the military, to ensure they were reminded of that. The first of these measures was the removal of Marshall Poll from his post as head of the Deres Space Forces. Of course, the commissioner would announce it was with great regret that after many years of faithful service Marshall Poll was tendering his resignation and although the commissioner pleaded with him to stay, he reluctantly bowed to the marshall's wishes. A move that the commissioner hoped would keep the honor of the marshall intact but still send the required signal to the military.

A sudden and violent change in the ground car's direction threw Aral up against the armored passenger window. Aral experienced a sharp pain and raised his hand to his head. Withdrawing it, he found a warm, sticky substance on his fingers. He was bleeding! The ground car bounced into the air and came crashing back to earth a moment later, throwing Aral into the rear of his driver's seat, but this time the strong arm of Galas, Aral's bodyguard, saved him from causing any more injury to himself. Galas was screaming at the driver. "The tunnel! The tunnel!"

Aral struggled against Galas' strong grip in vain as he tried to sit upright. "What is happening?"

"The capital is under attack, Deputy. Now stay down and let me do my job!"

Aral was flung forward again and the ground car's tires screamed as the driver brought it to a halt in the middle of the tunnel. Galas touched the controls, which darkened all the vehicle's windows and sealed the ventilation system. With deft movements, Galas secured the emergency restraints around Aral before doing up his own. Galas began speaking, but Aral realized it wasn't to him. His bodyguard was speaking into his concealed radio. "Deputy Aral is in his ground car stationary in the middle of the Zelek tunnel three Jils from the capital building..." Aral could hear the muted tones of someone on the other end of the radio interrupting Galas. The way the bodyguard's face hardened, Aral knew it wasn't good news.

"Impact imminent, Deputy. Hold on."

Aral's world shook as if the entire planet was coming apart. A few seconds later, a howling like that of a thousand screaming poltergeists filled the tunnel and the ground car was battered as if by a thousand fists. Through the armored windows, Aral could see the other cars in the tunnel fold under the tremendous pressure, their windows imploding and slicing into their unfortunate occupants before an invisible hand picked up the cars and threw them around like toys. Aral opened his mouth to scream as, through the front windscreen, he saw a cargo truck barreling toward them in midair.

For Aral, everything went black.

#

TDF NAM RIVER - EDGE OF 23 LIBRAE SYSTEM
83.7 LIGHT YEARS FROM EARTH

The urgent beeping of the comms terminal by his bed brought Vusumuzi Mkhize to instant awareness. Pushing the accept key before his eyes even fully opened, the commander of Cruiser Squadron 1.2.2 swung his legs out of the comfortable bed and onto the floor as the anxious face of the duty watch officer, Commander Li Ming Liou, filled the small screen.

"Commodore. Communications has intercepted an all-frequencies signal from Director Boone on Planet IV. She states she has armed Deres soldiers entering the base. The signal was terminated at that point."

Mkhize started to get dressed as he spoke to the terminal over his shoulder. "Anything from the *Henry Moseley*?"

"Negative. I launched a comms drone on receipt of the message from Director Boone, but so far no reply."

Mkhize sat down as he pulled his boots on. If the *Henry Moseley* hadn't replied, he had to assume it was lost. "Time for Director Boone's signal to reach us?"

"At this distance it takes... er...forty-three minutes for a radio signal to reach us."

He guessed this was the beginning of a general push by Deres forces and the seizure of the base on Planet IV and the destruction of the *Henry Moseley* were the opening shots. "OK, Li, let's prep the surveillance drones. I want to know what the status of both the Deres and Nilmerg fleets are. If this is the start of a general conflict, then fleet movement will be a key indicator. Bring us to battle stations and warn the rest of the squadron to prepare for a fold back to Planet IV. As of now, we are operating as peacekeepers, but let's be ready for anything."

Mkhize cut the link and headed for the bridge as the battle station's alarm began to wail throughout the cruiser. He was reasonably confident his four cruisers were a match for anything either side could fling at him, but if the Deres had already captured the base on Planet IV, they had hostages, and Mkhize was simply not equipped to handle a surface rescue operation.

#

OFFICE OF THE PRESIDENT - GENEVA
EARTH - SOL SYSTEM

"...That's the situation as of thirty minutes ago, Madam President, Councilmen," concluded Senior Force Leader Tolas from his post in Central Command under the towering Mont Salève.

In her office in the center of Geneva, President Coston allowed herself a silent curse. The Deres incursion couldn't have come at a worse moment. With Admiral Jing on Alona trying to head off a conflict between the Commonwealth and the Alonan Empire, the Persai in the middle of selecting a new head of the Council of Twelve, and the Garundans so heavily committed to their mission to relocate and secure the Others POWs, Janus was still totally reliant on Commonwealth forces until it established its own defense forces and President Crothers estimated this could take him anywhere up to a year to do. This left only the forces of Earth and the Benii in a position to react to Marshall Poll's occupation of the joint base on Planet IV. The faces of the five ministers, one from each of the member states of the expanded Commonwealth which made up the Commonwealth Council regarded her blankly from the holo cube. The Council offices were only across Lake Geneva, but for propriety's sake, they had chosen to show their independence by joining the conference call from their own sanctum.

"What are your recommendations, Senior Force Leader?" asked Rebecca, although she already knew she was not going to like what the Persai Deputy Chairman of the Combined Joint Chiefs of Staff in the holo cube was going to say.

"Cruiser Squadron 1.2.2 assumes a blocking position beyond the weapons range of the Deres ship currently in orbit, with orders to halt the progress of the advancing Deres fleet that undoubtedly plans to reinforce Marshall Poll. If we can deny him reinforcements, then it at least gives you the chance to reach a negotiated settlement and the release of the hostages."

"Do we have any idea of the intentions of the remainder of the Deres fleet, Senior Force Leader? Are they making any aggressive moves?" Minister Yalus of Garunda asked.

"Commodore Mkhize's surveillance drones are picking up contradictory orders coming from multiple sources. It is our assessment that following the destruction of the House of the People and the death of Commissioner Malas and most of the Deputies, no one is quite sure who is in charge. Units loyal to the marshall are moving to secure key points, while those units which may remain loyal to the elected government are either fighting piecemeal or are sitting out the fight to see who comes out on top. To be honest, Minister I can't really blame them."

"And where are the Nilmerg in all of this?" The question came from the newest member of the Council, Tracy LeBlanc, representing Janus.

"Ambassador Isa is currently on Nilmerg, preparing for the upcoming peace talks. She reports the Nilmerg have increased their readiness state but are waiting to see if the Commonwealth will stand by its position as guarantor of the current ceasefire before taking any independent action."

The holographic Persai face of Minister Tovana leaned closer into the pickup. "As the humans would say, 'the ball is in our court'. Assuming we prevent the marshall's forces from linking up, what do you believe our chances are of securing a peaceful outcome, Senior Force Leader?"

"You have all seen the same video recording I have. I believe the marshall is sincere in his statement that if we interfere in any way, then he will begin executing the hostages."

To one side of the holo cube in her office was a still image of the smiling face of Marshall Poll, holding a pistol to the head of Director Boone as he transmitted his demands to the Commonwealth cruisers. Poll had given the Commonwealth until his fleet arrived in orbit around Planet IV to leave the system or he would begin executing his hostages.

"Are you saying we have no choice but to initiate a rescue attempt?"

Tolas hesitated before answering but when it came his voice was firm. "I do not see how we have a choice, Madam President. If we wait and call the marshall's bluff, then I believe the next video recording we receive from him will be one showing us a dead hostage and any window of opportunity to launch a rescue mission will have gone."

"How long until the Deres fleet reaches our cruisers?"

"At the current rate of advance, we can expect contact in a little under seven hours, Madam President."

The room lapsed into an uneasy silence as Rebecca looked from one holographic face to another until her eyes finally came to rest on the image of Sarah Boone. If she did nothing, then there was the chance the marshall would do nothing but... Rebecca stared at the image for another few moments and the look in the marshall's eyes was enough to convince her he was a man who could not be reasoned with. Time to throw the dice and hope your luck held.

"Ministers. It is the recommendation of Earth's government that you authorize the Senior Force Leader to use any and all force necessary to secure the release of the hostages and to enforce the provisions of the peace treaty of which the Commonwealth is the guarantor."

As it was Garunda's turn to chair the Commonwealth Council, it fell to Minister Yalus to take the next step. "I think we can all agree time is of the essence, so I call for a vote. The question before us is, do we authorize the Commonwealth forces to take steps to secure the release of the hostages, regain control of the joint base on Planet IV, and prevent any further Deres aggression? How say you, Minister Tolas?"

"Pars says aye."

"Minister Weinberg?"

The senior civil servant, having already heard what his president had to say on the matter, knew his vote was a mere formality. "Earth says aye."

"Minister Wakk?"

For the first time, the Benii were being asked as full members of the CUOP for their opinion and Rebecca noted Minister Wakk had chosen to remain silent during the briefing, so it was anyone's guess which way they would vote.

"Benii says aye."

"Minister LeBlanc?"

"Janus says aye."

"As the representative of Garunda, I vote aye. The vote is unanimous. Senior Force Leader Tolas, under Article 52.4

sub-paragraph six of the Commonwealth Union of Planets Charter, the Council authorizes the deployment of such forces as the Combined Joint Chiefs feel necessary to secure the release of the hostages and to regain control of the joint base on Planet IV and to prevent any further Deres aggression. The authority shall remain in place until such time as this decision is either endorsed or revoked by the respective heads of state of the Commonwealth Union of Planets."

Tolas let out a gruff "Thank you, Ministers. Now if you will excuse me, I need to get to work." The link to Central Command terminated and with a nod to the Council ministers, Rebecca terminated her link to them. Alone in her office, Rebecca stared at the last remaining image in the holo cube. A smiling Marshall Poll holding his pistol to the head of Sarah Boone. *Keep smiling Marshall, but we're coming for you!*

CHAPTER FIFTEEN
The Sound of Thunder

ZARMINA - 20.3 LIGHT YEARS FROM EARTH

The noise of hundreds of voices in the auditorium struck Brigadier General Vladimir Egnorov like a wave as he entered through a side door. Waiting for him was his Second in Command, Colonel Andreas Kendale. The German gave a curt nod to the Regimental Sergeant Major standing at the side of the auditorium's stage. The RSM brought himself to attention and raised his not-inconsiderable voice to ensure he was heard.

"Regiment! Regiment attention!"

The sound of 300 pairs of feet slamming into the floor threatened to bring the walls down as the massed troopers of special operations unit Thunder came to attention. Accompanied by Andreas, Vladimir made his way to the center of the stage. Halting, he let his gaze take in the massed ranks before releasing them from the position of attention.

"Please be seated, ladies and gentlemen."

Giving the troopers a few seconds to settle themselves, Vladimir looked over at the RSM who complied with the unspoken order and sent troopers from Thunder's intelligence shop scurrying throughout the auditorium, delivering PADs to the gathered officers and senior noncoms.

"Troopers. Thunder has received orders to immediately deploy to Planet IV of 23 Librae system, where approximately 125 hostages are being held by a force of Deres numbering approximately a battalion's-worth in strength. The PADs being handed out contain the most up-to-date intelligence we have. This intelligence is being updated as and when new information comes in from the cruiser squadron on station in the system. The hostages are being held by soldiers under the direct command of Marshall Poll, commander of the Deres space forces. There are also reports that naval units believed to support the marshall have carried out a missile strike on the Deres capital city, killing the Deres Commissioner and all of the civilian representatives. These naval units are now en-route to Planet IV and will arrive in under six hours."

From the audience came a few muttered oaths and some not-so muttered. The troopers in the auditorium were considered the toughest the Commonwealth had to offer, but even they balked at the callousness it took to carry out a missile strike on a civilian target. Privately, Egnorov shared his troopers' sense of disgust, but he had a job to do and time was short.

"Time is against us, so this will not be the well-planned, well-practiced, small-unit operation we are used to. This will be a maximum effort. We are going to rely on stealth, surprise, and the natural aggressiveness of the Thunder trooper."

That got a few "Oo-rahs" from the audience and

Egnorov smiled proudly at his troopers' confidence.

"The PADs you have also contain combat team orbats and load outs. Everything else we'll work out on the fly. Admiral Glandinning has given permission for us to use some of the new toys I know some of you have been drooling over. We fold out in two hours. Senior non coms, go and get your boys and girls moving. Officers, stay put. Colonel Kendale and I want to go over the outline plan with you and get your thoughts. Let's go get our people back! Dismissed!"

Thunder was on the move.

#

PLANET IV - 23 LIBRAE SYSTEM
83.7 LIGHT YEARS FROM EARTH

The muzzle of Vladimir Egnorov's plasma rifle slid snake-like through the tall grass and came to a stop just as it cleared the last stalk, enough to allow the passive optical sight mounted on it to give him a clear view of the flat plain below and the clear plasteel dome housing the captured base. So far, the operation was going like clockwork. The two specially modified Excalibur-class assault ships the navy put at Egnorov's disposal to carry his Thunder troopers to 23 Librae system had worked as advertised. For months, the scientists and engineers on Zarmina had been redesigning and reengineering the Excaliburs to tailor them to Thunder's specific requirements. The ability to insert a large force of troopers and all their equipment into a target and get back out without being detected. The Excaliburs reentered normal space on the opposite side of the planet from the base and the Buffalo troop shuttles ferried his troopers from low orbit and flew below the radar horizon of the base until they reached Egnorov's chosen landing zone in a valley only eleven kilometers from the target. There had been no sign of the Deres ship in orbit above the base having detected the

Buffalos approach, no doubt due once more to the inventiveness of the Zarmina research teams, who had added a few tweaks of their own concoction to the standard Chameleon stealth units integrated into the Buffalos.

On arrival at the landing zone, the Buffalos powered down every nonessential system to reduce any chance of detection while the Thunder troopers disembarked and formed up, ready for the approach march to the objective. The Wraith suits worn by the troopers adapted to the environment around them, and within moments each trooper disappeared like a ghost into the misty rain that was beginning to fall, their individual footsteps muffled by the damp ground. Without the aid of his suit's sensors, Egnorov would never have been able to tell that he was surrounded by 300 of the best soldiers the Commonwealth had to offer.

Back to business. It appeared Andreas' interpretation of the thermal scans was correct. Evenly spaced around the perimeter of the dome were Deres weapons emplacements reinforced by earth works and sporting a heavy machine gun and infantry section. By the main airlock, guarded by yet another weapons emplacement, were four shuttles, their crews milling around the rear loading ramps. Hanging from each of the sharply raked wings was a weapons' pylon with six evil-looking missiles. At either side of the cockpit windows was an ovoid protrusion with a hole pointing forward. If Egnorov was to make an educated guess, each of those protrusions was rapid-fire cannon of some sort. The navy's thermal scans had shown six of these shuttles in use by the Deres, so where the hell were the other two? In answer to his silent question, his suit's external pick-up brought him the sound of rapidly approaching turbo fans. Seconds later, two Deres shuttles screamed low over the long grass concealing his position, and banked sharply. One shuttle continued its turn, gaining height, and began a long, lazy circling of the base. The second shuttle's nose dipped as its pilots brought it to a hover before slowly descending to touch down a short distance from the other, already-grounded shuttles. As the engine noise died, Egnorov saw a group of soldiers rushing forward under a cajoling officer who quickly formed them into a perfectly straight line. The rear ramp lowered and barely had a chance to touch the wet ground before a large Deres was out, his head scanning left and right like a bird of prey searching for its next victim. *Bodyguard!* Egnorov thought. Somebody important must be on the shuttle. Seemingly satisfied, the Deres stepped to one side and a second figure descended the ramp at a more sedate pace. The waiting soldiers sprang to attention and presented arms. With a dismissive wave that passed for a salute, the senior officer strolled past the assembled soldiers and, accompanied by the bodyguard and the officer from the arrival party, he headed for the airlock leading into the base. Egnorov tracked their progress through his weapon's sight until he lost sight of the small party as they entered the airlock. The double tone in his ear bug focused his attention onto his suit's heads-up display. Andreas was signaling that all the assault teams were in position. In the top-left corner of the display, the numbers of the countdown clock marched on remorselessly. Twenty minutes until the approaching Deres fleet were within weapons range of the Commonwealth cruiser squadron. If the Deres were still in control of the base and its hostages when the clock reached zero, then Commodore Mkhize would be forced to withdraw and the Deres would have won. Thunder and Egnorov were here to ensure this did not happen. With a final check on his troopers' positions, Egnorov activated his suit's link.

"All Thunder units, this is Egnorov. Strike! Strike! Strike!"

In a split-second, all hell broke loose. This was no silent

assault. Thunder was coming in noisy. Each of the Deres weapons emplacements had its own dedicated Thunder fire team assigned to it. At Egnorov's order, the emplacements fell under plasma rifle fire from the concealed troopers. The boiling plasma cut through the earthen defenses as though they were nonexistent. The Deres soldiers staffing them were given no chance to react before the hail of incoming fire cut them down. However, Egnorov was taking no chances, and a volley of High Velocity Missiles streaked forward. The HVMs pummeled the emplacements to dust.

From the high ground above the shuttle landing area came more withering plasma-rifle fire targeted at the hapless shuttle crew. They died where they stood. The circling shuttle didn't have to wait long to share the same fate as its grounded comrades. Egnorov had no way of knowing how many of the Deres shuttles would be airborne when he began his assault, so in the tradition of more is better than less, his plan called for two anti-air teams per shuttle. With only the one shuttle in the air as the assault launched, all twelve teams turned their missiles onto the sole remaining air threat. Team three would later claim to have downed the shuttle, but with twelve missiles accelerating past Mach three in the few seconds the shuttle had to react, no one would ever know. What Egnorov did know was that the ear-shattering explosion and ball of flame and falling wreckage meant that the Deres air threat was dealt with.

With the perimeter defenses down, the dome assault teams moved up. The assault teams were not going to waste time cycling through the dome's airlock. Instead, they made their own doors. Troopers carrying frame charges placed them against the plasteel dome walls and stepped back out of the shaped charges blast area. With muffled bangs, Thunder blew eight large holes in the dome and the troopers went pouring through, ignoring the air escaping from the dome as nature fought to equalize the pressure differential. Assault teams headed for their assigned objectives.

"Let's go, RSM." Egnorov cried over his link. Eager to join the assault, he stood and headed for the nearest breach, trailed by the RSM and the two other troopers making up his escort. The Wraith suit's powerful artificial muscles pushed him along at forty kilometers an hour. Reaching the breach, the heavy, armored hand of the RSM on his shoulder momentarily restrained Egnorov as he bent to enter the gloom.

"Ladies first, sir, if you don't mind," said Sergeant Nesy Preuss as she pushed through the breach, rifle up and hunting for anything even resembling a possible threat to her boss. "Clear!"

Egnorov stepped through the shattered plasteel with the RSM and Staff Sergeant Semple at his heels. The sight that greeted Egnorov was one of cold, clinical death. Scattered around the breach lay dozens of Deres soldiers. The Thunder troopers' orders were simple and explicit. Every Deres in uniform was to be treated as a combatant and was to be neutralized with extreme prejudice. The sight of so many dead Deres was testament to those orders. Egnorov didn't give his order a second thought. This was combat and his mission was the safety of the hostages first. Over the open command link, he heard the call he was waiting for.

"Red Team. Building Four secure. Two X-Rays dead. Five Yankees alive and well."

Egnorov let out a silent *yes*! Building Four was the power station. X-Rays were enemy soldiers and Yankees were hostages. Red Team's success was quickly followed by more as the Thunder troopers spread out over the base.

"Blue Team. Building Seven secure. Five X-Rays dead.

Four Yankees alive and well." That would be the medical center and its staff.

"Yellow Team. Building Two secure. Four X-Rays dead. Thirty-eight Yankees alive and well." Egnorov said a silent *thank you* to God. Yellow Team's objective was the main mess hall and the naval data had shown it to hold the largest concentration of thermal signatures, leading Egnorov and his planners to believe this was where the majority of the hostages were being held. The message from Yellow Team confirmed this.

"Green Team. Building Six secure. One X-Ray dead. Fifteen Novembers alive and well." November was the designation which had been given to the Deres scientific party that has been working on the base when the Deres soldiers overran it. Fifteen would account for all but one of them.

"White Team. Building Five secure. Two X-Rays dead." That would be the entrance to the elevator shaft leading down to the cavern holding the Saiph library five kilometers below them.

"Orange Team. Building Three secure." The supply building. Egnorov was not expecting it to be guarded as it held nothing of any value, but a team was assigned to it in case any Deres soldiers had decided to hole up in it.

With only one building left, Egnorov did a quick head count. By his math, he was short two Yankees and one November. The echoing sound of automatic weapons fire told him where he was likely to find them.

"OK, RSM, sounds like Black Team is having some trouble getting into the Operations Building. Let's head over there and see if we can give them a hand, shall we?"

Egnorov was sure he heard the RSM use a derogatory

term regarding officers over the open link before his mind switched gears and he raced for the sound of the gunfire. Sliding to a halt at the corner of the mess hall, he decided it would be better to use the optics mounted on his rifle to see around the corner, rather than stick his head out. Pushing the muzzle of the weapon around the building's edge, his HUD gave him a clear view of what awaited him. Deres soldiers firing from the top floor of the two-story Operations Building pinned down the majority of Black Team. A small number of team members were trying to infiltrate the flanks of the building, but every time they exposed themselves, they were forced back by the sheer weight of fire. Egnorov zoomed in on the ground floor windows and he was able to make out the unmistakable shapes of armed Deres, waiting patiently to fire on anyone attempting to approach from this side. Egnorov estimated that the Deres had maybe a twenty-meter clear field of fire around the entire Operations Building. Yeah, if he were going to hole up anywhere, then this would be the place. A movement in the HUD and a split-second later the corner of the building Egnorov was sheltering behind began taking fire. Back-pedaling away from the hail of fire, Egnorov weighed up his options. With the rest of the base secure, he could just wait out the Deres who were holed up in the Operations Building. It wasn't as if they could go anywhere. On the other hand, they still had two hostages and one noncombatant in there. What if they decided to execute the hostages as they previously threatened to do? The countdown clock in the HUD was down to seven minutes. Seven minutes separated the success of the mission from failure. No, the building had to be taken.

"RSM, here's the plan. You and Preuss take up sniper positions on this roof, it should give you a good angle onto the side of the Operations Building facing us. Semple, you're with me. Hope you remembered your flash bangs."

With a small chuckle, Semple patted his suit's leg pouch. "Never leave home without them, sir."

Inside his helmet, Egnorov grinned. "Good man. Suit. Command channel. Black Six. Black Six. Egnorov."

The frustrated voice of Captain Barshai, Black Team's commander came back. "Go for Black Six."

"In thirty seconds I want you to lay down covering fire on the north and west aspects of your target. Watch for friendlies approaching from the east."

"Understood thirty seconds."

"Egnorov clear... RSM?"

From the tone in his voice, it was obvious the RSM was unhappy with the way things were unfolding. "Overheard, sir. We've got your back."

"I would expect nothing less, RSM."

A fusillade of plasma rifle fire from Black Team told him it was time to move. Crouching low like a sprinter, he burst out of cover and ran for all he was worth for the Operations Building, Semple by his side. The Deres standing guard at the windows caught sight of him and brought their weapons up to fire. Still ten meters to go. He wasn't going to make it. The Deres heads exploded in a fountain of blood and bone as single, precision shots from the RSM and Preuss serviced their targets. Breathing heavily, Egnorov crashed into the wall of Operations Building. The actual Operations Room was located on the upper floor of the building, so Egnorov was hedging his bets that that was where any hostages would be held. Keeping a wary eye on the nearest window, he called to Semple.

"Breacher!"

Semple was ahead of him. The staff sergeant was already pulling the coil of explosives from his left leg pouch and was pressing it hard against the wall in a rough oval, large enough for a Wraith-suited person to fit through. When he was finished laying the breaching charge, Semple reached into his other leg pouch, extracted two grapefruit-sized objects, and passed them to Egnorov. Another two appeared and were duly attached to his waist. Flash bangs. The weapon of choice when entering a room that contained both X-Rays and Yankees, the flash bang was a type of concussion grenade. Flung into a room, it exploded with a blinding light and a high-pitched sound, which blinded, deafened, and disoriented anyone in the room. The effects, though instant, were also temporary, so no permanent harm was done, but it did give assaulting troopers a window of a vital few seconds to enter a room and deal with any threats.

"Ready, Semple?"

"Just like old times, sir."

"Let's do this!" Egnorov activated the link to Black Team and the RSM. "Breaching lower level now, switch fire to upper floors."

Semple tapped a command into his suit and the breaching charge went off, rocking the two troopers back on their heels. With the debris still flying through the air, Egnorov was through the breach and into the smoke-filled room beyond. Two Deres soldiers were on the ground, trying to struggle to their feet. Egnorov's rifle barked twice and they stopped moving.

"Two X-Rays dead, east room, ground level."

Semple moved past him to the open doorway. Flattening himself against the wall, he stuck his rifle barrel around the door frame and swept the corridor in both directions.

"One X-Ray at either end, sir. Stairway to the right. Door to another room to the left."

Egnorov stepped over to him, placing himself so they were now standing back to back.

"Three. Two. One. Step."

Like a well-practiced dance team, Egnorov and Semple took a single side step, placing themselves square in the middle of the corridor, weapons already lined up on their targets. The Deres were too busy concentrating out the windows to even notice that the reaper was ready to take them. Egnorov and Semple fired simultaneously.

"Two X-Rays dead, corridor, ground level."

Flash bang in hand, Egnorov approached the closed door to the remaining ground floor room. Semple braced himself, and with a kick the door flew open. His mechanically assisted kick actually took the door clean off its hinges, sending it flying into the room and into a hapless Deres soldier waiting to target anyone coming inside. With a deft lob, Egnorov sent the flash bang into the center of the room. Prepared for what was coming next, the two troopers had their visors dimmed and their external audio turned down. The Deres weren't so lucky. The blinding flash and high-decibel scream caused them to drop their rifles as hands flew, too late, to protect ear drums and eyes squeezed shut to no avail as black spots continued to dance on their retinas.

Egnorov and Semple entered the room on the heels of the detonating flash bang, methodically working targets from opposite corners in toward the center of the room. It was all over in a matter of seconds.

"Three X-Rays dead, west room, ground level. Moving to upper level. Black Team, check fire! Check fire!"

With the check fire order, both Black Team and the RSM would stop firing on the upper level of the Operations Building, leaving only Egnorov and Semple to deal with any Deres they encountered.

The two Thunder troopers moved back into the corridor and headed for the stairwell, reloading their spent rifles' charge packs as they moved. Switching to thermal vision, Egnorov scanned the stairwell and the ceiling directly above him. The brighter red of two heat sources showed up plainly against the cooler blue permacrete. Two Deres were in ambush position covering the top of the stairs, waiting to greet the unwary. *Well, two can play at this game,* thought Egnorov. Throwing the image across to Semple's suit he raised his rifle and aimed at the ceiling. Taking his cue from Egnorov, Semple also took aim at the ceiling.

"Full auto on three. Two. One. Fire!"

The narrow corridor filled with the ear-shattering sound of two plasma rifles discharging superheated rounds into the permacrete roof as fast as the weapons systems could cycle. The plasma tore through the permacrete, the waiting Deres soldiers, and carried on through the roof of the building. Egnorov plunged into the thick dust, relying on his thermals to guide him up the stairs. With the threat now negated at the head of the stairs, he leapt over the two large holes in the floor, which had just held the Deres waiting in ambush for him. On his right was a partially open doorway. Slowing his head-long dash, he palmed a flash bang through the gap. Semple saw Egnorov's action and held himself at the stairwell for an extra second before bounding forward. As he cleared the demolished floor, the flash bang detonated and Semple took the door at the run, Egnorov swooping in behind him.

Plasma rifles spat and more enemy soldiers were sent to meet their fate.

"Two X-Rays dead, west room, upper level."

That confirmed it. The hostages must be in the Operations Room. Egnorov was out of flash bangs, so it would be his turn to be doorman. Bracing himself, he raised his leg and smashed it into the door, which splintered and fell off its hinges. Semple was ready and two flash bangs followed the door. But whoever was in the room must have had the reactions of a cat. Egnorov didn't have time to get clear of the doorway as machine-pistol rounds hammered into his chest armor, knocking him off his feet. Semple saw him go down as the flash bangs detonated. He didn't hesitate. Rifle up, he flung himself into the Operations Room. Standing directly opposite the doorway was the biggest Deres he had ever seen. Grasped in one large hand was a compact machine pistol. The other hand rubbed at his eyes to clear his vision. Semple didn't give him the chance. His finger caressed the trigger of his rifle. One round took the Deres in the center of his chest, punching through his rib cage, and exiting his back, taking the contents of his chest cavity with it. The second round removed his head from his shoulders. Spinning in place, Semple's rifle sighted on his next target. An older Deres in a more flashy uniform was trying to push himself behind a human female while struggling to pull a pistol from its holster. Two paces forward and Semple grabbed the Deres by the throat. The Wraith suit's motors whined as the unfortunate Deres was picked up and flung across the room. Egnorov regained his footing and was entering the room, searching for targets. The sight of the flying Deres in uniform was enough as his combat instincts kicked in and his rifle seemed to fire of its own accord. The Deres was dead before he hit the ground.

The suit's external audio pick-up came back on

following the flash bang's detonations and the unmistakable sound of a screaming human female's voice came to him.

"Don't shoot! Don't shoot!"

Turning his head toward the sound, he was confronted by the scene of Semple in his Wraith suit trying to grab another Deres from behind a Nilmerg, who was punching and kicking out at the trooper while a human female was hanging off his back with one hand while punching at his armored shoulders with the other.

"Stand down, Semple, I think this particular Deres is our missing November."

Semple stepped back and his sudden change of direction caught the human female unawares. She fell ungracefully to the floor. Egnorov approached her as his suit automatically ran facial recognition on the red-faced, sweaty form. The name "Sarah Boone" flashed up in his HUD. The Nilmerg still lay prostrate over the last remaining Deres as they both eyed the unmoving Semple warily. The suit identified the Deres as Gils Sarar and the Nilmerg as Ull Fors, giving their roles as co-expedition leaders.

"Two X-Rays dead, Operations Room upper level. Two Yankees and one November alive and well. Black Six, send a couple of troopers in here to escort our guests to the mess hall. Break. Suit. Naval channel. Send mission successful. Signed Thunder."

#

BRIDGE - TDF NAM RIVER

"Commodore. Signal from Thunder. Mission successful." The call from the comms officer broke the tension that had subsumed the bridge ever since the first Buffalo launched nearly two hours before. The sensors of the

Nam River had been able to follow the approach of the Buffalos carrying the Thunder troopers only intermittently, due partially to the terrain, but Vusumuzi Mkhize suspected it was mainly due to whatever adaptation the eggheads at Zarmina had made to the assault shuttles. The Deres Q Ship was still in geostationary orbit directly over the base and Mkhize was prepared to blow it out of space if he got even the slightest suspicion it had detected what was happening on the planet's surface and made any move to intervene. When the Buffalos reached the landing zone and went to minimal emissions, the *Nam River's* sensors had lost them completely, so it had been a pensive wait for Mkhize. Every minute he waited for Thunder to complete their mission was another minute the Deres fleet had gotten closer.

The tactical holo showed how close it actually was. Half an hour earlier, the surveillance drones he had ordered to keep a watch on the remainder of the Deres fleet reported all the remaining ships had formed up and were heading his way. The original fleet of Deres destroyers was only three minutes from entering his weapons range. Mkhize extended his arms out before him, fingers interlocked, and cracked his knuckles, allowing a smile to break his lips as he caught the inevitable wincing of some members of the bridge crew. The Deres might be three minutes from weapons range, but they were already well within range of Mkhize's four Lynx cruisers, as he was about to make them realize.

"Tactical. Highlight the fleet flagship."

In the holo cube, a single Deres destroyer was highlighted.

"OK people, time to remind the Deres we are here to enforce the ceasefire. Tactical. The squadron is to go active on all weapons systems. Make the flagship your primary target."

"Aye-aye sir. Weapons systems are on line. Electronic Counter Measures are active. Ready to engage on your command."

"Very well. Comms. Hail the Deres flagship audio and video."

#

Aboard the *Volar* Fleet, Admiral Toro fought to keep his face impassive as the computers shouted out their warnings. Looking around his bridge, he could see barely concealed panic in the eyes of the crew. Toro had promised them that the Commonwealth ships would withdraw from the system rather than risk the lives of the hostages held by the marshall. As the distance between his ships and those of the Commonwealth reduced with no sign of Commonwealth ships maneuvering from their blocking positions, the first shadows of doubt clouded his confidence. Now though, not only did they have the impertinence to lock weapons on his ship, but they were jamming his communications with Marshall Poll on the planet's surface and his ship in orbit. With a mental shrug, he dismissed the Commonwealth ship commander's actions for what they could only be: a final act of defiance to save as much face as possible before he turned tail and ran back to his worthless Nilmerg allies.

Lieutenant Rana was once more seated at his post in front of the Communications Section, so it was he who alerted Toro to the incoming signal from Mkhize.

"Fleet Admiral. The Commonwealth commander wishes to speak to you directly."

Toro face reflected his unconcealed pleasure. *A-ha! So the mighty Commonwealth have rattled their sabers and now wish to inform me that they are going to accede to our demands. This is a moment to savor.* With a flourish, Toro said, "Please put him through. I have business to complete and I have had about enough of this Commonwealth game of bluff."

On the large forward view screen, the face of Mkhize appeared and without prelude began speaking. The interpretation program took a few seconds to catch up and when it did, any thoughts of an easy victory fled from Toro's mind.

"Deres fleet commander. This is Commodore Vusumuzi Mkhize, Commanding Officer of Cruiser Squadron 1.2.2. Your actions on Planet IV and your presence here are clear violations of the ceasefire brokered in good faith between both your government and that of Nilmerg. The Commonwealth Union of Planets, as the guarantor of the said ceasefire, orders you to immediately reverse course and return to Deres. Failure to do so will result in your destruction. You have sixty seconds to comply."

As Mkhize's words sunk in, Toro could see the panic-stricken faces around him. They knew the Commonwealth forces outnumbered them four to one, and it was more than likely that if they engaged the Commonwealth cruisers, they would be lucky to survive. Toro had to regain the upper hand and quickly, before he lost the crew's confidence.

With all the swagger he could muster, Toro addressed the image of Mkhize on his screen. "Do not try to order me around. It is I who will be giving the orders here today. As you very well know, Marshall Poll has hostages, Commonwealth citizens amongst them. Now get out of my way, or their blood will be on your hands."

For the first time in hours, a large, toothy smile spread across Mkhize's face. "Your beloved marshall and all his soldiers are dead. The hostages are free and once more under the protection of the Commonwealth. You now have forty-five seconds to comply."

The view screen went dark as Mkhize terminated the video link. Toro had the wind taken out of his sails. He crumpled into his command chair as though punched in the stomach, oblivious to the noise erupting around him as the bridge crew realized their gamble had failed. Their glorious future as heroes of the Deres people was reduced to tatters. Through it all, the computer continued to interpret the audio signal being received from the Commonwealth ship.

"Fifteen...fourteen...thirteen...twelve...eleven...ten"

Someone grabbed Toro by the shoulders and shook him hard. Raising his head, Toro looked straight into the eyes of Rana. Rana's mouth was moving and his spittle wet Toro's face. Eventually, his words managed to penetrate Toro's numbed brain.

"Admiral! Admiral! Your orders!"

Whatever Toro was about to say became inconsequential. The Commonwealth countdown reached zero. Four Lynx cruisers fired their main energy weapon batteries on the *Volar*. The massed fire struck the ship along its entire length. Battle armor evaporated at their touch as the deadly grazers penetrated deeper and deeper. Metal, flesh, and bone became nothing more than superheated gases at their touch and in seconds the *Volar* became – for just a moment – the brightest star in the sky as the ship and its crew gave themselves up to space in a flash of heat and light.

#

Commodore Mkhize kept his eyes steadfastly on the outside view projected into the main holo cube filling the center of his bridge as the last gaseous remains of the Deres flagship dissipated into the cold vacuum of space.

"Comms. Raise whoever is now in command over there, I want to speak to them. Maybe this time I'll be able to get them to see reason before they run out of ships."

The comms officer turned back to his board and a blinking incoming signal alert caught his eye.

"Incoming signal from the Deres, sir."

Mkhize's deep laugh filled the bridge. "Now that was quick. Our little firepower demonstration must have encouraged some smarter thinking over there."

The confused look on the comms officer's face made him pause. "It's not coming from any of the destroyers, sir. It's a general signal being broadcast on all frequencies from the lead ship of the second group of Deres ships."

"Let's hear it."

With a few commands, the image of the holo cube changed and instead of the blackness of space, Mkhize was looking at a Deres dressed in what passed for an official-looking suit. Mkhize noted the left side of his head was swathed in bandages.

"... of Deres. You have been deceived. Marshall Poll and Fleet Admiral Toro have been stripped of their ranks by order of the House of the People. Troops loyal to the government have put down the attempted coup and restored order. The People's Prosecutor, following my orders as the senior surviving Deputy, has issued arrest warrants for the criminals known as Poll and Toro. The charge is mass murder. The final cost of their murderous attack on the capital is still not known and will probably not be known for many days, but we estimate we have suffered over 17,000 dead and perhaps 100,000 injured. Even in the darkest days of our long conflict with the Nilmerg, we have never seen such losses amongst our civilian population. Our search-and-rescue services are doing their best, but the task before them is so great, even their strenuous efforts will not be enough to reach many survivors in time to render aid. In an act of friendship I found deeply touching, the Anala of Nilmerg has offered all the aid his people can provide. Through the offices of the Commonwealth Ambassador, I have accepted his kind offer. I am now personally leading loyal ships in pursuit of the criminals and I call upon all true Deres to look into their hearts and see the truth of how you were deceived by Poll and Toro. Lay down your arms, I beseech you. You were only following the orders of the men who preyed upon your fears and uncertainty of the future. No charges will be brought against any man if he follows my orders. I, Deputy Aral Lex, promise you... Soldiers of Deres. You have been deceived..."

Mkhize made a throat-slashing gesture and the voice of Aral Lex cut off. The bridge remained silent as Mkhize considered his next move. He still faced fifteen destroyers and at least some of their crew must still be loyal to Poll and Toro, but which ones?

"Tactical. Keep a weapons lock on those ships but do not fire unless we are fired upon."

Now we wait and see, thought Mkhize as he attempted to relax. The first indication the Deputy's message was getting through came ten minutes later. A destroyer at the very edge of the fleet powered down all its systems with the exception of life support. As if that ship had been the first crack in the dam, a second and then a third ship quickly followed suit. Over the next half hour, all the remaining destroyers powered their systems down as their crews awaited the arrival of the loyal forces.

Mkhize pulled himself out of the seat he felt he had occupied for days and suddenly realized he was hungry.

"Tactical, bring the squadron down from battle stations. I'm going to get some food if anybody needs me." With one final look at the fifteen destroyers floating serenely in space before him, Mkhize headed for the mess. He was under no illusions about how close he had come to taking a lot of innocent lives today and was relieved that in the end, he did not have to.

CHAPTER SIXTEEN
Janus

JANUS - 4.7 LIGHT YEARS FROM EARTH

Thomas Crothers sat with his back to the highly polished oak desk, a gift from Rebecca Coston, as one president to another, and lounged in his comfortable chair taking in the view from his office windows and clearing his mind to ready it for the imminent meeting he knew would be a complete sea change for his world and its people. The view outside was very different from what it had been just a scant few years before when the Janus colony had been nothing more than a collection of ramshackle prefabs. The glinting glass-sided edifices that now dwarfed his own offices would soon enough be dwarfed in turn by the new construction springing up as far as the eye could see. Humanity's first extra-solar embryonic colony was expanding rapidly. Money and people were pouring in at a prodigious rate as humanity realized the gravity of the threat to its own existence represented by the Others and any more races like them. Thus, they threw their resources into building a self-sufficient colony so that if the worst did come to pass and Earth suffered the same fate as so many other worlds the Others had attacked, at least the human race would go on in some shape or form.

In what many still regarded as a minor miracle of organization and sheer focused determination, Janus rapidly grew into what it was today. A planet with a population of over ten million souls and counting. An established agricultural and industrial base, which not only provided for the planet's inhabitants but had become a major exporter to other Commonwealth worlds. Its industrial base had proved its worth when the Others' attack on Earth destroyed the Deimos shipyards. The Janus shipyards were able to step in and provide much needed repair facilities to the badly damaged TDF fleets.

No one would disagree that the driving force behind the success of Janus was its governor, Thomas Crothers. A quiet, unassuming man whom most people would have passed in the street without a second glance. Inside, though, was a calculating mind, which could work any problem to a successful conclusion. There was also a willingness to succeed that others fed off and became invigorated by. People soon became justly proud of what they had achieved and were never shy in telling anyone who would listen that they hailed from Janus. So it came as no great surprise when a plebiscite was held and the people of Janus voted for independence from Earth. It also came as no surprise when Thomas Crothers was elected as the first president of Janus with an overwhelming majority.

The opening of his office door brought Thomas out of his seat. He quickly covered the short distance to warmly embrace his guest. The image of the short, balding president hugging the tall, thin, auburn-haired woman was one any news vid crew, if they had been present, would have paid good money for. Releasing his embrace, Thomas stood back and indicated the comfortable-looking chairs and the low coffee table with its waiting cups and coffee service.

"It's good to see you again, Patricia. How was the trip?"

Patricia Bath gratefully sunk into the seat as Thomas poured them both a steaming cup of coffee.

"To be honest with you, Mr. President, all this business of sneaking around is more tiring than you can imagine."

Thomas let out a soft chuckle. "Not cut out to be a modern-day Mata Hari eh, Patricia?"

"That woman was made of sterner stuff than me, Mr. President. I left Geneva at some godforsaken hour this morning to avoid any awkward questions and then was sequestered in an anteroom on Gateway Station for five hours until the courier ship was ready to leave. When we arrived in Janus space I was grateful to be able to board your Coast Guard shuttle so I could at least stretch my legs. I've never realized how small those courier ships are. No, Mr. President, I'm definitely not cut out for the spy business. I like my creature comforts too much."

"Don't we all, Patricia. Don't we all." Placing his cup down on the table, Thomas pushed an encrypted PAD over to Patricia, whose demeanor became instantly business-like. "Here is the information you requested," he said. "I told my advisers I wanted a worst-case scenario and that's exactly what they provided. If Earth was to withdraw from the Commonwealth, then they believe the consensus of opinion is that an Earth First government would try to regain control of Janus. This would be unacceptable to the majority of the Janus population and I would agree with them. It would be my government's policy that Janus should remain within the Commonwealth. If we did, we could expect economic and military sanctions to be imposed by Earth, but my advisers are confident that we could make up any shortfall by increasing our trade with the remaining nations of the Commonwealth." Thomas paused, as if unsure how what he was going to say next would be received.

Patricia sensed his uneasiness. She had known Thomas for over five years and considered him a friend.

"Please continue, Mr. President."

Setting his jaw, Thomas went on. "That brings us to the issue of colonization. Any aggressive colonization program by an Earth First government would, as a matter of course, have an impact on Janus as Earth's closest neighbor. Janus would have no choice but to counter this by enacting our own colonization program at the earliest opportunity. We expect such a program to bring Janus into direct competition with Earth and as such, there will need to be a similar expansion of our military forces..."

Patricia's face drained of blood. "Mr. President. Do you really think it would come to that? Human against human?"

Thomas shrugged his shoulders in reply. "Times have changed, Patricia. I have to look out for the best interests of my people now and the rhetoric these Earth First people are spouting quite honestly scares me. Right now, Janus relies on Admiral Lewis and Second Fleet for protection. Janus doesn't have a substantial space navy of its own. A few destroyers and frigates belonging to the Coast Guard, yes, but nothing to match the firepower of a battleship or even a modern cruiser. I'm coming under increasing pressure to increase the Coast Guard's funding to allow it to build more capable ships..." Thomas made eye contact with Patricia and she could see the anguish in them.

"The funding is set to be approved. We expected to take more responsibility for our own defense sooner or later, so all we are doing is bringing those plans forward. A good many sailors and marines who are leaving the service have laid down roots here. They have families here now and a number of them have asked to stay and the government is inclined to let them. We find we are in need of their particular skill sets now more than ever. The first battleship of the Janus Space Navy is set to begin construction by the end of next month. Tell Rebecca I'm sorry, but I have to think of Janus first now."

The two friends sat in silence, each absorbed in their own thoughts as the future path of the human race came to its first fork in the road. Differing directions that would not easily be reconciled.

#

The secretary softly closed the door behind Patricia and as if on cue, a side door leading to the president's Chief of Staff's office opened to admit two civilians and a single uniformed officer. If anyone had seen the three enter the room, they might have found it odd that the officer wore the uniform of a Terran Defense Force admiral.

Thomas remained in his seat as he gestured for the others to sit. Doing so Thomas' Chief of Staff wasted no time in asking the question whose answer they all wanted to know.

"So, what was her reaction, Mr. President?"

Thomas hesitated before answering Chin Lee's question, still wondering if they were doing the right thing. Independent or not, Janus still retained deep cultural and economic ties with Earth and those were not going to simply dematerialize overnight. However, thought of the effect the Earth First movement's plans to split from the Commonwealth and its pursuit of isolationist policies could have for Janus, and any other colony established by Earth in the future, was something Thomas was not willing to risk.

Janus was his home and he had to think of its people first.

"As well as we expected her to, Chin. It will be a blow to President Coston and will only serve to give Grant and his campaign ammunition to use against Kris Madkin, but it can't be helped. The time for Janus to stand on her own two feet has come. Talking of which, Rayner, how long before we are able to reveal the illustrious new Janus Space Navy to the world?"

The larger-than-life National Security Adviser seemed to fill the entire chair he was sitting in and, as always, a bead of sweat trickled down his forehead. "The Articles of Independence gifted the independent government virtually the entire planetary defense grid, including the surveillance and weapons platforms in orbit. The TDF retain control of Second Fleet, but only so far as the actual ships themselves. All support facilities are similarly gifted to Janus, so the only thing we lack..."

"Are ships," finished Thomas wearily, "And of course the personnel to crew them."

"We already have the Coast Guard cutters, Mr. President and they are fully crewed by Janus citizens," interjected Chin in an attempt to raise the president's spirits.

Thomas turned his head to look at the sole uniformed man in the room. "A mere drop in the ocean compared to the firepower you have at your disposal, Admiral Lewis."

Admiral Robert Lewis, CO Second Fleet, TDF sat looking unperturbed as the politicians in the room slowly sank into despair. "Mr. President, the combined firepower of the entire Coast Guard is less than one of my cruisers. However, I do think you are underestimating your lack of available trained personnel."

Chin Lee cocked a dubious eyebrow at the admiral. "My numbers come directly from the Department of Defense, Admiral and I would like to hope they know how many people they have working for them."

The chuckle that escaped Lewis caught the others in the room by surprise. "You may have a point there, Mr. Lee, but have they talked to the Department of Immigration lately? The Earth First movement is not only scaring the politicians. There are rumblings within the fleet. A lot of officers and crew are not happy with their views and a large percentage of those sailors are due to complete their tours of duty in the near future, and the prospect of going back to an Earth run along Earth First lines is not filling them with end-of-tour joyfulness. Many are looking for an alternative and Janus is the obvious choice. If you were to offer some sort of package to help them relocate their families, I can pretty much guarantee the majority would take it. You still wouldn't have the trained personnel to crew anything the size of Second Fleet, but you would have enough to crew probably one BatFor, maybe more, and of greater significance, it would provide a core of experienced officers and ratings to build on."

Chin Lee sat forward, enlivened by Lewis' suggestion. "This could work Mr. President. We have been looking into how we should screen immigration now that Earth's government can't tell us who we can and who we can't take. It would not be unheard of for a nation to award points to an applicant based on the needs of the country. We can easily place military personnel in the highest point bracket and I'm sure a few words from yourself in the ears of the Treasury Secretary could free up the needed cash to fund a relocation package, which we can then deduct from the wages of those serving over a span of a tour of duty."

Thomas looked to Rayner, who gave an approving nod.

"Well, that's settled then. It only leaves us with the question of who we can get to run our shiny new toy. By your presence here today, Admiral, I take it you have considered my proposal and find it agreeable?"

"Your assumption would be correct, Mr. President. I have spoken to my wife and she and I are in agreement. Janus is the place we would both like to retire to when the time comes for that, so perhaps we should do something to ensure it is still here when that day is upon us." Reaching into his pocket, Lewis withdrew two pieces of paper and handed them to Thomas. "Mr. President, before attending this meeting I dispatched my letter of resignation to the Secretary of the Navy. My wife will do the same later today. Please accept both my wife's and my own application for Janus citizenship."

Thomas leapt to his feet and took Lewis' hand, pumping it enthusiastically. "Welcome to Janus Fleet, Admiral Lewis." Thomas gave his National Security Adviser a sideways look. "And I believe Rayner here is looking for someone to head up... What is it you are calling it, Rayner?"

"The Office of Naval Intelligence, Mr. President."

"Ah yes, so it is. Although I don't think we can guarantee adjoining offices, Admiral." Thomas chuckled at his own joke.

"Believe me, Mr. President, I would rather be in a different star system than have to have an office next door to my wife. Absence makes the heart grow fonder and all that."

All four men laughed as another step in separating Janus from Earth was taken.

CHAPTER SEVENTEEN
Project Bright Star

TANIL - PLANET IV
STAR SYSTEM 84137 - 320 LIGHT YEARS FROM EARTH

The being that had come to be known throughout the Commonwealth as simply one of the Others stared blankly at the diminutive Garundan who sat on the opposite side of the metal table. Bolov wasn't fooled by the Other's near comatose expression. He knew firsthand that, without the steel shackles securing the Other's wrists and feet to the table and floor, the seemingly unresponsive Other would be over the table in a second, attempting to murder Bolov with his bare hands.

The last time Bolov attempted to interrogate a member of this race, no such restraints were in place. It was only Bolov's extensive experience in interrogating pathological murderers, a hangover from his previous job as a consultant psychiatrist for the Capital Police, that allowed him to see the warning signs. As it was, he barely avoided the fingernails trying to scratch his eyes out before vise-like fingers wrapped around his throat, squeezing with all their might as they tried to throttle the very life from him. His vision filled with black spots as his brain was starved of life-giving oxygen and the strength fled his muscles as he tried vainly to fend off his attacker. Then the interrogation room door burst open and guards with stun batons raised rushed to his aid and that was Bolov's last memory of the incident. He eventually regained consciousness in the compound's medical center, his throat was wrapped in cool, pain-relieving healing gel. It took three days for the gel to do its work and allow Bolov to speak without pain again.

Hence the Other before him sat securely attached to the metal table and chair welded to the floor with additional fixture points for the Other's leg restraints.

With a final glance at the PAD in front of him, Bolov began.

"Ak-an. I am Doctor Bolov and it is my greatest hope that you might be willing to aid me in my understanding of your people." If Ak-an was at all surprised Bolov knew his name, then outwardly he showed no reaction, he simply continued to stare off into space seemingly unaware of the doctor's very presence. However, Bolov knew Ak-an's semi-comatose state was an act. The Garundan knew that Ak-an was fully aware of his surroundings.

"I wish to learn of the Ehita..."

With a speed that gave Bolov no time to react, Ak-an lunged forward, his teeth bared and eyes wide, coming to a stop only centimeters from the doctor as the sturdy chains reached their limit, Ak-an's muscles quivered as he struggled against them. "Only the Chosen People may speak of the Ehita! You are not worthy, heretic, and on the day of the Creator's return you will feel his wrath while the Chosen People follow him to Aseena."

Recovering quickly, Bolov raised a hand to signal to the

guards watching on the holo pickups that he did not require their intervention. *It appears speaking of the Ehita gets a bit of a violent reaction,* thought Bolov, *maybe I should change tactics*, "If we cannot speak on this subject, then perhaps you would be so kind as to tell me of the Creator and perhaps give me a greater understanding of his work."

At the mention of the Creator, Ak-an closed his eyes and dipped his head and his whole body seemed to relax, slowly he lowered himself back into his seat. For a few moments, Ak-an's lips moved without a sound coming from them before his eyes opened and his head once more rose. "In the end, the Creator will be victorious over the heretics and you will all perish in his name." Ak-an tried to raise his hands to the small amber jewel at the base of his skull but the restraints would not allow him. "Blessed be the Creator." Returning his arms to his sides, he took a breath. "I see no harm in telling you of the Creator."

"Thank you, Ak-an," said Bolov in his most conciliatory tone. This was the furthest he had gotten with any of the prisoners. By this time in interviews, the subject had been stunned by the guards and returned to the general population. Time to tread carefully. "Perhaps you could tell me how the Creator first came to your people?"

Ak-an's lips twisted as he tried to control his anger. "The Creator did not come to my people, heretic, he made us as he made all things... even you." A glob of spittle issued from the side of Ak-an's mouth, as if he was tasting something which wanted to make him wretch.

Bolov took a moment to process what Ak-an had just said. "But Ak-an, we are of different worlds, which are separated by light years."

"Distance is of no significance to the Creator. The

Creator breathed life into the universe and then visited Balach and the other worlds and blessed them with the gift of intelligence before returning to Aseena to sleep and wait until the fruit of his labors had grown and matured enough so that, one day, he could welcome them into Aseena and share its bountiful and never-ending beauty with him. But while he slept, the poison of heresy seeped into the minds of his creations. When the Creator awoke, he saw how the poison warped his creations and only on Balach did he find a small group, the Chosen People, who were still free of the poison. The Creator sent his angels to save the Chosen People in his mercy and to remind us of what awaited us, he transported the Chosen People to Aseena to stand before him."

"The Chosen People have met with the Creator?"

"Yes, heretic, we have. The Creator stood before us as we looked in awe upon the never-ending lush fields of Aseena, bathed in the faint red light of its star and it was there he proved to those who may still doubt his power that he was the Creator and master of all things."

Bolov was totally captivated by the story. "And how did he do this?"

A smile creased Ak-an's lips, the smile a parent would give a child who could not possibly understand what they were saying. "He extinguished the star and told the Chosen People we must follow the Ehita until the poison of heresy was cleansed from the universe. Only then would he allow the star to shine again and welcome us back into Aseena."

This information was gold dust. Never before had anyone gotten one of the Others to speak so freely about their origins. *I really hope the recorders are working*. "Please continue, Ak-an."

"The Creator led us to Durav, the planet from which we

were to conduct the Ehita. He gave us the Coltus so that we may communicate with him and seek his guidance in the way of the Ehita. Finally, he blessed us with the symbol of the Chosen People, the Gift Stone. When the original Chosen People arrived on Durav, they found the Creator had already marked them as his people. It was the Coltus that instructed us in the use of the Gift Stones."

"The small gem at the back of your necks. This is the mark of the Creator?"

"Yes, Doctor. Every pregnant female visits the Atistes, the house of the Creator, where the Gift Stone is passed over them. Any child of the Chosen People who is born and does not bear the mark of the Creator, we know to be the spawn of evil poisoned by heresy and sent to lead the Chosen People away from the path of the Ehita and the Creator."

As Ak-an stopped speaking the silence in the room stretched on until Bolov asked the question he knew he had to, even though he dreaded the answer. "But Ak-an, there are no Gift Stones here on Tanil. What will happen to any child born without the mark of the Creator?"

Ak-an leaned forward again until the restraints held him in place and an evil, predatory smile spread across his face. "They, like you heretic, will die at the hands of the Chosen People."

Words failed Bolov as he stared back at the smiling Ak-an in utter horror. The regime within the camps was reasonably lax, the Garundans had thought it better if the Others were allowed to associate freely, live as family units. It was the Garundans hope that by allowing them to do so the Others would recognize that their captors actually bear them no ill will. But this, the deep loathing for all that was not of the Creator up to and including the murder of innocent new born children. Bolov knew what he must do. All new born children would have to be removed from their mothers for their own protection.

#

CARSON CITY - EARTH – SOL SYSTEM

The top floor office of Admiral Aleksandr Vadis, head of the Naval Intelligence Service, gave a commanding view of the Sierra Nevada Mountains. A truly breathtaking sight, but right now he and the other two occupants of his spacious office had eyes only for the three meter-wide holo cube currently filled with the interview of the Other called Ak-an.

The interview came to its conclusion a second time. It had been watched in its entirety twice without a single utterance from the group. The aging admiral rose out of his chair at the head of the small wooden conference table he retained for his more intimate meetings and padded across the deep-pile carpet to the small liquor cabinet, which some unseen aide had thoughtfully furbished with his favorite whiskey. He poured one for himself and his two guests without asking their permission. Making his way back to table, he placed a full glass down in front of each before retaking his seat.

He allowed himself an appreciative sniff before taking a sip with closed eyes, allowing the alcohol to slowly warm his throat and chest. With his eyes still closed, he addressed his guests. "Thoughts?"

Elizabeth Wilson raised her glass and indicated for the portly man opposite her to start the discussion. Brigadier General Earl Statham was one of many retired officers who had been subjected to recall under the Emergency Powers Act by the then-Admiral Olaf Helsett before his move to Secretary of Defense.

Statham had run Admiral Jing's intelligence shop in First Fleet, before Jing's promotion to the Combined Joint Chiefs of Staff, and more recently Vadis had quietly moved Statham to head up the secretive Department of Special Projects. Not even Wilson was entirely sure what this particular department did, but she gathered its fingers were in an awful lot of pies and the aforementioned Brigadier Statham appeared to have a lot of pull. She was not at all surprised to see him at this classified meeting.

"I think this is yet another piece of the puzzle Aleksandr, and one which may at last give us a starting point."

Elizabeth tried to hide her surprise at a mere one-star brigadier calling a three-star admiral by his first name. Elizabeth, as a Rear Admiral (lower half), had a star of her own, but even though she knew and had worked closely with Vadis for nearly a decade, she didn't dare call him by his given name without his permission and definitely not in the company of strangers. Even more surprising was the lack of reaction from Vadis, not even a raised eyebrow at what she saw as a major breach of etiquette.

In fact, his eyes were still closed as he replied, "So you think young Wilson may be on to something?"

"Yes, I do."

Now Elizabeth was completely confused. Since when did the admiral refer to her as *young* Wilson?

"You may be a jarhead, Earl, and much as I hate to admit it, I'm inclined to agree with you." This elicited a chuckle from the brigadier as he took another sip of his drink, mumbling something about squids, a rather derogatory term used by marines for navy personnel. Vadis opened his eyes and pointed a finger at Elizabeth, "What about you,

Elizabeth? What's your take on this Creator legend?"

Ignoring the friendly, she hoped, exchange of insults between her boss and Statham, she concentrated on giving her best analysis of the Ak-an video, "If, and it's a big if, we are to believe even a part of what the prisoner told the good doctor, then it gives credence to the theory of the existence of another race. A race who saved a select few from the bio-weapon used on Balach, then transported them to Durav, where they used advanced AIs to educate them beyond their natural evolutionary level, to a point where they could travel amongst the stars and wipe out any other intelligent species they came across to clear the way for the return of what they believed to be their god."

Elizabeth moved to take another drink from her glass but her hand paused mid-ascent, and she instead replaced the glass on the polished table. "Although this is the first I've heard of their transportation to the Creator's world of Aseena and their meeting with him. On the other hand, there are numerous examples in human history where various religious groups claim to have met their deities. This could all be just religious dogma." This time, Elizabeth managed a slug of smooth whiskey and as she put her glass back down she noted that Statham had a "cat who got the cream" look on his face.

With a resigned sigh, Admiral Vadis tilted his head back and closed his eyes again. "Go on, Earl. Make your pitch."

Elizabeth looked confusedly between Vadis and the still-grinning Statham.

"What would you say if I could supply you with a time machine which would allow you to go back in time and see whether this so-called Creator actually did make a star disappear like the legend says?"

Elizabeth stifled a laugh. "Then I would say you have

invented a machine which science fiction writers have been waxing lyrical about for thousands of years and I would strongly suggest you get down to the patent office as soon as it opens tomorrow. You could make millions."

Vadis nearly choked on his whiskey as he tried unsuccessfully to swallow and laugh at the same time.

"Now I see where young Wilson gets his sense of sarcasm from," Statham said between chuckles of his own.

Ah, so it's my nephew Terrance the marine was referring to, thought Elizabeth. This raised another question. *What does he have to do with this?*

"I'll ensure I do that first thing... Now, back to the point. If I could identify a star that somehow unexpectedly stopped shining on or about the same time we know the population of Balach was decimated by the bio-weapon, would you agree that there was a good chance that star could be the one from the Creator legend?"

Elizabeth stared at the marine brigadier in disbelief. He was serious about this. Elizabeth took a few seconds to gather her wits. "I would have to concede that a star suddenly disappearing would certainly lend credence to the legend, but this is all theoretical. We cannot travel back in time. It's impossible."

Statham displayed that grin again as he looked intently toward Vadis like a dog would its master while awaiting permission to do something. The admiral gave him a simple nod and the marine reached into his briefcase and extracted a secure PAD, which he passed to Elizabeth. "Welcome to Project Bright Star."

#

GATEWAY STATION - EDGE OF THE ASTEROID BELT SOL SYSTEM

Gateway Station was a hive of activity as the multi-million ton freighters, warships, science vessels, colony transports, and every other kind of flotsam and jetsam required to service the interstellar nation Earth had become buzzed to and fro like angry bees as their captains maneuvered them in the congested traffic lanes under the wary eyes of the controllers aboard the station. There had been several near misses in the two years Gateway Station had been operational and no one wanted to see what would happen if one of those massive freighters collided with a colony transport carrying hundreds of colonists. So although it may appear to the untrained eye that the various ships' movements were chaotic, they were actually performing an intricate ballet with the station traffic controllers keeping a tight rein on events.

The scene outside the station's thick battle armor was of little concern to Lieutenant Terrance Wilson as he walked down yet another identical corridor in search of the correct docking bay. He had taken the time to study the route from his arrival dock to his destination dock when he stepped off of the intersystem transport which brought him to Gateway Station, but after forty minutes of walking and two different inter-ship cars which whisked him from the upper decks to the lower decks and out to the restricted military docking area, he was beginning to doubt his eidetic memory. Had he possibly read the schematic wrong? Rounding a corner of the never-ending sterile white corridor, he was relieved to find a personnel tube with a marine standing guard in front of it. Inscribed in blue, meter-high letters above the bulkhead door was the letter G and the number 18. *At last!* At the lieutenant's approach, the marine came to attention but his hand hovered close to his holstered PEP pistol all the same.

His job was simple. No unauthorized personnel were allowed access to the ship at the far end of the personnel tube and it looked as if this particular marine took his job seriously.

"Lieutenant Wilson reporting for duty aboard the science vessel TDF *Tycho Brahe*." Terrance passed over his ID card which the marine accepted with his left hand, right still free to draw his PEP if required. Inserting the ID card into the reader on his belt without ever moving his wary eyes from the naval officer, the marine waited for the double beep of recognition before removing the card and returning it to Wilson.

Identity confirmed, the marine saluted Terrance. "Welcome aboard, sir. The XO has left orders that you are to report to Briefing Room Two on your arrival. Your escort will meet you at the other end of the personnel tube."

Terrance returned the salute as the marine stood aside and the bulkhead door slid open, allowing Terrance to set off down the personnel tube. Making his way along the tube, Terrance battled to suppress the butterflies he felt in his stomach. Unlike many of his compatriots, Terrance had never even served on board a ship before, never mind a ship that was in the main crewed by civilian scientists. Instead, he was plucked directly from the Naval Academy and deposited in the skyscraper building housing the headquarters of the Naval Intelligence Service and it appeared that was where he was destined to remain. Until he had reviewed the now-infamous Ak-an recording. While putting the story of the Creator legend together with his research into the origins of the Others, he wrote a report for his boss in which he came up with a solution to finding the location of the fabled world of Aseena. To Terrance, the answer was simple. If Ak-an was to be believed, then Aseena's star showed a distinct shift in the red light spectrum. Using the data that Terrance had put together, they knew the Others must have visited Aseena and stood before the Creator in roughly 1000 AD. If the legend was to be believed, all you needed to do to locate the Creator was to find a red shift star that had suddenly disappeared on or around 1000 AD. Simple. *Oh, how I should have kept my mouth shut,* thought Terrance as the bulkhead leading into the *Tycho Brahe* let out a slight hiss of hydraulics as it slid aside. Stepping into the airlock, Terrance waited patiently as the outer door closed and locked before the inner door opened. The smiling face of a young twenty-something lanky ensign greeted Terrance.

"If you will follow me sir, the XO is waiting."

Terrance set off after the ensign, who made some banal chatter about this being his first ship after graduating the Academy and how excited he was about heading out into unexplored space. Terrance tuned him out as his thoughts fleetingly turned to Maggie and the four-month-old son he was leaving behind on Earth for the duration of this mission. Mentally berating himself for his sudden somber mood, Terrance fixed a smile on his lips as he pretended to listen to the ensign. The one-sided conversation lasted through a short elevator ride up to Deck Four and the walk to the entrance to Briefing Room Two. Knocking politely, the ensign opened the door and stepped to one side saying:

"I'll wait here for you. When you are finished I will escort you to your quarters, sir."

Terence mumbled a thank you as he stepped past him and entered the spacious briefing room where a balding, slightly chubby, harassed-looking lieutenant commander was surrounded by a sea of PADs.

"Lieutenant Terrance Wilson reporting for duty, sir." Terrance came to attention and saluted the executive officer.

The XO's head didn't rise from the PAD he was studying

as he waved a hand at tray of coffee and pastries at the far end of the table.

"Help yourself to some coffee, Lieutenant. I just have to finish this cargo-loading schedule update before another irate scientist demands that his precious science experiment gets priority loading over some other experiment. I swear, you would think that they thought we poor navy men had never prepared for a long cruise before."

Pouring himself a cup of the steaming brew, Terrance took a seat opposite the XO, taking the opportunity to study the oak-clad walls of the room, which were adorned with framed pictures of elegant sailing ships through early steam and turbine vessels to ultramodern, state-of-the-art gravity drive starships. Above the head of the table was a reproduction of Tycho Brahe, the Danish nobleman and astronomer the ship was named after. Tycho Brahe was most famous for his discovery of what became known as Tycho's Supernova in the constellation Cassiopeia, which burst into the Earth's sky in 1572. The sight of the austere Danish nobleman with his full beard and mustache staring down at Terrance with his fixed eyes completely engrossed Terrance and it took him a moment to become aware that the XO was now regarding him with an amused look on his face.

"Don't worry, Lieutenant, he has the same effect on all of us. I'm Lieutenant Commander Darel Apter, XO of our little flying observatory. The captain sends his apologies for not meeting you in person but he's been delayed in a meeting with Doctor Sarkisian and the department heads. Apparently there's a last-minute hitch with the Deployable Stellar Detection Grid and since the primary purpose of our mission is the detection and analysis of the evolution of stars, then the key piece of equipment we are going to use to detect those selfsame stars being kaput before we even start could mean we have a very short mission." Apter chuckled at his own joke and Terrance couldn't resist the urge to join in.

"But seriously. As far as your own work goes, only the captain, myself, Doctor Sarkisian, and Ensign Burkett, he's the one who escorted you here, know your true mission. Locating the star this so-called Creator extinguished. Your cover will be as liaison officer between the navy and the scientific staff on board. This should give you free access to any of the scientific departments and a plausible reason to speak directly with the captain and Doctor Sarkisian. Burkett may look like he belongs back in school but he already has degrees in astrophysics and cosmology and his IQ is probably the highest on the ship, with the exception of Doctor Sarkisian."

Never judge a book by its cover, Terrance reminded himself.

"The current mission parameters call for us to fold out to a point 500 light years from Durav where the DSDG will be deployed. Subsequent folds will be in the range of fifty light years until we reach a maximum of 2000 light years. If, as you speculated, a star with a red shift is detected, then we will decrease the distance of each fold and target destination until we ascertain the star's location. I must say, Doctor Sarkisian was not overly happy when the Department of Special Projects hijacked her expedition, but she cooled down some when it was explained to her the seriousness of the mission and, to be honest, I think she sees it as a bit of a challenge. Our best reckoning is each deployment of the DSDG and interpretation of the data it gathers should take about two weeks. Doctor Sarkisian reckons that we should know whether your theory holds water by the 1200 light year point so that would put us at week fourteen of the mission."

"My own best guess was between the 800 light year and 1200 light year window, sir, so it seems the good doctor and myself are singing off the same song sheet," agreed Terrance.

Apter stood and Terrance took this as his cue the meeting was over. "Once again, welcome aboard the *Tycho Brahe,* Lieutenant. Burkett will get you settled in and introduce you to the key department heads. If everything is on schedule, we can expect to fold out day after tomorrow."

CHAPTER EIGHTEEN
Direct Action

RUE MUZY - GENEVA – EARTH – SOL SYSTEM

"And you promise next time you will supply me the recipe for crispy eggplant and mozzarella, Roberto?"

"Ah, Signore Madkin, you know the recipe has remained a closely guarded family secret for generations, although, if the beautiful Signora Madkin was to grace my poor restaurant with her presence, I would be unable to resist her charms."

"I fail to see how your restaurant can be so poor with the prices you charge." Clement Bradshaw said in a deadpan voice.

Roberto looked aghast, his arms wide in fake affront. "Signore Bradshaw, I have many children to feed and my wife likes to enjoy the finer things in life. What is a man to do?"

All three men shared a knowing laugh as the stony-faced bodyguard held the restaurant door open and the chill of an early December night's wind pierced their heavy coats as though they were made of the thinnest paper.

Stepping out onto the sidewalk, both men were glad of the awning that hung off the building and protected patrons from the falling snow. The outside temperature was well below freezing and both men's attention was on the ground car and the warmth the vehicle's interior promised. Its rear door was being held open by a second bodyguard as the wind tried to push it closed again.

From an alley to the left came the loud, piercing cry of a cat. Madkin, Bradshaw, and the two bodyguards turned their heads in the sound's direction. It was an entirely natural reaction, one that anyone would have had, but it was also fatal.

Out of the shadows to the right, a nondescript figure stepped into the light flooding from the restaurant's large windows. He slipped the remote control for the noisemaker back into his left pocket and his right hand came up smoothly, the light glinting off the metal in his hand. The canopy over the restaurant's entrance prevented the assassin's preferred long-range shot, so he was forced to resort to the messier close-quarter assassination. More risk was involved, but his pay master had the funds to cover the added expenses and he had never failed to pay in full before. Besides, watching your target die close up was somehow more... fulfilling.

The trailing bodyguard never knew what hit him as a burst of supersonic, needle-sharp metal flechettes entered the back of his skull and exploded out the front, ripping his face to shreds as they exited, bone and brain barely slowing their progress.

Kris Madkin had once been a marine and the sound of a flechette pistol was one he had heard before and never expected to hear again. His survival instincts took control, adrenalin poured into his system as he grabbed Clement roughly by the coat collar and propelled his startled friend with all his might through the open rear door of the waiting car, crouching as he spun to face his attacker. He was just in time to see the second bodyguard cut down by a hail of flechettes, which turned his upper chest and throat into a mess of splintered bone and ripped flesh, the man's blood cascading from his body in a fountain of red, covering Kris' face and obscuring his view of the advancing angel of death.

The bodyguard's falling body landed heavily on Kris, knocking him to his knees and banging his head off the car door's edge. The pain of the impact was nothing compared to the sudden searing pain ripping through his left shoulder as another salvo of flechettes from the attacker sought to end him. Kris tried to stand but the dead weight of the bodyguard across his legs was preventing him. Kris went to push him off but only his right arm would respond and he felt his energy leaching from his body as his blood spilled out onto the sidewalk. Kris raised his chin and looked defiantly into the face of the assassin standing only a few feet from him. The business end of a flechette pistol was pointed squarely at his head.

"You should have stayed out of the way, Madkin. I might have let you live..." Whatever he was going to say next was forestalled by the driver's door opening as the final bodyguard made his move, PEP in hand. The driver's shot went wild and the assassin adjusted his aim to engage the new threat. A single thought screamed through Kris' brain. *I will not die here today! Not like this!* Summoning up the last of his failing strength, he pushed at the dead man's shoulder straddling his legs but it was no good, his rapidly weakening muscles failed him. Stars were beginning to dance in front of his eyes. The sweet embrace of unconsciousness was beckoning him. The limp bodyguard rolled back and his jacket fell open, revealing the PEP pistol partially drawn from its holster. The whining of the flechette pistol and a sudden cry signaled the end of the driver. With the last dregs of his being, Kris reached for the PEP, feeling its cold metal grip as his fingers wrapped around it. The restaurant lights were blocked out as the assassin leaned over his slumped body and a gravelly voice came faintly through the blood rushing in Kris' ears.

"Mr. Anderson sends his regards, Bradshaw..."

Kris pulled the trigger of the PEP. Once. Twice. Three times before blackness finally claimed him.

#

THE PRESIDENT'S PRIVATE RESIDENCE
OUTSKIRTS OF GENEVA - EARTH – SOL SYSTEM

The loud knocking on her bedroom door startled Rebecca Coston from her slumber. Sitting up, she rubbed the sleep from her eyes as she checked the illuminated clock on the bed stand. 0217.

Her husband Bill was away for the weekend, skiing in the Alps with their teenage children and she was taking the opportunity to get a rare early night. *So much for that idea*, she thought as she kicked off the bedclothes before shrugging on her robe. She padded over to the door and pulled it open.

Standing in the well-lit hallway was Joane Goode, Deputy Chief of Staff, and alongside her was Issac Sounder, head of the president's protection detail. Trepidation crept into Rebecca's still-groggy brain, "What is it, Joane?"

Joane's voice caught in her throat and she cleared it loudly. Seeing Joane struggling with whatever she wanted to say, Rebecca turned her attention instead to Issac. Issac had been head of her Presidential Office of Security detail since the first day she stepped into the shoes of retiring President McMullan. Rebecca had never known him to shy away from telling the facts, no matter how ugly they were. She expected nothing less right now.

"Madam President. Approximately thirty minutes ago, the POS communications center lost contact with Mr. Bradshaw's protection detail. While attempting to reestablish contact, they intercepted a call from local law enforcement reporting shots fired outside a restaurant. The restaurant was Mr. Bradshaw's last known location." Isaac took a breath.

"I authorized the immediate deployment of the POS Crash Team who were on scene within ten minutes. On arrival, they found all three agents of Mr. Bradshaw's detail dead. Senator Madkin is seriously wounded and is on his way to hospital for emergency surgery. His condition is unclear at this time. Mr. Bradshaw is shaken but unharmed. He refused to leave Senator Madkin's side, so I have Crash Team members in the ambulance with him and the remainder of the team will follow to secure the hospital until I can replace them with more discreet security."

Rebecca weakened at the knees. She held on to the doorframe for support. Clement Bradshaw was her oldest friend in politics and for sure he had been in the game a long time and made a lot of enemies along the way but that's what happens in politics. You don't extract revenge by killing someone.

"Who did this, Issac?"

"The attacker was also killed at the scene, Madam President."

"Well at least one of your men got him. Not much consolation, but it's something at least."

"The Crash Team leader believes it was actually Senator Madkin who killed him, Madam President. According to local police who were first on the scene they recovered a POS-issue PEP pistol from Senator Madkin's hand before he was transferred to the ambulance."

Despite the dreadful news of the loss of the agents, a wry smile formed on Rebecca's lips. "Once a marine, always a marine, Issac."

"Apparently so, Madam President."

Banishing the last wisps of sleep from her mind, Rebecca straightened herself up and began issuing orders. "Joane. Wake up the Director of the FIB, I want his best investigators on this and he is to make it his number-one priority. No excuses. Next I want you to arrange a meeting of the National Security Council for...Ah, call it eight AM. This attack is not only an attack on Clement Bradshaw, he is my Chief of Staff and therefore an integral part of my government, and that makes this an attack on the very fabric of our nation. I want to make it very clear to both the intelligence and the investigatory agencies that I will not abide any infighting when it comes to the hunt for whomever was behind this, because mark my words, there is someone else behind this."

"Yes, ma'am."

"Issac, I'm going to get dressed. By the time I am, I want transport waiting to take me to the hospital and you leave the Crash Team in place for a while. Maybe the sight of heavily armed, battle armored men will convince the world and whoever instigated this plan that I'm taking the death of three agents and the shooting of an Earth Senator seriously. Very seriously indeed."

Rebecca spun, the door slamming closed behind her,

heading toward the dressing room. Kill her agents and injure Madkin would they! Attempt to kill her oldest friend! *Somebody just made a huge mistake and I'll damn well make sure it's their last one.*

#

The presidential flyer landed amid a flurry of activity on the landing pad adjacent to the main entrance to Geneva General Hospital. The first of the security detail barely got his feet on the ground before Rebecca Coston was out of the flyer and striding off at a pace that was distinctly unsightly for a national leader.

The president and her entourage swept through the entrance and reception area like a tornado, leaving staff and visitors aghast at the site of the POS in a place that was usually calm. The first vid reports of the attack were only now being broadcast and people were looking from the large screens to the president in shock. Rebecca ignored them as she was ushered into an elevator with her detail. The rest of her entourage would just have to wait for the next one, or take the stairs.

When the doors opened, Issac stood to one side to allow the president to exit and her steps faltered as she was confronted by the sight of a seven-foot-tall, jet-black, armored monster holding an equally oversized plasma rifle in its armored gauntlets.

"The Crash Team are equipped with the latest issue marine Wraith suit, Madam President," Issac whispered in her ear.

Recovering her composure, Rebecca headed off down the corridor but came to a sudden halt at the sight of Clement Bradshaw flanked by two more armored giants with his head in his hands, sitting on a flimsy plastic chair, his clothing covered in blood . With no regard for presidential demeanor, Rebecca ran to him. Kneeling in front of him she gently took his blood-encrusted hands in hers.

"Clement, are you OK? You're covered in blood. Do you need to see a doctor?" Rebecca shared a swift look with Isaac who went to activate his comm to call for medical assistance but Clement's shaking head stopped him.

"It's not my blood Rebecca, it's Kris'. I did my best to stop the bleeding..." Clement's head lowered again and his voice dropped to a whisper. "...There was just so much of it. He just came out of nowhere. Just started shooting. Kris flung me into the car. Stood in the doorway. He used his own body to protect me, Rebecca." Clement's body shook as his body finally succumbed to the shock of the events that had occurred on the dark sidewalk. Rebecca took him in her arms, holding her quietly sobbing friend close. Eventually the sobs subsided and the older man wiped at his eyes with a blood-stained shirt cuff.

"He's gone too far this time, Rebecca. First Harriman and now this."

The president's face reflected her confusion. "I'm sorry, Clement. I don't understand. You know who ordered this?"

Clement fixed his eyes on Rebecca's and his voice was firm. "Seaton Anderson."

#

The room sat in deathly silence as the recording from the restaurant's security vid cameras replayed the scene from the street the night before. The would-be assassin appeared out of the darkened doorway before coldly and clinically taking down the two bodyguards. You could clearly see Kris Madkin throwing Clement Bradshaw into the safety of the vehicle before turning to face the attacker and then going down under the combination of the weight of the dying bodyguard and the attacker's fire. The driver's attempts to defend his charge and finally the attacker's slow, almost lackadaisical walk to the rear door to finish off Bradshaw before the assassin's body contorted unnaturally as Madkin fired his pistol. The video paused with the image of the assassin flying backwards under the impact of Madkin's shots. As the lights returned to normal, those gathered turned their heads to the head of the table and the impassive face of President Coston. They all knew that this was not a time to mince their words.

Edward Munro, FIB Director, was the first to speak. "Madam President. The assailant has been identified as this man." A holographic image of a thirty-something male appeared above the table, "Jordell Ferrett. Dishonorably discharged from the army after serving time for assaulting several members of his own platoon. He is a trained sniper and we believe that on his release he sold his skills to the highest bidder. The last few years he has kept a low profile. Rumor has it he now only takes on jobs for a single client who pays him to remain exclusive. Who that client is we have yet to ascertain..."

A raised hand from Rebecca stopped his narration. "Play the recording, Issac."

The POS agent tapped a key on his PAD and after a moment, a gravelly voice emanated from the room's speakers.

"Mr. Anderson sends his regards, Bradshaw."

Rebecca could see the shock on the faces of the gathered men and women. "This is an enhanced recording of what the microphone in the rear of the car picked up. It clearly identifies a 'Mr. Anderson' as the man behind this. I believe this man to be Seaton Anderson and your job is to get me a watertight case that will see Seaton Anderson sent to the deepest, darkest hole of a prison we possess. Not a word of what we know leaves this room. This individual has attacked the state and he will be treated as an enemy of the state and so will anyone helping him. Am I clear?"

The nodding heads and mumbled acknowledgments from around the table reassured Rebecca that they got the message. As she stood, the rest of the room got to its feet.

"I shall leave you to it, then."

Rebecca was met outside the room by Joane Goode who matched her pace as they headed back to the president's office.

"Senator Madkin is out of surgery and expected to recover well. With the pioneering nanite regeneration processes, the doctors expect him to regain full use of his left arm and shoulder within a few months. The doctors will keep him in for observation for a couple of weeks..."

Rebecca stopped walking and faced Joane. "Yes, yes, but the longer he spends in the hospital, the longer the presidential race is effectively being controlled by Grant, or should I say more correctly, Senator Dikul. By the time Kris is back on his feet, the race will be all but over. The question is... how do we keep Kris in the running? The vid reporters can't get anywhere near him in the hospital..."

"Excuse me, Madam President." Issac Sounder's unexpected interruption was something so rare, it took a moment for Rebecca to realize it was he who spoke.

"Of course, Issac, what is it?"

Issac looked unusually hesitant to speak, but when he

did he did so with his usual matter-of-fact voice. "The footage of the incident was taken from the vid cameras which are the property of the restaurant and the restaurant owner has no obligation under law to keep those recordings private. They are his to do with as he will."

The political machine that was the brain of Rebecca Coston whirred into action. "You, Issac, have missed your calling as a political hack! Joane, why don't you make a call to a few news outlets and happen to mention while giving them an update on Senator Madkin that the authorities are examining video recordings of the incident. That should be enough of a hint for them to start searching for the footage themselves. Let's see how Grant and Dikul try to spin footage of Madkin not only saving Clement's life by putting himself in the line of fire, but taking down the attacker while mortally wounded himself!"

For the first time that day, Rebecca felt the spring returning to her step.

CHAPTER NINETEEN
Fanning the Flames

SELENE SYSTEM - 272 LIGHT YEARS FROM EARTH

Sub Leader Norava adjusted his position in his command chair on the small flight deck of the Persai destroyer *Hovval*. It felt like he had been in the seat since time immemorial, but knew it had only been some fourteen hours by the ship's clock, which advanced ever so slowly. Only another two hours until he was relieved by his second in command, Tollan, and he could head off for some well-deserved sleep. Sitting on the edge of a system where the occupants had made it clear you were not welcome was not good for one's nerves. Never mind the fact that virtually every electronic system on the *Hovval* was closed down to minimize any chance of stray electronic emissions. This extended to the lighting on board and it had turned the whole ship into something resembling a cold, dark morgue. This thought brought a bare-toothed smile to his face. If the Turak caught them sneaking around out here, there was a very good chance the *Hovval* would indeed be his and his crew's final resting place. When the orders came down from the fleet for Norava to take his little destroyer to the Selene system, he had queried them but when he was informed the orders came directly from Chancellor Volak's office, he had immediately complied.

The *Hovval* had been floating here on the edge of the system for nearly two weeks now and his passive sensors were recording constantly. The four Turak cruisers which the humans faced down when the Turak had first made their appearance were long gone. In their place was what Norava was sure was a slow but steady naval buildup. Even at this extreme distance, the computers were able to tell him that the Turak were busily constructing an orbital station and surface support facilities. A space elevator was being built which would link the station to the surface and a steady flow of freighters emerged from fold space to dock with the station. Of more concern to Norava was the growing number of warships that were entering the system. *Hovval* was too distant to make out any sort of fine details, but the size and energy readings the ships were giving off put them in the heavy cruiser/smaller battleship range and there were a lot of them. Some twenty-five at the last update. The Commonwealth only knew the areas bordering the Commonwealth that the Turak laid claim to. They still had no idea of the true size of Turak space or what resources they were able to bring to bear, but from what he had observed it was apparent they fielded a significant navy.

An unexpected flurry of activity around the tactical section caught his eye.

"Report!" He called gruffly.

The fixed features of the section chief turned to face him as the remainder of the section continued to work frantically.

"Sub-leader, we are reading multiple nuclear explosions and energy weapons fire emanating from the area of the

Turak space station and the nearby shipping. Our passive equipment is not good enough to give a clear image of what exactly is happening but everything I am reading here points to a battle taking place."

Norava's boredom vanished instantly. "How long before we can get visual imagery?"

"6.2 hours at this distance, sub-leader."

"Very well. Ensure all recorders are running and I want the communications probe constantly updated in case we need to launch. Engineering. Get our drive back on line but keep energy output as low as possible. For the time being, we will wait and see what happens and hope no one stumbles across us."

#

The battle, and the sensor and imagery data left Norava in no doubt that that was what it had been, had ended eight hours ago. It had lasted less than twenty minutes. Norava could still picture the holographic images of mighty warships, their color as dark as night and weapons' pylons jutting out from the flattened, broad hulls as they emerged from fold space almost directly atop the Turak space station. Without hesitation, powerful grazers spat their murderous beams and the station rocked as the colossal amount of power contained within the energy fire lashed at the station's armor. In what seemed like only seconds, the station came apart under the intruders' withering fire. With the station gone, the warships switched their fire to the Turak ships. Norava could only imagine the blare of the alarms as the ships' crews raced to their battle stations. Many never reached them. A wave of missiles speared out from the black ships and caught the majority of the Turak before even their point defenses became operational. It was a slaughter. Ship after ship succumbed under the impact of nuclear-tipped missiles. Hulls buckled and failed. Explosions racked the damaged ships until they could withstand it no more and the ships and their crew joined those of the space station in the cold embrace of the long night. The few Turak ships that did manage to put up a fight did so in an uncoordinated and sporadic fashion. How they fought! Energy beams flashed across the vacuum of space to strike at the intruders. Missiles darted back and forth. In the end though, it was all for naught. The intruders' hulls seemed impenetrable. Energy weapons fire seemed to have no effect and nuclear detonations, which completely enveloped more than one of the intruders, were useless. The intruders emerged from the nuclear fire apparently undamaged. Outnumbered and outgunned, the remaining Turak soon joined their brothers. With the warships dealt with, the intruders split their force. One half began the methodical slaughter of the defenseless freighters, while the other half began a surface bombardment of the planet. The atmosphere was soon obscured by the radioactive dust clouds as debris was flung high into the stratosphere. Their mission of destruction completed, the intruders formed up once more and disappeared into fold space.

As the black angels of death fled the system, Tollan urged Novara to take the ship in closer to the planet. His second-in-command argued that now was a golden opportunity to recover pieces of the floating Turak debris. The intelligence that could be gathered from recovered hull plating, interior design, weapons and power systems and perhaps, the holy grail, complete or partial body parts. The Commonwealth still had no idea of the genetic make-up of the Turak and if Novara was to return to Pars with even a DNA strand, then the plaudits he would receive from the Chancellor would allow him to choose any ship he wished as his next command. Novara, however, wavered. He could see the benefits of Tollan's argument but against this he must way up the reaction time of the Turak. What if one of the destroyed Turak ships or the space station had managed to get off a communications drone and a Turak force was even now on its way here? The destroyer would be swatted like a fly by a single cruiser. No. Better to remain here at the fringes of the system and observe. Let us see how the Turak react and in what force. Tollan again voiced his opinion, as was his duty as second-in-command. Let them wait twenty-four hours before returning to Pars. If a Turak relief force had not arrived in the system by then, it was a safe bet it was not coming. Novara saw the logic of the suggestion, so the crew of the *Hovval* settled down for a tense wait.

The wait lasted less than an hour and a half. From fold space emerged a flotilla of the largest ships Novara had ever seen. Six behemoths, which made the smaller battleships and cruisers that surrounded them look like minnows swimming alongside whales. Novara had fought against the Others and he had seen their mighty Vulture class battleships up close but even those ships at 2300 meters long and weighing in at 330,000 tonne seemed medium-sized in comparison to these Turak vessels.

Without moving his eyes from the tactical hologram that showed the Turak flotilla, Novara called out to his Tactical section. "Tactical, tell me you're getting all this."

"Yes, Sub-leader. All data recorders are running... Standby! Aspect change! The Turak flotilla is dispersing... it looks like they intend on carrying out a sweep of the entire system, Sub-leader."

Novara had no intention of letting the Turak find him. "Navigation. Plot us a course for home and fold when ready." Novara sat back in his command chair with a sense of satisfaction edged with apprehension. The Chancellor had been correct in his decision to send the *Hovval* to keep watch on the Turak. The sensor data they had managed to gather was a veritable gold mine for the intelligence analysts, who would hopefully use it to identify the strengths and weaknesses of both the Turak and the mysterious black-finned warships. The appearance of the second flotilla of Turak ships was an unexpected bonus that had given them good sensor reads of the larger elements of the Turak fleet. The Chancellor's gamble had been well worth it. Time now to head home with their winnings. The familiar disorientation of the shift into fold space enveloped Novara as the *Hovval* vanished from the Selene system.

#

DAGGER STATION - ASTEROID BELT - GARUNDA SYSTEM

Rear Admiral Pallas was quietly pleased with the progress the construction crew were making on the station that would be the lynch pin in the defense of the Garundan system, not that he would ever let them know this. The Garundan admiral was always an unwelcome sight as he conducted his unannounced spot inspections of the nearly completed station and more than one construction foreman had been the object of his scathing remarks when one piece of welding or siting of framework was not up to his standards of excellence. Pallas cared naught for what the builders of Dagger Station thought of him. Garunda may still not have the vast industrial or technological base of some of the other planets of the Commonwealth, which was why Dagger Station was built in the system's asteroid belt rather than the Kuiper belt like its Terran equivalent, Gateway Station. No matter. He was determined to ensure his station would be seen as a shining example of how far Garundan technology had come from when humans had first introduced the people of Garunda to the wonders of space travel. Garunda would be forever in their debt. It was a measure of the high regard in which his planet and his people held the humans that this very station was named for the human frigate whose captain and crew had risked their very lives in the First Battle of Garunda to prevent the Others from laying waste to his home world.

With a touch of a key, his desk and the seat he was on began to rotate ninety degrees and one entire wall of his office receded into the roof to expose the humming brain of Dagger Station. The Central Operations room. Located at the very core of the massive station, rows of terminals manned entirely by native Garundans filled the expansive room, which was broken down into four key sections. One area was responsible for traffic control. Maneuvering and prioritizing shipping that intended to proceed sun-wards toward the inner system, or transship their cargo in one of the hundreds of large docking ports adorning the skin of the station. Another section commanded the growing fields of weapons platforms armed with ten centimeter grazers, high velocity anti-ship and anti-missile missiles and, more importantly, the buoys which generated the disruption field and which allowed no gravity drive ship to operate beyond the asteroid belt and extending inward to blanket the entire inner system. When completed, these weapons would form the outer shell of the station's defensive belt. Pallas still considered it an error not to equip the station with a Garundan home-grown version of a space fighter as the humans had their Gateway Station, but the men who held the purse strings informed the navy point-blank that there simply was not the money at this time to design and build a Garundan space fighter, so that was the end of the argument. A third section of the room housed the operators who controlled the station's integral weapons systems. Mounted on the hull of the station were over 200 heavy grazers, the like of which was found only on the heaviest Nemesis class battleship. Complementing the array of energy weapons were the armored missile silos, which covered the outer hull like sea barnacles. Their missiles were easily capable of hitting a target out to a range of three million kilometers from the station. And finally, there was the

Engineering section, which ensured the vital organs of the station, the power plants which supplied the light and heating, the atmospheric recycling plants which provided air for all aboard to breathe and the thousand and one other things which were required to sustain life in the inhospitable habitat of space. This station would be the most powerful piece of military hardware anywhere in the quadrant when it was completed. The thought brought a frown to Pallas' forehead. He knew more than most that until the station was completed, it was still vulnerable. This was why he had requested Vice Admiral Kerta to station elements of Third Fleet adjacent to Dagger Station until such time as Pallas was satisfied the station was fit to take over the role of guardian to the gateway of the Garundan system. The sight of BatFor 3.2 floating serenely 500,000 kilometers from the station was one Pallas was glad to see. Only another three or four months, and the station would be able to dispense with their protection. Pallas sighed quietly to himself as he touched the key that would lower the wall back into place while he returned to the reports that were stacked on his terminal and seemed to grow more numerous every day.

A few tedious hours later and Pallas was ready for a break. The digital clock showed it was early afternoon and the admiral decided to sample the fare of the officers' mess. Closing down his terminal, he stood and stretched his weary muscles. *Too much time sitting at your desk, Pallas* he berated himself mentally, promising himself an hour in the gym later in the day. He headed out of his office and it was only a short walk to the elevator bank, which would whisk him up the twelve levels to the mess. He was a few short steps from the elevator when the screaming of the battle station's alarm resounded down the corridor. Spinning on his heel, he quickly retraced his steps, entering Central Operations just as the solid weight of the battle armor door slid into place with a loud bang, sealing the room off from the outside. Striding through the sea of sailors still scrambling to their posts, Pallas made a beeline for the duty command officer's position located on a raised gantry giving them a commanding view of the entire room.

Commander Oolas was the duty officer this shift and as Pallas approached he could see Oolas' head darting from side to side as he rattled off orders into his pick-up while his fingers were a blur on his terminal's keypad as he tried desperately to assess all the information threatening to swamp him. Pallas stepped up beside him and his experienced eye quickly assessed the situation. A large group of ships that the computers were designating warships had entered normal space two million kilometers from the station. Sensors indicated a surge in power output indicative of weapons systems coming on line. BatFor 3.2 was coming to battle stations in response as every freighter that thought it might end up in the line of fire was maneuvering wildly to clear the combat area. According to the terminals tell-tales, the fields of weapons platforms were bringing their grazers to full power and the missile platforms were signaling they were ready to accept targeting data. Weapons crew on the station itself were buttoning up as fast as they could and slowly but surely the status lights were blinking from standby to ready. Pallas tapped a key on his wrist comm, patching him into the command net. The sudden cacophony of voices made him flinch involuntarily. It seemed like every captain of every ship, be it military or civilian, was attempting to speak at the same time, with the result that one call was cutting up the preceding call, so no one could get a complete message through. Scanning the board in front of him, Pallas found the key he was looking for and depressed it with gratefully. Instantly, all conversation ceased as the powerful transmitters of the station blanketed the airwaves with an ear-piercing two second whine. This was the warning that a priority transmission was imminent and all others were to cease their use of the communications link.

"Attention all ships. A number of unidentified vessels have entered the military exclusion zone. Until such times as their intentions can be clarified, all civilian shipping is to forthwith move into staging areas Alpha and Gamma and await further instructions. That is all. Dagger Station clear."

As the civilian traffic moved to comply with his instructions, Pallas turned his attention back to his unannounced visitors.

"Computers are calling them fourteen battleships, twenty cruisers, and thirty-two smaller ships, possibly destroyers or frigates, Admiral. BatFor 3.2 is moving to intercept and Admiral Tolo is transmitting in the clear that he welcomes them to Garunda and requests they state their intentions...."

Pallas was mesmerized by the ships' strange flattened hulls with the vertical pylons extending above and below the main body. Their color of space-black made it hard to make any details out by eye alone. When Oolas stopped his report in mid-sentence he turned his head to see a confused look cross the commander's face. "Something wrong, Commander?"

Oolas worked his terminal for another few seconds before replying. "Fire Control are having a hard time getting a solid lock sir... We're not detecting any active ECM from them but something is definitely interfering with our systems..."

Pallas leaned closer to the commander's shoulder to check the computer readouts himself when, without warning, the intruders opened fire. The battleships' energy weapons reached out across the distance separating them from BatFor 3.2 and wherever they touched they left devastation in their wake. Two Nemesis battleships were pierced through and through by thick, green beams and in a heartbeat they and their crews were nothing more than expanding clouds of debris.

Pallas struggled to keep his voice level as he gave his next order. "Platform weapons free, Commander. Fire at will."

Seconds passed slowly as the order to fire was transmitted to the platforms and in those vital seconds another three Garundan ships shook and shuddered before succumbing to the lethal, energy fire and exploding in violent fireballs, the remains spinning off into the night.

But the enemy did not get it all their own way. Individual ships of BatFor 3.2 began to return fire, fire which increased rapidly as ship after ship joined in. Energy fire crisscrossed the space between the two fleets, the distance closing as BatFor 3.2 pressed closer and closer.

"Where are my platforms, Commander? We need to get into this fight!" Shouted Pallas in frustration.

"We can't get a target lock, Admiral!" Cried Oolas.

More Garundan ships fell to the black monsters who just hung there, holding their ground, making no attempt to maneuver. An action that flew in the face of all the rules of space warfare. *Well, if they are just going to sit there in one big bunch*, thought Pallas.

"Forget targeting individual ships. Concentrate your energy fire on the center of mass and fire. Flush the missiles and program them for proximity detonation. If we don't do something soon, then our ships are finished."

Finally the station's weapons platforms belched fire into

the heart of the enemy. A single, hapless enemy battleship was unlucky enough to be at the intersection of the massed ten centimeter grazers. The resulting explosion briefly illuminated that entire section of space as if it possessed its own mini star before dissipating.

"They are moving, Admiral! Headed straight for us"

"What about the missiles, Commander? How much damage are they doing?"

"Ah... minimal, sir. We have confirmed detonations but we are seeing no damage to the enemy ships. Sensors are reporting what appears to be some sort of strange energy field enveloping each ship. It's deflecting the blasts."

"And our ships?"

When Oolas failed to answer, Pallas grabbed him by the arm and shook him. "Commander! Our ships, what are they doing?"

Pallas watched in horror as the blood drained from Oolas' face. "They're gone, sir. They have all been destroyed."

Pallas released the commander's arm and used his now free hand to steady himself against the terminal, his mind numbed by the news that an entire BatFor had just been erased from existence in front of his eyes. His gaze fell to the status boards and the gaggle of freighters in the staging areas. If the intruders could defeat top of the line Garundan warships so easily, the freighters would be easy meat. Reaching past the commander, Pallas keyed the all-ships link.

"Attention all ships. This is Admiral Pallas, Commanding Officer Dagger Station. You are ordered to evacuate this area of space at best speed. I do not believe we can contain the enemy ships. Good luck. Pallas clear."

"Vampire! Vampire! Enemy missile separation!" Pallas' head snapped up at the call and he focused on the tactical display, expecting to see waves of missiles headed toward the station. Instead, a single, blinking red icon closed rapidly on the station. Laser defense clusters spun in their turrets to engage the approaching missile but once more the computers failed to get a solid lock and so refused to fire. Oolas moved to command the computers to override and use barrage fire to bring down the missile, but it was too late.

The flash of light was reminiscent of a mini supernova as the anti-matter warhead detonated and the millions of tonnes of space station representing the peak of Garundan technological and engineering innovation was swallowed whole by the wave of superheated plasma and expanding gas. The pressure wave expanded rapidly from the point of detonation and struck those civilian freighters which had not immediately heeded the admiral's warning. Their hulls crumpled and broke apart before being swept into the asteroid belt with the wave which turned mountains of rock into dust as it passed.

The silent, black intruders sat perfectly still as the all-powerful wave approached them. The wave roared over them and continued on its way to reveal the black ships sitting as pristine as they had been before the wave engulfed them. A faint sparkling-like residual electricity flickering along their hulls.

Without a word, the black fleet pivoted and accelerated into fold space.

CHAPTER TWENTY

Seeds of Confusion

PARS - PERSEUS ARM - 6400 LIGHT YEARS FROM EARTH

Force Leader Tolas was ushered into the private office of Chancellor Volak for what Tolas believed was an unscheduled security briefing of the Chancellor following the attack on the Garundan system two days previously. Two days, which had seen Tolas travel aboard the lead Persai cruiser of the flotilla which the Chancellor authorized deployed at the request of the Commonwealth Council. Earth, Janus, and Benii had all made similar gestures of support and now a full Commonwealth fleet patrolled the space around the Garundan system while Garunda's own Third Fleet in orbit around Garunda remained on high alert. Tensions were running high throughout the Commonwealth and Tolas had been forced to squash rumors among his own staff that perhaps these mysterious black ships were some form of Alonan Empire secret weapon or possibly a Turak first strike. Having seen the devastation in Garunda for himself, Tolas requisitioned a courier ship to take him to Earth, where he met with the Chairman of the Combined Joint Chiefs of Staff, Admiral Jing. The meeting had seen more level heads discuss the situation. The sensor data which had been hastily cobbled together from the civilian freighters which survived the attack had been analyzed and it quickly become apparent that these black ships were of the same design and gave off the same power signatures as those which carried out the massacre of the Alonan colonists on Balat eight months previously. As far as Jing was concerned, this ruled out the Empire as a likely suspect. This then only left the Turak or an as-yet-unknown third party. Tolas and the other members of the Joint Chiefs could not fault Jing's logic but that still did not solve the strategic problem of where this enemy may strike next. The meeting ended with the unanimous decision to increase patrolling among the colonies bordering Turak and Commonwealth space, while bringing the various home fleets to an increased state of preparedness. With nothing further to be done at this stage, Tolas boarded a ship and returned to Pars to review his own fleet's defensive posture and update the Chancellor.

Perhaps it was the two days of traveling interspersed with the intense meetings and staff planning sessions, but as Tolas entered the room, he did not immediately notice the small, for a Persai, figure of Caran, head of the Persai intelligence service, seated in the shadow of the open door. As it swung closed, Caran literally jumped to his feet to welcome Tolas, startling him and getting Caran a fanged, deep throated growl before Tolas recognized him and realized he was in no danger.

"My apologies, Chancellor, Caran. I expected to be meeting with you alone."

Chancellor Volak let out a short, barking laugh. "No apology required, Force Leader Tolas. Caran here seems to excel in surprising people and it is for this very reason that I have called you here today. Please sit. Caran, if you would."

"Of course, Chancellor." Tolas took his seat, wondering what nugget of intelligence the spy chief was in possession of which got him a private audience with the Chancellor and the head of the Persai armed forces. Caran remained standing, taking a step to one side to clear the floor-mounted holographic projector, while drawing a small control from his sleeve as he did so. The image of the four black ships that had carried out the raid on the world of Balat appeared.

"Chancellor..." began Caran. "These are the images supplied to us by the Humans of the ships the surveillance platform observed in the Balat system, some 60000 light years from Pars. At this stage, I have no doubts as to the veracity of these images..."

"I'm sorry, but why would we even consider doubting these images? The Humans are our allies. We fought side by side with them throughout the long war against the Others," interrupted Tolas, a tone of incomprehension in his voice.

Volak tapped a long finger on his desk, garnering Tolas' attention. "Force Leader, please let Caran continue. All will become clear momentarily."

"Thank you, Chancellor. As I was saying, we have a visual image of the warships and the Humans supplied us with the sensor records, so we were able to get a good read on their power and weapons signatures. Now this..." A touch of the control and the image changed to the blurry readings from a much lower-grade sensor package. "This is the image we have managed to download from one of our own freighters that was actually present during the attack on Dagger Station and managed to escape. My people have confirmed that although the visual image is of poor quality, the power and weapons signatures are identical to those that were employed at Balat..."

Tolas interrupted again, his frustration obvious by his tone. "We know all this, Caran. I have received the same briefings on Earth by Admiral Jing's intelligence staff."

"Indeed, Force Leader. Indeed. But what you have not seen is this." With a flourish that would have done the best stage magician proud, Caran waved an arm at the floating hologram and touched the controller. The frozen scene of battle was unmistakable. Mighty warships were hacking away at each other with powerful energy beams while missiles darted among the deadly beams as they sought out their prey. Tolas rose from his seat and walked slowly toward the image as if in a hypnotic trance. Halting before the image, he studied it in minute detail. After a few moments, he turned to Caran and this time his voice held the urgent tone of a man demanding answers.

"Where did you get this from, Caran? Those black ships are identical to the ones that attacked Garunda but those are not Garundan ships they are fighting. Those are Turak."

The spy's face remained implacable. "The intelligence services ran an operation which placed a Persai ship on the outer edge of the Selene system to observe Turak movements in the system. Three days ago, the ship was a witness to this attack and the Turak response to it."

Tolas spun on the smaller intelligence man, making no attempt to hide his anger. "You used one of my ships to spy on the Turak! Are you mad? I gave strict orders no Persai ship was to enter into Turak space without my explicit approval. You know as well as I the Turak have already made it quite clear that any infringement on their territory will be met by force. Are you trying to start a war? How dare you..."

"Enough, Force Leader." The raised voice of the Chancellor cut Tolas' vitriolic tirade off in mid-sentence. "I approved the operation personally and, seeing the results, I am glad I did so. Does this not prove beyond doubt that the Turak were not responsible for the Garundan attack? Indeed, they too have been the victims of these mysterious black ships."

Tolas felt the anger leeching from him. The Chancellor was correct. The question now was what to do with the information.

"We must share this with the other members of the Commonwealth immediately, Chancellor. If the Turak think we were responsible for the events in the Selene system, then they may decide to launch an assault on the Commonwealth at any time. And if they do, we will find ourselves in a war neither of us started. It is the story of the Nilmerg and the Deres all over again."

"Something that I would hope nobody on either side wishes for, Force Leader." Chancellor Volak intoned solemnly as he stood up and walked around his desk. He placed his powerful hand on Tolas' shoulder while giving Caran a barely perceptible nod. Caran handed a small data crystal to Tolas, who took it and looked at it quizzically as the Chancellor spoke.

"The data crystal holds all the sensor readings and imagery taken by our ship in the Selene system. A courier ship is waiting to take you back to Earth. Share the data with our allies. They and the Turak need to know who was responsible for what happened at Selene."

Tolas bowed deeply to his Chancellor and with a passing nod to Caran, he headed for his waiting ship.

#

OFFICE OF THE PRESIDENT – GENEVA
EARTH – SOL SYSTEM

Rebecca Coston was still contemplating the short briefing she had just sat through with Admiral Jing and Secretary Aaron Beckett. The data gathered by the Persai had come as a bombshell to the military planners. Admiral Jing was sure the Turak's next move would be to strike at the Commonwealth and, having seen the size and power of the Turak ships which arrived in the Selene system in response to the black ships' attack, he insisted the president seek an immediate meeting with the other heads of the Commonwealth to call for a resolution to instigate a state of emergency. Such a resolution would give the military priority on all engineering and manufacturing facilities, release all budgetary constraints, and allow the local military commanders power to overrule minor and mid-level government officials. Rebecca saw the need to implement the admiral's demands but it was a move that, in the dying days of her presidency, was something she did not want to be her legacy. Instead she agreed to a further raising of the alert level which called for the cancellation of all leave and training. The Terran Defense Forces moved onto what by any other name was a war footing. A disgruntled Jing had been tempered by the president's decision, realizing this was as far as the politician was willing to go which was why her next decision caught him somewhat by surprise although it really should not have. Rebecca directed Aaron Beckett to assemble a diplomatic mission, which would be dispatched forthwith to the Selene system to make contact with the Turak and share the Persai data with them. Her hope was that by sharing the information with the Turak, she could forestall any misguided retaliation. Jing's initial reaction had been to argue with her. Revealing the Persai data would only confirm the Commonwealth had indeed been spying on them and it would also give the Turak the chance to assess the level of

Commonwealth surveillance technology. In the end though, he was forced to admit the diplomatic mission should be given a chance to succeed. They had all seen the imagery of the massive Turak warships that the Persai witnessed appearing in the Selene system and Jing was in no hurry to send his forces up against the firepower those ships represented.

The meeting ended and Rebecca had been left alone for a few moments. Her isolation came to an end as there was a polite knock on her door and the Deputy Chief of Staff, Director of the FIB, Attorney General, and the Secretary of Defense were shown into her office. Joane Goode steered the group toward the compact conference table off to one side and they all waited politely while Rebecca left her desk to join them at the head of the table. Sitting, she indicated for the others to do the same before she spoke.

"Ladies and gentlemen, I called you here today for an update on the assassination attempt on Clement Bradshaw and I intend to keep this down to the pertinent facts only, no sugar-coating and no procrastination. Understood?"

Nods of understanding from the Director and the AG, while Joane Goode sat motionless and Olaf Helsett, Secretary of Defense, kept his own counsel. The request for his presence at this meeting had come as he was about to board a naval courier for an inspection tour, which would give the official seal of approval signaling the activation of Admiral Radford's long-anticipated CSG *Itus*. Olaf had actually been looking forward to seeing the Mosquito space fighters going through their paces but when the president calls, everything else is put on hold. Sitting now with the FIB Director and the AG, he had to admit that the sense of bewilderment on first arriving at the president's office was not dissipating.

"Go ahead Edward, let's hear it."

"Madam President. My investigators have managed to trace bank deposits to Jordell Ferrett from a number of dummy corporations. The trail is complicated and so far the investigators have seized the records of fourteen shell companies. There is still a long way to go before we will have a rock-solid case, years possibly, but everything I have seen so far points at the money man being someone high up in the Zurich Lines hierarchy. The problem will be proving it."

The president shifted her gaze to the Attorney General. "Is what the Director has, along with the audio recording, enough?"

Olaf Helsett looked sharply from the president to the AG, his mind racing to catch with the conversation. Audio recording. What audio recording? This was the first he had heard of such a recording existed.

Edvard Dietel had been one of the most well-respected prosecutors in the business before his appointment as AG, so his uncharacteristic hesitation was not missed by those seated at the table. "Madam President. Seaton Anderson has the best legal team money can buy. They have managed to tie the courts up in so much legal red tape over the episode with Daya Thomas that we'll be lucky if he ever sets foot in a courtroom and unless the FIB can get a written confession out of him then I have no doubt our efforts to link him to the assassination attempt will be equally fruitless."

Rebecca expected as much but she needed to hear it from the horse's mouth. Pushing herself back from the table Rebecca brought herself to her feet. The others all stood in response.

"Thank you for your candor. Joane will see you out. Olaf, if you could remain for a moment, please."

As Rebecca and Olaf were left alone in the room the

Secretary of Defense could no longer contain himself. "You think Seaton Anderson was behind this, Madam President?"

Rebecca screwed her eyes closed and a hand went to her brow. The weight of what was coming next hung heavily on her. "Ferrett named Anderson before Kris killed him."

Olaf was lost for words. The revelation that Seaton Anderson was behind the attempt to kill a presidential candidate and a sitting president's Chief of Staff was inconceivable. While Olaf processed the information, Rebecca moved behind her desk and pulled open the top drawer, retrieving a PAD. Lifting it to eye level, the PAD automatically activated an iris scanner confirming that Rebecca was who she said she was before holding the PAD out to Olaf, who took it in slightly clammy hands.

"The PAD contains a Presidential Finding that Seaton Anderson presents a clear and present danger to the state and authorizes the Secretary of Defense to take executive action against Seaton Anderson at the earliest opportunity."

Olaf raised his eyes from the PAD and into those of his president. His own eyes hardened as he saw the steel will behind hers. It was not the first time Olaf had held the fate of a man in his hands. He had spent virtually all his adult life in the navy sending men and women under his command into battle. This, though, was something else; but his president was giving him an order and he would carry it out, so he answered in the only way he knew how to:

"Aye-aye, Madam President."

CHAPTER TWENTY-ONE

Out of the Shadows

EDGE OF THE ASTEROID BELT - SOL SYSTEM

"Sir, there it is again. I know we're flying awfully close to some of these rocks but I would bet my last credit that what I'm seeing is not a sensor ghost, it's a ship hiding out there hoping the metal in the surrounding asteroids will hide it from us. They must be operating on minimal power. Our passives aren't detecting any unusual electromagnetic radiation so I'll bet they're using only their passive systems just like us. They probably have no idea we're even here."

Lieutenant Commander Celene Yasuda and the destroyer TDF *Tiger Shark* had been doing a routine clearance patrol of the asteroid belt four million kilometers from Gateway Station when the Tactical Station alerted her to what they first designated a sensor ghost. Yasuda was under strict orders to investigate every anomaly, so *Tiger Shark* cautiously entered the asteroid field and began its search. Seven hours later, it looked like she was coming to the end of her hunt.

"Very well. XO bring the ship to battle stations. Tactical, let's light everything up, go active on all sensors." The battle station's alarm whooped through the destroyer as, from the fire control systems, tens of thousands of watts of energy poured out, blanketing the surrounding asteroids.

"Target identified! Bogey One. Small craft low on the starboard bow. Range... 700 meters... Power spike! Computer is calling it weapons coming on line."

Yasuda struggled to keep the excitement from her voice as her brain involuntarily ordered the dumping of adrenalin into her system. "Arm forward plasma cannon and fire as she bears!"

"Target acquired... Firing... A hit! Power readings dropping. Bogey One appears to be tumbling out of control sir."

"Cease fire. Navigation brings us alongside. XO let's get the magnetic grapples ready, we'll drag the ship clear of these rocks and see what we have here."

The operation to tow the damaged ship clear of the asteroid belt was a precarious and time-consuming one, which called for all the skill of the *Tiger Shark's* navigator. Five hours of gentle nudging and pulling saw the *Tiger Shark* and her prize floating freely in open space, allowing the XO and his salvage team to don armored space suits and carry out a much more detailed, hands-on inspection of the little ship. Yasuda sat nervously in her command chair, her eyes glued to the holographic projection floating in the center of the bridge as it relayed what the XO's helmet cam was seeing.

"There's a lot of damage to the outer hull, Skipper. Looks to me like our cannon most likely impacted the asteroid they were hiding on and they were hit by flying debris. From the number of strikes, I doubt very much if any of the crew survived."

The damage the XO was referring to was obvious on the camera view. The matte-black, once-smooth surface of the craft was now torn asunder by hundreds, probably thousands of high velocity impacts. The hull had taken on the consistency of a good Swiss cheese.

"Have you identified a hatch yet, XO?"

The camera panned to the left and another space-suited figure came into view a few meters more to the rear of the ship. The figure was bent over a blinking control panel and was working away with a cutter.

"Chief Santos thinks she’s identified an airlock and reckons it’s still got some power flowing into it. Perhaps from some emergency backup, because we're getting minimal power readings. If she can get it working, we can avoid cutting our way through the hull."

"OK, XO, let’s see if the chief can get it open. If not, we go back to Plan A and cut our way in."

Chief Santos was as good as her word and only minutes later the hatch she was working on slid smoothly aside to reveal an airlock just big enough for two space-suited humans. The XO and Chief Santos squeezed in and the outer door closed, but the inner door stayed resolutely closed as well. The chief worked her magic again and the inner door opened to give them their first view of the cramped interior of the small craft illuminated by the bright lights mounted on the spacesuit helmets. Here and there the occasional panel flickered with the last gasp of power.

"This corridor appears to run the length of the ship, Captain. We're going to follow it and see if it leads to some sort of cockpit or bridge."

As the XO and the chief advanced steadily down the narrow corridor, Yasuda caught glimpses of what could have been a galley and sleeping accommodation. *This ship was definitely not built for comfort,* thought Yasuda.

The corridor came to an end and another sealed hatch faced them. Chief Santos bent to work and after a short time, the hatch began to move, only to halt after a few centimeters. Yasuda watched as the XO and the chief managed to get their armored fingers into the opening and through the bridge speakers came grunting sounds as the two suited figures pried the door open with sheer muscle power. As the gap slowly widened, a dark object floated through from beyond the door, startling the two humans who jumped back in surprise. Yasuda was on the edge of her seat as she strained to make out what it was.

The XO stepped forward, his helmets harsh lights bringing the object into stark relief. It was a body. The XO slowly spun the body until the camera was able to get a clear image of the face. A face covered in light brown fur, two round eyes set in a slightly pointed heads with the ears mounted higher up the head than a human's. The mouth and nose protruding slightly. A short thick neck leading to a barrel chest. Yasuda knew that her mouth was agape with total astonishment but right now she did not care if anyone saw her. If she had taken the time to look, she would have seen no one on the bridge was paying her any attention. Every eye was fixed on the holograph as it showed the image of a body of a member of what humanity thought to be a long-dead race. The Saiph!

#

CENTRAL COMMAND - MONT SALÈVE - EARTH

President Rebecca Coston and Admiral Ai Jing sat in

silence as the video recording from the *Tiger Shark* replayed for the third time. As it reached its conclusion and the corpse of the dead Saiph was replaced by the steady image of the Terran Federation flag, Rebecca absentmindedly rubbed her eyes.

"There's no doubt?"

Patricia Bath, standing off to one side, answered the president's question. "None, Madam President. DNA samples are a 100 percent match. The three bodies recovered are Saiph."

The room lapsed back into silence as the president struggled to assimilate the new reality. The race that had been responsible for ensuring every member of the Commonwealth and the Alonan Empire came to be the top of their planet's evolutionary chain was still out there amongst the stars. Those same benefactors were responsible for the deaths of the colonists on Balat, the destruction of Dagger Station, and attacking the Turak in the Selene system. The same two questions kept coming to Rebecca. Where have they been and why come out of hiding now? No matter how hard Rebecca wracked her brain, the answers would not come to her.

"Madam President. The Saiph ship has been shipped to Zarmina, hopefully Doctor Moore and his team will be able to shed some light on this mystery. The ship did suffer extensive damage, but we hope to be able to recover some useful data from the undamaged systems. At this point, anything which may be useful in combating their ships would be invaluable."

Rebecca spun to face Jing. "You really think it is going to come down to a shooting war between the Commonwealth and the Saiph, Admiral?"

Jing kept his face impassive and his tone neutral. "I would say we were already in a shooting war, Madam

President. The attacks on Dagger Station and the Turak had to have been coordinated. They were obviously designed so the Turak would think we attacked them while we were meant to believe the attack on Dagger Station was the Turak. Tensions were already running high in both camps. It would only require a single spark for the whole border area to burst into flames."

"I don't see how Balat fits into it. The Alonan Empire is 60000 light years away, what possible gain would they reap for destroying an Alonan colony?"

The admiral shrugged his shoulders. "To draw off resources. Make us station ships around Waypoint 4 for fear the Empire decide to blame us for Balat and retaliate. Whoever is in charge of these Saiph is obviously attempting to start a three-way war between the Commonwealth, the Empire, and the Turak. When it's all over, the Saiph can just roll in and take over."

"You really think it's that bad?" Asked Rebecca, knowing she was not going to like the answer.

"Madam President, the Saiph took out Dagger Station with one missile. One! The Turak at Selene didn't even scratch their paintwork!"

"But the Garundans destroyed one of their cruisers."

"Yes they did, Madam President. With the combined fire of a dozen or more grazer platforms. We have to face facts. We have nothing in the fleet that could stand toe-to-toe with them and come out on top."

Rebecca felt the clouds of despair enshrouding her. "Worse case, Admiral. If the Saiph arrived in the Sol system today, what are our chances?"

Jing did not answer immediately as he ran the numbers in his head. With a barely noticeable clearing of his throat, he faced Rebecca. "Our system defenses are the strongest in the Commonwealth and I am confident if a force equivalent to what the Garundans faced were to attempt to engage Gateway Station, then we could defeat them."

Rebecca's mind's eye saw the first rays of sunshine break through the clouds, until Jing spoke again.

"But that would not be enough, Madam President. Earth can't just hide behind its defenses while the rest of the Commonwealth and our colonies burn. We need to meet them on the field of battle and defeat them. Prove to our people, the Commonwealth, the Empire, and the Turak that the Saiph are not almighty. We need to take the fight to them."

"We need to find them first, Admiral." Patricia's comment was followed by a stony silence, she saw Jing ignoring her and keeping his eyes locked on Rebecca. The president gave the admiral a slow nod before Jing turned to face Patricia.

"Doctor. What I am about to tell you is highly classified. Some months ago, the navy began a covert operation which we called Project Bright Star..."

#

TDF TYCHO BRAHE - INTERSTELLAR SPACE 900 LIGHT YEARS FROM EARTH

Lieutenant Terrance Wilson sat patiently as the inbuilt encryption program on his terminal decoded the latest coded message from Central Command. The ready tone sounded and Terrance brought up the message:

'From: Chairman, Combined Joint Chiefs of Staff

To: Lieutenant Wilson, TDF *Tycho Brahe*

Message begins:

Project Bright Star is now the priority. Cease all other activities until mission objective is achieved.

Message ends.'

CHAPTER TWENTY-TWO

The Dragon's Den

TDF CUTLASS - SELENE SYSTEM
272 LIGHT YEARS FROM EARTH

TDF *Cutlass* emerged from fold space at the outer fringes of the Selene system and broadcast its hail. Nicholas Schamu understood the risk in sending a Commonwealth cruiser into the system but he agreed with Aaron Beckett, in all likelihood the information held on the PAD, resting in the inside pocket of his impeccable tailored suite, contained the last and best chance of avoiding war.

"Turak ships exiting fold space at 186 mark 4 distance 15000 kilometers, Captain. Its four heavy cruisers, sir, and their weapons are," the tactical officer scanned his screens, " coming online."

"Keep a cool head, Lieutenant. Double check our sensors. I don't want us transmitting a single erg which may be mistaken for a fire and control system," spinning in her command chair an anxious Denise Parks faced Nicholas, "all yours Ambassador, if this doesn't work they've got us cold."

Nicholas gave a small cough before depressing the stud on his chair which activated the voice link. "Turak vessels, this is Ambassador Nicholas Schamu. I carry important information concerning the identity of those who are responsible for the attack on your ships in the Selina system, which I wish to share with you. I am transmitting the data now." The data flew across the empty void and Nicholas prayed the Turak would take time to review the data before blowing the *Cutlass* out of space.

Interminable seconds passed and became minutes while Nicholas and the crew of the *Cutlass* held their collective breaths. After an eternity a single word response arrived.

"Standby."

#

The bridge crew fiddled and fussed over their terminals. Captain Parks browsed the ship's daily reports, although, Nicholas noted, the same static page displayed on the captain's screen for the last fifteen minutes. Even Nicholas, a life-long diplomat and used to hours of patient waiting neared the end of his tether. An over five hour standby tether.

The comms officer broke the monotony. "Incoming signal, Captain. It's a set of coordinates and instructions to fold immediately."

"Show me the coordinates," Parks squinted at the main holo display, "mmm... must be almost 150 light years from our current location which takes us well inside Turak controlled space. Navigation, any idea what's at the coordinate's location?"

The navigator ran through the star charts and found the correct system. "The coordinates are a match for system 90159. It's a star much like our own sun but older. That's all,

Captain, no further references found in either the Saiph or Commonwealth databases."

Captain Nicholl wrinkled her nose as she often did when faced with a difficult decision and, after glancing once more at the holo cube, she turned to face Nicholas, "Well, Ambassador, it's your call."

Nicholas ignored the ominous wrinkle, not one to squander his invitation to begin dialog with the Turak he said, "Captain, we should comply with the Turak request."

"Folding 150 light years further into space," her wrinkle deepened, "held by a race who threaten to destroy us if we infringe their territory," she shifted in her seat, "Ambassador, I'm far from happy, but that's why we're here." She spun her seat forward. "Navigator, plot the coordinates and fold when ready. Let's do this." The *Cutlass* surged forward into fold space and disappeared from the Selene system.

"All stop!" called the captain as the ship blinked back into existence 150 light years away, in the heart of system 90159.

"All stop, aye."

"Tactical. Let's scan the area and see where they've brought us."

Sensors gathered data at lightning speed, passed the information to the ship's computers for parsing and projection to the main holo cube.

In all its glory, the surrounding space revealed a sheer cacophony of energy and mass returns which brought silence, broken only with gasps of surprise from the bridge crew. The tactical officer broke the temporary quiet.

"My god! This has to be one of their main worlds. Check out the shipping! I don't remember seeing the space around Earth being so busy. I'm reading a mix of civilian and military ships. Computer has identified three of the monsters the Persai observed in the Selene system, after the black ships attack, holding station amongst a number of smaller ships. Ha! And by smaller I mean Bismarck class battleship size. This suggests a major fleet base, excluding the space stations orbiting the nearest planet, two of them make Fortress Command resemble a kid's toy."

Captain Parks hovered on the edge of her seat as she sucked in the information displayed in the holo cube. "Tactical, concentrate your efforts on the warships. Let's get as many passive scans as we can, if the ambassador's mission fails we may be fighting these guys pronto."

"Please, Captain, let us not be so pessimistic at this early juncture." Nicolas said.

"Captain," The comms officer halted what would have been Parks' snappy return. "Message from the orbital station, we're being ordered to approach the station and dock."

"Very well. Navigator, take us in nice and steady. I suggest you get your First Contact Team ready, Ambassador, your wish for face-to-face talks with the Turak is granted."

Nicholas acknowledged his captain's words with a nod and a smile then slipped from his seat and strode from the bridge to gather his team while the *Cutlass* continued its journey toward the orbital station.

Cutlass slipped silently passed imposing ranks of Turak warships. On their final approach the true scale of the construct became apparent. The station resembled a giant spinning top, approaching 1500 meters at its widest point and slightly under one kilometer from top to bottom, rotating above a planet the *Cutlass'* sensors deciphered as heavily industrialized.

Nicholas did not doubt his tactical officer's veracity when he identified this planet as a major Turak world and not a startup colony. The infrastructure alone must have taken decades to establish, maybe more.

The navigator identified the correct docking port and as they closed in, the captain called up the view from the outside vid cameras allowing an impromptu examination of the hull of the impressive station.

Struck with an oddity Denise switched from camera to camera and confirmed her suspicions. Each of the view ports were closed and sealed denying the humans a tantalizing glimpse of the space station interior. *These people sure appreciate their privacy! Well, won't be much help when the ambassador enters the station and sees all... assuming they allow him to enter the station.*

"Mooring clamps secure, Captain. The Turak are extending a personnel tube it will mate with Airlock 14 on Deck Three." Said the navigator.

"Very well. Comms, my compliments to Major Flynt, detail a couple of marines to escort the ambassador. Mention this to the major, if the ambassador argues, the marines are to remind him of my orders in regard to his safety from Admiral Papadomas."

#

Two conspicuous marines dwarfed Nicholas Schamu and the other two members of the First Contact Team as they stood in the airlock. Stripped of their ubiquitous Wraith suits, the marines stood at the ready with PEP pistols holstered at their waists.

No doubt Major Flynt has a whole marine company on standby in full armor and ready to move at a moment's notice, Nicholas sighed and waited for the airlock to complete its cycle.

He heard the invisible locks clunk and on release, the whole door swung open to one side, allowing him his first view of the Turak - a solitary squat figure dressed all in scarlet.

An enclosed full face helmet rendered the Turak's head barely decipherable, although, two pinpricks of glowing red hinted at a pair of unblinking eyes. A matching form fitting body armor enclosed the torso and two arms hung by the Turak's side. Nicholas' eyes followed the length of the armor covered arms which ended, unsurprisingly, with armored gloves. Nicholas' eye's widened as he drank in the shape of those gloves. Two thick sausage like fingers topped with a smaller thumb. *No Saiph meddling here*!

The Turak carried no weapons, at least none Nicholas discerned. *A good sign? Perhaps the body armor is the formal uniform of the Turak*?

A speaker mounted in the Turak armor crackled to life. "Human, follow me. Do not deviate, if you do not comply, you die." He turned on his heel and set off.

Nicholas hesitated for but a millisecond before he adhered to the stark orders and followed the scarlet clad figure down a corridor. His companions followed in his wake.

Nicholas' longer stride meant he caught the Turak posthaste, though, he made no attempt to introduce himself. Nicholas read nonverbal communication as well as the next man. No insightfulness was required to understand this particular Turak's lack of interest in speaking to humans. His job, if he was a he, was to deliver them... somewhere.

They passed many closed hatches along the corridor until after a short distance the group reached a set of double doors. On their approach the doors swooshed open and revealed a bijou carriage equipped with up to a dozen seats.

The Turak entered the carriage, took a seat at one end and poised his fingers over the nearby compact panel. He waited for the humans to comply with his silent request. The humans read their cue and each grabbed a seat while the Turak entered a series of key strokes in the control panel. The doors closed. Moments later, Nicholas saw doors flash by the carriage windows. They were moving, but at such velocity he lost count of the flashing doors and became almost dizzy.

A short time passed before the carriage slowed and came to a halt. The Turak stood as the carriage doors opened and he strode off as fast, as his short steps allowed, down another deserted corridor. They walked in silence for another few minute until their unwilling guide reached a doorway covered in ornate gold motifs. The symbols reminded Nicholas of ancient Nordic runes.

The doors slid open and the scarlet clad Turak stepped to one side. "Enter. Approach the clan lord, human. Be respectful or face the wrath of Clan Orlak."

Nicholas, now used to such threats, did not bat an eyelid. He and his party entered.

Wow! There was no comparison to the sterile corridors they had just walked to get here. A marine let out a low whistle at the sight of the opulent state room. Decorated in exquisite rugs and throws, gold, platinum and rare gems glinted and sparkled, lit only by secreted wall lights. Equidistant along the walls stood statuesque Turak, dressed in distinctive scarlet body armor and hung across their chests they carried an ugly rifle type weapon with a wicked, half meter long blade attached to the barrel.

Eyes drawn to the center of the room Nicholas drank in the view of an imposing lone high-backed chair upon which sat another Turak, adorned in the now familiar figure hugging armor, topped with a gold embellished helmet and a matching gold sash fitted snuggly around his waist.

At last! Perhaps now we can get to talk.

"Human, share this information and leave the space of Clan Orlak and all Turak."

Perhaps not.

Nicholas surmised this race to be a subset of the Turak, *Clan Orlak? Is this the chief?* "Clan Lord. I am Ambassador Nicholas Schamu and…"

The Turak half rose from his seat, "Who you are is not my concern, human!" His deep voice echoed around the room. "Do not waste my time. Give me the information you say exonerates your puny Commonwealth of the murder of my clansmen." He returned to a seated position and gestured towards Nicholas. "Give the information to me! Then leave before my goodwill is exhausted and I extract it from you and return your lifeless body to your master."

In unison the marines' hands dropped to rest on their PEP pistols in their holsters. The clan lord inexplicably let out bellowing laugh. "Humans with fighting spirit? I will see what sort of warriors you are. Come! Battle with me!"

Nicholas stepped in. He had no wish to witness combat and much preferred diplomacy to war. He slipped the PAD with the recordings from the Selene system and the vid images of the recovered Saiph ship from his suit pocket.

"Clan Lord, the evidence showing The Commonwealth did not attack your clansmen in the Selene system is held on this device." He pulled the recordings on the PAD and got ready to play. "We too, were attacked by those ships and many of our own are dead. This device," he held the PAD out towards the clan lord, "also holds a video recording of the interior of a ship belonging to our attackers which we recovered. We identified the crew of this ship as a race we know as the Saiph…"

This time the Clan Lord rose to his feet and he pointed at Nicholas. "Lies! The Saiph are dead! Their world is gone. You waste my time. How can dead Saiph do these things?"

The clan lord's words startled Nicholas, the Turak had knowledge of the Saiph!

"You say you suffered at the hands of these black ships? I will do your dead the honor of reviewing this information, but, you must return to your ship and leave our space! I will refrain from extracting my clan's vengeance until I am satisfied of the origins of the black ships."

The state room's entrance doors swooshed open and their talkative guide stood awaiting them. Nicholas placed the PAD on the floor before turning to leave.

His head spun with the gems of information his brief audience gave him. A glimpse into the structure of the Turak clan based system, their natural aggression touted by confrontational language and the compulsion to prove physical prowess. The Turak also knew of the Saiph and their ignominious fate at the hands of the Others.

The Turak understood more about Commonwealth space and history than a modest spattering of Standard English.

Nicholas and his superiors had much to ponder.

CHAPTER TWENTY-THREE

Settling Accounts

SLIVINO VALLEY - NORTHERN ITALY – EARTH – SOL SYSTEM

The New Year had come to the Slivino valley and winter's harsh weather returned with a vengeance. Temperatures plummeted well below zero and the snow and ice was thick on the ground. Seaton Anderson had been forced to postpone his daily treks through the woods but even the luxurious surroundings of the house became too much for him, so he requested his favorite stallion saddled up and headed out into the cold with the sound of the wind his only companion.

Conditions were worse than Seaton expected and after only half an hour he decided to cut his outing short and return to the warmth of the house. Turning the horse around, he glimpsed the towering spires of the estate through the trees when without warning, the horse reared up on its hind legs. Seaton lost his grip and fell hard onto the frozen forest floor. Dazed, he lay still for a few seconds before the stars receded from his vision to see the stallion galloping off down the track back toward the estate house. Seaton let out a silent curse as he struggled to his feet. It was an hour's walk at least back to the welcoming fires of the house. A fleeting image in the corner of his eye made him turn his head in its direction. The sight of a blurry white ghost filled his vision before a strong arm locked around his neck, followed by a quick twisting motion. A sickening crack rang out.

Seaton Anderson was dead before he hit the ground. Victim of a fatal riding accident. The ghost disappeared into the forest, its job done.

#

OFFICE OF THE PRESIDENT – GENEVA EARTH – SOL SYSTEM

"...And once more our top news story of the day. The tragic death in a riding accident of multi-planet business mogul Seaton Anderson on his estate in Northern Italy has been met today with heartfelt condolences from many in the business and political community. Many believed Seaton Anderson was responsible for bankrolling the Grant campaign and had used his influence to promote the Earth First movement. Pollsters are already predicting his loss will be a body blow to the Grant campaign. With only three months until Election Day, Senator Kris Madkin is beginning to open a gap that many predict will quickly become a gulf Grant will not be able to close. In other news..."

Rebecca Coston touched a control, muting the sound of the news announcer with a feeling of grim satisfaction.

CHAPTER TWENTY-FOUR
Mosquito Swarm

GUZMAN SYSTEM - 47.5 LIGHT YEARS FROM EARTH

Commodore Neil Bekker watched with a sense of relief as the shuttle bearing the Guzman Colony Administrator left the Rosa Island boat bay and headed toward the surface of the planet Guzman.

Guzman was the second of a six planet system and orbited its G2-5V type star, roughly, around the middle of the star's habitable zone at 0.82 AUs, giving it a year length of 350 days. The corporation, which won the colonization license, considered Guzman, the most Earth-like world within fifty light years of Earth, a major prize despite having twenty-three percent less landmass than Earth. The unspoiled wilderness and lack of large predators attracted many inquiries from potential colonists and investors.

Neil could easily imagine himself on Earth if he disregarded the second moon and differing constellations. A number of his officers and crew had even discussed off-world retirement plans here, although, several were put off by the incessant bureaucracy and reliance on the colonization corporations.

Neil held no ill will toward the administrator of Guzman, but this was the fifth colony he and his four cruisers of Cruiser Squadron 1.6.4 had visited in the past month, as part of Admiral Jing's colony reassurance policy.

Neil's command spent one week in orbit around each colony world, entertained the local administrator and gave tours of their ships. Meanwhile, Neil fielded the bombardment of complaints. Ah! The complaints...

"We've no parts for repairs"

"Where's our supply ships?"

"We've no food"

The lists seemed endless and repetitive. Resigned, Neil realised there was no sense explaining to the various administrators that responsibility for their complaints lay with the colony's sponsors and not the TDF. He learned to nod, make the appropriate sounds, empathize and finally request a list of gripes which he assured would be included in his next dispatch to Colonial Support Command.

The paper pushers at the Hub were welcome to chase the corporations. Good luck with that! A grin tugged at Neil's lips. A double tone from his wrist comm reminded him of a staff meeting in a half hour to discuss the rotation of the Haig and the Montgomery.

The two older Vulcan class cruisers, unlike his own Lynx class cruiser Rosa Island and its squadron mate the

Lexington, were nearing the end of their cruising endurance. Rather than carry out an underway replenishment or UNREP, Central Command had instructed the ships to fold to the Sol system, to meet their maintenance and resupply schedule, and in return Cruiser Squadron 1.6.4 would receive two 'new' fully fitted and supplied Vulcans to complete the final months cruise.

Neil looked forward to the day the independent cruiser squadrons were fully equipped with the Lynx class. Losing two cruisers which the squadron had diligently integrated into their slick, efficient machine, only to be forced to repeat the integration process with two completely new ships was a royal pain in the ass.

Reaching his ready room Neil was already raising one hand to grasp the collar of his uniform jacket in preparation for a nice quiet lunch when the cries of the battle stations klaxon sounded throughout the ship. He took ten extra steps which saw him go past the marine guard and entered the bridge.

"Situation, XO?"

Commander Ra slipped out of the captain's chair and stepped to one side as Neil strode across the bridge.

"Sensors report four heavy cruisers have exited fold space beyond the orbit of Planet III. We lost them as they entered the planet's shadow but we got a good look at them before they moved behind the planet…" Ra's hesitated, drawing Neil's focus from the tactical display. "They're Black Ships, sir... It's the Saiph."

Neil understood Ra's hesitation, after all, they had all seen the recordings of the Black Ships' actions against the

Turak at Selene and Garunda's Dagger Station. Four against four, may seem like evens, but Neil did not believe these odds for a second. The Black Ships outgunned them and Neil knew how ineffective the Commonwealth's energy weapons were against the enemy's shields. The safe option was to fold, leave the system. But what of the Guzman colonists' fate? His duty left him no choice, he would stay and fight.

Neil stared at the tactical holo for several seconds, tuning out the noise of the bridge, his mind whirring as he formulated his plan of action before snapping out his orders.

"Communications! Contact the administrator and tell her to put her evacuation plan into effect. Warn her to get the colonists as far from built up areas as possible, they will be the enemy's first target. Next, launch two drones for Gateway Station, append our logs and my intention to delay the enemy from reaching the planet, and request immediate assistance.

Navigation! Plot a course that puts Guzman's second moon between us and Planet III.

Tactical! Deploy a surveillance drone, I want to see what they're doing behind that planet.

Two can play at hide and seek. If they spotted us when they entered the system and can no longer find us, they may think twice about heading straight for the planet."

#

TASMANIA - EARTH

The month of March was officially winter in the northern hemisphere, but on the most southern tip of the island of Tasmania March was the height of summer. A stifling 69.8 degrees Fahrenheit. The midday sun beamed from a clear blue sky on to the perfectly formed ranks which filled the parade ground.

Brigadier General Karen Mills felt the urge to scratch the annoying itch on her thigh. The doctors had assured her that, in time, her brain would adjust to her synthesized leg, a complete copy of the original she had lost at the hands of the Others on 70 Ophiuchi.

Forcing herself to ignore the phantom itch, she concentrated on the stationery rows of the immaculately turned out graduates.

The band struck up the Anthem of Terra and the lead rank stepped off in perfect unison, led by the top recruit. As she drew level with Karen, who stood on the raised reviewing stand, she said. “Eyes! Right!” the loud confident voice drew the appropriate response from the ranks and a flash of white followed as the recruit’s gloved hand came up to the peak of her white cap, her blue eyes fixed on Karen.

Karen returned the salute and held the pose as the graduating class completed its march past. Out of the corner of her eye she saw Vice Admiral Christos Papadomas, his face beamed with pride as his daughter Philippa, the top recruit, led her graduating class in revue.

Sitting beside Christos were Philippa’s siblings, Maia and Odysseia. A smaller woman, that Karen did not recognize, sat with them, her face filled with happiness, although, from the furtive glances she gave Christos she seemed more pleased with Christos’ smiles than Philippa’s graduation.

Other unusual events involving the Papadomas family had occurred recently. In the week leading up to graduation

Karen's office had received calls from the Garundan, the Persai, and the Edasich. Each had asked to send a representative in a 'private capacity' and Karen had, of course, granted the requests but also ensured the Diplomatic Corps were informed. Then, this morning, as the recruits' family members arrived, Karen received an urgent call from the Duty Officer. "There's a shuttle on final approach, sir, with Ambassador Jelav, Felan of the Edasich, Force Leader Verus and Fleet Admiral Jing, onboard." Karen thought, for a second, the Duty Officer was joking before she realized it was true.

Her second in command, Colonel Rollison, had rushed to the main shuttle pad with a side party of marines and welcomed the VIPs, while Karen's leisurely plan of dressing and enjoying a last cup of coffee before facing the families was throw into complete disarray. She only just managed to reach the Officers Mess as the VIP party walked through the door.

Much to Karen's relief, Jing took her quietly to one side and explained they were there for a flying visit to see the graduation before heading to Zurich for the presidential inauguration ceremony later. Karen secretly suspected that Jing enjoyed watching a one star general run around like a headless chicken, but she kept her thoughts to herself and moved on to meet and greet the families.

Back on the parade square, Karen saw Christos' pride in his daughter's achievement echoed in the family's stand, packed with mothers, fathers, wives, husbands and children all gathered to watch their loved one take their place as a fully commissioned officer in the Terran Defense Force Marine Corps. The last six months had been long and grueling.

As 'Mustangs' they had already spent at least three years in the corps and the marine drill instructors, or Dis, expected them to already be experience in tactics, weapon handling, wraith suit maintenance, and platoon level administration. Any who fell short of the DI's benchmarks were given one single chance to improve. If they did not, they were RTUd and being returned to unit was difficult to live down.

The memory of Karen's own graduation day came to mind. She had not been honored as Top Recruit, nevertheless, she remembered the pride and the relief, if she was honest, of completing her officer training. She had searched the mass of faces in the family's stand for her father and she would never forget the huge smile she had seen on his face.

A retired navy master chief, he had not been impressed when she turned eighteen and, the same day, arrived home enlisted in the corps. He had been so angry, his face had turned a deep shade of purple and he barely spoke to her. Throughout her teenage years, her father had regaled stories of how he made life difficult for every marine with the misfortune to cross his path, so, Karen's decision to join the enemy, as he saw the marines, was a betrayal. Nevertheless, Karen had been undeterred.

As a direct entrant she had spent the better part of eighteen months ensconced in the Marine Officer Training Academy. She and her mother had kept in contact through vid letters and both avoided the subject of her father. As the day of her graduation had drawn near, Karen had sent an invitation for two, but fully expected only one seat to be filled.

On the morning of the graduation parade she had taken her place amongst the ranks of soon-to-be officers. In those days the corps, and the entire TDF, had been much smaller in numbers. They had held only one graduation per year and usually only forty or so from the original 200 hopefuls graduated. Subsequently the number of graduation guests was never more than a couple of hundred.

Karen remembered the moment she had marched past the reviewing officer, on command she had snapped her eyes right and almost missed a step, for standing beside her mother in the family's stand was her father. Proud as punch, in his blue navy master chief's uniform decorated with his medals and awards. His smile had brought the hint of a tear to Karen's eye because that was when she realised the old goat was proud of her.

"Eyes front!" Philippa's command brought Karen out of her reverie and Karen dropped her saluting arm back to her side.

The graduating class continued its steady march around the parade ground until, once more, they paraded in front of the reviewing stand.

They came to a halt, boots slammed into the compacted ground with the force and sound of a firing cannon. They paused and with no command, the class left turned to face the reviewing stand.

Another pause, then Philippa did an about face while the center rank held their ground, the front took a single pace forward as the rear took one backward. Heads snapped to the right and feet shuffled as the class measured off exactly one arm's length from the next person.

Another pause, then heads spun to the front while Philippa performed another precise about face to face the reviewing stand.

Another pause.

"Sir! The graduating class is in open order and awaiting your inspection!" Bellowed Philippa.

Karen stepped down from the reviewing stand and was met by the senior drill instructor and two further DIs at the base of the steps. Together they marched in perfect formation until they halted in front of Philippa. The senior DI stepped to Karen's right while another DI took up post to her left cradling a silk cushion in his arms. The rows of single silver bars reflected the Tasmanian sun.

"Officer Cadet Papadomas." Said the senior DI.

Karen lifted a single bar and, reaching forward, carefully attached the officer's bar to Philippa's collar.

"Congratulations, Lieutenant Papadomas." Karen said as she shook Philippa's hand.

"Thank you, sir. Permission to fall out and escort you during your inspection."

"Permission granted, Lieutenant." Karen took a step back as Philippa turned smartly to the right and led the way to the first rank.

"Officer Cadet Matthews." Introduced Philippa.

"Congratulations, Lieutenant Matthews." Karen shook his hand and pinned a bar on his collar.

"Officer Cadet Chin."

"Congratulations, Lieutenant Chin." And so the ceremony continued until each member of the class was presented their hard earned officer bar. Now they were all officially first lieutenants in the marine corps.

Philippa returned to her place at the front of the class as Karen and her escort made their way back to the reviewing stand. Karen's foot just touched the first step when she became aware of a small commotion in the family's stand.

Her eyes fell on Admiral Jing talking urgently into his wrist comm as he made his way toward the rear of the stand where a car awaited. In the distance Karen picked up the high pitched whine of shuttle engines warming up. Something's up, she thought.

#

CARRIER STRIKE GROUP ITUS
GATEWAY STATION - SOL SYSTEM

"Admiral on the bridge!" Called the first officer to spot Vice Admiral John Radford as he strode on to the Flag Bridge of the TDF's first operational carrier, TDF Itus.

Although not quite as big as the Bismarck class battleships each of the Colossus class carriers could do something a Bismarck could not. The Itus could launch the Mosquito space fighter and was home to seventy two of the deadly two-seaters.

John seated himself and activated the repeater displays which showed him all of the strike group's available information. The strike group was rapidly moving to battle stations in reaction to the flagship's signal. John spared a look at the fleet's readiness state. His eight Bismarcks were slower to react than the smaller cruisers and destroyers but one by one there status updated with green lights by their names.

"What do we have, Tactical?"

"Sir, eight minutes ago Gateway Station received a flash signal from the Rosa Island a Lynx cruiser and the lead ship in Independent Cruiser Squadron 1.6.4. The squadron is conducting a port visit in the Guzman system. They say that four suspected Black Ships have entered the system. The squadron commander is unsure if the Black Ships are aware of his presence but he has moved his ships into positions to intercept any move on the colony."

"Thank you. Strike group status?" Asked John as he caught sight of Captain Taw entering the bridge and making for the flight operations team. The female Benii's long legs ate up the distance in easy steps.

Retaining a Benii as his Commander Air Group, CAG, in charge of his six fighter squadrons had ruffled a few feathers. But, the Benii had a wealth of experience in carrier and fighter tactics and to John it seemed the height of stupidity not to exploit her expertise, especially as the Itus was a carbon copy of the Benii carriers.

Built around a central flight deck used to recover the fighters and launch and recover the larger shuttle type craft. The Mosquito fighters launched from four rows of launch tubes, two top side port and starboard. A further two were located lower side port and starboard. A design which should mitigate any damage to a single area of the ship impacting on flight operations.

"All ships report ready, sir."

“CAG, how are we doing?”

“Alert fighters are in the tubes and ready to fly, Admiral. Alert plus ten are moving into the tubes now and we’re generating a full anti-shipping strike. I recommend we hold position until the strike package is complete, then we can launch in a single flight rather than in separate waves. Fifteen minutes to launch ready.”

“Understood, CAG.” John tapped commands into his chair and a schematic of the Guzman system appeared in his holo cube. He overlaid the downloaded information from the Rosa Island on to it. Four red icons appeared behind Planet III, while four blue icons representing the TDF cruisers, appeared behind the second moon of the colony world. John assumed the Black Ships were still behind Planet III and had not already made their move and engaged the defending cruisers. Fifteen minutes was a long time onboard a cruiser that was out gunned by an enemy ship with Saiph energy shields.

John glanced at the image of the flight deck displayed in the holo cube above flight operations. He saw Mosquito fighters being armed as quickly as humanly possible, the pilots sat in their cockpits as the ground crew maneuvered them into their launch tubes.

At the far end of the flight deck he saw the wavering energy field that kept the vacuum of space from engulfing the entire deck but allowed transit from the outside such as recovering fighters or shuttles. A Benii invention. Unfortunately neither the Benii nor the scientists of Zarminda had yet perfected the sort of energy shielding the Saiph were able to employ, therefore, during combat operations a pair of massive battle armored doors sealed the flight deck.

John raised his head from the display, a drop in the steady hum of words between various stations alerted him to the entrance of Major Olaz, the Empire of Alona's military exchange observer or spy, and, as always two steps behind, the imposing figure of marine brevet Major Vanderhoek.

In different circumstances John would have found amusement in the exchange program which paired a six foot four, 240 pound marine with a five foot two ninety eight pound Alonan.

The Alonan and marine had been a constant presence on the flag bridge since their arrival two months ago. John had always wondered how the marine knew exactly when, and where, the Alonan intelligence operative would want to go next. Later! Thought John, I have a battle to win.

Another set of commands and the space around the colony and Planet III was covered in overlapping spheres… just. John sent the data from his terminal to Tactical.

"Tactical. Review the data I've just sent you. I want a cruiser equipped with a dampening field generator assigned to each of those spheres. We must hold the Black Ships in the system until we can close and engage. Assign a single Bismarck and an Ageis to each cruiser. If that generator was the only thing preventing me from escaping the system I would take it out."

"Aye-aye, sir."

"Navigation, plot a course for the remainder of the group. I want us to come out half way between the colony and Planet III. CAG, what's the flight time of your birds from there to the Black Ships last known location?"

"Fifty Six minutes," Taw mentally calculated, "on super cruise, leaving them forty minutes of combat operations over the target with sufficient fuel to return safely without tanker support."

On John's display the tactical team's revised ops plan popped up. Each of the disruption sphere's location and separation had been refined and ships assigned to each as he instructed. A flashing diamond indicated the task groups expected arrival coordinates.

John's brain went into over drive as he refined his tactical options, spitting data packets to the tactical section as he ran through the likely moves of his enemy and how he would counter them. The planning teams of CSG Itus had gamed out hundreds of scenarios over the last six months and John adapted these, on the fly, to best fit what awaited him in Guzman.

The precious minutes flew by. Ground crew rushed to get the carrier's fighters ready to launch. After an age, the orotund voice of Taw cut across the flag bridge. "Strike package complete, sir. Birds are in the tubes and ready to launch."

John's head came up, his eyes flicked to the chronometer before settling on the Benii standing proudly by her operations team. "A full strike package ready with four minutes to spare, CAG. Very impressive." John took one more look around the flag bridge before flexing his fingers on his armrests. Time to see if the faith Admiral Jing had in the carrier strike group concept would bear fruit.

"Navigation, *Itus* will fold on your mark."

"Aye-aye, sir. Fold in five…four…three…two…one…Fold!"

#

GUZMAN SYSTEM - 47.5 LIGHT YEARS FROM EARTH

In one moment the space between the Guzman colony and Planet III was empty, in the next, space was filled with millions of tonnes of battle armored warships. As the ships of CSG Itus positioned themselves and their sensors swept the system, Itus was pinged by a communications whisker laser.

"Admiral, we're receiving a data stream from the Rosa Island… it's a relay feed from a surveillance drone they have skulking in the dark side of Planet III… There's four cruiser size vessels in low orbit, they're Black Ships!"

The blood red icons of the four Black Ships sprang into life in John's tactical display. "How old is the data, Tactical?"

The commander checked his display and confirmed, "Four point three minutes, sir."

Ok we can do this, thought John.

"Communications. Signal the dampening field ships to begin transmitting immediately. I don't want those ships able to fold out of here. Tactical. We'll go with Savannah Two."

A press of a stud on his armrest and the head and shoulders of Vice Admiral Gregory Rowe, commander of the strike group's battleships entered the holo cube in front of John. "Greg I'm going with Savannah Two. Assume command of the ships approaching from system north, I'm taking those from system south. My fighters are launching now…"

John raised his eyes to Captain Taw and gave her a single curt nod, the Benii spun and began issuing orders. Seventy-two Mosquito space fighters spat into space, formed up and accelerated toward the unseen enemy ships.

"We need to be smart, Greg. They might only be cruisers but they have those damned energy shields, but, if we pummel them hard enough we know they fail. With the dampening fields flooding the system we've effectively taken out their long range fold missiles…" John scowled. "However, it's a double edged sword and we must close with them to bring our conventional missiles and energy weapons into play."

Greg Rowe was no fool, he knew a bloody battle was imminent. "Don't worry, Admiral. They're messing with the TDF and it's high time we taught them the error of their ways."

Despite himself John smiled at his subordinate's remark. "I like your thinking, Greg. Good luck and good hunting." Terminating the link John sat back in his chair as the Itus surged forward at full power following in the wake of her fighters.

#

Commander Bo checked her instruments, as her Mosquito and the other eleven fighters that made up VFA-101, 'The Mailed Fists', skimmed at barely a few hundred meters above the cloudy, toxic atmosphere of Planet III. They were closing fast on the last reported location of the Black Ships.

"How are we doing back there, Charlie?"

"Everything is looking good, Commander. The clutter from the atmosphere should mask us until we get within missile range. Assuming the ships are still where we think they are."

Bo glanced down at her display which showed virtually real time coverage from the surveillance drone, now that they were close to their target. Yeah, they're still hovering less than five minutes from us, Bo thought.

Charlie was back on the intercom. "Radar horizon breach in thirty seconds… ECM coming online…weapons systems all in the green."

Bo activated the link to the other Mosquitos under her command. "Mailed Fists. Mailed Fists lead. Weapons hot! Remember we need to get in real close to do the damage. Stay in your pairs and watch your backs. Follow me in!" Bo forced her throttles to the fire walls and the Mailed Fists lunged forward, closely followed by every Mosquito of CSG Itus.

#

John Radford was on the edge of his seat as the Itus cleared Planet III and he got his first good look at his quarry. His tactical holo display was filled with flashes of energy weapons as the enemy cruisers flayed at the swarming Mosquitos.

Missiles designed to seek and destroy the large ship killers, fired by capital ships, filled the space around the cruisers but the agile Mosquitos darted between them and released their own smaller, less powerful missiles before strafing the enemy with their rapid fire plasma cannon and needle lasers.

Green energy shields flashed in near constant brilliance as time and again the Mosquitos' weapons hit home. Unfortunately, it was plainly obvious that the small fighter's weapons were not powerful enough to penetrate the enemy's shields. Well, thought John, let's see how they do against the big boys.

"Tactical. Fire Plan Gamma. Concentrate fire on two enemy cruisers only, Admiral Rowe will get the other two.

CAG, recall and rearm your fighters. The Black Ships know we have capital ships in the system, I fully expect them to make a break for it and clear the disruption generator bubble. Your fighters must be available to chase them down if we can inflict significant damage on their shields."

The battleships and cruisers of CSG Itus launched their first wave of conventionally powered missiles toward the static Black Ships. The Terran missiles closed on the enemy cruisers and flashes of coherent light came from the targeted ships as they flushed their own anti-missile missiles in reply, an attempt to beat back the avalanche of nuclear tipped warheads bearing down on them.

Missiles crossed and inter penetrated as space was filled with explosions large enough to wipe any earthly city from existence, but, as the plasma cleared, the four Black Ships remained unscathed.

Then, three of the cruisers gathered momentum and slowly moved off, leaving their sole squadron mate in orbit. John slapped his hand hard on his armrest, causing a few furtive looks from his bridge officers before they quickly returned to their duties.

A feral grin spread across the admiral. One down, three to go, thought John. "CAG, how long before you're ready to launch a second strike?"

"Twenty minutes, Admiral." Replied Taw as she continued to coordinate the mosquito recovery operation.

John stared at his tactical display. The remaining three Black Ships were accelerating for all they were worth, pulling clear of the battleships' and cruisers' weapons range.

He had gambled on the enemy being primarily equipped with long-range fold powered anti-ship missiles, leaving the smaller short range anti-missile missiles to fend off his own heavy missiles. Frustratingly, however, his gamble hadn't quite paid off, he needed to buy another twenty minutes so his fighters could re-engage.

"Tactical. Detail two cruisers to continue the bombardment of the stranded enemy ship, then send our destroyers in pursuit of the other three. Primary target is the enemy ship's engines. We need to slow them down."

For a moment the commander at Tactical looked as though he was going to question his orders. The destroyers certainly had the legs to catch the fleeing cruisers, but there was only a half dozen of them against the three cruisers who's weaponry outmatched them and still had their energy shields intact. The commander took one look at the determined face of his admiral and changed his mind.

The six destroyers of CSG Itus broke from their places alongside the hulking battleships, like the lithe greyhounds they were, eating up the distance between them and the fleeing Black Ships. Within minutes they had gained enough ground that they entered the effective range of their missiles but they held fire and closed further. In space battle terms they were in knife fighting reach.

As one, they flushed their missiles all aimed at a single fleeing cruiser while their energy fire battered its shielding. With a blinding flash the energy shielding failed and a twenty megaton missile detonated scant meters from the cruiser's main drive. The resulting explosion ripped the entire stern from the Black Ship, the bow tumbled, bleeding atmosphere and flames.

Then the tactical officer's fears came true.

The last two Black Ships suddenly slowed their headlong escape and maneuvered broad side on to pursuing destroyers. Energy armament opened fire and the destroyers were wracked by millions of ergs of laser and grazer fire. It was a one-sided fight. As John and the bridge crew watched the Black Ships' fire laid waste to the pitiful armor of the destroyers. John steeled himself to watch the sacrifice of the brave ships' crews, promising he would forever remember their unquestioned faith and obedience they had shown him.

"Mosquitos are re engaging, Admiral!" Shouted the CAG.

"The enemy are in missile range again, sir. Admiral Rowe has opened fire."

The enemy commander had made a mistake by turning to fight the destroyers and it was one John intended to make him pay for. "All ships are to engage as they bear. Let's finish this!"

#

The fight was over and John sat silently in his command chair. The subdued voice of the flag bridge reflected his own anguish at the costly victory. Four Black Ship cruisers destroyed, but he had lost two battleships, five cruisers, six destroyers and thirty eight fighters. The numbers said it more eloquently than he ever could.

Unless the Commonwealth found an answer to the enemy's energy shielding soon, the outlook was bleak for any Commonwealth ship that took on a Black Ship fleet.

The Black Ships and their Saiph masters had shown their superiority in weapons and ships. They had devastated an Alonan colony, vanquished the Turak at Selene, wiped Dagger Station and its Garundan defenders from space. Now they had humbled the new jewel in the TDF's crown. CSG Itus. The Saiph had shown that they controlled the most powerful units in space and John had a bad feeling that they were only flexing their muscles.

CHAPTER TWENTY-FIVE
Foram

ASTEROID F815B - FORAM SYSTEM
36 LIGHT YEARS FROM ALONA

Calan breathed heavily inside his helmet, despite the increased oxygen flow, and a bead of sweat rolled into his left eye. He blinked repeatedly in an attempt to clear his vision.

Not for the first time, since he and his mining team landed on this metal rich asteroid, he cursed the maintenance crew who failed to spot the faulty power unit on the equipment hauler. Calan and his team had been forced to maneuver the last of the survey units into position by hand. The one hour job had soon became three.

Calan had briefly considered abandoning the survey and returning to the yard to swap out the equipment hauler, but the six hours wasted on this round trip journey would put him well behind schedule and if there was one thing his boss, Major Dola, did not appreciate was falling behind schedule. Major Dola waxed lyrical about the importance of the raw materials the asteroid mining teams provided to the Empire's classified research and construction yards secreted here, in the Foram system.

Calan's mind's eye conjured an image of the pretentious Dola standing on the gantry of the boat bay. Like some feudal lord he looked down, figuratively and literally, on the men and women of the mining teams and bored them to death with his nasal speech, outlining the mining sections and therefore his own, importance. No raw materials, no scientific experiments and the shipyards could not breathe life into the draftsperson's and scientists' vision of ships. Without the ships the Empire could never achieve parlance with the Commonwealth. Calan really couldn't suffer the speech again, so he and his team used good old fashioned brute force to shift the final pieces of survey equipment into position.

"Lieutenant Calan, sir." Harad's tone over comms indicated a problem. Calan sighed deeply. To expedite the survey equipment deployment Calan had allocated one miner per location to run the set up procedures, freeing the others to move the remaining equipment and although Harad was one of the most inexperienced miners in his team, Calan had been confident enough to leave Harad unsupervised. Seemingly now a poor decision.

"Go ahead, Harad."

"I think we've a fault with number four. Whenever it comes out of set up mode it indicates a massive concentration of refined metals a little way below the surface."

Calan forced the frustration from his voice. If number four really was faulty it meant unpacking the spare back on the shuttle, powering it up, running diagnostics, powering it down, hauling it to its designated location, setting it up, running another diagnostic in situ before, finally, dragging the faulty unit back to the shuttle. Would this day never end?

“Hang on, I’m on my way.” Calan set off with graceful bounces in the micro gravity of the asteroid, covering the distance quickly. Calan cleared the visible horizon and Harad came into view. He saw the young miner punching commands into the glowing green control panel, no doubt running yet another diagnostic on the errant machine. Well, at least he isn't standing around waiting for me to sort his problems!

Landing in a small puff of dust, Calan pointedly ignored Harad as he eyed the instrument display. The diagnostic cycle completed and reported the equipment was functioning properly.

“You see, sir,” said Harad, “the computer says every thing’s working properly but it can’t be. Refined metals don't occur in nature.”

Calan silently agreed while punching commands into the obviously faulty equipment. Maybe by changing modes he could identify the fault. With a final tap Calan activated the ground penetrating radar mode. Complying with Calan’s instructions the survey equipment sent a millimeter length radar pulse in a short arc deep into the asteroid before displaying the results on a small screen.

“Odd...” Calan mumbled, while Harad tried to peer over his superior’s taller shoulder.

The radar showed a structure barely one meter under the surface. Calan adjusted the arc of the radar sweep to its maximum coverage before initiating another pulse. Moments later the return displayed on the small screen. Calan’s heart raced as his logic battled to make sense of the grainy image he saw - sleek lines interspersed with vertical and horizontal ones at regular intervals.

Calan stumbled back from the display, his eyes involuntarily scanned the surface of the asteroid as if his unaided eyes could see through the fine gray powder. His brain struggled to process what he knew to be true. A scant few meters below him was a spaceship.

#

Calan and his team stood silently alongside the fussing Major Dola, while Calan tried to tune out the major's staccato orders, "... move that equipment... one meter to the left it looks untidy there! ... The general's coming... clean up... I don't care where… move it!"

It had little effect on the miners who had descended en mass to the location of Calan's discovery.

At first Major Dola was incredulous and dismissive. Calan's report was, "... no more than a junior officer blowing a malfunctioning equipment's reading into something it isn't!"

Until Calan's team carefully excavated the area directly above where the alleged false image was taken. They had dug only a single meter before their tools struck the outer skin. Carefully, they exhumed it and revealed a smooth, silver surface which sparkled brightly in the blue of the portable work lights Callan had ordered to the site.

Unsurprisingly on receipt of Calan's video of the dig, the usually disdainful Dola ordered a halt to proceedings and immediately departed from his shipyard office. He proceeded to round up every available miner under his command, cram them and as much equipment as he could aboard shuttles and headed for the asteroid.

On reaching the asteroid, Dola quickly assumed command of the dig and ordered a complete survey using the extra ground penetrating radar he brought with him. The arduous work was worth the effort, for it revealed the assumption a ship was buried within the asteroid was wrong.

The ship was the asteroid! And it was massive - over 700 meters long, sixty at the beam and over forty from the keel to the tip of the single protuberance which broke its perfect lozenge shape. It was anyone's guess which end was the bow and which the stern, for all Calan and his fellow miners knew they were looking at the ship from its side. They could only presume each end of the lozenge was the front and the back. Further investigation proved the ship was coated in a layer of asteroid material varying in depth from a couple to up to ten meters in places. Someone or something spent a great deal of time on this camouflage.

The quandary was: Who built the ship? And why did they hide it?

Calan noticed Dola finally halting his flapping movements as he stood to the best effort of attention his vacuum suit allowed. Following Dola's line of sight Calan spotted a mob of suits were bouncing gracefully toward them. Calan put two and two together and stood to attention, as much as his semi rigid suit allowed, for the arrival of the general. Calan's loyal team followed his lead.

The approaching group came to a halt. Dola tried but farcically failed to salute the lead figure. Calan smirked as he caught a chuckle on the open radio channel. Dola chose to ignore it as he spoke.

"Welcome General Lura, Chief Scientist Kilor. As you can see..." The chief scientist stepped right past Dola, giving him a taste of his own dismissiveness. As he teetered at the edge of the excavated area Kilor drank in the sight of the seamless and beautiful metal hull reflecting the artificial light. Meanwhile Dola spluttered on "... Ah... Yes... Well... as you can see," he cleared his throat, "I have revealed an area of what we believe to be the top half of the hull and have awaited your arrival before attempting to gain entry."

The scientist finally spoke. "This is fascinating." He turned towards the general and implored. "We must get inside, General, look!" He turned back to the shiny hull. "It's impeccable... Untarnished… Undamaged... and there's no clue as to how long it's been here."

"Is it Commonwealth, Kilor? Have they placed this ship here to spy on us?"

"No, General." The scientist shook his head. "I'm fairly confident whoever built this is not Commonwealth. We chose the Foram system for its isolation from colonization routes. It has no habitable planets and there's no reason for anyone to come here. Besides, I have certainly never heard of them disguising one of their ships as an asteroid, have you?"

"Can't say I have, Kilor." The general nodded. "Very well, we'll treat this as an alien construction, until we know otherwise. Major Dola."

"Yes, sir?"

"Have your teams assist Chief Scientist Kilor. He's to get whatever he needs. You have full authority to requisition anything and anyone you feel necessary to fulfill his requirements. If anyone argues, refer them to my office."

"Yes, sir."

Calan involuntarily rolled his eyes, Oh God, that pompous ass has even more power now! That meant one thing, he would be even more insufferable.

"Lieutenant Calan."

"Sir?" Calan stood straighter as he replied.

"Well done to you and your team. The Empire prides itself on rewarding good work and as such each of your team is promoted one grade. Congratulations, Captain Calan."

Calan, dumbfounded by his sudden unexpected promotion stuttered, "Uh… Th… Tha… Thank you, sir."

General Lura let out a short laugh. "And as you'll soon discover, Captain, with promotion comes responsibility. You're on detached duty with immediate effect. You will work directly for Chief Scientist Kilor and, when the time comes, you'll have the honor of being the first to enter the ship."

Calan beamed unseen within his helmet. He was almost bursting with pride.

"Sir, it will be my honor."

"Don't thank me yet, son. We've no idea what we'll find inside there… Very well!" General Lura turned and headed to his ship, leaving Calan to stare at the glinting metal skin and wonder what awaited him inside.

#

Chief Scientist Kilor's enthusiasm to enter the mysterious ship was tempered by caution. To minimize damage to the hull and protect its interior, Kilor had ordered another complete set of radar imagery before agreeing to the painstaking removal of the asteroid material. To minimize further delays, Major Dola had organized the various mining teams into round-the-clock shifts. Though, in a rare moment of consideration, he had used his newly granted authority for the benefit of his hard pressed subordinates by requisitioning a large cargo hauler and converting the empty bays into reasonably comfortable ad hoc sleeping and catering areas. The growing number of scientists, technicians and the need for laboratories, soon forced Dola to requisition a second ship and Calan began to see a different side to Dola. He would always be a pompous ass but, it turned out, he was an efficient administrator and earned a modicum of respect from miners, scientists, and technicians alike.

Nevertheless, Kilor's cautious approach proved its worth when, on removing a particularly stubborn section of asteroid material, the miners uncovered an airlock, but, instead of entering the ship, Kilor chose to continue the excavation of the outer covering and forced the miners, much to their frustration, to continue with their hard graft for a further week. The result was a completely exposed, glittering ship of burnished silver metal. A smooth hull, which reflected distant stars, hovered freely in space for the first time in who knew how long and permission was finally granted to enter the mysterious ship.

#

Calan and his two man team floated beside the airlock door attached to the hull by magnetic tethers. All attempts to power up the door had proved unsuccessful and with no visible hinges or mechanisms on the outer door Calan had opted to use a thermal lance to cut his way inside.

Knowing everyone from General Lura down was listening to his transmissions, Calan swallowed and tried to wet his dry mouth and throat.

"Go ahead, Jara."

Jara, the experienced ship worker brought in especially for this moment by Major Dola, activated the lance and with remarkable ease, rotated the bulky contraption to plant it against the airlock's metal skin. Within seconds the superheated plasma began to slice through the airlock. Minutes later he deactivated the lance and secured it and its power pack to the hull before placing three magnetic clamps on the free-floating section he had cut. He attached one end of a tether to the coupling point on each clamp and the other to the front of his suit. When all three were fixed he used the thrusters on his maneuvering pack to pull the section of cut away airlock free. Spinning around, he gently placed the section on the hull and secured it in place. Jara gave Calan a nod.

Calan's heart raced, "I'm entering the airlock now." He called confidently over his suit radio. Calan passed through the hole, mindful of snagging his suit on the ragged metal and risking sudden decompression.

It was pitch black.

Calan illuminated the interior with his suit lamps. "Uh… it looks like a standard airlock, nothing much different to ours. Hold on, I'll see if I can find a control panel... Got it! I've a panel with a sequence of colored touch controls and… it looks like we may have a faint power reading…"

Without warning the airlock filled with a bright white light. Calan's visor immediately darkened and he felt a thud through the magnetic boots holding him to the airlock floor. Spinning around, he saw a second door had closed behind him, isolating him from his team on the hull.

The urgent tones of Kilor broke the stillness.

"Captain Calan, what's happening? We've lost your video feed. What is your situation? We have indications the ship's power is coming online." The general and Kilor had been following Calan's progress on the banks of monitors in their makeshift control room aboard the freighter.

Calan took a closer look at the door which had closed behind him, it was of similar composition to the outer door, which they had burned through and he saw no control panel to open it. He tried to make sense of events.

"May be the ship reads our cutting through the outer door as a hull breach and has activated some sort of emergency protocol? This second door could be used simply to protect the integrity of the ship."

#

Kilor liked Calan's logic, airlock failure safeguards, simple. "Calan, back away from the second door. Jara will cut another hole and we'll get you out of there…"

"Excuse me, sir."

Kilor hunted the room until he found the technician monitoring Calan's suit's readouts who had the temerity to interrupt him. "Yes?!"

The tech shrank in his seat a little, at Kilor's irritated tone. "The sensors show the airlock has a breathable atmosphere."

"What? Confirm that… Then check again." Kilor eyes met those of General Kula for a brief second. "Calan, check your suit systems. We're reading a breathable atmosphere in the airlock. Jara could cause an explosive decompression if he cuts through the door while the airlock retains an atmosphere. Give us a few minutes to work the problem and I'll get back to you." Cutting the link to the stranded captain, Kilor faced General Kula.

"Well, our exploratory mission seems to have morphed into a rescue mission."

"Indeed! So how do we rescue our good captain without causing any more damage to the ship?" Major Dola cleared his throat loudly.

"You wish to say something, Major?"

"Sir, if I may," the major didn't wait for approval, "during my last tour of duty I was stationed aboard the Emperor Yalo IV spaceport as Section Head of Damage Repair. One of our regular training scenarios was a breach of the outer hull causing a full or partial depressurizing of particular sections, while the rest of the section remained pressurized. Our procedure was to erect a secondary airlock around the damaged section, which could then be cut away with no risk to any trapped survivors."

Kula and the general nodded, it seemed to be a workable solution.

"Do you have the equipment to build another airlock, Major?" Asked the general.

"I don't need to build one, sir." Dola smiled, enjoying his moment.

"Get on with it Major, or you'll find yourself reduced to the rank of private before you leave this room!"

The major blanched, unaccustomed to such threats. "The mining team transport shuttles come equipped with an extendable personnel tube. The personnel tubes have an integrated airlock on each end. If we move a shuttle close enough to the damaged airlock we can fabricate a makeshift docking collar to seal the airlock and allow us to cut through the inner door without the danger of an explosive decompression."

The general looked to Kilor who nodded in agreement. "How long to get the shuttle in place and fabricate the docking collar, Major Dola?"

"No more than two to three hours I would think."

"So ordered. Get to it, Major."

As Dola scampered out of the control room, Kilor reestablished his link to the stranded Calan to keep him appraised of the rescue plan, however, the increasing power levels registering throughout the floating ship drew his attention. Section after section showed signs of coming to life and if the scientist interpreted the data correctly then within a fleeting moment the entire ship could have life support and power. What in the Emperor's name was happening over there?

#

Calan had exactly the same thought. Kilor had cut his radio link only moments ago and Calan was sure the control room was doing everything in their power to ensure his rescue. But his rescue was not his main concern at the moment, as the airlock pressurized, sound traveled freely and from beyond the inner airlock door he was certain he heard movement.

At first, he dismissed the noises as his wild imagination, but then came a bang so loud the small airlock reverberated. No trick of the mind! He activated his radio link, no longer fearful of looking stupid to the crew. Calan received only static.

Bang!

There it is again.

Bang! Bang! Whoosh!

The inner airlock door retreated into the roof and Calan faced two aliens in tight fitting green uniforms carrying large boxes. Their large round eyes widened matching Calan's surprise. For what seemed an eternity, the trio stared across the meter or so separating them, before the aliens let out a fusillade of high pitched squeaks and hopped from foot to foot. Calan held up his hands in what he hoped was a peaceful gesture, the aliens stopped screaming and seemed increasingly fascinated by his hands.

Swapping confused looks the smaller of the two gingerly stepped forward and raised its hand as if to place it against Calan's. Their palms met and the alien jerked backwards sparking another animated conversation.

The smaller alien, the one Calan thought was in charge, tapped at its neck and spoke for a few moments then cocked its head as though listening to a reply. More squeaking ensued, followed by more head cocking. Calan reasoned they were equipped with a communications device, perhaps this one was speaking to the captain of the ship? Calan smiled wryly as he imagined this conversation.

Excuse me, sir, you know that airlock you wanted fixed? Well, I found a stow away... Yes… Yes… What, sir? Throw him overboard, sir? Yes, sir, right away sir! Calan's thoughts were interrupted with the whoosh of the inner door. The aliens had stepped out of the airlock and sealed Calan, once more, within. Calan frantically activated his radio link to Kilor, but got only an earful of static. Damn! He suspected his alien friends had jammed his signal, all he could do was sit tight. He did not have to wait long.

The inner airlock door retreated into the roof and revealed a single alien. The uniform was different. This alien wore a dark blue one and at his waist was a weapon, Calan was sure, about the size of a standard pistol.

The alien gazed quizzically at Calan.

Son, you gotta look a man square in the eyes if you want to get his true measure, Calan's father's word replayed in his mind. He hoped the same principle applied to this alien.

Calan reluctantly released his helmet clamps, gingerly removing his helmet before laying it at his feet. The alien fearlessly watched Calan as if he were a curious exhibit in a freak show. It reached up with its arms and motioned a vertical line down its chest, like dragging a zipper, then wiggled its shoulders. Are you kidding me?

“I’m not taking my suit off!” Calan broke the silence and put his hands on his waist staring at the unwavering alien. Dammit! Calan shook his head and looked away as he considered his options. One, remove his pressure suit and the alien opens the outer door leading to the cold, nasty end of Captain Calan. Two, ignore the request and the alien opens the outer door and Captain Calan still meets a nasty end. Three, remove the suit.

Calan reasoned he’d already removed his helmet, there was no chance of him replacing it in time if the alien decided to flush the airlock. He sighed. What’ve you got to loose, Calan? Calan worked his gloves off and wriggled out of his awkward suit. Stripping down to his inner thermal layer, Calan felt naked before the implacable alien.

The alien stepped forward, apparently satisfied Calan was no threat and Calan noticed, for the first time, their similarity of height and build. The alien grasped Calan’s right wrist and turned Calan’s hand palm up before it placed its own palm on it. The breath caught in Calan’s throat as he looked at the five lightly furred fingers wrapped around his own. In shock, his jaw slackened, he drew his eyes from the gripping hand into the now playful eyes of the alien. *My God, he’s a Saiph*!

###

Connect with PP Corcoran

Like my page on Facebook: facebook.com/ppcorcoran
Follow me on Twitter: twitter.com/ppcorcoran
Visit my website: ppcorcoran.com
Blog: ppcorcoran.wordpress.com
Email: info@ppcorcoran.com

COMING SOON

The K'Tai War Series
Invasion, book 1

The Carters have a past.
A secret past.
A past that the K'tai didn't reckon on.

Dave and Sue Carter have just moved to the frontier planet of Agate on the border of human and K'tai space. Tensions between humans and the K'tai heighten over the discovery of large deposits of the precious mineral Redlazore on Agate.

Yet the Carter's new lives are peaceful, just as they hoped. Dave commutes daily to his mid-level exec post in the city and Sue counsels in their local suburban High School, much to their twin teenager's distaste. In the midst of diplomatic talks the K'tai invade Agate.

It's unexpected, it's violent and it's chaotic.

The Carters are separated by just eight miles, but it quickly becomes a battleground. The seemingly impossible mission to reunite this family through the bloodshed begins.

Visit www.ppcorcoran.com

Praise for CHRIS KENNEDY'S Science Fiction:

"Chris Kennedy takes humanity, the most recent newcomers to interstellar space -- and the reader -- on a roller coaster exploration of alien cultures with ancient animosities and startling technologies. There's action and skullduggery in plenty, and along the way Kennedy gives the reader a look inside questions of morality, ethics, and the true meaning of personal responsibility, not simply to others, but to one's self."

- **David Weber, Author of the Honor Harrington and Safehold Series**

CHRIS KENNEDY'S JANISSARIES

The war with China was over and Lieutenant Shawn 'Calvin' Hobbs just wanted his life to get back to normal. The hero of the war, he had a small ream of paperwork to fill out, a deployment with his Navy F-18 squadron to prepare for and a new girlfriend to spend some quality time with. Life was good.

Until the aliens showed up.

They had a ship and needed to get to their home planet, but didn't have a crew. They had seen Calvin's unit in action, though, and knew it was the right one for the job. There was just one small problem—a second race of aliens was coming, which would end all life on Earth. Calvin's platoon might want to do something about that, too.

Having won a terrestrial war with 30 troops, winning an interstellar war with nothing but a 3,000 year old cruiser should be easy, right?

"Janissaries" initiates "The Theogony," a trilogy that will take Lieutenant Hobbs and his Special Forces platoon to the stars. It will also show them that there's much more to Earth's history than is written in the history books!

The following is an

Excerpt from “Janissaries” Book 1 of The Theogony:

Janissaries

Chris Kennedy

Available Now from Chris Kennedy Publishing

Chapter Twenty-Three

Bridge, TSS *Vella Gulf*, Tau Ceti System, May 25, 2019

"Vipers are approaching the fourth planet," said the operations officer. The sporadic power spikes had continued for several hours, but due to the random nature of the source, Arges hadn't been able to triangulate it. It was coming from the direction of the fourth planet or its small moon, but he was unable to determine which. Arges had asked Captain Deutch to launch a couple of Vipers with sensor gear; the next time the power source activated, he would be able to triangulate it.

"Very well," said Captain Deutch. Looking at the helmsman, he asked, "Our position?"

"We are holding at 125 million miles from Planet Four, as ordered," replied the helmsman.

"Vella Gulf, *this is* Viper 02," radioed Lieutenant Steve 'Gecko' Smith, the Weapons System Officer for the flight. *"We are approaching the planet, but do not see anything abnormal yet. We are not picking up any energy readings at this time."* At that distance, radio waves would have taken over 11 minutes to make the journey from the fighter to the *Vella Gulf*. With the Psiclopes' faster-than-light communications system, it was almost instantaneous.

"I'm starting to pick up readings of large concentrations of metal on the other side of the moon. The metal appears to be processed. We're coming over the horizon where we ought to be able to see it. There is enough...Wait! I've got

radars tracking us!...VAMPIRE, VAMPIRE, MISSILES INBOUND!" Gecko screamed.

"Missile launch from the moon of the fourth planet!" called the defensive systems officer from the Security position. "Six missiles launched...five are tracking *Viper 02*, and one is locked on *Viper 03*..."

Onboard *Viper 02*, Tau Ceti System, May 25, 2019

"Break right!" yelled Gecko as he released two decoys. He looked at his display. "What the fuck did we do to you?" he muttered as five of the six missiles turned to guide on him. He smiled as one of them attacked the thermal flare that he had released. The missile detonated, and the blast destroyed the flare...and one of the other missiles that were tracking them.

The pilot of *Viper 02*, Flight Lieutenant Ken 'MOSA' Smith, had the throttles of the little ship at maximum and was flying as straight away from the missiles as possible. Any maneuvering only let them catch up with him more quickly and shortened the time that Gecko had to defeat them. He jettisoned the four missiles the ship was carrying to get rid of the unnecessary mass and saw that he was now accelerating at 655 G's, which was 5 G's higher than what the fighter was rated for. MOSA hoped that the missiles tracking him would run into the ones that he dumped, but that wish went unanswered. Space was just too big.

"Three missiles still tracking us," said Gecko with tension in his voice. Even though the fighter was accelerating at over 650 G's, the missiles were accelerating at over *100,000 G's*, and they were catching up fast. He put the defensive laser on automatic, and it began trying to target the missiles that were rapidly overhauling them. "Break left!" Gecko yelled as he fired out another round of decoys.

MOSA turned the ship hard left and was rewarded with one of the remaining missiles changing its targeting to the decoy. The other two kept coming.

"Fifteen seconds to impact!" cried Gecko as MOSA rolled the craft back level, and the laser began firing again. "Ten seconds!"

"Nine!"

Before Gecko could say "Eight!" the fighter's laser hit the missile that was closest to them, and the missile exploded. The fighter's sensors were unable to track the remaining missile, and Gecko momentarily hoped that it had been caught in the explosion.

But it hadn't, and as the sensors cleared, Gecko saw that it was almost on them. The laser began firing again.

"Three seconds!"

"Two!"

"One!"

"*GLUCK AB*!" Gecko transmitted as the missile closed on them.

Bridge, TSS *Vella Gulf*, Tau Ceti System, May 25, 2019

"*Viper 02* has been destroyed," said Steropes as the sensors on *Viper 03* detected the 25 megaton nuclear explosion. He had taken over for Arges, who had become very pale at the beginning of hostilities. "I do not think there will be any survivors."

***Viper 03,* Tau Ceti System, May 25, 2019**

"We've got a missile headed toward us," said Bullseye, the WSO of *Viper 03*. He launched a spread of decoys. "Break right!" he called, and *Viper 03*'s pilot, LT Carl 'Guns' Simpson, turned the fighter hard to the right.

The missile neither followed them, nor did it attack the decoys. It continued in the direction that it had originally been heading, away from where the *Vella Gulf* lay waiting, as it continued to accelerate at over 120,000 G's. "Where the hell is it going?" asked Guns.

"No freakin' clue," replied Bullseye, "but wherever it's going, it's getting there *fast*." He watched the missile's trajectory for a second. "Hey Guns," he said, "let's go follow it and see where it's going."

Guns turned the fighter onto the vector of the outbound missile. After about 30 seconds more, Bullseye was unable to track it any longer as its motor went out. Guns started calculating the amount of fuel that he had left. "Umm...how much longer do you want to follow it? We're getting kind of low on fuel..."

"Not much further..." he stopped as his sensor registered a gate activating. As fast as the missile was going when it hit the gate, the activation was significant, and Bullseye was easily able to pinpoint the position of the gate. "OK, we're good," he continued. "I figured it was headed for a gate, and I wanted to get the position of it. Let's get back to the ranch before something ugly comes through it."

"You don't have to tell me twice!" agreed Guns as he turned the fighter back toward the *Vella Gulf*.

* * * * *

Catch up with Chris Kennedy at:
Amazon: http://www.amazon.com/-/e/B00E4MIJA8
Website: http://chriskennedypublishing.com/
Facebook Fan Page:
https://www.facebook.com/chriskennedypublishing.biz
Twitter: @ChrisKennedy110

Printed in Great Britain
by Amazon

50249539R00197